FLOOD WATER

BLOOD WATER

Flood Water

by
Peter Ling

Magna Large Print Books
Long Preston, North Yorkshire,
England.

British Library Cataloguing in Publication Data.

Ling, Peter
  Flood water.

  A catalogue record for this book is
  available from the British Library

  ISBN 0-7505-0757-8

First published in Great Britain by Random Century Group, 1992

Copyright © 1992 by Peter Ling

Cover illustration © Len Thurston

The right of Peter Ling to be identified as the author of this work has been asserted by him in accordance with the Copyright, Designs and Patents Act, 1988.

Published in Large Print August 1995 by arrangement with Random House U.K. Ltd.

Magna Large Print is an imprint of
Library Magna Books Ltd.
Printed and bound in Great Britain by
T.J. Press (Padstow) Ltd., Cornwall, PL28 8RW.

*This book is dedicated, with gratitude,
to David Gemmell,
who opened a door for me.*

AUTHOR'S NOTE

Again, I must thank Chris Lloyd and his team at the Bancroft Library for their help in research; and I am indebted to books by local authors, including *Ben's Limehouse* by Ben Thomas (Ragged School Books) and *Pull No More Bines* by Gilda O'Neill (The Women's Press.)
And let me repeat that some of the locations in this book and all the characters are imaginary; to my knowledge, there has never been any organisation resembling 'The Brotherhood'.

THE JUDGE FAMILY

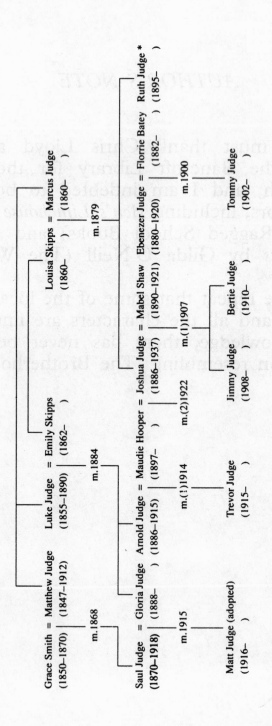

*see O'Dell family tree

THE O'DELL FAMILY   THE KLEIBER FAMILY

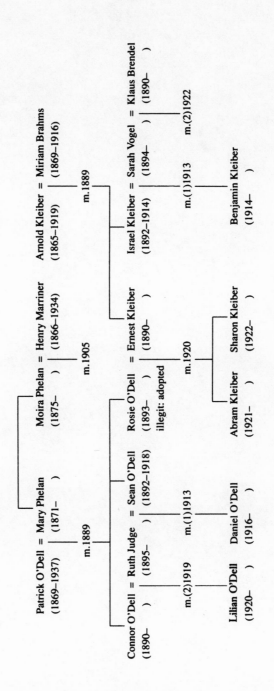

Patrick O'Dell = Mary Phelan
(1869–1937) (1871–   )

Moira Phelan = Henry Marriner
(1875–   ) (1866–1934)
m.1905

Arnold Kleiber = Miriam Brahms
(1865–1919) (1869–1916)
m.1889

m.1889

Connor O'Dell = Ruth Judge = Sean O'Dell
(1890–   ) (1895–   ) (1892–1918)
m.(2)1919   m.(1)1913

Rosie O'Dell = Ernest Kleiber
(1893–   ) (1890–   )
illegit: adopted
m.1920

Israel Kleiber = Sarah Vogel = Klaus Brendel
(1892–1914) (1894–   ) (1890–   )
m.(1)1913   m.(2)1922

Lilian O'Dell
(1920–   )

Daniel O'Dell
(1916–   )

Abram Kleiber
(1921–   )

Sharon Kleiber
(1922–   )

Benjamin Kleiber
(1914–   )

PART ONE

THE TWENTIES

Sunday, 29 February, 1920

It was half-past midnight, and some time before
sunrise Ebenezer Judge knew that he was going
to die.

Where the dock opened on to the river, the
port and starboard lights winked red and green,
reflected in the puddles. Eb could not scream
for help, because his jaws were gagged with a
handful of dirty cotton-waste, and every time he
slipped on the wet paving-stones, they hauled
him back to his feet with a blow and a curse,
dragging him with them. He tried to break free,
but he could not; there were too many of them,
manhandling him along the narrow jetty.

The Punishment Squad had got him, and
there could be no escape.

He did not put up any resistance when they
flung him down on the rainswept slabs, and
tied his ankles with a thick cord. This was
the worst sentence of all; the retribution for
any man convicted of treachery towards the
Brotherhood. He longed to protest, 'It's all
a mistake! I never broke my oath—I swear I
never turned against you!'

But they had stopped his mouth, and he could
not speak in his own defence.

He knew what would happen to him, because
he had seen it all before. In the old days, he
and his brother Josh had been in charge of the

15

Punishment Squad. He remembered how Izzy Kleiber had fought and kicked right to the end—until the moment when they lifted him up, then lowered him over the outer wall of the harbour, where the greedy river licked its oily lips and waited, invisible in the darkness below... That was when Kleiber had given up the struggle and collapsed, limp and helpless as a rag doll.

Now Ebenezer Judge understood what he must have felt, as a dozen willing hands hoisted him on high, held him for an instant in mid-air, then let him down, inch by inch, until the back of his head knocked against the stone wall and the freezing water lapped over his boots. He remained like that for a few seconds longer, while they tied his wrists to a pair of iron rings bolted into the wall, and then they let him go and left him dangling there—half in, half out of the river.

Somewhere above his head, a deep voice intoned the ritual words: *'For the Judas who turns against his Brothers—the man who betrays us by revealing the innermost secrets of our Guild—the punishment shall be as follows... Such a man shall be exposed to wind and weather, suspended between the high and low tidemarks, from night until morning—so that he may take time to consider his wickedness, and repent...'*

The tide was on the turn now. Within the next few hours the water would rise, and his body would turn to ice as he was submerged, inch by inch, in the merciless waters of the Thames.

His chest—his shoulders—his throat would be covered by the rising tide, and then... *Oh, Jesus!*

An unexpected wave broke over his head. The water rushed into his mouth and nostrils, and he could not breathe. He fought for air—his lungs were bursting—the pain was unbearable—he knew that he was drowning... *'Dear God Almighty, have pity. Help me—help—'*

His wife, Florrie, shook him awake.

'What is it, Eb? What's the matter?'

For a moment he did not know where he was: the darkness lay upon him like a leaden weight, crushing him as if he were under a ton of river-water. His heart hammered as he choked out the words: 'Drowning... Dreamed—I was drowning...'

'You're soaked through with sweat, right enough. Let me fetch you a clean nightshirt,' said Florrie, throwing back the bedclothes.

'No!' He stopped her, his chest heaving. 'Wait a bit—don't leave me... Get me breath back...'

'You've been having a nightmare, that's all,' said Florrie. 'What was it all about?'

'I thought they'd hung me up by my arms,' he began, and then he stopped short, remembering that the Punishment Squad could not do that to a crippled man with one arm.

Ebenezer Judge had resigned from the Brotherhood when the Great War began; he volunteered for the army, and was sent to Flanders. Years later, he came home with his right arm blown off by a shell, and ragged lungs after a poison-gas attack: he would never

17

work on the docks again.

'Well, go on.' Florrie was still trying to understand what had upset him. 'Tell me about it.'

Now he was breathing more regularly, but he shook his head. 'Nothing to tell,' he said.

It wasn't the first time he'd had this nightmare; it was happening more often nowadays. But how could he tell Florrie, without explaining what had happened on that night, long ago? When Izzy Kleiber was punished for his treachery, they only meant to give him a cruel ducking and a bad fright; no one had taken into account the heavy rains. The tide had risen a foot above the usual highwater mark, and when they came to cut him free in the morning, they found him hanging on the outer wall—drowned.

Eb Judge had carried that secret with him ever since. He couldn't confess it to Florrie; he could never talk about it to anyone except Josh, who had been there with him—and he was not on very good terms with his brother, these days.

Unlike Eb, Josh had come back from the war in one piece, hale and hearty. No doubt he slept soundly at night—Josh wasn't the sort of man to be tormented by bad dreams.

'All right then,' Eb said at last. 'Go and fetch me a dry shirt, then p'raps we'll get some rest.'

A little more than half a mile away, on the other side of the Isle of Dogs, Ebenezer's sister Ruth was also awake.

She tried not to make a sound, because

she didn't want to disturb her husband. As landlord of the Three Jolly Watermen public-house, Connor O'Dell worked long hours and needed his sleep. She wouldn't wake him—but she wished her nagging pain would go away.

'Ruth—are you awake?'

She was startled by his deep Irish brogue, so close to her ear. 'Yes.'

'I thought as much. I could tell by your breathing.' He rolled a little closer on the big feather mattress in the big brass bedstead, and put his arms round her—carefully, because he had to take special care of Ruth now.

'What's wrong with you at all?' he asked. 'D'you have a guilty conscience, maybe?'

She relaxed, safe within the circle of his embrace—the familiar warmth of his body, his hands holding her, stroking her tenderly. In spite of his great strength, after nearly a year of marriage she was still surprised and touched by his gentleness.

'I dare say that's it.' She smiled a little in the darkness. 'It must be my sins making me restless, unless it's something I ate.'

He lifted himself on to one elbow, looking down at her; a finger of light from the street-lamp outside crept between the curtains, touching her face.

'Are you telling me you've a pain?' he asked anxiously.

'Only a bit of one. I expect it's indigestion—I shouldn't have had that bread and cheese so late.'

'You're sure that's all it is? You don't want

19

to go taking chances in your condition.'

'Go along with you!' she teased him. 'I'm as strong as a horse, you know that. Anyone'd think I'd never had a baby before.'

'You never had *my* baby before,' he said quietly.

For Ruth had been married to Connor's brother Sean, and her first child—a fine boy called Danny—had been born four years ago. Sean was the first man who ever made love to her, and Ruth had thought she loved him too, but it was not a happy marriage and when Sean was killed in France, just before the Armistice was signed, she realised that she had been denying her true feelings for years. She had loved Connor from the day she set eyes on him; and he loved her too, though as long as she was his brother's wife, he would never admit it.

When she became a widow, everything changed. As soon as he was out of uniform, Connor applied to take over the management of the public-house from his parents—Mam and Da were getting on in years, and Da wasn't a well man—but the Brewery were not prepared to lease the pub to a bachelor. So Connor declared his feelings at last, and in due course he and Ruth were married and now, almost a year later, she was going to have his child.

'Will I make you a hot drink?' he suggested. 'If it's indigestion, that might help.'

'Are you sure you don't mind?'

'Why would I mind?'

He got out of bed; Ruth heard him pulling on

his old flannel dressing-gown and thought once again how very lucky she was. If only this pain would go away, everything would be perfect.

Quietly, Connor crossed the room, opening the door cautiously so as not to waken his parents in the big bedroom at the other end of the landing.

That was when they heard the sound of breaking glass. It was not a loud noise, just a muffled thud, followed by a faint tinkle.

'What was that?' asked Ruth.

It might have been a cat knocking an empty tumbler off the bar—except that they didn't keep a cat, and all the glasses had been washed up and put away before they went to bed.

'I'll go and see,' said Connor.

He knotted the cord of his dressing-gown and left the room. For a powerful man, he could move very quietly when he had to. He took the stairs slowly, trying to remember if it was the third or the fourth step from the bottom that creaked when you put your weight on it. Taking no chances, he avoided them both in one long stride.

At the foot of the stairs, he paused. Straining his ears, he could just hear a metallic scratching noise. A draught whipped his bare legs, and he glanced over his shoulder, along the passage; there was a hole in the little window beside the back door, just large enough for a hand to come through and turn the key in the lock... And through the archway that opened into the saloon, he saw a flicker of light.

He advanced warily, without making a sound.

21

In the bar, a single candle threw grotesque shadows across the ceiling. Two men with their backs to him were trying to force open the cash-register. The taller man had worked a knife-blade into the drawer. It sprang open, and he cursed under his breath.

'If you'd asked, I could have saved you the trouble,' said Connor pleasantly. 'We empty the till each night at closing-time.'

Startled, the intruders whirled round, backing away. It was clear which of them was the leader—broad-shouldered and heavily built, he lifted the knife menacingly and said, 'Where d'you keep it? Where's the money?'

'Have a bit of sense! If you know what's good for you, you'll make yourself scarce before you wake the whole house... Better cut and run before the coppers arrive.'

'Shut your face!' The man took a step towards him, and Connor saw his hands were shaking; candlelight glittered on the shivering blade. 'Hand over the cash, or you'll be sorry.'

Connor laughed, and went to meet him.

As the knife flashed down, aimed at his heart, Connor deflected the blow with his left forearm. The blade skidded aside, ripping the thin material of his dressing-gown and grazing his shoulder, but he scarcely noticed it. The knife clattered to the floor, and he threw in a right-hook to the jaw that sent the man reeling back against the counter, gasping, 'Pick it up, Mike—quick!'

His accomplice hesitated a second too long, and Connor kicked the weapon into the corner, then followed up his advantage.

It was a while since he had used his fists in the fairground boxing-booths or in the army regimental championships, and a thrill of excitement surged through him—but his opponent's reactions were sluggish, and his lumbering attempts at counter-blows had no weight behind them.

Connor drove home a pile-driver blow to the solar plexus; the man's knees buckled, and he sank to the floor, with no fight left in him.

'You leave him alone!'

The voice behind him surprised Connor; it was a boy's voice, with an uncertain crack in it. Looking round, he saw that the young accomplice had retrieved the knife and was pointing it at him like a gun, stammering: 'You'd better let him go, d'you hear?'

'Mother of God—you're only a kid. Give me that before you land yourself in worse trouble.' Connor held his hand out, looking into the boy's eyes, adding, 'Mike—is that your name? Right, now, give it here and don't be a damn fool.'

After a moment of uncertainty, the boy lowered his head, unable to meet Connor's steady gaze, and handed the weapon over.

'Thanks. How old are you?'

'Fourteen,' said the boy huskily.

'And how'd you get mixed up with that layabout? He'd no right to drag you into this sort of caper.'

'Don't you talk about my dad like that! He could break you in pieces, only he's not been well... Since he came home from the war, he can't get any work, see? There's me and Mum to keep, and no money coming in.'

The man on the floor was staggering to his feet and Connor understood why he could not defend himself—he was half-starved.

'Don't talk so much, son—don't tell him nothing.' He threw a sullen glance at Connor. 'Wotcher going to do with us? Police, is it? Keep me here if you want, but let the boy go. He's done you no harm.'

By way of reply, Connor walked across the room, drew back the bolts on the street door and flung it open.

'Get out, the pair of you, before I change my mind.'

The man didn't need telling twice, and as the boy began to follow him, Connor suddenly remembered: at some time during the evening, when the saloon till ran short of change, he had put in some silver of his own and taken out a fiver—then stuffed it in a pewter tankard on the shelf for safekeeping.

On impulse, he called the boy back. 'Mike! Take this, and try to talk some sense into your dad if you can. And don't let me see your faces round here again—understand?'

The boy pocketed the money and ran out of the pub after his father.

With a sigh, Connor shut the door and bolted it, then blew out the candle and went upstairs.

He felt a trickle of blood down his arm from the scratch on his shoulder, and pulled the torn sleeve more tightly round it, hoping Ruth wouldn't notice the damage and make a fuss. Then he remembered the hot drink he'd promised her. Well, he'd see to that presently, after he'd explained the delay. Entering the bedroom, he wondered how much he should tell her—but there was no need for that.

Ruth was sitting on the edge of the bed, a towel in her lap and her nightgown bunched up round her waist. In the dim light from the street-lamp her face was very white—and the stain of blood upon the sheets looked almost black.

Instantly, he was at her side. 'Dear God, what's happened?'

'I don't know. The pain's been getting worse and I can't stop the bleeding.'

'I'll go for the midwife!'

'No—a doctor. I need a doctor, Con. I'm afraid I—I might be going to lose the baby.'

The rain was pouring when Ebenezer banged the doorknocker of his brother's house in Denmark Place. Raindrops hit the surface of the road and danced upon it like spinning coins. Standing on the front step, Eb felt a rivulet of ice-cold water run down the back of his neck, and found that he was underneath a leaking gutter.

He pulled up his coat-collar and edged closer to the door, muttering impatiently, 'Get a move on, can't you?'

Footsteps approached along the passage, and Josh's wife Mabel appeared in the doorway, looking surprised. A plump, foolish woman of thirty, with a turned-up nose, Mabel passed through life with an expression of permanent astonishment.

'My goodness gracious!' she exclaimed. 'Fancy seeing you, Ebbie—and on a day like this, too!'

'If you'd be good enough to stand aside, I'd be obliged,' he said sharply. 'This weather does my chest no good at all.'

'February Fill-dyke—isn't that what they say?' She stood back to let him in. 'Can I help you off with your coat, or aren't you stopping?'

'Of course I'm stopping!' One-armed, Eb resented having to depend on other people to assist him. 'You don't think I came over here just to say good morning, do you?'

'I didn't know what to think.' She removed his wet topcoat, and gave it a shake before hanging it on the hall-stand. 'We generally see you in Chapel, Sunday morning—and it's not even ten o'clock yet.'

'I want to talk to Josh first. We'll go to Chapel later on.'

'If you say so. He's in the kitchen, with the boys. Would you like to go through?'

Eb brushed past her and entered the back-kitchen. Joshua, in vest and trousers with his braces dangling, was at the scullery sink with half his face covered in lather, peering at his reflection in a cracked mirror and wielding a cut-throat razor.

'You're quite a stranger and no mistake,' he greeted his brother over his shoulder.

At the kitchen table, twelve-year-old Jimmy and ten-year-old Bertie were playing a game of

Snap. They looked up curiously at Ebenezer, but said nothing.

'You let them play cards on a Sunday?' commented Eb sourly. 'What would Father say?'

'What the old man don't know won't hurt him,' said Josh. 'Budge up, boys, make room for your uncle. Pull up another chair.'

Eb interrupted him. 'I'd be grateful if Mabel and the boys would go round to our house for a while. I want a word with you in private.'

They all turned and stared at him.

'You mean now?' Mabel looked more astonished than ever. 'But I haven't even put the joint in the oven yet. We've got a nice piece of beef, and it'll take two hours at least.'

'You can attend to that presently, can't you?' snapped Eb. 'Put your coats on and go round to Jubilee Street—Florrie will give you a cup of tea and a biscuit. I told her to expect you.'

'But, Ebbie...' She began to argue, but he cut her short.

'When we've had our talk, we'll come round and join you—it shouldn't take long. Chapel-meeting doesn't start till eleven; you'll have plenty of time.'

Mabel looked helplessly at Josh, hoping for support, but her husband wiped the lather off his cheek with a corner of the dishcloth and said doubtfully, 'I dunno, I'm sure. What's this all about, Eb?'

'I told you—I've got to talk to you in private. It's a Brotherhood matter.'

'Oh? Well, in that case, I suppose...' Josh

shrugged. 'you'd better run along, Mabel. Come on, boys, look sharp. Get your coats on.'

It took several minutes before they were ready to leave, and even then Mabel hovered in the doorway, saying plaintively, 'You won't be long, will you? That joint's got to go on by a quarter to, or goodness knows what time dinner will be ready.'

'We'll be as quick as we can.' Eb was making himself comfortable at the head of the table. 'Thank you—off you go.'

As the front door slammed behind them, Josh finished drying his face and hands and began to put on a clean shirt and a stiff collar.

'Well now!' he said. 'I can't remember when you last came round here on Brotherhood business—what's this in aid of?'

Eb's yellow face set into hard lines. Before the war, he had been one of the most prominent members of the Dockworkers' Guild, acting as principal deputy to their father, the Chairman, but after he was disabled and discharged from the army, he was forced to take other work, helping Florrie to run their Aunt Emily's corner grocery shop. In his heart, he still regarded this as women's work, and felt humiliated that it was now Joshua who acted as Marcus Judge's chief assistant at the dockyard.

'It's only partly Brotherhood business,' he admitted unwillingly. 'But it is personal. Very personal.'

'Something to do with Father?' An unwelcome thought occurred to Josh, and he looked alarmed. 'Here—you're not going to tell him, are you? About the boys playing cards?'

Eb permitted himself a half-smile. 'I dare say I might manage to forget that,' he said.

It amused him to think that, although Marcus Judge was no longer taking an active part in the running of the Brotherhood, leaving most of the day-to-day organisation to his son, Josh was still afraid of the old man.

But perhaps it was not so surprising. For twenty years Marcus Judge had been the most powerful figure on Jubilee Wharf, second only to the Wharfmaster himself. It was Marcus Judge who had created the Brotherhood and selected likely candidates for it, and it was Marcus Judge who decided upon punishment when a man's work was unsatisfactory, when he was guilty of negligence, dishonesty or—worst crime of all—treachery.

Marcus never carried out these punishments himself; he gave the orders, and his trusty 'inner circle' of officers carried them out. Small wonder, then, that Marcus Judge was still feared and hated by so many men in the Isle of Dogs.

Joshua broke in upon Eb's reflections. 'Are you going to tell me what's up, or aren't you? You look as if you're a bit under the weather, Eb—not feeling too grand, p'raps?'

'No, I'm not feeling too grand, as you put it.' Eb felt his chest constrict and snatched a breath, then croaked: 'I had that dream again last night.'

'What dream? What are you talking about?'

'You know very well what dream!' He began

29

to pant. 'I dreamed about Izzy Kleiber and the Punishment Squad, only in the dream *I* was Izzy Kleiber, and I was drowned...'

Josh's face darkened. 'Well, what about it? Like you say, it's not the first time—and it's only a dream, for God's sake!'

'You dare to take His name in vain?' Eb's voice had an underlying note of hysteria. 'Are you no longer a god-fearing man, Joshua?'

Irritably, Josh knotted his tie and straightened it. 'I do my duty, if that's what you mean. I go to Chapel every Sunday and I say my prayers, but I'm not superstitious like some people I could mention—and I don't believe in dreams!'

'Don't you make mock of dreams.' Eb leaned forward, lowering his voice. Between every phrase, his lungs wheezed like broken bellows. 'The Scriptures tell us to beware of dreams—think of Joseph and his brethren. Dreams are the key to understanding—that's why I must find out what my dream means! Is the Almighty sending us a warning? Am I in danger, Joshua? Is the Brotherhood in danger?'

'Get away—don't talk so daft!'

'*Listen to me!*' Eb's hand shot out, clutching his brother's arm and pulling him closer. 'Suppose it's a sign that everything's going to come to light? Suppose the police were to find out what really happened to Izzy Kleiber?'

Josh pulled himself free and straightened up. 'You must be soft in the head. How could anybody find out? Anyway, it was an accident. We never meant to finish him off.'

'No sin goes unpunished. I believe there's

trouble ahead for us, Joshua. I believe the whole story's going to come out.'

'Pull yourself together, man! How could it come out, after all this time? The only one who might have talked was Cousin Saul—and he's dead and gone, too.'

Saul Judge was first cousin to Eb and Josh. A man of various talents, he had run a ramshackle ship-chandlers establishment at Cyclops Wharf on the West Ferry Road. He augmented his meagre income by plying for hire as a wherryman, ferrying passengers across to Greenwich, and sometimes he followed a more grisly trade. He was nicknamed 'The Resurrection Man' because he would row up and down the river by night, fishing up floating bodies—and picking their pockets before he handed them over to the police and claimed his reward.

It was Cousin Saul who took charge of Izzy Kleiber's corpse, and then 'found' it some time later—the victim, apparently, of a riverside accident. And it was Cousin Saul who had blackmailed Ebenezer, extorting money from him in return for his silence about Kleiber's death.

'Saul could have reported us, but now he's six feet under, so we're safe as houses,' concluded Josh. Then his face changed, and he added reluctantly, 'Unless...'

Eb picked him up quickly. 'Unless what?'

'You don't suppose your young Tommy might talk, do you? I always did say you were a fool to tell him.'

Eb and Florrie Judge had one son, Thomas, and when Tom was sixteen he discovered that Saul had some hold over his father. When Eb told his son the truth, Tom went to Cyclops Wharf, determined to put a stop to the blackmail that was making his father's life a misery. There was a quarrel and in the struggle, Saul was killed. Tom ran away to sea to start a new life, under a new name, in America.

'Tom would never say a word.' Eb's breath rattled, and he could hardly speak. 'He'd do anything for me—even killed a man for my sake.'

'Then you've got nothing to worry about, have you?' Joshua put on his black jacket and checked his reflection in the mirror; the picture of a respectable Chapel-going citizen. 'Stop working yourself up over nothing, and let's be on our way.'

'No, wait—hear me out. Why do I have this dream about drowning? It must mean *something.*'

Fetching his hat and coat, Josh began to laugh. 'P'raps it means you're going to be drowned' he suggested playfully. 'Come on, let's go!'

Ruth lay on her back and tried not to move, because even the slightest movement was torment, but when the spasms of pain stabbed her it was hard to keep still. She clenched her fists, determined to suffer in silence. Everyone had told her she couldn't be in a better place, but they kept saying she must be patient a little while longer—and she didn't know how much longer she could bear it.

When Connor threw on some clothes and left the Watermen at a run, in search of a doctor, he left his mother to hold Ruth's hand and try to comfort her. She had no idea how long they waited like that, with Mary O'Dell wiping the sweat from her face with a cool washcloth, speaking gently in her soft Irish singsong as if Ruth were a child, for by now her memories had blurred together; faces swam into focus through waves of pain, then disappeared.

She remembered Con coming back with a doctor she had never seen before. He examined her swiftly and impersonally, and sent for an ambulance.

After that everything got very confusing. She had an impression of being lifted up from the bed—she had cried out in agony, feeling as if she would break in half—and laid upon a stretcher. As they bundled her down the stairs she must have fainted, because the next thing she could recollect was being wheeled along an endless corridor that smelled of disinfectant. There were lights at regular intervals in the ceiling, with patches of shadow in between, and stripes of light and dark followed each other overhead as they trundled her along.

Then she remembered someone taking off her nightgown, and a brisk woman in a white starched uniform saying something about going into the theatre—and she saw the doctor again, talking earnestly to a man in a long white gown who was pulling on a pair of rubber gloves...

And suddenly, there was Con, looking quite out of place in these surroundings, and strangely unlike himself. He was holding her hand and staring down at her with an extraordinary expression on his face that she had never seen before.

She licked her dry lips and managed to whisper, 'What's going to happen now?'

'They're going to operate. But it's going to be all right—there's nothing to worry about. You'll be all right.'

'And the baby?' She forced out the question. 'What about the baby?'

He didn't seem to hear her but kept repeating, 'All right. You'll be all right...'

But she knew that he was lying to her.

'Am I going to die?' she asked. 'You must tell me!'

He shook his head, and said nothing. That was when she understood why he looked so strange. It was the first time she had ever seen fear in Connor O'Dell's eyes.

She wanted to pray, but she was so exhausted, the words wouldn't come out right. Instead, she heard herself saying, 'Where's Mum? I want my mum—where is she?'

It was nearly midday when the worshippers came out of the Emmanuel Chapel after the prayer meeting.

The heavy rain had subsided during the morning, but the pavements were still wet underfoot and a fine haze of moisture hung on the wintry air. On the other side of the

34

road, a taxi waited in the drizzle, its black hood glistening.

The Reverend Mr Evans stood under the shelter of the porch, shaking hands with his congregation as they emerged.

'Powerful sermon, Reverend!' said one man. 'Plenty of food for thought in that.'

Some people were already turning their thoughts to food of another kind, impatient to get home. Florrie tugged at the empty sleeve of her husband's coat, pleading, 'Do hurry up, Ebbie. You know you don't like roast potatoes if they're overdone.'

'*Our* dinner won't be ready yet,' fretted Mabel, following them out. 'It didn't go in till nearly eleven.'

Behind her, Joshua said cheerfully, 'It won't hurt us to eat a bit later for once. I might go for a stroll to get up an appetite—the exercise'll do me good.'

'In this weather?' Mabel looked more astonished than ever.

'I dare say you won't be walking very far,' said Eb, smiling at his brother. 'Down to the Ferry House public bar and back again. That's your idea of exercise, eh, Josh?'

Joshua glanced anxiously over his shoulder. Their father disapproved of alcohol at any time, but to enter a public-house on the Sabbath was completely unthinkable.

'Keep your voice down, can't you?' he murmured, but his two sons had sharp ears.

'Can we come too, Dad?' asked Jimmy. 'We

35

don't mind waiting outside the boozer, do we, Bertie?'

His chubby young brother jumped up and down. 'Buy us a ginger-pop, Dad. Go on, be a sport!'

'Quiet, the pair of you!' barked Joshua. 'Don't let Grandfather hear you talking like that.' Then he broke off as a newcomer appeared, working his way through the throng of people leaving the Chapel, against the tide.

They all fell silent as they recognised him. Bare-headed, his dark curly hair sparkling with raindrops, Connor stopped in front of Joshua and said urgently, 'Where's your mother? I've got to speak to her.'

Joshua bristled angrily. 'What the hell are you doing here?'

'Language, dear!' Mabel squeaked in dismay. 'Remember where you are!'

Ebenezer moved closer to his brother, facing Connor. 'What gives you the right to ask for our mother?' he wanted to know. Connor ignored him, addressing Joshua. 'I have to see her—it's urgent. Isn't she here?'

'That's no concern of yours. You know well enough you're not welcome in this family,' began Joshua.

'Throw him into the gutter, Josh!' urged Ebenezer. 'Go on—teach him a lesson!'

Slowly, Connor closed his fists, and Joshua's muscles tensed, while the two boys egged him on.

'Go it, Dad. Give him what for!'

'What is the meaning of this?'

36

The voice was unmistakable, and they all turned towards the figure in the doorway. As he came out of the Chapel, his sons stood back to let him pass.

Over six feet tall, and square-shouldered, Marcus Judge was still an imposing character. Although at sixty he was becoming a little stooped, and his hair and beard that used to be jet-black were turning to silver, the force of his personality was undeniable.

'You are in the shadow of God's house,' he reminded them sternly. 'How dare you engage in a brawl?' His voice was not loud, but so penetrating that every syllable was distinct.

'We were sending this chap about his business,' explained Ebenezer.

Joshua chimed in, 'It's O'Dell, Father. Ruth's husband.'

'I know who he is.' Marcus came up to Connor, face to face. 'We have met before—and we have nothing more to say to one another.'

'I've no time to argue with you,' said Connor. 'I've a taxi-cab waiting across the road.'

'What are you saying? What do you want with me?'

'It's not what I want. It's for Ruth—she's in the London Hospital, in Whitechapel Road. She wants to see her mother.'

'Ruth? What's happened to her?'

Unnoticed, a little apple-cheeked woman with white hair had come out of the Chapel, and now she took her husband's arm.

'Don't distress yourself, Louisa.' Marcus patted her hand. 'If Ruth is unwell, that's very

37

regrettable, but there is nothing we can do for her. Come along, my dear, we must go home.'

He tried to move away, but Louisa clung to his arm, saying, 'No, wait, Marcus. If Ruth's ill...'

'Your daughter is asking for you, Mrs Judge,' said Connor. 'I've come to take you to her.'

Marcus Judge glared at him under beetling brows. 'Must I tell you again? We have no daughter. The day Ruth walked out of this family—when she went over to the Roman Church—she cut herself off from us. Even so, we would have taken her back, like the lost lamb that went astray, but she spurned our forgiveness. There is no more to be said.'

Louisa Judge held her ground, asking Connor, 'What's wrong with her? Is it something serious?'

He nodded. 'She was expecting our baby. They say it's in the wrong place. She's in a bad way—bleeding, and in terrible pain. They have to operate... The doctor says it's her only chance, but it's touch and go, seemingly, and she's asking for you.'

Marcus Judge lifted his face to the dark rain-clouds, and intoned: 'She is in the hands of the Almighty. May He have mercy upon her. Come, Louisa.'

But she removed her hand from her husband's arm and said, 'You'd better go home, Marcus. I'll see you later.'

Staring incredulously at his wife, he began to protest. 'Louisa, I forbid you—'

She did not give him time to finish. Holding her head high she met his gaze, saying simply,

38

'Don't be silly, dear. If Ruth needs me, I must go to her.' She turned to Connor. 'Did you say you had a cab waiting?'

By the time they reached the hospital, it was all over.

Ruth was no longer in the operating theatre; she had been moved into the maternity ward, and the Sister came out to meet them.

'Mr O'Dell? Your wife's very tired—she's bound to be weak, after losing so much blood—but you can see her for a few minutes.' She glanced at Mrs Judge. 'I'm afraid she's not allowed any other visitors.'

'I'm her mother,' said Louisa.

'Ah, I see. Well, in that case...'

Connor burst out impatiently: 'How is she? Is she all right?'

'She's come through the operation very well. And so has the baby.'

'A baby?' He could not believe his ears. 'But I thought—I was afraid that—'

'You've nothing to worry about, Mr O'Dell. You have a fine daughter.' The Sister smiled. 'You should be very proud of them.'

2

'What a lovely day.' Ruth lifted her face to the sun. 'And just look at those flowers—it feels as if the winter's really over at last.'

'Don't you believe it,' grunted Connor.

'There's a biting east wind off the river. Let that sunshine fool you into taking off your coat, and you'll be in bed with pneumonia before you know it.'

'Tell your Dad from me he's a gloomy old moaner.' Ruth smiled at her son who skipped along beside them, swinging on Connor's hand, while Ruth pushed the new baby in her shiny new perambulator.

'Gloomy old moaner!' repeated Danny gleefully. 'Dad's a gloomy old moaner.'

Of course, Connor was not Danny's father, but since the wedding a year ago the lad had taken to calling him 'Dad', and seemed to have forgotten Sean altogether.

'Fine thing, encouraging the children to poke fun at me,' Connor grumbled.

'Ah, why not crack your face and give us a smile?' Ruth teased him. 'You should be feeling cheerful—Easter Sunday's a special day.'

They didn't often have a chance to leave the pub together, but this afternoon she was determined to have a family outing, so as soon as the dinner-things were washed up, they had come for a walk to the Island Gardens.

At the southernmost tip of the Island—which wasn't an island at all, being surrounded by the Thames on only three sides—a little strip of greenery had been preserved as a public park. Today, buds were bursting on the trees and in the flowerbeds a show of early daffodils danced to the tune of the river breeze.

'Listen!' Ruth lifted a finger. 'I can hear music... Didn't I tell you this was a special

40

day? There's a band playing, just for us.'

'Is it 'cos of my birthday?' Danny wanted to know.

He had celebrated his birthday a couple of weeks earlier with balloons and four candles on an iced cake, and he was hoping the festivities might be going on indefinitely.

'Not likely,' said Connor. 'Some poor devils trying to earn a few coppers, by the sound of it.'

The music grew louder, and the O'Dell family stopped to watch the band as they went by. They were a motley crew—half a dozen young men in shabby clothes, some still wearing khaki tunics and caps and one of them with a placard across his chest saying: *Ex-Service—please help.*

One played a bugle, another scraped a fiddle and two more blew on combs-and-paper, while the percussionist thumped a bass drum with a cymbal attached to the rim. Their leader played no instrument, but sang a set of unfamiliar words to a familiar war-time tune:

It's a long way to the pawnshop—
It's a long way to go.
It's a long way to the pawnshop—
Where all our mothers go.
Goodbye, coat and weskit—farewell, watch and
chain.
If you don't keep an eye on your trousers,
They'll go there—the same!

He rattled a tin cup as they passed. 'Spare a tanner, guv'nor. Ex-soldiers, down on our luck.'

41

Connor plunged his hand into his pocket and produced a few coins, which he tossed into the cup. The man touched the peak of his cap and the band moved on, striking up *Roses of Picardy* as they wandered away.

'Thank you, Con.' Ruth slipped an arm through his. 'I know you don't approve of giving money to people in the street, so that was nice of you.'

'Nice?' He spat out the word like poison. 'Myself, I'd call it disgusting. They shouldn't have to go round begging! The Government ought to take care of them, it's the least they could do...but as long as there's eejits like me to fork out a bob or two, the authorities won't do a thing.'

'You see, Danny?' Ruth turned to her small son. 'He may be an old moaner, but he's got a heart of gold.'

'Not at all.' Connor allowed himself a crooked smile. 'I gave 'em the price of a pint or two, in hopes they might come and spend it at the Watermen! Maybe it'll keep them from breaking in and rifling the till.'

Ruth threw him a warning look, which meant: 'Not in front of Danny!'

When she came home from the hospital, she had noticed new locks and bolts on the doors, front and back. Eventually Connor told her about the intruders and they had agreed not to discuss the burglary in front of Danny.

Now he said firmly, 'I don't believe in running risks. Matter of fact, I'm thinking of having a telephone installed as well. That way, we can call the police if there's any trouble, or send for an ambulance if we've a need to, which God forbid.'

By now they had reached the end of the Gardens, and found several people admiring the view across the river. On the opposite bank, Greenwich Palace shone in majesty; the sun was setting, turning the white walls a glowing pink.

'How about a nice portrait, sir?' The voice had a slight foreign accent. 'You and your good lady, with the Palace in the background?'

A bespectacled street-photographer was working his way through the crowd, trying to persuade them to have their pictures taken. Seeing the two young children, he redoubled his efforts.

'Now there's a bonny baby, and the boy's a handsome little chap. You'd make a very fine group.' Then he looked more closely, and exclaimed: 'Ruth—I didn't recognise you at first!'

'Ernest, how are you?' She greeted him warmly, and turned to her husband. 'Con, you remember Ernest Kleiber?'

'We have met,' said Connor, as they shook hands. 'Though I knew your brother better. We worked together on the docks in the old days, before—'

Ernest's smile faded. 'Before Izzy was killed. Yes, I know.'

Six years had done nothing to soften the horror of Israel's death; Ernest Kleiber would never come to terms with that. But he made an effort to put it from his mind, asking, 'And so—these are your children?'

'Yes. This is Danny. Say "how d'you do", Danny,' Ruth urged.

'How do you do?' Danny shook hands with the stranger, then introduced his sister. 'This is our baby. I'm four, and she's nothing.'

'He means she isn't one yet. She's only five weeks old—born on the twenty-ninth of February.'

'Upon Leap Day?' Ernest smiled. 'Does that mean she only has a birthday every fourth year?'

'Yes, it'll be a big saving in presents,' Connor remarked dryly.

'Don't be so mean!' Ruth scolded him. 'She'll celebrate her birthday on the twenty-eighth, won't you, my lovey?'

Only the tip of a pink nose was visible above the cot-blanket, but Ernest declared, 'She is a beautiful child, to be sure. What is her name?'

'She's Lilian Mary O'Dell,' Danny told him.

'Lilian, because it's my mother's second name—and Mary, after Connor's mother,' Ruth explained.

'That's very nice. Do you remember Izzy's wife?'

'Sarah? Of course—I was with her the day her baby was born. His name's Benjamin, isn't it?'

'Ah, yes, Ben will be six in August. You must come and see us—we're still in my parents' old house, just off Poplar High Street. It needs a lot of work, I'm afraid, but perhaps one day, when our ship comes in...'

The Kleibers had come over from Germany

some years before the war, and settled in Poplar. Old Aaron Kleiber built up a little tailoring business, and for a time Ruth had worked for him as a seamstress, together with Sarah Vogel, another immigrant, and Rosie O'Dell, Connor and Sean's half-sister. In due course, Izzy and Sarah were married, but when the war broke out there was a lot of anti-German feeling in the East End. Their house was attacked by a mob and the family were interned for the duration of the war as 'enemy aliens'.

'I believe your mother died while she was in the camp—I was sorry to hear that,' said Ruth. 'I hope your father is keeping well?'

'Alas, my father died also, soon after we returned to Poplar. The new upheaval was too much for him; his heart could not stand the strain.'

Ruth made the sign of the cross. 'May he rest in peace.'

'Oh, yes—I am sure my parents are both at peace now. It was the end of a long struggle; there will be no more bespoke tailoring or fine sewing in the old workshop.'

'You never thought of following in your father's footsteps?'

'Oh, I've no talent in that line!' Ernest indicated his old-fashioned camera and tripod. 'All I can do is take pictures.'

'You used to run a little photographic shop in Silmour Street,' Connor remembered. 'Have you started up again?'

'I wish I could. That would take capital, and I do not have much money. Street-photography is all I can manage, these days.'

'Well, we'd be very pleased to have our picture taken,' Connor told him. 'How about doing one now?'

'Oh, please.' Ernest was embarrassed. 'Don't feel you have to.'

'But it's a good opportunity! Lift the little 'un out of the pram, Ruth, and we'll all have our picture taken.'

So the family posed stiffly, gazing into the camera, while Ernest removed the lens-cap and vanished under the black velvet hood.

'Watch the birdie! Don't move, please—quite still. Thank you—that's all.'

'I didn't see any birdie,' said Danny suspiciously.

'He must've flown away so quick, we didn't spot him,' said Connor.

'I hope the exposure was long enough. The light's beginning to fade.' Ernest packed up his camera, folding the legs of the tripod. 'I should have a print for you in a day or two. Why don't you call in on Wednesday afternoon, Ruth? Sarah will be so pleased. You know where we are, don't you?'

'Of course. Is it just the three of you living there? You and Sarah and Benjamin?'

'We also take in paying guests from time to time,' said Ernest awkwardly. 'It helps to make ends meet.'

'What a good idea. But I really meant,' Ruth hesitated, then took the plunge, 'isn't Rosie with you, then?'

The name fell into the conversation like a

46

pebble dropped in a pond. For a moment no one spoke, and the rings spread out, fading slowly.

'I have not seen Rosie since the war,' said Ernest in a low voice. 'You remember? I came to the Watermen to ask if you had any news of her.'

'When she left the Island, she turned her back on the family and we've never heard from her since. She went up West, to look for a job in one of the big department stores. You said you would try to find her.'

'I did try—many, many times. Day after day, I walked up and down Oxford Street, Regent Street, Kensington. I went to all the big shops, but it was hopeless. Nobody had heard of Rosie O'Dell; I was looking for a needle in a haystack.' He shivered a little, and turned up the collar of his mackintosh. 'It is turning chilly now the sun has gone down; your baby mustn't catch cold. I will tell Sarah you are coming to visit us on Wednesday afternoon. I am so glad to have met you again.' He bowed slightly, then shouldered his camera and was soon out of sight.

As they watched him go, Connor said, 'It makes you think. A few years ago he had a flourishing little business going in that shop of his, and now look at him. On his uppers.'

'A few years ago, he had Rosie with him.'

'Who's Rosie?' asked Danny inquisitively. Something about the way they spoke of her aroused his interest.

'Aunt Rosie's your Dad's sister,' Ruth told him.

47

The small boy frowned. 'If she's Dad's sister, why doesn't she live in our house? Lilian's *my* sister—and she lives with us.'

'Your Aunt Rosie had to go away,' said Connor. 'Come on, it's high time we were heading for home ourselves. It'll soon be dark.'

As they retraced their steps, Ruth couldn't help wondering if they would ever be able to tell Danny and Lilian the truth about their Aunt Rosie when they grew up. It was not a story they were proud of

For Rosie O'Dell was not Mary O'Dell's daughter. Mary had a sister, four years her junior—bright, stylish Moira Phelan. Moira studied shorthand and typing and got a job as a secretary in the office of Mr Henry Marriner, a successful businessman. When she found that she was pregnant, she turned to her older sister for help, and since the O'Dells knew that Mr Marriner had been paying court to Moira, they assumed he was responsible for her condition. When the baby was born, the O'Dells adopted her—a darling little girl, dark and pretty—and brought her up as their own, with Connor and Sean.

Eventually the truth came out. Rosie had been the result of one reckless moment of love between Moira and Mary's husband, Patrick O'Dell; an occasion never repeated and best forgotten—until twenty years later, when the shocking news exploded like a time-bomb. The revelation almost destroyed the O'Dell family. It was a long while before Mary could forgive her husband's infidelity, and she had never seen or

48

spoken to her sister since then.

But the one most deeply hurt was Rosie herself. Not only had her real mother rejected her at birth and given her away, but worst of all, her adoptive father whom she had loved so much now turned out to be her real father, a cheat and a deceiver. Ashamed, confused, uncertain of her own identity, Rosie O'Dell had walked out of the house and never returned.

For some time she stayed with the Kleibers. When Ernest set up shop as a photographer, she had gone to work as his assistant and their friendship blossomed into romance. If war had not broken out, they would have married, but when the Kleibers were sent away to prison-camp, her last hope of love and security collapsed; that was when she left the Island and went up West.

Ruth shook her head, trying to put these unhappy memories from her mind. When the little family reached the Watermen, Connor unlocked the side door of the pub and helped Ruth in with the pram.

'What's for tea?' Danny sniffed the air. 'Gran's been making a cake!'

He roared down the passage to the back-kitchen, where Mary O'Dell hugged him and promised him a slice of fruitcake still warm from the oven, if he was a good boy and ate up all his bread and butter first.

Lilian was fast asleep again, and Ruth managed to lift her out of the pram without waking her.

'I'll take her straight upstairs and put her in

49

her cot,' she began, but Connor put out a hand, stopping her.

'You're still brooding about Rosie, aren't you?' he said.

'I can't help it. She was always a good friend to me. I hate to think of her now—alone and unhappy, perhaps.'

'Maybe she's not unhappy—maybe she's not alone either,' said Connor. 'If you ask me, it's Ernest you should feel sorry for. He's the one who's lonely and unhappy. He's still in love with her.'

On Tuesday morning, in Jubilee Street, Florrie carried out her daily chores—with one minor difference.

She fried a rasher of bacon, a sausage and a slice of bread, then cut them up small enough for Eb to eat with a fork. Generally, he came downstairs to wash and shave while she was doing this, but today she took him up a tray so he could have his breakfast in bed. Florrie did not eat anything herself—a cup of tea was all the breakfast she ever wanted—and as soon as she had finished, she put on her coat and hat and left the house. Then she made her way to the little corner grocery shop, five minutes' walk from Jubilee Street.

This was the shop which had been run by Eb's Aunt Emily ever since she was widowed, thirty years earlier. Emily had never had a head for figures, and her brother-in-law, Marcus Judge, had kept an eye on her finances from the beginning, gradually acquiring a controlling interest in the business.

When her son Arnold went off to war, Emily felt completely at a loss, and was grateful for any help that was offered her. As Ebenezer was also serving in the army, Florrie moved into the flat above the shop, together with her schoolboy son and Arnold's young bride, Maudie. Before long, Maudie had a baby—and soon after that, a telegram arrived saying that Arnold had been killed in action.

The next few years were difficult for them all, but when Eb came home, gassed and disabled, he had done his best to put the shop back on a business footing—going in every day to work behind the counter, keeping the books, and not letting customers run up bills they couldn't pay.

Today, when Florrie arrived at the corner-shop and rapped on the closed front door, Aunt Emily lifted the roller-blind and peered shortsightedly at her through the glass.

'All on your own, dear?' she said, when she unlocked the door. 'Isn't Ebbie with you?'

'No, he'll come on later. I said he should have a bit of a lie-in; he had another bad night again. Moaning and groaning in his sleep, he was—I felt quite worried for him. But I thought I'd come round first, to help you open up and get things straight.'

'Thank you, dear.' Emily lowered the blind again. The shop didn't open till eight, but there was a lot to be done before then. She rambled on, 'We had a broken night, too. Little Trevor was sick three times—too many sweeties before bedtime, I expect, so I'm all behind like the cow's tail this morning. Maudie had to change his nightie twice. She's still upstairs, getting him dressed.'

Florrie took off her hat and coat and hung them up, saying, 'I'll make a start on the bacon, shall I?'

'If you would, dear, then I can weigh out some packets of tea. Mind yourself on that machine—the blade's ever so sharp.'

Emily always repeated this warning, although she was the only one who had ever cut herself on the bacon-slicer. As they went on with their work they gossiped happily, like two birds twittering to one another from different branches of a tree.

With a rat-tat at the door, a few envelopes dropped on to the doormat.

'Postman's early today,' said Emily, going to pick them up. She turned them over one at a time, trying to decipher the handwriting. 'Oh dear, more bills from the wholesalers, by the looks of them. Hello—this one's got a funny stamp on. I've never seen one like this before, have you? Oh, I do believe it's American... Would that be a picture of George Washington?'

'Shouldn't think so. Hasn't he passed on by now?' said Florrie, craning over her shoulder.

'I don't recognise the writing,' began Emily and then, as Florrie gasped and took the letter from her: 'Why, whatever's the matter?'

Florrie was staring at it, open-mouthed and trembling, unable to reply.

'You've gone quite pale, dear. Are you feeling poorly?' Emily fussed over her. 'Shall I get you a glass of water?'

'No, I'm all right. It's just...I know that handwriting.'

'How could you? We don't know anybody in America.'

Florrie nodded slowly. 'Yes, we do. Josh told me once, that's where Tommy went. His writing's more grown-up—well, he'd be two years older now—but I'd know it anywhere.'

'Are you sure?' Emily's hand fluttered helplessly to her face, fingering her lips. 'Oh dear, Marcus said we must all try and forget about Tommy. Ever since that awful night when Saul died, and—Tommy went off, Marcus says he's not one of our family, not any more. We must put him out of our hearts for ever, he said.'

'How could I do that? I'm his mother!' Florrie gazed at the letter in her hands. 'But I'm not the one he's written to—it's not addressed to me. It says: *Mrs Maudie Judge.*'

Emily screwed up her eyes, trying to focus on the envelope. 'So it does. Oh, Florrie—how dreadful.'

'I don't understand. Why should he write to Maudie instead of me?'

'I think perhaps they'd begun to get rather fond of one another. Too fond, I mean. You know the pendant she always wears round her neck, shaped like a heart? He gave her that for Christmas, just before he ran away. I said it wasn't proper for her to keep it, but she wouldn't listen.'

Florrie looked up, wide-eyed. 'You mean there was something going on between them? But he was only a boy! He'd just turned sixteen—and she was a married woman, with a child.'

'A widow,' Emily corrected her. 'And not much more than a child herself—only five years older than Tommy.' Then, as Florrie stuck her finger under the flap of the envelope and began to tear it open, 'Oh, do you think you should? It's not meant for you!'

'He's my boy—I've a right to know what's become of him!' Florrie scanned the letter, her lips moving silently. When she had finished, she turned to Emily in blank dismay. 'Whatever shall I do?'

'What does he say?' Emily asked.

Florrie held out the letter, but Emily shook her head. 'I left my glasses upstairs—I can't make out his writing. You tell me what's in it.'

Laboriously, Florrie began to read aloud. '*My dearest darling, I don't know whether I should be writing this to you, but I still think of you every day of my life, first thing when I wake up and last thing before I go to sleep. You are never out of my mind.*

'*I would have written sooner, but I was afraid of getting you into some trouble. Then I remembered you always get up in the morning before Aunt Emily, so I'm sure you will find this before anyone else sees it; and I want you to know that I am alive and well. As you see from my address, I'm living in Yonkers now, and have a pretty good job* in a cannery, working in the packing and despatch department.

'I rent a room in the house of our foreman, living as one of the family, which was a stroke of luck; a boarding-house would cost more. This way, I live cheap and put some money in the bank every week. When I've saved enough, I plan to come home and marry you, like I said I would.

'I don't spend much—I stay home most nights. Don't worry, I have no lady-friends; there will never be anyone but you, Maudie. Loving you was the best thing that ever happened to me: I could never go with anyone else.

'I promise I will come back to you one day. I realise I must be wanted by the police for Saul Judge's death, but it was not murder. I had to do it in self-defence, or else he would have killed me. One day I will tell everyone the truth about that night, and clear my name.

'We must be patient till then. Wait for me, my dearest darling. You are mine and I am yours. I will always love you. Yours ever. Tom.'

Emily held on to the edge of the counter to support herself and whispered, 'I was afraid this would happen. I was afraid they'd been carrying on.'

'You should have put a stop to it!' said Florrie accusingly. 'Why didn't you tell me?'

'At first I didn't suspect anything. Only afterwards, when Tommy disappeared and Maudie seemed so heartbroken, then I began to wonder. What are you going to do with that letter?'

'What do you think I should do?'

55

Emily racked her muddled brain, and had a sudden inspiration. 'I tell you what. Give it to me, and I'll take it round to Louisa, presently. She'll know what to do for the best.'

They agreed that for the moment they would say nothing about it to Ebenezer. There was always the danger that he might mention it to his father—and that was bound to lead to more trouble. They both felt that, as Marcus's wife, Louisa could be relied upon to give the best advice.

Some time after the shop opened, Eb arrived for work, grey-faced and haunted. Emily gave Florrie a meaning look and said, 'Now you're both here, you won't mind if I slip out and do a little shopping? I've one or two calls to make as well.'

As fast as her rheumatic legs would carry her, she toddled round to the Rope Walk, to the house where Eb and Josh and Ruth had been born and brought up.

Louisa opened the front door, and saw at once that her sister was upset. When they sat down at the kitchen table, Emily perched on the edge of her chair, and her hands were never still. She kept fidgeting with her bonnet, dropping her hat-pin, taking off her gloves and putting them on again. At last Louisa could stand it no longer.

'What's wrong?' she asked. 'Are you going to tell me or aren't you?'

'Oh dear, it's so unfortunate...' Emily glanced over her shoulder and lowered her voice. 'Marcus isn't at home, is he?'

'No, of course not. He's gone to the Wharf, as usual.'

The routine at Jubilee Wharf remained unchanged. Each morning at seven the members of the Brotherhood presented themselves at the dock-gates, and Josh called out their numbers, allowing them in one at a time to report for work. Though Marcus no longer took part in this process, he never missed a single morning; he liked to know everything that was going on—how many cargo-ships berthed for loading or unloading—how many hours taken to clear each one—how many men needed on every job.

'Marcus won't be home till tea-time,' said Louisa. 'Why do you ask?'

'Well, Florrie and me, we were wondering what we should do. You see, *this* arrived today—first post.' Diving into her beadwork reticule, she produced the letter with the American stamp, and slid it across the red chenille tablecloth.

Picking it up, Louisa said, 'But it's addressed to Maudie.'

'I know, that's what makes it so awkward. Florrie opened it... You'd better see for yourself.'

Louisa frowned. 'I don't like prying in other people's letters. Who's it from?'

'Tom,' whispered Emily. 'He's in America. You've got to read it.'

Something in her face made Louisa unfold the letter. When she had finished reading it, she looked up, asking, 'Has Maudie seen this?'

'No. We didn't know whether to give it to her or not. What do you think?'

'It's addressed to her—that makes it her property.'

'But it says such shocking things!'

'That's no business of ours. This is between Maudie and Tom; you've no right to keep it from her.'

Louisa put the letter on the table, but Emily was reluctant to pick it up. It lay between them, a scrap of paper that had travelled halfway round the world, and could finish up as evidence in a murder trial.

They had been so intent upon it, they never heard the back door open and shut, or saw the shadow at the scullery door until Marcus Judge said, 'Good morning, Emily. I didn't expect to find you here. I dare say you weren't expecting to see me, either?'

Emily gave a little moan of fear, and Louisa said quickly, 'What's happened, Marcus? Why aren't you at the Wharfmaster's office?'

'There were no boats in or out today. After the Easter holiday, you'd think the Wharf would be twice as busy, but trade's getting worse all the time. It seems the country can't afford imports, and we've precious little to export, either, so we had no work to give our men. Joshua had to send them home empty-handed.'

While he was speaking, Emily tried to pick up the incriminating letter and slip it into her bag, but Marcus stopped her.

'May I see that letter, Emily?'

Still fumbling with the clasp of her bag, she

gasped, 'No, Marcus. It's nothing—nothing of any importance.'

'The letter, if you please,' he repeated inexorably.

She had to hand it over. He read it in silence, then looked from his wife to his sister-in-law, and back to his wife again.

'So, I come home to find you plotting behind my back. What were you intending to do with this letter, Emily?'

'I came to ask Louisa's advice. You see, Tom sent it all the way from America, so I thought—'

'Perhaps I haven't made myself clear. Thomas Judge is no longer a member of this family. He has put himself beyond the pale—I have forbidden you to speak of him.'

'He's still Florrie's son,' Louisa cut in gently.

'Florrie has no son! Don't you understand what I say? Thomas Judge does not exist.'

He walked to the old-fashioned kitchen range, where red-hot coals glowed behind the bars of the grate. Crushing the letter into a ball, he dropped it in. It flared up, then became black ash.

'That belonged to Maudie,' said Louisa.

'Maudie? Ah, yes.' He turned to Emily. 'Had Maudie read it?'

'No. I brought it straight here.'

'Very well. You will not tell her. You will speak of this to no one.' Returning to the table, he put his hands together in an attitude of prayer. 'You will repeat these words after me: *I hereby solemnly swear before Almighty God...*'

59

They echoed each phrase as he continued: '...*that I will never mention the existence of any such letter to anyone else—now, or at any time in the future, so help me, God.*'

Obediently, they bowed their heads and he dusted his hands as if they had been contaminated. Then he turned to his wife and addressed her in words that cut like a knife.

'I did not expect this from you, Louisa. I am bitterly disappointed.'

'Can we leave the table, please, Mutti? We've finished our tea.'

Benjamin Kleiber gave his mother a pleading look, and pushed aside his plate.

'Benjamin, you must not be rude. Daniel is our guest—perhaps he would like some more cake.'

Danny O'Dell shook his head, and Ruth prayed that her son would not say with devastating candour: 'Your cake tastes funny' —then breathed again as he said politely, 'No more, thank you, Mrs Kleiber. Can we go and play now?'

'Very well. Take Daniel to your room, Ben, but you mustn't make a noise. Miss Hoffmann is resting.'

The two small boys scrambled down from their chairs and raced for the door. Ben was almost two years older than Danny, but small for his age, while Danny seemed likely to take after his father, so they were very nearly the same height.

'I am glad they get on well together,' said

60

Sarah Kleiber. 'Ben is a solitary boy; he needs to make new friends.'

The two youngsters shouted gleefully to one another as they raced upstairs. Their feet clattered on the uncarpeted boards, and Sarah threw up her hands in mock despair.

'Poor Miss Hoffmann! Why can't small boys be still and good, like your daughter?'

Ruth looked down fondly at Lilian, who lay placidly on her lap sucking her thumb, and she smiled. 'Oh, this one can make herself heard when she wants to, believe me! Is Miss Hoffmann one of your paying guests?'

'That's right. Most of our lodgers go out to work during the day, but Miss Hoffmann is not in good health. She was interned, like us, and the hard winters were specially trying for her. She has never been really well since then. That is why she spends so much time in her room. I asked her if she would like to come down and have tea with us, but...'

Sarah looked round the long dining-room. Bare, and sadly in need of redecoration, it was not very welcoming. She sighed. 'You must see great changes since you were here last.'

Ruth did not know what to say. It was not only the house that had changed. Once, Sarah had had a kind of beauty—pale-skinned and dark-haired, with big lustrous eyes. Now the light had faded from those eyes, and her complexion was sallow. She looked drawn and tired, as she asked: 'Can you remember how it was, when Aaron and Miriam were alive?'

'I remember it very well. There used to be

a round dining-table here—mahogany, wasn't it?—and a sideboard along that wall.'

'That was where they kept their best china; Miriam was so proud of her dinner-service. Of course, that all went during the war.' Sarah began to stack the plates from the table—plain white china, cheap and practical. 'We needed a bigger table anyway. This is an old trestle-table Ernest found in the workroom at the back, when he opened up the house again. It was used as a sewing-bench in the old days, but we're glad to have it. Sometimes we sit down as many as seven or eight for breakfast or supper.'

'But what became of the Kleibers' furniture —and the dinner-service?'

Sarah shrugged. 'When the house was standing empty, people came and smashed the windows. After that, they broke in and began to steal whatever they could carry away—little things at first, like crockery and silver, but later on the furniture went as well. When Ernest came home, he could not believe his eyes. There was damp everywhere. The paper was peeling off the walls, ceilings coming down...'

She tried to smile. 'We've done the best we can to put things right. I learned how to put up wallpaper—I became quite expert at it! But the house still needs a lot of work, and at present Ernest cannot afford it.'

'I was hoping to see Ernest here this afternoon,' said Ruth. 'What a pity he had to go out.'

'It's a fine afternoon—and early-closing day, so he decided he should take his camera along to the Tower of London. There are always sightseers there—sometimes they like to be photographed with the Beefeaters.'

'What a good idea...' Ruth looked round for a clock, but there was no clock in the room. 'What time do you expect him to come home?'

'Not until quite late. It's a long walk from the Tower to Poplar.'

'He walks? It must be miles—why doesn't he take a bus?'

'He doesn't like to waste money on bus-fares. And he says he enjoys walking; he often goes for long walks by himself.' Sarah seemed as if she were about to say something else, then thought better of it. Standing up, she began to load the tea-things on to a tray.

'Do you mind if I clear the table? I must get ready for supper; our lodgers will be coming in presently.'

'Let me help with the washing-up,' said Ruth. 'I'll put Lilian back in her pram, then I can wipe while you wash.'

'Oh no, you mustn't. You're a visitor!'

But Ruth wouldn't take no for an answer, so Sarah went to put the kettle on. When Ruth followed her into the kitchen, she looked around; like the rest of the house, it was clean but very sparsely furnished. It could not be easy to produce meals for seven or eight lodgers under such spartan conditions.

Putting the remains of the cake back into the larder, Sarah asked anxiously, 'Did you think it tasted a little stale? I always keep it in a tin, but even so...'

Ruth assured her that the cake had been delicious, and they made a start on the washing-up. Looking through the window over the sink, Ruth could see the little paved yard leading to the workroom where she had struggled to learn the craft of fine hand-sewing, so long ago.

'Does Ernest use the workshop now?' she wondered.

'There's not much of it left. You remember it had a glass skylight? Before we came back, Ernest had such plans. He hoped to convert it into a photographic studio—and then he found that there was not a single pane of glass left, and the rain had got in. It was a big disappointment.'

'Poor Ernest. It's all so terribly unfair.'

'Yes, poor Ernest.' Sarah tipped the last of the washing-up water down the drain and said shyly, 'If you don't mind me asking, do you ever hear anything of Rosie these days?'

Ruth shook her head. 'Ernest asked me that. We haven't been in touch with her for years.'

'I'm so sorry—he didn't tell me that. In fact I'm surprised he asked you. He never speaks of her, now. It's a subject we do not talk about.' She dried her hands on the kitchen towel, adding, 'I worry about Ernest. It is not right he should live as he does in this house, with nobody but strangers to talk to. He is so very lonely.'

'But he has you for company,' began Ruth.

'He does not talk very much to me. I have a separate life of my own. I'm lucky, I have Benjamin but Ernest has nobody. When he came out of the prison-camp at the end of the war, he believed Rosie would be waiting for him and when he could not find her, I think it broke his heart.'

For a moment Sarah fell silent, then she suddenly turned to Ruth. 'But how stupid I am! I talk of Ernest, and forget the most important thing of all. Before he went out, he made me promise to give you this.'

She opened a drawer of the kitchen-dresser and pulled out a photograph, which she gave to Ruth. It was the family portrait they had posed for on Easter Sunday afternoon: Connor, Ruth and Danny, staring glassy-eyed into the camera. Only Lilian, safe and snug in Ruth's arms, looked completely at her ease.

'It's wonderful,' said Ruth. 'Now, where did I put my handbag? How much does Ernest charge for a group photo?'

'There's no charge,' said Sarah. 'It is a present for you and your family, with Ernest's very best wishes.'

'He's a professional photographer—I must pay him for his work!'

'He would be most offended. He said you have always been a good friend to him; he is very happy to do something for you, in return.'

Next morning, when the O'Dells sat down to breakfast, the photograph had pride of place on the kitchen mantelpiece. It had been much admired, for Mary brought it out time and again to show to favoured customers in the saloon bar.

'I'll have to get a frame for it,' said Connor, 'before you wear it to pieces, passing it around.'

'Don't you be so cheeky!' said his mother. 'And you watch yourself with that fried egg. I'll not let you go to visit the Company with dribbles of yolk all down the front of your suit.'

Across the table, Danny giggled and Connor quelled him with a look. 'Stop your nagging, Mam. I won't disgrace you, never fear.'

Once a year, the landlord of the Watermen had to put in an appearance at the Head Office of the Brewery in Farringdon Street. It was more of an annual rite than a business meeting, and always concluded with expressions of mutual goodwill and handshakes all round—provided the pub continued to show a profit. Nevertheless, visiting the Company was an important occasion in Mary O'Dell's calendar; when her husband was the landlord, she always fussed over him beforehand, ironing his best shirt, starching the collar, sponging his blue serge suit and tucking a clean handkerchief into his top pocket. Now that her son had taken over, she showed every sign of treating him in the same way, much to his discomfort.

Ignoring Connor's assurances, Mary turned to Ruth. 'And when you get there, make sure he goes to the Gentlemen's Cloakroom and has a good wash before the interview. Those Underground trains are always black with soot, and they're bound to notice if he's got grubby hands.'

The landlord's wife was expected to accompany him on the trip to Head Office. Although

66

Mary had gone to Farringdon Street each year with Patrick, and was always greeted cordially when they arrived, the actual interview was a strictly male affair. She had to sit in the waiting-room, on a slippery horsehair sofa, while it was going on.

Con exploded. 'For pity's sake, Mam, you'll be telling her to wipe my nose next!' which sent Danny off into another fit of giggles.

'He won't let you down, I promise,' Ruth chimed in soothingly.

'I sincerely hope not,' said Mary. 'Anyhow, *you're* looking very nice, my dear. I always like you in that blue dress.'

'You're sure you can manage without us this morning?' Ruth continued, 'because I'm sure the Company don't really want to see me. I could easily stay here to help out in the public, if you like.'

'Not at all. I shall be running the saloon—it'll be like old times, and we've the new barmaid in the public. We'll manage fine.'

'If you have any awkward customers, you can call up the potboy from the cellar, can't you?'

'There'll be no awkward customers as long as I'm in charge!' said Mary grimly. 'And you'll be back soon after midday, I expect.'

'A bit later than that,' said Connor. 'I've been thinking, it's a long time since the two of us went out together, so I'm taking Ruth for a bite to eat. Da tells me they used to do a decent lunch at the chop-house by Holborn Viaduct.'

'Oh, we don't have to eat out. It's a terrible waste of money,' began Ruth.

'Don't interrupt me, woman—I've not finished yet. When we've eaten, we're going to do some shopping. That blue dress of yours looks well enough, but you've had it a while now; you need something new to wear. You presented me with a daughter lately—it's high time you had a present yourself.'

'A new dress?' Ruth's face glowed. 'Oh, Con—it's a lovely thought, but I really don't need it.'

'Don't go talking him out of it,' said Mary. 'It may be a long time before you get another offer like that!'

'No more arguments, Mrs O'Dell—my mind's made up,' said Connor. 'I thought we'd see what Gamages have to offer. It's only a hop and a skip from the Viaduct, and they have a good selection of the latest fashions.'

'And how would you know that, might I ask?' Ruth enquired.

'Rosie once told me Gamages was the best. I don't know if she ever bought anything there, but she enjoyed window-shopping.'

'Fancy you remembering,' said Mary. 'It's true enough—Gamages was her favourite.'

'I never knew that,' said Ruth. A silence fell, and then she pushed back her chair and stood up, saying, 'Very well. If you're set on it, we'll go to Gamages.'

On the journey, she sat in the Underground carriage next to Connor, saying very little, watching the other passengers.

'You're quiet today.' Connor glanced at her. 'Not worrying about the children, are you?'

'Oh, no. Your mam's so good with them —she'll make sure Danny doesn't get into mischief and see that Lilian has her bottle at the right time.'

'Then what are you pondering so deeply?'

Ruth smiled. 'Nothing special. I'm enjoying a day out with my husband, that's all.'

Her reply was truthful enough, but it was not the whole truth. She did not want to tell Connor that she had a private plan in mind; it was such a very long shot, and might come to nothing.

The visit to the Brewery Company presented no problems, and they were in and out of the office within half an hour; when they went into the chop-house on the stroke of twelve, they were the first customers.

Ruth looked down the menu and was scandalised. 'I could cook you the same food for a quarter of the price. Honestly, it's a wicked waste.'

But he told her to stop grumbling and enjoy herself, and she had to admit that the spring lamb with mint sauce was very tasty.

It was still early when they went in to Gamages and headed for Ladies' Gowns. Ruth wandered through the department, studying the dresses on display—and the young ladies behind the counters as well—but she could not see a familiar face.

Eventually she found a dress that appealed to her. It was low-waisted, in deep chestnut georgette with touches of lace at the collar and cuffs—smart enough for evening wear but simple enough for the daytime, too.

'I'll have to try it on, to make sure it suits me,' she told Connor.

'Fair enough—I kept you waiting at the Company office. But don't be too long, will you? I feel like a bull in a china-shop, with all these young women gawping.'

One of the assistants took Ruth into a fitting-room and helped her into the dress, then stood back to admire the effect.

'Oh, yes, madam—it might have been made for you. And the colour goes with your hair, don't you agree?'

'It's perfect...but I wonder, while I'm here, could I have a word with the lady in charge of the department?'

The assistant looked alarmed. 'Our manager-ess? Is there something not to your liking, madam?'

'No, no. It isn't about the dress at all—it's a personal matter.'

Puzzled, the girl went off, and a few minutes later a grey-haired woman in black entered the cubicle.

'Can I help you, madam? What seems to be the problem?'

'There's no problem. I like this dress very much, and I'm sure my husband will like it too, but I'm hoping you might be able to help me. I'm trying to trace a member of our family who moved to this part of London during the war, looking for work. She was always interested in fashion, and this was her favourite shop, so it's quite likely this would be the first place she'd come to.'

'How long ago would this have been?'

'Almost exactly five years—in May, 1915. She was twenty then, a pretty, dark girl with curly hair and an Irish brogue.'

'Could you tell me her name?'

'Rose O'Dell. Everyone called her Rosie.'

'Rosie O'Dell...' The manageress nodded. 'As soon as you described her, I felt sure it must be Miss O'Dell. Yes, she worked here for a time.'

'But not now?'

'I'm afraid not. She only stayed for a few months, then she became unwell and had to give up the job. We all liked her. We were sorry to see her go.'

'You mean she never came back? Did she leave any forwarding address?'

'No, nothing like that. She went quite suddenly. We never saw or heard from her again.'

Ruth's hopes, which she had built so high, collapsed like a house of cards. There was only one crumb of comfort; she was very glad that she had not said anything about it to Connor.

3

As the spring tides rose, flowing into summer, the Island began to blossom: pots of geraniums appeared on windowsills and girls sewed new ribbons on to last year's straw hats. Hearts beat

71

faster, and along the streets, footsteps lightened and quickened on the paving-stones.

Only Ebenezer's heart grew heavier, and his steps dragged and faltered.

The women at the corner-shop remarked upon the change that had come over him, and could not account for it.

At midday, he always took a half-hour break, sitting in the kitchen armchair with his feet up on a stool, nibbling toast and dripping and preparing for another long afternoon behind the counter.

Today Florrie and Emily, busy cutting bread and making cups of tea, exchanged glances.

'Another slice, Ebbie?' suggested Florrie.

'No, I don't want any more.' He pushed his plate away, the remains of the dripping toast congealing, half-eaten. 'I've no appetite at all.'

'How about a nice cup of tea, dear?' said Emily, filling the teapot. 'I'm sure you won't say no to that.'

'I'm not thirsty either,' he rasped, and his breath rattled in his lungs, reminding him of the dream that kept coming back, night after night.

'You ought to force yourself to have a little something,' his wife told him. 'You're doing no good, starving yourself like that.'

'Will you leave off nagging?' he snarled at her, and she took a step back. 'I'll eat and drink when I feel like it! It's no concern of yours what I do.'

'She's only telling you for your own good, dear,' Emily interposed.

He looked as if he were about to turn on his auntie as well, but at that moment they were interrupted by a clatter and a crash and the wail of a child.

'Dear me!' Emily was glad of an excuse to change the subject. 'There's little Trevor in the wars again—what's he up to now?'

'Mischief, as per usual,' grunted Eb, but she was already on her way to her beloved grandson.

'What is it, ducky? Tell Gan-gan what's the matter.'

While the others snatched a midday break, Emily's daughter-in-law Maudie took her turn of duty in the shop, and she always had her small son with her so she could keep an eye on him.

Unfortunately Trevor was a restless child, and easily bored. Today, while Maudie was filling a grocery order to be delivered by hand, he had decided to amuse himself by trying to clamber up the shelves, and succeeded in pulling down several tins of treacle. Worse still, one of them had lost its lid and a sluggish, syrupy lake was already spreading across the floor.

'It wasn't Trev's fault. He didn't mean to—it was an accident,' said Maudie, all in one breath.

'It can't be helped, dear. I'll clean up the mess,' sighed Emily then, more urgently: 'Oh no, Trevor. Don't tread in it, whatever you do!'

But she was too late: Trevor was already paddling in the treacle, and Maudie swooped down to pick him up.

73

'I'll give him a good wash, and change his socks and shoes,' she said. 'Then he can come with me while I run these groceries round to Marbury Road. It'll do him good to get out for a while; it's being cooped up indoors all day makes him fidgety.'

As she passed through the kitchen on her way upstairs with a protesting armful of Trevor, Eb asked darkly, 'How soon does that child start school?'

'He's down for next September,' Maudie replied over her shoulder, and vanished quickly up the stairs.

'The sooner the better—perhaps they'll teach him how to behave!' Eb struggled to his feet. 'If Maudie's going out, I suppose that means I've got to get back behind the counter. No peace for the wicked, as they say.'

'You stay where you are, Ebbie,' his wife told him. 'Emily and me can take care of the shop; you have a rest while you can—you look quite washed out. Here, why don't you have a nice read of your newspaper?'

'Load of rubbish.' Eb tossed the daily paper on to the floor, as he slumped back into his chair. 'I'm sick and tired of reading the news. Country's going to the dogs—men out of work everywhere—there's no money about... This shop's takings are down by half, compared to this time last year. When are we going to be told some good news for a change?'

Florrie gave him a long, searching look. With every day that passed, he seemed to grow more depressed, and she was trying to think of something—anything—that might cheer him up. Suddenly she made up her mind.

Closing the door into the shop, she glanced up the stairs to make sure Maudie wasn't within earshot.

'I can tell you one bit of good news,' she began nervously.

'You can?' Eb looked her over and gave a mirthless laugh. 'You know something the newspapers haven't got hold of, is that it?'

'Yes, I do. I'm not supposed to tell you, 'cos your father said as how we'd all got to put it out of our heads, but...' she leaned down towards him, like a conspirator. 'A letter came from our Tommy the other day. He's alive and well in America—at a place called Yonkers. Funny name, isn't it?'

'Tom wrote you a letter? Show it to me!'

'I can't do that. Your dad burned it in the stove and he made your mum and Aunt Emily swear not to talk about it no more. But I never had to promise, so that's why I thought it might cheer you up a bit. Tommy's doing all right out there, working in a factory and saving money. And he says as soon as he can afford the boat ticket, he's going to come home.' She hesitated, then decided to skip the details concerning Maudie. 'He's going to explain he never meant to kill Cousin Saul that night. He did it in self-defence. That's why he wants to tell the police the whole story—everything that happened—then he'll be able to clear his name and be a free man again. There, that's good news for you, isn't it?'

75

She looked at her husband hopefully, expecting to find an answering smile on his face but he remained as he was, sunk back among the cushions of the armchair, as if turned to stone. On his face was an expression of absolute terror.

He drew in several great gulps of air before he had enough breath to gasp out: 'Don't say any more. Don't ever mention the boy's name again. You mustn't tell a living soul what you just told me. Not a word—understand? *Not one single word...*'

'How d'you want it done this time? Your usual?'

Ruth sat on an upright bentwood chair in front of the washstand in her bedroom, and stared at her reflection in the looking-glass.

'Yes, just a shampoo and set,' she said.

'I can do you some nice curls at the sides as well,' added Gloria. 'I've brought my tongs with me today.'

'Oh, you needn't bother about that,' said Ruth. 'Con says he doesn't like my hair frizzed up too much.'

'I never frizz your hair!' Gloria bridled. 'You know I don't...but a few soft curls over each ear look very becoming—everyone says so.'

'Well, I'm not sure.'

'Trust me!' said Gloria firmly. 'Don't worry, I won't heat the tongs too much and singe your hair off. I know what I'm doing, just a gentle hint of curls—no more than that. By the time I've finished, your husband's going to fall in love with you all over again.'

Ruth laughed. 'All right, then. Just a gentle hint.'

Her cousin shook out a towel and tied it deftly round Ruth's shoulders, then unpacked her combs, brushes and scissors, laying them out on the dressing-table along with the setting lotion and the curling-tongs.

She poured some warm water from the washstand jug into the basin, tipped in a little shampoo, and began to work up a lather; and as she worked, she talked.

'How's all the family keeping? How's Connor? And the two kiddies?'

'They're all very well. Con had to go to the Magistrates Court this morning.'

'Oh, no. He's not got into trouble, has he?'

'Certainly not—what an idea! He's got to apply for an extended licence so we can stay open an extra hour on August Bank Holiday, that's all. So Mary's looking after the children while I have my hair done.'

'Yeah, I caught a glimpse of your ma-in-law on my way in. She lifted her lip at me—I think she meant it for a smile.'

'Don't be so unkind. Mary O'Dell's a blessed angel—I won't hear a word against her.'

'Oh, she's been good to you, I'm not denying that, but she can't stand the sight of me—never could. And I'm sure I never gave her any reason to be so high-and-mighty!'

Ruth said nothing. She was not going to dig up ancient grievances or remind Gloria of days gone by, when she used to come into the Watermen with half a dozen different gentlemen-friends in tow or, which was even worse, unaccompanied and on the look-out for a lonely man who might take a fancy to her.

At that time, Gloria had caused her mother, Emily Judge, a great deal of shame and sorrow. She had walked out of the corner-shop and set off on the primrose path, which led rapidly downhill. A year later, she finished up in hospital, sick and disillusioned, rejected by the so-called friends she had picked up along the way.

That was when Ruth got to know her better, and to like her better; and a few months later, Cousin Saul had married Gloria, taking her to live at the ramshackle old warehouse on Cyclops Wharf.

After two major operations, Gloria could no longer have children, but one day Saul brought home a baby he had found abandoned on the mud-flats at low tide. They adopted the child and brought it up as their own, christening him Matthew after Saul's late father.

'And how is Matt?' Ruth enquired politely, with her head in the basin as Gloria washed her hair, then rinsed it with another jugful of water.

'Right as ninepence. I left him with our next-door neighbour—she's very good with him.'

'No prospects of selling the warehouse yet, I suppose?'

'Not a whisper. And the longer we wait, the more dilapidated the old place looks. It'll fall down round our ears one of these days, if we don't watch out! When you think how optimistic I was, this time last year...'

When Gloria had got over the first shock of Saul's horrifying death, she put the warehouse up for sale, together with the contents of the ship-chandlers shop on the ground floor, confident that she would soon find a purchaser. The property proved hard to sell, however. It needed too much spent on repairs, and the stock was old-fashioned and out-of-date. The only offers Gloria received were absurdly low, and she rejected them indignantly.

All the same, she realised she had to earn a living to support herself and Matt, and hit upon the idea of setting herself up as a hairdresser. She had always been interested in beauty culture and hair-styling, so she took a job with a small hairdressing parlour in Stepney to learn the tricks of the trade and when she felt she knew enough, gave in her notice and advertised her services: *Lady clients visited in the comfort and privacy of their own homes.* Naturally, one of her first customers was her Cousin Ruth.

'Now then—you can start to dry yourself with that towel, while I heat up the tongs.'

Gloria had brought a portable spirit-lamp with her. She lit it, then arranged the curling-tongs upon the little grid at the top, asking: 'By the by—how's Mr O'Dell? I never seem to see him around the pub these days.'

'Poor old Pat—he hardly ever leaves his bedroom now. He's got so much older these last few years.'

'How old would he be exactly?'

79

'Funny you should ask that. He'll be fifty-one tomorrow.'

'Lord save us, d'you call that old? Fifty-one's no age at all!'

'I know, but he's not well. It hit him very hard when Rosie left home—and then when Sean got killed in the war... He seemed to turn into an old man before his time.'

'Awful how it takes some people.' Gloria wiped the tongs clean with a scrap of paper, twirling them in a circle until they had cooled slightly, then she coiled a strand of Ruth's hair round the tongs and when it was tightly curled, fixed it in place with two hairpins. Suddenly she exclaimed, 'Ooh, that reminds me of something I meant to show you.'

She put down the tongs, and began to rummage through her bag. 'There's a picture in the latest *Ladies' Companion.* I buy it every month—well, I have to keep up with all the latest styles, don't I?'

She flicked over the pages of the illustrated magazine. 'Where's the dratted thing got to? I'm sure this is where I saw it... Ah, here we are!'

Folding back the page, she passed it to Ruth. 'This season's evening-gowns—direct from Paris,' she explained, pointing to a large photograph.

Three young ladies posed against a rose-covered arbour, showing off three daringly low-cut dresses.

'Very smart, but I don't think they'd be quite suitable for pulling pints in the saloon, do you?' remarked Ruth, about to hand the magazine back.

'Never mind the dresses, I'm talking about the girl! That dark one on the right—doesn't she put you in mind of anybody?' Ruth looked again, and caught her breath, while Gloria chattered on. 'It was you mentioning her just now, reminded me. I suppose it couldn't be her, could it? If not, it's her double.'

'That's Rosie,' said Ruth. 'No doubt about it.'

'Think so? They haven't printed her name. Besides, what would she be doing, wearing Paris gowns and getting her picture in the papers?'

'I don't know—but I'm going to find out.'

'How can you do that?'

'The magazine must have an address and phone-number. Would you leave it with me? I can get on to them and ask.'

'Oh, yes—you're on the telephone now, aren't you? I'd feel a proper fool talking into one of those things, but I suppose you're used to it.'

'Well, we've had it for several weeks now.' Ruth was not going to admit that she had never actually made a phone-call herself, but there had to be a first time for everything, and since Connor was out, this would be the ideal opportunity.

When the shampoo and set was finished and Gloria had gone, Ruth went into the little office behind the saloon and closed the door carefully. Then she sat at the roll-top desk with the magazine in front of her, took a deep breath and lifted the receiver off its hook.

81

The girl's voice in her ear startled her; it was so clear and so close. 'Number, please?'

'Oh, yes. I want the office of the *Ladies' Companion,* please—in Fetter Lane.'

Patiently, the operator asked: 'Do you have the phone-number, please?'

'Oh, I'm sorry—yes, I've got it here.' She read it out from the printed page. 'It's Central—one thousand and twenty-one.'

'Central one-oh-two-one. Hold the line, please.'

Ruth waited for what seemed a long time. There were various clicks and buzzes and the peal of a bell, followed by a different female voice. *'Ladies' Companion.* Good morning, can I help you?'

Ruth explained as briefly as possible that she was trying to get in touch with a relative—the young lady on the right of the group in the picture on page twenty-two.

'I'm sorry, I can't give you that information. We only publish the photographs. That one was taken for us at Kristof Laszlo's studio—you'd have to ask him about it.'

'Oh, well.' She had done it once, she could do it again. 'Do you have his telephone number?'

'Mr Laszlo's a very busy man; he doesn't care to be disturbed. I think it would be much better if you wrote a letter in the first instance. I can give you the address of his studio, if you like.'

So that was that.

When Ruth replaced the ear-piece on the candlestick telephone, she reread the address she had copied down: Manette Street, off

Soho Square. She began to compose a letter in her head, then rejected the idea. To write and receive a reply would take so long—her letter might be ignored completely. There was only one thing for it; she would have to go to Manette Street and enquire personally.

'...And finally, brethren, let us ask the Almighty to look down upon us and our endeavours with His special favour, beseeching Him that He may send a blessing upon our daily tasks, and that in His infinite wisdom He may smite our enemies, and destroy those who would destroy us. Amen.'

The assembled group of men repeated Amen after him, and Marcus Judge resumed his seat.

There was a reverent silence, broken only by the hissing of the gas-jets in the wall-brackets, and then Josh stood up, acknowledging his father's prayer.

'Thank you, sir. Well, gentlemen—the evening's business is now concluded, and I am hereby closing the meeting.'

The Inner Circle of the Brotherhood broke up, scraping back chairs and muttering to one another as they filed out of the Guild Office.

Marcus turned to his son. 'Are you ready to leave, Joshua? Perhaps you'll accompany me as far as the Rope Walk?'

'Not tonight, Father, I'm staying on to do some work. There's the question of the membership to be sorted out. We've too many men on our books and not enough work to go round. We're going to have to cut back.'

Marcus knitted his brows. 'I sincerely hope it will not come to that. Our strength lies in numbers, Joshua. Put your trust in our Lord and Master, and He will provide. Didn't you read the newspaper? Now that Poland has decided to wage war upon the Russian Bolsheviks, she has turned to our Government for assistance. That means that arms will be sent to the Baltic—more work for us all. Another war...it's the very thing we need to keep us busy. An answer to prayer, my son—never forget that.'

Remembering his own recent war-service, Josh was tempted to argue but knew it would be a waste of breath. He simply said, 'Yes, Father—I dare say. But I think I'll stay and get on with some paperwork all the same, if you don't mind. Good night.'

His father nodded curtly and went out without another word. Josh stifled a yawn and opened the Register of Membership, running down the long list of names and pencilling question-marks against those who were old or infirm or generally unreliable.

After a while, he heard a tentative knock at the door and looked up. The man in the doorway was certainly old and infirm, and none too reliable either, but when he ceased to be of any use to the Guild as a working docker, they had found him a sinecure job as nightwatchman on the Wharf.

'Yes, Fred? What is it?'

'Begging your pardon, Mr Josh, sir.' The old man hobbled into the circle of light, turning his cloth cap in his hands. 'I didn't like to interrupt when you're busy, but I thought as you ought to know—we got an intruder hanging around. I'm sure I heard footsteps, down by the jetty.'

'The main gates were locked, weren't they? How could anyone break in? Unless he came over the wall—and there's broken glass along the top.'

''Scuse me, sir—when the meeting finished and the other gentlemen went off home, the gates was left open for a few minutes. Somebody could've slipped in then without me noticing.'

'I see.' Josh sighed. 'All right, I'll take a look round. Lend me that lamp, will you?'

Fred handed over the old bull's-eye lantern he was carrying, and asked, 'D'you want me to come along with you, sir?'

'No, thanks, Fred. You get back to your hut—I think I can manage.'

Not for the first time, Josh wondered how much use an aging and lame nightwatchman would be in an emergency, but he put this thought aside and set off on a tour of inspection.

The night was very dark. Low cloud blotted out moon and stars, and there was a damp mist off the river, shrouding the dock like a blanket. The beam of the bull's-eye lantern did not penetrate the gloom very far, and Josh decided to switch it off. It would not be of much help to him, and it would alert any intruder that he was on his way.

He moved stealthily through the darkness, making his way cautiously towards the jetty.

The mist was cold and clammy, but at least it wasn't raining tonight. He tried not to think of

85

that other night, more than five years ago, when he and Ebenezer had walked this same path, on their way—or so they thought—to release Izzy Kleiber. The image in his mind's eye was as sharp as ever. He could still recall the sodden weight of the man, hanging from the iron rings upon the outer wall—the struggle to haul him up—the rush of water spewed from the gaping mouth as they turned him over...

Jolted out of these memories, he was startled by a movement a few yards ahead, along the jetty. A face emerged, staring at him, greenish and hollow-eyed, and the hair at the back of his neck stood on end...

'My God!' exclaimed Josh.

'Josh—is that you?' asked Ebenezer simultaneously.

Relief and anger swept through Josh. 'What the hell are you doing here?'

'I've been waiting for you. I waited till the meeting was over, then I came in—the gates were still open. I've got to talk to you, Josh.'

'For Christ's sake, can't you leave me alone? If you're going to tell me about that bloody dream again—'

'It's not the dream. Something's happened...' Eb broke off, racked by a fit of coughing.

'You must be barmy, hanging around on a night like this—you'll catch your death. Here, come indoors and get yourself warm.'

The two brothers went back into the Guild Office, and Ebenezer began to gasp and splutter, telling his story as best he could: what Florrie had said to him about Tom's letter—and what Tom had threatened to do...

'He's going to come back to London. He's going to tell everything he knows—clear his name, he calls it. It's all going to come out, Josh, every bit, when he tells the police what he and Saul were fighting over. He doesn't care if he drags us down with him, as long as he clears his precious name! A dutiful son—turning against—his own father!' he panted, clutching at his brother for support.

Josh tried to calm him down. 'Take it easy, man, you'll kill yourself if you carry on like this. Look at you—shivering with cold and wet. What you need is a good stiff drink inside you, to warm you up.'

Eb shook his head violently. 'You know I'm teetotal. If Father could hear you now...'

'This is strictly between you and me, Eb. I'm going to take you to a little place that'll sell us a bottle of scotch in the back room, and nobody any the wiser. That's what you need—whisky, for medicinal purposes. Come on, no arguments. You may be my elder brother, but for once you're going to do as you're told!'

When the Watermen closed its doors, Connor locked up for the night and made his way upstairs.

He found Ruth already in bed, leaning against the pillows in the gentle yellow glow from the oil-lamp on the dressing-table.

'Now there's a pretty sight,' he said, as he

began to undress. 'You look like a princess, so you do!'

'Stop your teasing,' she told him. 'You're only saying that because Gloria did my hair so nicely this morning.'

'Nothing of the kind.' He sat on the edge of the bed to take off his boots. 'You know I don't like to see it all frizzed up like that.'

'Well, I'm sorry, but I like it like this,' she said. 'Anyhow, the curls never stay in long. Listen—I've had an idea about your da's birthday.'

'Don't you start! Hasn't Mam been on about it every day this week?'

'Yes, she said he needs some new pyjamas—his old ones are so worn through they're hardly decent—so I went out and bought him a pair.'

Grinning, Connor pulled off his shirt and stepped out of his trousers. 'Meself, I don't know why he bothers with such things at all. As far as I remember, the wearing of pyjamas isn't mentioned anywhere in the Ten Commandments, is it?' Naked, he climbed into bed beside her. Ruth fended him off, holding him at arms' length.

'No, seriously—listen a minute, will you? I've been thinking, we really ought to persuade your father to get dressed and come downstairs sometimes. If we keep giving him pyjamas and dressing-gowns, we're simply encouraging him to stay in bed all day long, don't you see?'

'Not exactly. What are you driving at?'

She tried again. 'Look, we've got him some pyjamas—all right, but why not give him

88

something else as well? How about a smart shirt, and a new tie? It might be a way of tempting him down to sit in the bar, sometimes.'

Connor nodded. 'Sounds like a good idea, but you've left it a bit late. It's his birthday tomorrow.'

'I know that. I thought, if you've no objection, I could slip up to town after breakfast and go to one of the big stores, and buy him a really handsome shirt and tie.'

'Aha! So that's your secret plan!' Connor pulled her closer to him. 'You're after an excuse to go on the prowl round those fashion-shops again—isn't that the truth of it?'

Smiling, Ruth gave in to him. 'Oh, you're too clever by half. How did you guess I'd got a secret plan?'

Half a mile away, in another bedroom, Mabel Judge opened her eyes to find her husband looming over her, silhouetted against the landing light.

'What time do you call this?' she asked. 'Wherever have you been?'

'I told you I'd be working late tonight,' he said. 'And then Eb called in. He was feeling a bit low, so I did my best to cheer him up.'

She sniffed. 'You've been drinking again. I can smell it on you.'

'Yes—I persuaded poor old Eb to take a drop, and it's done him a power of good. He's as happy as a sandboy now.'

'Eb drinking?' Mabel looked astonished. 'What will Florrie have to say about that?'

'Florrie's not going to know; I've brought

him back here. He can have Jimmy's bed for tonight.'

'But where's Jimmy going to sleep?'

'He can double up with Bertie when he gets back. I told him to get up and put some clothes on—he's on his way round to Florrie's now, to say that Eb's staying with us. And I'm going to carry Eb upstairs and get him settled. Don't worry, I've got it all organised!'

Ebenezer was dimly aware that he was being carried up the narrow staircase. His head banged against the wall when they reached the landing, but for some reason it didn't hurt at all. He smiled foolishly as Josh undressed him and put him to bed; he was feeling blissfully contented, but he couldn't focus on anything very clearly. When he closed his eyes, the room seemed to be turning over and over, like the Big Wheel at the fairground...

Still, what did that matter? He lay on his back, waiting for sleep to overtake him. He just felt slightly sick—a little bit nauseous...

Then he slipped into a deep sleep, and all at once the warm feeling of happiness deserted him and his stomach heaved as he recognised the same old nightmare returning: the walk along the jetty, the cruel hands dragging him to the edge, the utter helplessness as they lowered him into the icy water, the wave that broke over his head—and at last, that terrible choking sensation. He longed for the dream to end, desperate to wake up and find himself safe in bed.

But this time it seemed that the dream would never end.

Early on Tuesday morning, Ruth took a train and was in the Gentlemen's Outfitting department at Gamages soon after the store opened. Fifteen minutes later, with a neat package under her arm, she caught an omnibus to Charing Cross, then completed her journey on foot.

When she reached Soho, a policeman directed her to Manette Street; a narrow alley between two tall buildings.

A small brass above a doorbell bore the words: *Kristof Laszlo, Photographer. Please ring.*—so she pressed the button. Somewhere inside the building, an electric bell shrilled but after that nothing happened. There was no sound except for a pigeon burbling to itself in the road, pecking at horse-dung.

Perhaps there was no one at home. Perhaps nobody had heard the bell. Perhaps Mr Laszlo was so busy he could not be interrupted. Screwing up her courage, Ruth rang again and was rewarded by the sound of footsteps.

Then the bolts were drawn and the door opened a couple of inches, as far as the safety-chain would allow—and Ruth's heart leaped.

Rosie O'Dell peered through the narrow gap, her eyes half-shut against the glare of daylight. She was still in her nightdress, with a paisley shawl thrown round her shoulders.

'Who is it? What do you want?'

'Rosie—it's me. May I come in?'

Rosie's eyes widened. She stared at Ruth, scarcely able to believe what she saw.

'Oh! Yes, of course. I never dreamed... Hang on a second.'

She fumbled with the chain. Released, the door swung open and the two women embraced, laughing, and on the edge of tears.

'Come in, come in! Oh, it's so good to see you...

Ruth followed her into the hallway and was immediately aware of disorder; open packing-cases and an assortment of clothes and furniture piled up in every inch of space. An ancient staircase led to the upper floors of the building, and beyond that, the long hall opened into a large, well-lit room. She caught a glimpse of a camera-tripod, and lamps in huge reflectors, surrounded by yet more boxes and bales.

'Have I come at a bad moment?' she asked. 'Is everything being packed up for the removal men?'

Rosie looked puzzled, then broke into a familiar, dimpled smile. 'You mean the mess? Take no notice—it's always like this. I tried to tidy up a bit when I first came to work here, but I soon found out I was wasting my time. Come on in, I'll find you a chair.'

She led the way into the studio. Rapidly clearing away some bric-à-brac—a fan, a mandolin, a rusty birdcage—from a velvet throne, she invited Ruth to sit down, and settled herself on the edge of a dress-basket.

'Now then—begin at the beginning. How did you find me?'

Ruth explained about the *Ladies' Companion* and her telephone-call, and went on to ask:

'How long have you been working as a photographic model?'

'Oh, a couple of years,' said Rosie vaguely. 'Before that I was modelling clothes for some of the best fashion-houses in London—and in Paris too, sometimes.'

'Goodness, that must have been exciting. How did it happen?'

'Oh, I just bumped into some people, who knew some people... It's all a question of luck, really.' She pulled a face. 'Mind you, I wasn't always lucky. I've done my share of drudgery along the way—waitressing, skivvying, working in shops.'

'I know you were at Gamages for a while. That's the first place I tried, when I started looking for you. They told me you didn't stay there long—you were taken ill, weren't you?'

'Like I said, I've had my ups and downs. But never mind about me—I want to hear about you! You're looking very well. How's Sean keeping?'

'Sean? Oh dear, I should have realised. There's so much you don't know.'

She told Rosie everything that had happened: how Danny was born, and how Sean was killed in France—and how, six months later, she had married Connor... And now they had a baby daughter.

Rose listened, open-mouthed, and at the end of this recital she jumped down from the wicker basket and hugged Ruth all over again.

93

'I'm so happy for you,' she said. 'And for Connor. Tell him from me, he's a lucky man... So the two of you are running the pub now?' Her voice altered. 'And what about the rest of the family? How are they?'

'Mary's very well. She's a proud grandma —you can imagine! As for your father...' Ruth hesitated. 'Did you know it's his birthday today?'

'I hadn't forgotten. You always remember things like birthdays, somehow. How is he?'

As gently as she could, Ruth told her that Patrick had taken to his bed many years ago, finishing, 'It seems as if he'll never get any better. He needs something to bring him back to life—something to live for. A *real* birthday present.'

'What do you mean?'

'I mean—Mary has forgiven him for what happened. Don't you think you might find it in your heart to do the same?'

There was a silence, and then Rosie said huskily, 'Dear God, what a thing to ask. It's been such a long time. So much has happened since then.'

'That's why I thought it might be worth suggesting. After all, it's water under the bridge now, surely?'

'I don't know...I'll have to think about that.' Rosie glanced down, and apologised belatedly for her attire. 'I'm sorry—I'm only just out of bed. We were rather late last night.'

Ruth looked round the studio. 'I thought this was where you work. Do you live here as well?'

94

'Um, yes, more or less. For the time being, I do.'

She broke off as a man's voice called from the staircase: 'What's all this dam' talking? Can't a man get any peace around here?'

It was an unusual voice—part Cockney, part mid-European—and the owner of the voice was equally bizarre. Short and square, with greasy black hair and a Van Dyke beard, he wore a sea-green smoking-jacket over a frilled shirt and wine-coloured velvet breeches. The shirt was unbuttoned, revealing a hairy chest, and his feet were crammed into a pair of Persian slippers with pointed toes.

Seeing Ruth, he stopped short. 'An' who is this young lady, please?'

'My sister-in-law, Mrs O'Dell. Ruth, this is Kristof—Mr Laszlo.'

'Charmed to be making your acquaintance, dear lady.' He bowed low, lifting Ruth's hand and brushing it with his lips. 'Such a delightful surprise.' Then he glared at Rosie, adding, 'But what you are doing in your night-clothes this time of day? Whatever will the dear lady think of you? You must get dressed immediate!'

'Yes, all right—I'm just going. Could you make Ruth a cup of coffee? I won't be two ticks.'

Rosie ran upstairs and Mr Laszlo beamed upon Ruth, revealing a row of gleaming white teeth and some gold fillings.

'You like coffee? Or you prefer something stronger? A glass of plum brandy, maybe?'

'No, really—nothing at all, thank you.'

'Suit yourself!' He shrugged, spreading his arms wide, then threw himself down upon a threadbare chaise-longue, his hands behind his head. 'This is big surprise for me. Rosie never tell me she has no sister-in-law.' He looked Ruth up and down, openly appraising her, to her great embarrassment.

'An' she never tell me she has such a beautiful sister-in-law, neither. Do you do the same line of work, maybe? Modelling for pictures—huh?'

'No, I don't. I help my husband run a public-house,' said Ruth, then added firmly: '*And* I look after our two children.'

'Pity. I could do a lot for you, my dear.' He gave a prodigious wink. 'If you ever change your mind, you know where to find me—huh?'

Ruth tried to steer the conversation into other channels. She asked, 'Have you been in London long, Mr Laszlo?'

'Ten bloody years ago, I come from Hungary,' he announced cheerfully. 'And four of those bloody years I spend in a bloody prison-camp—if you'll pardon the expression. What for they want to lock me up? They think maybe I'm going to throw a bomb at the King and Queen, or what?'

It was a relief when Rosie rejoined them, now wearing a smart dress in cherry-red shantung, and a black hat with a saucy feather. She came into the studio, apologising for keeping Ruth waiting, and pulling on a light summer jacket.

'You going somewhere?' asked Mr Laszlo. 'Why you not tell Kristof?'

'Because I only just made up my mind,'

96

replied Rosie. 'It's my dad's birthday today—I'm going to wish him many happy returns.'

'Oh, Rosie, he'll be so pleased!' Suddenly Ruth had an idea. 'Before we go, do you have a telephone? I think perhaps I should talk to Connor first, so he can break the news gently to Patrick and Mary. It might be too much of a shock if we burst in on them without any warning.'

Going back in the train, Ruth made sure that no one else was listening, then ventured to say: 'I know it's none of my business, but are you and Kristof—you know what I mean—together?'

'Of course not! Well, anyway—not like you mean.' Rosie averted her face. 'At least, it's nothing serious. He's never serious about things like that. Oh, we get on well enough. As soon as he found out I knew about cameras and all that, he realised I could make myself useful round the studio, so I sort of moved in. It was what you might call convenient—for both of us.'

Ruth said, 'I gather he was interned during the war, as well?'

'Yes, he was, but that's not the reason I—' Rosie stopped, then began again. 'That's just a coincidence. It doesn't mean anything.'

'Doesn't it? I notice you never once asked me about Ernest.'

Rosie turned to her. 'Have you seen him? Is he all right?'

'I've seen him; I don't think he's very happy. He still misses you dreadfully. He'd give anything to see you again.'

'No.' Rosie's voice was hard, and very definite. 'I could never do that. You mustn't tell him you've seen me—that's all over and done with.'

'Don't say that. I'm sure he still loves you.'

'Don't you understand—*that's why!* I let him down, Ruth. I should have waited for him... But it's too late now—I won't ever see him again.'

At noon, Florrie couldn't wait any longer and went round to Josh's house to find out what had happened to Ebenezer.

Mabel ushered her in, speaking in hushed tones. 'Josh told me not to disturb him. He'll be sleeping it off all morning, he said.'

'But it's nearly dinner-time! He's not still in bed, surely?'

'I'm afraid so.' Mabel sighed. 'You know how men are when they've had a glass too many. He'll be like a bear with a sore head when he gets up.'

'Are you suggesting my husband's been *drinking?*' Though she was usually timid, this accusation outraged Florrie. 'He's a Rechabite, you know that! He never touches alcohol—he's signed the pledge!'

'I expect that's why it hit him extra hard—not being used to it, you see. Josh only gave him some whisky for his own good. He'd got chilled to the marrow last night and he needed a drop of something to keep out the cold.'

'I never heard such a thing! I don't care what Josh says, I'm going to wake him up. He's supposed to be at the shop. Me and Aunt

Emily's been working our fingers to the bone, waiting for him.'

Pushing past Mabel, Florrie climbed the stairs and knocked angrily on the door of Jimmy's bedroom. There was no reaction from within.

'I told you, didn't I? He's dead to the world,' said Mabel, over her shoulder.

'We'll soon see about that,' retorted Florrie, turning the handle.

The room stank of bile and alcohol. Mabel pulled back the curtains, and sunlight streamed in. Florrie gave a faint, inarticulate cry.

Still in his underclothes, Ebenezer lay sprawled across the bed, his head hanging down over the side, his one hand clawing at his throat. His eyes were wide open, staring blindly at the ceiling—his face was a mottled blue.

A doctor was summoned at once, but it was too late to save him.

Some time between midnight and dawn, Ebenezer Judge had dreamed his dream to the end, and choked to death—drowning in his own vomit.

Ruth and Rosie arrived at the pub as it was closing for the afternoon. Rosie was very nervous and Ruth did her best to reassure her, promising to make the reunion as simple as possible.

In fact, it all went off smoothly. Connor had already prepared the way for them, and Mary was in her best dress, with baby Lilian on her lap and Danny at her side when they walked into the kitchen.

'Hello, Mam,' said Rosie quietly. 'How are you?'

'All the better for seeing you,' began Mary, in a voice quite unlike her own, hoarse with unshed tears. She stood up, handing the baby to Ruth, and took Rosie in her arms. 'I should be very cross with you—worrying us the way you did.'

Then the tears came at last, and she couldn't say another word. The two women held one another, laughing and crying at the same time, while little Danny pulled at Ruth's skirt, wanting to know, 'Who's that lady, Mam?'

Mary broke free, dried her eyes, blew her nose and informed him, 'This is your Aunt Rosie... She's come home.'

Rosie too was wiping away tears; she gazed round the old familiar room and asked, 'Where's Connor? I thought he'd be here.'

'He'll be back directly. I think he had to go and see a man about some business,' said Mary. 'So now—do you feel ready to come upstairs and say hello to your da? Ruth will have told you—he mostly spends the day in bed, but as this is such a special occasion...'

When they went into the big bedroom, Patrick was seated in an armchair facing the door, dressed in his blue serge suit—waiting for Rosie. With great difficulty, he levered himself on to his feet.

'No, no, I need no help at all—I can manage on my own,' he grunted, short of breath, letting go of the chair. He opened his arms to his daughter. 'Come and give us a kiss, my darling. It's great to see you.'

They clung to one another as if they could never be parted again.

There was so much to say—there was too much to say. Mam and Da wanted to know everything about Rosie's life since they saw her last—where had she been, what had she done—but she only shook her head. There would be plenty of time for all that later.

'You'll not be running away again just yet?' Patrick asked anxiously.

'Not just yet,' Rosie told him.

Meanwhile Ruth was downstairs, looking after her children. She glanced up with a smile as Connor came in, but her smile disappeared when she saw who was with him.

'What's wrong?' asked Connor quickly. 'She's not gone already?'

'No, she's upstairs, but...'

'But what? I had to go and find Ernest, didn't I? He's as much right to be a part of this as anyone.'

Awkwardly, Ernest bowed to Ruth. 'I hope you don't mind me intruding upon a family occasion, but Connor explained—'

'Yes, I understand.' Ruth could not think what to say to him. 'It's only, when I suggested to Rosie that she might like to see you...' She could not go on, and Ernest's face fell.

'I see...I should not have come. Forgive me.'

Ruth tried to soften the blow. 'I'm sorry, but she's bound to feel a little strange at first. She

101

probably says things she doesn't mean...I do think it would be better if you went home now, Ernest.'

'If you say so.' His shoulders drooped and he turned away.

'Stay where you are!' Connor's face darkened. 'I invited you here—if anyone's at fault, it's myself. Why wouldn't she see him, for God's sake?'

'It's not fair to spring this on her without any warning,' began Ruth. 'Perhaps if we give her a little more time?'

Then the door opened again and Rosie burst into the room, her face radiant: 'What d'you think? Da says he's going to come down for tea with—'

She could not continue; at the sight of Ernest, her voice failed her. He looked so much older than when she last saw him—tired and thin—his hair receding, a pair of wire-framed spectacles upon his nose. She threw an agonised, reproachful look at Ruth and seemed about to run out of the room, but with three words Ernest stopped her.

Ignoring everyone else, he walked up and took her hands in his, saying simply: 'I love you.'

Unable to look into his eyes, she hung her head, whispering, 'I thought I'd never see you again.'

'I prayed that I would see you again,' he said, 'so I could ask the question I should have asked five years ago. Will you marry me?'

4

Gloria came to do Ruth's hair on the first Monday of every month. When she arrived at the beginning of July, they had a great deal to talk about.

'You remember Con's sister, don't you?' Ruth asked, with a twinkle in her eye as Gloria walked into the saloon bar.

Wearing an apron, with her sleeves rolled up and her hair tucked under a duster, Rosie stopped polishing the brasswork on the beer-pumps long enough to throw her a cheerful smile.

'Hello!' she said. 'How are you keeping?'

Gloria stared, her mouth agape, then turned to Ruth in bewilderment. 'I don't understand. I thought you said—'

Ruth laughed. 'Well, don't look so surprised! It's only because of you that she's here at all. You're the one who spotted Rosie's photo in that magazine.'

'You mean that's how you managed to find her?'

As briefly as possible, Ruth told the story and Rosie chimed in, 'But now I've left Soho, and moved back with the family, to help out as a part-time barmaid.'

'Now I know you're pulling my leg!' exclaimed Gloria. 'Don't tell me you've given up being a fashion model!'

'I have so,' Rosie assured her, 'and believe it or not, I've never been as happy in my whole life.'

She did not propose to gratify Gloria's curiosity any further; the memory of her meeting with Ernest was too precious to talk about—the most terrifying moment of her life, and the most wonderful.

She could still see him standing there, blinking shyly through his glasses and saying, 'Will you marry me?'

She did not even notice when Connor and Ruth took the children out of the kitchen, closing the door softly behind them; she could see nothing but the hope and the love that shone in Ernest's patient, trusting face. In abject misery, she lowered her head.

'Please don't say that,' she begged. 'Don't ask me.'

'Why shouldn't we be married?' He drew a sharp breath, as a new and appalling idea struck him. 'Do you mean there is another man? You love somebody else?'

'No, it's not that...' She tried to find a way to explain without hurting him too much. 'I was so afraid, when you went away. I thought it was the end of everything—I thought I'd be alone for the rest of my life. And then, after a while—well, I made new friends. Other men...'

He could hardly hear her; he came closer still, putting his hand under her chin and lifting her head.

'You don't have to tell me any more,' he said. 'That's all finished now. I love you more

104

than anyone else could ever love you. You and me—we belong together. Forget about the years in between. You're here at last—nothing else matters. Only say that you still love me.'

Their faces were a few inches apart—and then they were in each other's arms and she whispered, 'Yes—I still love you. Yes—I will marry you. Yes...'

The next day, she and Ruth went back to Manette Street to pick up her belongings and she explained to Kristof that she had decided to return to her family.

He took the news philosophically. He had been fond of her, but there were other pretty girls in the world, waiting to be photographed. He told her she was a fool, and wished her luck—then he gave her a gold sovereign and a bottle of champagne as a farewell present. They drifted apart as casually and amicably as they had drifted together in the first place, with no ill-will on either side.

And, as Ruth told Gloria later, 'She's got something else to look forward to...her wedding day.'

By now they were upstairs in the front bedroom, and Gloria was pouring hot water into the washbasin, preparing the shampoo.

'Is that a fact?' Gloria tested the temperature. 'Ow! That's nearly boiling—I'll put in a drop of cold. So she's only here temporary, so to speak. Well, that explains it. Some rich toff she met up West, I dare say?'

'Not at all. She's going to marry Ernest Kleiber. You know, he used to have a photographic shop at Cubitt Town.'

'Oh yes, of course! She lived there with him over the shop, didn't she? So that's all on again, is it? I never could understand what she saw in him—a bit thin and weedy, to my way of thinking. What a waste. A pretty little thing like her, with her picture in the papers—she could have had her pick of men. Still, there's no accounting for tastes.'

When Ruth's hair had been washed, she noticed Gloria getting out the curling-tongs and stopped her. 'You won't be needing those—I don't want curls today.'

'Why ever not? The last time you said you liked them.'

'Yes, I know, but Con's not very keen so we won't bother.'

'Well, it's up to you, of course, but I think curls give you a bit of sparkle. You're looking rather washed-out today, if you don't mind me saying so. Perhaps it's 'cos you're in black—black doesn't suit some people.'

'I thought I ought to. For a few weeks, anyhow, as a mark of respect.'

'You mean on account of Ebenezer? Yes—sad, wasn't it, him going off like that. Mind you, he'd never been in good health, not since they sent him home from France.'

'Did you go to the funeral?'

'No, I didn't. Well, Eb and me wasn't that close. He didn't approve of me, and to be honest I never much cared for him, either. Besides, I didn't fancy going to the Chapel and having all the family looking down their noses at me. You

106

didn't go yourself, did you?'

Their eyes met in the mirror above the washstand; Ruth shook her head.

'I wouldn't have known about it at all, except that Mum sent me a little note to tell me he'd passed away—in his sleep, she said. I knew I wouldn't be welcome at the funeral so I sent some flowers, and I got Father Ryan to say a mass for him instead.'

'That's nice. Of course, there was a lot of carry-on about the way Eb went, from what I hear. Seemingly, the night it happened, your brother Josh bought a bottle of scotch and got Eb squiffy. Naturally, he tried to hush it up after, but your dad got to hear of it from the doctor and he didn't half go for Josh—you can imagine. But then those two don't see eye to eye about anything these days. There's been a lot of trouble at the Brotherhood, they say—them two quarrelling at meetings...'

'What do they quarrel about?' asked Ruth.

'Ask me another. Could be political, perhaps —there's been a lot of rows about politics lately.'

As a rule, political matters were not discussed at the Three Jolly Watermen.

That evening, Connor was behind the counter in the saloon when he heard angry voices in the public bar. Leaving Rosie in charge, he went to investigate and found a three-cornered argument in progress.

A stocky, energetic young man with a shock of red hair was thumping on a table-top and proclaiming in a strong Welsh accent: 'I'm simply asking, when are we going to get our rights, like we was promised? A fair rate for the job and a standard working week—answer me that!'

Facing him, an older man tried to shout him down. 'You don't know what you're talking about, you and your Bolshevik friends! The dockers have got a national rate of pay now, and a forty-four-hour week—what more do you want?'

Sitting at a table between the two men, uncomfortably close to this violent exchange, Patrick O'Dell tried to pour oil on troubled waters. 'Give it a rest, lads, for pity's sake! Agree to differ, and shake hands on it, eh?'

Since Rosie's return to the Watermen, Patrick had had a new lease of life. He was up and dressed every day, and spent each evening in the corner of the public bar with a pint pot in front of him, keeping a benevolent eye on the satisfied customers.

But tonight, the customers were not all satisfied. The Welshman pointed an accusing finger at his opponent, retorting, 'What's the good of a national rate if we can't afford to live on it? You know as well as I do that the Wharfmasters are living off the fat of the land on their company profits, but how are the dockers expected to support their wives and kids on seventy-two shillings and sixpence a week?'

Behind the counter, a young barmaid tried to make herself heard. 'Let's have a bit of hush, gents, if you please!'

Unheeding, the Welshman went on, 'How are their wives expected to feed a family on a lump of cheese not big enough for a mouse, and a handful of peas that wouldn't satisfy a guinea-pig? As Ernest Bevin said at the Labour rally the other day—'

A roar went up from the customers, some of them calling out: 'Hooray for Ernie!' and others yelling: 'Down with the Bolshies!'

Patrick O'Dell pulled himself up from his chair, trying to intervene. 'We'll have no politics in this house, so will you shut your row, the pair of you!'

'You stay out of this—it's none of your business!' The Welshman shook him off impatiently. 'Who d'you think you are, to lay down the law?'

That was enough for Connor. In one stride he crossed the bar, and had the young man's collar in one hand, the other knotted into a fist beneath his jaw.

'I'll tell you who he is,' he said. 'He's my da and he's the boss here—and if he tells you to shut your row, you'll do as you're told.'

A hush fell over the room, and the young man pulled back, staring at Connor. Then his face changed, and he said in an awestruck tone, 'I know you... You're Connor O'Dell.'

'What's that to you?' Connor let him go, and settled his collar with ironic courtesy, arranging it round his flaming scarlet necktie. 'I know you too, my bucko—you're a troublemaker.'

'And we'll have no politics and no religious disputation here—that's the rule of the house,' said Patrick, sinking back into his chair, still a little flustered. 'You tell him that, son.'

'I've no wish to argue with you,' said the young man, with the beginning of a smile on his lips, 'but I'll be proud to shake you by the hand, Connor O'Dell.'

Rather at a loss, Connor said, 'Very well—shake hands and that's an end to it.'

'I hope not. I hope it will be my privilege to buy you a drink as well. What will it be?'

Still more mystified, Connor replied, 'Since you're feeling generous, I'll take a half-pint of our best bitter...but if we've met before, I have to admit I don't remember the occasion.'

'A half of best for Mr O'Dell!' They moved across to the bar together, and the stranger explained, 'No, we've not met, but I've watched you a good many times—in the ring.'

Light dawned at last. 'You've seen me fight?'

'Of course. The first time was when you were at Poplar, in the boxing-booth—it must be seven years ago. I was thirteen then, and you were a hero to me in those days. A bit later on, I saw you touring round with the army recruiting drive, giving demonstration bouts. I wanted to join up, like you—I even tried lying about my age, but I didn't have any luck.'

'That's a matter of opinion,' said Connor. 'Come and sit down, and let me introduce you to my father.'

They settled with their drinks at the corner table and the young man shook hands with Patrick, apologising for his bad manners.

'Think no more about it, my lad.' The old man nodded and smiled. 'You're very welcome—haven't the Irish and the Welsh a lot in common, when all's said and done?'

'Whereabouts do you come from, Mr—?' Connor hesitated.

'I was born in the Rhondda valley, at a little place called Treorky—and the name's Pritchard, Huw Pritchard.'

'And what are you doing so far from home, Mr Pritchard?'

'My dad was killed in the pit, and my ma died soon after, so Gran sent me to London. She didn't want me to get work at the colliery, and she had cousins in Limehouse—the Williamses, in Three Colt Street.'

'Of course!—the Welsh Dairy!' said Connor. 'So you came up to London when you were still a boy?'

'To begin with, I worked for the family, pushing the churns round the streets on the milk-cart, but then I got too old for that, and I applied for work with the Dockworkers Guild at Jubilee Wharf.'

'You're talking of the Brotherhood?' Connor raised an eyebrow. 'They don't take kindly to outsiders as a rule.'

'No, but Mr Evans spoke up for me. He's our Minister at the Emmanuel Chapel—the family are all Baptists, see? I was very grateful when Mr Judge took me on.'

'From what I heard you say a few minutes ago, you're not feeling quite so grateful for the job now.'

'Oh, the job's not bad—I'm not complaining. The trouble is, I'm a member of the Dockworkers' Union as well, and the Brotherhood doesn't always fall in with what the Union recommends. According to Mr Bevin, our Deputy Leader, we ought to—'

Patrick cleared his throat loudly and Huw broke off, grinning. 'Sorry, I'll get off my soapbox. All I'm trying to say is that the Brotherhood think they're a law unto themselves. They only stick to Union regulations when it suits them.'

'In that case, wouldn't you do better to apply to another wharf?'

'I suppose I might. But I like the crowd I work with—some of them, anyhow. I'd rather stay in the Brotherhood and try to persuade them to adopt the national agreements.'

'I wish you luck,' said Connor dryly. 'You're going to need it.'

'But let's not talk politics now,' said Huw impatiently. 'There's a thousand things I want to ask you, Mr O'Dell. I thought when the war was over, you'd go back to prizefighting. You could have been a British Champion by now—why did you give it up?'

Connor took a long swig of beer and wiped his mouth before replying.

'That's a long story,' he said finally.

At the end of the evening, Mary O'Dell came downstairs and found Ruth making cups of cocoa for the bar staff.

'You'll have a cup too, won't you?' Ruth

asked. 'How about Mr O'Dell—would he like one?'

'I won't say no for myself, but the old fellow won't stay awake long enough to drink it,' said Mary. 'I helped him into bed, and he was half asleep before his head touched the pillow.'

'Did you hear any sound from the children's room when you came past the door?'

'Not a murmur. I peeped in, and they're both far away in dreamland.'

Rosie came in and joined them, flopping into the armchair. 'I'm dead beat! I've been run off my feet tonight. I was helping Con in the saloon, and then he went off to sort out a spot of bother in the public, and I've hardly seen him since. He'll be in directly—he's just going round locking up.' She stretched out her arms and yawned. 'Oh my, I'm not used to all this hard work. I've got out of the habit.'

'It won't be for much longer,' Ruth encouraged her. 'Another couple of months and you'll be a lady of leisure again. Have you settled on the wedding day yet?'

'Some time in September, that's all I know. Ernest's got to fix the date with the Registrar. The sooner the better, as far as I'm concerned—I can't wait!'

As Ruth passed round the cocoa-cups, Mary said unhappily, 'I wish you'd wait a little longer, my darling. What's the hurry? Why does it all have to happen so quick?'

'What is there to wait for?' asked Rosie. 'Ernest loves me—I love Ernest. We want to get married as soon as possible.'

'Yes, but in a Registry Office... I'm sorry, I know you think I'm old-fashioned, but I can't bear the thought of you not marrying in church—not having God's blessing upon the pair of you.'

'But Mam, you know very well we can't do that—Ernest being Jewish, and me a Catholic.'

'What kind of Catholic do you call yourself, being married by a civil servant?' demanded Mary. 'I'm only saying, why not take a bit more time before you make up your mind? Maybe Ernest will come round. He might see the light and be received into the Faith.'

'He'll never do that. He's been brought up strictly, he goes to synagogue—I respect him for that. In fact, after we're married I shall probably start going there myself.'

'You're not serious?' Horrified, Mary crossed herself. 'You don't mean you'd change your faith?'

'I might—what's wrong with that? If it's all right for Ernest to change his religion to marry me, why shouldn't I do the same for him?'

'It's not the same at all!' The words burst from Mary. 'How could you turn away from Our Lord Jesus Christ and His Mother? Jews worship the God of Moses, I know that—but what about the New Testament? How could you live without Bethlehem—without Gethsemane—without the Resurrection? How could you pray in a church without a statue of Our Lady—without the blessed Saints—without even a crucifix?'

She turned helplessly to her daughter-in-law. 'Ruth, say something! Can't you explain to her?'

114

Ruth shook her head. 'I'm the last person you should ask. You were happy for me when I changed my religion—shouldn't we be happy for Rosie?'

Diplomatically, she tried to shift the conversation to firmer ground. What was Rosie going to wear for the ceremony? What did they want for a wedding present? Where were they planning to hold the reception afterwards?

'If you haven't already arranged something else, I know Con would be glad to let you have the wedding breakfast here in the Watermen,' she added.

Rosie said she felt sure Ernest would be very pleased. She began to count how many guests they had to invite: members of the immediate family, of course, all their old friends and neighbours...

Greatly daring, Ruth said, 'Can I make a suggestion? There's one person you may not have thought of, and this would be the ideal opportunity to invite her. To hold out the olive-branch, so to speak.'

Rosie and Mary both turned to look at her. Ruth did not have to finish what she had begun to say; she saw from the look in their eyes that they understood her.

'No,' said Rosie, her happiness fading.

'Never,' said Mary.

They knew that Ruth was about to suggest Mary's sister Moira—Rosie's natural mother.

'If she ever set foot in this house, I'd walk out of it,' Mary continued.

She did not raise her voice, or express any

115

anger; it was a plain statement of fact. Rosie was equally adamant.

'I don't ever want to see her again,' she said.

It was useless to argue. Picking up her cup of cocoa, Rosie said, 'It was just an idea. I think I'll go up now—tell Con I've gone to bed, will you?'

Lying in bed, she thought back over the conversation, blaming herself for having interfered in such a private matter. But she had been fond of Moira, and guessed how much anguish the rift in the family must have caused her. It seemed unfair that Mary, Patrick and Rosie had all been reconciled, and that Moira alone was excluded—banished from their affection for ever.

'I suppose I shouldn't have mentioned it,' she told herself. 'After all, it's no business of mine.'

She wondered if she should confess to Connor what she had tried—and failed—to do, but when he came into the bedroom at last, she felt at once that this was not the right moment. He seemed preoccupied, hardly looking at her as he got undressed.

Trying to break through his silent mood, she said, 'Gloria did my hair this morning. How do you like it?'

He glanced at her briefly, hardly seeing her. 'Very nice,' he said, with no expression whatever.

'I told her I didn't want any curls this time... What do you think?'

116

'Very nice,' he said again, and got into bed, still immersed in his own thoughts.

'I'm glad you like it,' she said in a small voice.

'Good night, Ruth,' he said, then he rolled over and went to sleep.

One Friday morning towards the end of the summer, Josh sat in the Guild Office, going through the wages list and making up the pay-packets to be doled out at the end of the day.

The only sounds in the room were the scratching of his pen-nib as he made each entry, and the chink of coins as he counted them out of the cashbox—and the heavy breathing of Marcus Judge, who sat at the other side of the desk, his eyes fixed upon his son.

Finally Josh put down his pen and asked wearily, 'Are you planning to stay much longer, Father?'

'Do you have any objection to my presence here?' countered the old man.

'No, not exactly, but there's nothing for you to do. And it's putting me off, having you watching me like a hawk all the time. I don't know how long I'll be—you'd much better get off home.'

'I prefer to keep you company. As long as I am with you, I can be sure that you will not be led astray by the demon drink.'

'For God's sake, Father, can't you ever let me be?'

Marcus rose to his feet, seeming to tower over

117

his son. 'How dare you take the Lord's name in vain? How dare you blaspheme before your own father?'

Josh set his jaw grimly, refusing to be browbeaten. 'I am not blaspheming. I asked you, in the name of Almighty God, to stop tormenting me and punishing me. Why can't you leave me to get on with my work in peace?'

'I shall never leave you, as long as you are caught in the toils of Satan.' Marcus's words came from deep in his chest, booming like the notes of an organ. 'I will not cease to wrestle for the salvation of your immortal soul.'

'All right! But while you're doing that, I'm trying to get the wages made up for—' began Josh, then exploded irritably as someone knocked at the office door: 'What is it now?'

The door opened, and Huw Pritchard walked in. They stared at him, for he had only reported for work half an hour earlier.

'Excuse me, sir—and you, too, sir.' Huw threw a polite nod in Marcus's direction. 'Could you spare a minute?'

'I'm warning you—if it's about the overtime payments again,' threatened Josh.

'It's nothing to do with pay, sir.'

'That makes a change. Well, what's the trouble this time?'

'I've just started work on the day-shift at Number Five Warehouse, loading the *Prince Albert*, sir.'

'I know that. Who gave you permission to take a break?'

'Nobody, sir. But I had to find out. The *Albert* is bound for Danzig tomorrow, on the morning tide, they say. Is that right?'

'Yes, she's going to the Baltic. Why?'

'We were given special safety rules—fire precautions—no smoking—all that. The lads say there's explosives in those crates—weapons and ammunition going to Poland.'

Josh's patience was wearing thin. 'What are you driving at, Pritchard? Yes, the Government's sending armaments to help Poland in her fight against the Soviet, but I can't for the life of me see what that's got to do with you!'

'Only this, sir. Me and my mates, we don't think Britain ought to be taking Poland's side against Russia. They've got trouble enough out there, I reckon, and that's why we're not working with any cargo that might be used against our Russian brothers.'

'Your Russian brothers?' Josh put his head in his hands. 'God give me strength!'

Marcus opened his mouth, but before he could speak, Josh cut in quickly: 'I mean that, Father. I'm praying that God will give me the strength to put up with this chap, spouting his everlasting Socialist claptrap.'

'I'm not trying to preach Socialism to you, Mr Judge, I'm simply telling you that as long as there's armaments being loaded from Number Five Warehouse, I won't be working there today. And neither will some of the others.'

'You can do as you please,' said Josh, through gritted teeth. 'You can go home and whistle for your wages, if that's what you want. As far as

119

I'm concerned, you and your Bolshie friends can do what you blooming well like—and that's *not* swearing, Father.'

Marcus walked majestically to the door and flung it wide open, saying to Huw Pritchard: 'You will leave this room at once. You will not report for duty again until you have apologised for your insolence. Now get out of my sight.'

Huw nodded calmly. 'Right you are, gentlemen. I'll be off, then. I just thought I should let you know how things stand, that's all.'

When the door shut, Marcus growled quietly, 'That young man must go. Strike his name from the list.'

Josh shook his head. 'No need for that. He's a good worker; he puts his back into the job and he gives value for money. He'd be a loss to the Brotherhood if we expelled him on account of his blessed principles.'

'He must not be allowed to glory in sinful pride and get away with it—'

'I didn't say he'd get away with it. There's more than one way to kill a cat... Don't you worry, he'll repent of his wicked ways all right, you leave that to me.'

The following morning, Connor went out for a stroll before breakfast.

One of Danny's birthday presents had been a puppy—a rough-haired mongrel with a dash of Airedale, the shaggy muzzle of an Irish terrier and paws like a wolfhound.

They couldn't decide what to call the animal, but Danny said at once that his name was 'Barker'—so that was that. Barker grew very quickly, and had to work off a tremendous amount of energy every day, and since Danny was much too young to take him out for walks, this duty fell upon Connor.

He pretended to grumble about it, but privately he enjoyed the early-morning outing across the Island to West Ferry Road and back again. On fine days, he took the long way round by Jubilee Wharf.

Today, as they approached the dockyard entrance, Barker began to yelp, sniffing excitement in the air. There were half a dozen men outside the gates, engaged in a noisy altercation. Some of them were carrying placards, with slogans that read: *Stop the war against Russia, No guns for Poland* and *Help for the Soviet people.*

The others were trying to drive the protesters away, and a fight seemed likely to break out at any minute, until a pair of uniformed police constables appeared, and stood watching them from the other side of the street.

Connor recognised one of the men on the picket-line, and hailed him. 'Morning, Mr Pritchard. Standing up for your rights again, I see?'

'Trying to, Mr O'Dell!' Huw waved his placard cheerfully. 'We've had some success already—turned away more than a dozen chaps, we did, once they understood what we were on about. They'll never get the *Albert* loaded before the high tide, now they're short-handed.'

'Another triumph for the working man, eh? Well, I wish you luck.'

Connor whistled to Barker, who was investigating a nearby lamp-post, and walked on. He was amused and oddly stirred by the Welshman's enthusiasm, but he couldn't help thinking that his triumph was likely to be short-lived.

As it turned out, he was mistaken.

The *Prince Albert* was not the only ship to be held up by a dockers' strike: at the East India Docks, the *Jolly George*, with a similar load of armaments for Poland, was prevented from sailing. The Labour Party made its voice heard, and a storm of protest blew up in Parliament. In Downing Street, the Cabinet began to have second thoughts.

At the Kleiber household in Poplar, these dramatic events passed unnoticed: Ernest and Rosie had more important matters in mind.

Suddenly the wedding day, which had seemed so far away, was almost upon them. Ernest felt unhappy about just one thing: he resented having to begin married life in this cheerless old house, under the same roof as Sarah and little Ben, together with any assortment of strangers who might happen to lodge with them.

'If only I had some money put by,' he told Rosie, as he was taking her home to the pub one evening.

They walked hand in hand through the warm summer dusk, their arms entwined, her head upon his shoulder, listening to the drowsy lullaby of ships' hooters from the river, and smelling the scent of soft tar upon the roadway.

'If I had a proper job, and a regular salary,

122

it would be different. I wish I could buy us a house—just a little place, big enough for you and me, where we could be all by ourselves.'

'One day we'll have somewhere of our own,' she told him. 'That's something to look forward to.'

When they reached the Watermen, Mary and Ruth wouldn't let Ernest into the kitchen, but made him wait in the bar. They had been working all the evening, sewing Rosie's wedding-dress, and it would be terribly unlucky if the bridegroom set eyes on it before the great day. They had bought a paper pattern, and followed the instructions carefully—it would be the most beautiful dress ever seen. Night after night they sat in the kitchen, adding frills of lace and clusters of tiny artificial pearls.

When Ernest left, Rosie tried it on and the two dress-makers stood back to survey their handiwork.

'The hem dips a bit on one side. Better take it up—you don't want to trip on it when you're walking up the aisle.' Mary broke off sadly. 'What am I saying? I don't suppose they have aisles in them Registry places...'

As devout Catholics, the O'Dells preferred not to attend the civil ceremony, but that didn't stop them doing everything they could to make the reception an unforgettable occasion.

The wedding breakfast was a feast, and the champagne flowed like water; the party went with a swing from beginning to end.

After the speeches and the toasts, someone began to play the piano in the saloon and Ernest led his bride into the middle of the floor, to lead the dancing. He had never had much practice as a dancer, and stepped on Rosie's toes once or twice, but she didn't care. He was the man she loved, and she felt as if she were floating above the ground.

At the height of the festivities, the street door opened and Huw Pritchard came in, looking for Connor. Patrick tried to explain that this was a family party and a private occasion, but Huw said, 'I know. I'm sorry, but I just heard some good news.'

Connor joined them, asking: 'What's happened now?'

'You were right, what you said about a triumph for the working man. It's in all the evening papers—look at this!'

He unfolded a copy of the *Star* and handed it to Connor. The news item was on the front page: the British Government, which had been sending aid and supplies to Poland to assist her fight against the Russian Soviet, had changed its policy. It would no longer be giving the Poles practical support in the war.

'And you feel this is all down to you, I suppose?' Connor teased him.

'I'm not saying that—but we did our bit, didn't we?'

Connor slapped him on the back. 'You did indeed. Sit yourself down, my lad. Private party or not, I'd say this deserves a drink.'

Ruth happened to be passing, and Connor stopped her, introducing the young man. 'Mr Pritchard, I'd like you to meet my wife. Ruth, this is Mr Huw Pritchard—a member of the Labour Party, a member of the Emmanuel Chapel congregation, a member of the jubilee Wharf Brotherhood—and a thorn in their flesh too, I shouldn't wonder! And I'm about to give him a beer, because he's got good reason to celebrate, this night.'

Connor went off to draw a couple of pints behind the bar, as Ruth shook hands with the young man. He had a fresh, open face, and stars in his eyes, and she took a liking to him at once. They tried to start a conversation, but it wasn't easy to make themselves heard above the music and chatter. By now everyone was dancing, and it seemed quite natural for Huw to ask: 'Would you do me the honour, Mrs O'Dell?'

When Connor came back with a pint pot in either hand, he found his wife in the arms of the young Welshman, and stood smiling, watching them dance together to a song that had become all the rage in the last few years:

If you were the only girl in the world,
And I were the only boy,
Nothing else would matter in the world today...

Half an hour later, Rosie was dreamily humming the same tune in the back of the taxi-cab that was taking her and Ernest home to Poplar; they had slipped quietly away from the party, leaving the pub by the side door.

Ernest kissed her gently, then quoted the words with a sigh. *'A garden of Eden, just made for two...* If only that were true.'

'Perhaps our wishes will come true, one of these days,' she told him. 'Perhaps we'll be able to start up in a shop again, like we did at Silmour Street.'

For a moment he said nothing, then asked quietly, 'Did you know that old shop's to let again? I walked past it the other day, and there was a board up outside.'

'What were you doing, walking along Silmour Street?'

'Nothing special. When I'm out for a stroll, I often go round by Cubitt Town. I like to remember the old days—when we were together, for the first time.'

He kissed her again. As the cab passed a street-lamp, the light flashed across his face; Rosie saw the unhappiness he was trying to hide, and asked, 'What's the matter?'

'Oh, I wasn't going to tell you this, but I went to the bank and asked to see the Manager. I explained about the shop; I thought he might give me a loan to set up in business again... I was hoping to surprise you—a sort of unexpected wedding present, but it was no good. He said money's very tight these days; he couldn't help us.'

She held him a little closer. 'It was a lovely idea, anyway. And we will get a place of our own one of these days—I'm certain of it.'

Back at the pub, Connor had been busy serving drinks all the evening, but by this time things were quietening down. He looked round for Huw Pritchard, but couldn't find him. Ruth was helping behind the bar, washing up glasses, and he asked her, 'Did the Welsh lad take himself off? I never saw him leave.'

'It was while you were down in the cellar, changing over the barrels,' she told him. 'He had to go—there's some sort of emergency at the Wharf, I think. Funnily enough, it was one of my nephews brought him the message—Josh's eldest boy, Jimmy. He said Mr Pritchard had got to report to the Guild Office right away.'

'This time of night?' Connor frowned. 'The place will be locked up.'

'Jimmy said they'd left the gates open specially...'

When Huw reached the entrance to the dock, the gates appeared to be shut, but as soon as he put his hand to them, they swung open and he found that the chain and padlock had been taken off.

He went through and crossed the yard. Outside, there had been occasional patches of light from the street-lamps, but in here, among the buildings, there was no light at all and he made his way uncertainly, groping through the darkness.

His footsteps seemed unusually loud on the cobblestones, setting up a confusion of echoes from the brick walls so that he had the eerie sensation that he was not alone, and that other solitary walkers surrounded him.

Huw felt an unaccustomed tremor of fear, and tried to shake it off. Who ever heard of a grown man being frightened of the dark?

He began to whistle a tune that had been

dancing through his head ever since he left the pub:

Nothing else would matter in the world today,
We would go on loving in the same old way...

But that did nothing to raise his spirits; ghostly reverberations of his own whistling returned to mock him, and he fell silent once more.

Then he stopped. He was almost sure he had heard another whistle, in a low key, somewhere ahead of him. He waited, listening, but it was not repeated so he pressed on.

When he reached the steps leading up to the front door of the Guild Office, he found the place in darkness, with no sign of life. Perhaps the boy had made a mistake—perhaps he was supposed to report directly to one of the warehouses instead. But he mounted the steps anyway, and knocked on the door to make certain: the sound was sudden and startling, but it died away quickly, with no response from within the building.

As he stood there, wondering what he should do, he caught a faint rustle—a movement, somewhere behind him. Instantly, fear welled up in him again, and he realised that he had walked into a trap. Before he could make a run for it, a voice said urgently: *'Right—get him!'*

Then they jumped on him, pulling him down the steps. He tried to fight back, but there were too many of them—he could not tell how many, for the attack came from all sides at once. They had wooden clubs in their fists and steel-capped toes to their boots, and they used them viciously.

Huw slipped and fell under the rain of blows, and pain exploded in his skull—and then the miracle happened.

A piercing whistle shrilled through the night air, and at the same instant the darkness was pierced by the white light of a bull's-eye lantern. Someone yelled in panic, 'It's the rozzers!'

Dazzled, shielding their faces, the gang of men scattered in disorder. They did not wait to be caught, but took to their heels in a moment of wild confusion and went clattering away across the cobbles.

Then, for a few seconds, nothing happened until the beam of light lifted and turned, shining across the face of the man with the lantern. Connor tucked the dog-whistle back in his breast pocket and said briskly, 'Right, my bucko. Let's see how much damage they've done to you.'

He helped Huw on to his feet. Dazed, the boy blinked at him, panting, 'Is it only you? On your own?'

'Sorry to disappoint you, but it's not the Metropolitan police force. Do you think you can manage the walk back to Three Colt Street, if I give you a helping hand?'

A month later, the boarders were sitting round the long table in the Kleibers' dining-room, having breakfast. The morning mail had just been delivered, along with the daily newspaper. As Rosie and Sarah passed the toast and the boiled eggs, Ernest turned to a visiting industrial engineer from Tallin, and said: 'This will interest you, sir. I see here that an armistice was signed on Wednesday, between Poland and the Russian Soviet. We must be thankful that another war is over.'

A murmur of general conversation broke out, in a mixture of English, German and Yiddish. Rosie touched Ernest's shoulder, and held out an envelope.

'This came for you.' She looked troubled, and pointed to the address printed on the back flap: *Horner & Hardiman, Solicitors.*

The names were vaguely familiar; he fancied he had seen them written up in gold lettering upon an office window in Stepney. Puzzled, he tore open the envelope.

It was not a long letter, written in an old-fashioned copperplate hand. He read it through once—twice—then stood up, pushing back his chair.

'Rosie, my dear, could I have a word with you in the kitchen?'

She followed him from the dining-room, and Ernest shut the kitchen door. She asked anxiously: 'Is it bad news?'

He shook his head. 'It seems not. See for yourself.' She took the letter from him, and read it silently.

Dear Mr Kleiber, I have been requested by a client to approach you, concerning a matter of business. I venture to write and enquire if you would oblige me by calling at this office, at some time convenient to yourself. I am not at liberty to

130

offer any further information at this juncture, but I think I may say that our meeting will be to your advantage.

I remain, sir, your obedient servant, K B. Hardiman for Horner and Hardiman, Solicitors.

5

'And to finish off, how about a group picture? Mothers and babies all together,' suggested Ernest.

'We're not babies!' said Danny indignantly. 'I'm five!'

Trevor smiled in a superior way, pointing out, 'Ackcherly, *I'm* nearly six!'

To avert an argument, Ruth cut in firmly: 'And Ben's nearly seven, so I'm quite sure Uncle Ernest knows you're not babies. He was thinking of Lil.'

Lilian, unconcerned at fifteen months, gurgled in her mother's arms.

Ernest threw up his hands. 'All right, all right! My humble apologies! Will the mothers—and the young gentlemen—and one baby—kindly take up their positions for a group picture?'

As they were milling about in front of the camera, Rosie said to her husband, 'Just think—at breakfast-time you were saying when we opened the shop, we probably wouldn't have any customers at all, and here they are, queueing up to have their pictures taken.'

The photographic shop in Silmour Street was looking very festive, with tulips and wallflowers in a vase, paper streamers across the ceiling and a banner in the front window, announcing: *Grand Reopening, 14 May, 1921.*

'Oh, we wouldn't have missed it for anything!' Gloria was taking good care that she and Matthew would be seen to advantage, making straight for the centre of the group. 'Push your hair out of your eyes, Matt, so we can see your face.'

Ernest looked through the lens and made some last-minute adjustments, then beckoned Rosie, who was standing to one side, watching.

'My dear, you must be in the picture as well. This is for the family album.'

It was certainly a family picture—four ladies seated in a row with their offspring cross-legged on the ground in front of them: from left to right they were Sarah Kleiber and Benjamin, Gloria Judge and Matthew, Ruth O'Dell, with Lilian on her lap and Danny at her feet—and Maudie Judge, with her hand on Trevor's shoulder.

'Oh, you don't want me in it,' protested Rosie. 'I look a sight—and besides, I'm not a mother.'

Trevor remarked knowingly, 'But you soon will be, won't you?'

Some of the ladies looked scandalised. Mortified, Maudie tried to silence her son. 'Trev, don't say things like that. It's rude.'

But Rosie only laughed. It was hardly a secret by this time; even her loose maternity dress could not disguise the fact that she was expecting a baby in six weeks' time. Good-naturedly, she took her place at the end of the line and when Ernest was satisfied with the arrangements, he said: 'Watch the birdie!'

Disillusioned, Danny turned to Trevor. 'There isn't any bird really.'

There was a pop!—a flash—and the group broke up, all talking at once. Under cover of the buzz of conversation, Rosie turned to Ruth.

'I bet it was your idea, wasn't it, getting them all to come this afternoon?'

'Well, why not? I thought it would get things off to a good start.'

Ruth had already decided to bring her own children to be photographed today, and then approached all her friends with young families, suggesting they might like to do the same—so it had turned into a children's party. In front of the studio backcloth of a painted garden, each mother in turn sat for a portrait with her offspring, and when that was done Ernest offered to take an extra group of them all, as a free gift.

'It's been marvellous.' Rosie had never looked so lovely; pregnancy agreed with her and she was glowing with happiness. 'So much has happened, these past six months.'

She remembered the day the letter arrived from Horner & Hardiman, last November. At first she and Ernest had been completely mystified, for how could some solicitors they had never met have any news for them which would be 'to their advantage'?

But obviously they had to find out what it was all about.

The same morning, Ernest went to the Post Office—which had a blue sign outside, saying in white lettering: *You May Telephone From Here*—and called the office at Stepney, making an appointment for the following day.

The meeting was arranged for ten o'clock; in their anxiety, they arrived twenty minutes early, and Ernest suggested that for politeness' sake they should walk up White Horse Lane and back, to kill time. But it was a damp, grey morning, and they hadn't gone far before it came on to rain.

Rosie, who was wearing her best dress, hat and coat for the occasion, said, 'We're not getting soaked to the skin for politeness, are we? Come on—let's go back indoors, out of the wet.'

When they returned to the office, a stiff-and-starchy female clerk told them they would have to wait. They sat on hard upright chairs in a draughty passage, and all the excitement they had been feeling drained out of them, seeping through the soles of their shoes and vanishing into the linoleum.

At exactly ten o'clock, the clerk informed them that Mr Hardiman would see them now, and they were ushered into his office. It was a gloomy room, with one small window that let in hardly any light, as it faced another building only a few feet away. The walls were lined with bookshelves, each shelf crammed with books, mostly in long sets of leather-bound volumes that looked as if they had not been read, or touched, or even dusted for a very long time. There were still more books and box-files and stacks of paper piled high on the tables that filled the room, leaving one narrow alleyway leading to the desk where, in a small pool of light from a green-shaded table-lamp, Mr Hardiman sat enthroned.

In such cramped surroundings, the gentleman himself seemed out of scale, for he was a large man, with a large head; a frill of silver hair surrounded a shining bald pate, beneath which was a large pink face, buttressed by several chins. Upon his Roman nose, a tiny pair of gold-rimmed spectacles might have seemed insignificant—but he made great play with them.

At first he peered over the top of his spectacles, eyeing his visitors severely. 'Mr and Mrs Kleiber? Quite so—pray be seated.'

He indicated two chairs in front of the desk, and they sat down. Then he peered through his spectacles at a sheaf of papers on his desk, turning the pages one by one, studying the information they contained. He appeared to be in no hurry, taking his time to consider each word with cautious deliberation, while Rosie and Ernest sat in silence, hardly daring to breathe.

At last Mr Hardiman took off his spectacles, produced a white silk handkerchief, and proceeded to polish the lenses; when that was done, he replaced them upon his nose, and looked over the top of them again.

'So!' he said. 'You have come in reference to my letter? I'm much obliged to you.'

135

'Perhaps, sir, you'd be kind enough to tell us what this is all about?' said Ernest tentatively.

'Perhaps I will, Mr Kleiber, perhaps I will. And possibly—I say possibly, mark you—when I have done so, it may be your turn to feel obliged to *me!*'

He uttered a short sharp bark, which made Rosie jump; she assumed it was a cough, then realised that it was intended as an expression of amusement. Mr Hardiman's large pink face convulsed for a moment into something very like a smile.

'When I tell you why I have asked you to come here, I think you may feel your journey has not been in vain,' he said, and his shoulders heaved, rising and falling with silent mirth. 'But I am acting upon the instructions of a client who chooses to remain anonymous, so I am not at liberty to give you as much information as you might wish. I say you *might*—because of course I cannot speak with any certainty upon that point—as you *might* wish to be granted. Permit me instead to put some questions to you. I fancy you are by way of being a professional photographer, Mr Kleiber?'

'Yes, sir, though at present I'm only—'

'Do not trouble yourself to elaborate your answers, sir; a simple yes or no will suffice. You are a professional photographer, and at one time you pursued your calling at certain two-storey premises in—um—Silmour Street, is that correct?'

'Yes, but that was—'

'Indeed—in Silmour Street, but that was

136

several years ago, as I think you were about to tell me?'

'Yes, sir.'

'Yes, it was. And you ceased to be the tenant and occupant of the said premises in the summer of 1915, did you not?'

'Yes, I—'

'Yes, you did. Very well; perhaps it may have come to your notice that those self-same premises are at present vacant, and advertised to be let?'

'I saw the board a few weeks ago, when I—'

'To be let—exactly. So far we are in accord upon all points.' Mr Hardiman took off his spectacles again, and waved them in the air as he continued: 'Now we come to a more problematic matter. I am instructed to enquire whether you would agree to recommence trading there, as you did six years ago, using the premises as a studio and dark-room, and as a shop for the sale of photographic goods—and occupying the upper floor for domestic purposes. Would you entertain the possibility of undertaking such a venture again?'

'I'd like nothing better, sir!' Ernest glanced at Rosie, his face alight. 'In fact, I've already tried to raise a bank loan in order to do that very thing—but I had no luck. And without some capital behind me...'

'Say no more, Mr Kleiber. If you are agreeable to the suggestion, the financial arrangements need not be a barrier to you. My client is prepared to supply the necessary capital, regarding it in the light of a reasonable business investment.'

'You mean your client would employ me as a manager, to run the shop for him?'

'My dear sir, you must not tell me what I do or do not mean. I myself will keep you fully informed of my meaning.' Mr Hardiman pointed the ear-piece of the golden spectacle-frame at Ernest, stabbing the air to underline the points as he made them. 'You would be the sole owner of the business; my client would be merely an investor in the scheme, providing sufficient funds for you to purchase your stock-in-trade, and paying the entire rental of the property. It would be exactly similar to a bank loan, to be undertaken on the same terms, and at the same rates of interest—if you are agreeable?'

'But that's amazing! It's just what I've been hoping for! Of course I'd be agreeable, more than agreeable.'

'Not so fast, Mr Kleiber. Kindly allow me to finish what I have to say. I was about to add: *If* you are agreeable—and *if* you are prepared to abide by certain conditions...'

'I don't understand. What conditions?'

'You must give me your solemn assurance on three counts: that you will not seek to discover the identity of my client, that you will not ask for any further assistance if the venture should prove to be unsuccessful and finally that you will not discuss this matter with any other person; this stipulation to include even members of your

138

own family and your circle of personal friends and acquaintances.'

Ernest and Rosie looked at one another again, at a loss for words, as he went on, 'If you are prepared to give your agreement to such an undertaking, I will give instructions to your bank without delay, and the necessary funds will be put at your disposal. Well, Mr Kleiber—Mrs Kleiber—what do you say to that?'

They did not ask for time to think it over; there was only one possible answer to such a proposition. They both said: 'Yes.'

After that, things moved with reasonable speed—that is, as speedily as anything can move, when it involves the law, or finance, or the transfer of property—and in due course the money was paid into Ernest's bank account, and he acquired a new lease on the Silmour Street premises.

The shop had been standing empty for some time, and needed a great deal of work. Ernest and Rosie tried to make a start on the repairs, but by then she had discovered that she was pregnant, and Ernest would not let her do any work that might involve strenuous effort. He had called in a local firm of builders to carry out the essential brickwork, plastering and re-tiling on the roof; after that, he took a hand in the redecoration personally, splashing on new paint and putting up wallpaper.

By the end of April 1921, the work was finished and they began to furnish the upstairs flat, mainly with items brought over from the house at Poplar, and to stock the shop with cameras, films and processing equipment.

Today—the Saturday of the Whitsun weekend —the shop had opened its doors to the public for the first time; and they had got off to an encouraging start.

'Sorry we can't run to champagne,' said Rosie, passing round sticky buns and pouring fizzy lemonade. 'But come back again in a year or two, when Ernest's made his fortune, and we'll have a real celebration!'

The children had no complaints about the refreshments, and when it was time to leave, they decided that it had been a pretty good party. Even Trevor said grudgingly: 'It wasn't too bad, except they didn't give us balloons.'

'Trev, don't be so ungrateful!' said Maudie. She shook hands with Sarah, whom she had not met until this afternoon, saying, 'It's been ever so nice talking to you, Mrs Kleiber. P'raps you'll come over to tea with us one of these days, and bring your Benjamin. It'll be lovely for Trev to have someone to play with.'

'Yes, thank you, we shall look forward to that,' said Sarah politely. She had not been favourably impressed by Trevor's arrogant display of bad manners, but kept her thoughts to herself. 'Ruth—will you be walking up Manchester Road?'

So Gloria and Maudie set off one way, towards West Ferry Road, while Ruth and Sarah went in the other direction. They walked slowly, for Ruth had to negotiate Lilian's pushchair up and down each kerb, and as they walked, they talked.

140

'I'm so glad everything has worked out for Ernest and Rosie,' said Ruth. 'But I expect you must be missing them, now they've moved.'

'That's true, but I keep busy looking after my lodgers,' Sarah explained. 'I don't have much time to feel lonely.'

Ruth wasn't sure this was altogether true. She suspected that life must be harder than ever for Sarah, left on her own with a small son to bring up and a houseful of strangers to cater for, and she made a resolution to visit Sarah more often.

'Anyway,' Sarah concluded, 'it's wonderful that Ernest was able to reopen his shop again.'

'Yes, although I never quite understood how he managed it. I know Rosie told me, soon after the wedding, that his bank wouldn't give him any help, so how did he finally raise the money?'

'I believe someone invested in the business,' replied Sarah vaguely, 'but he never told me the details, and I didn't like to pry.'

Further along Manchester Road, their paths divided and they said goodbye to one another. When she reached the Watermen, Ruth wheeled Lilian in through the side door, calling, 'Con—we're back!'

There was no answering shout, and as they entered the kitchen, Mary O'Dell said: 'He's out in the backyard with that friend of his—the Welsh fellow.' She began to unfasten the baby's harness, lifting her out of her chair. 'Go and tell Con to tidy himself up, because tea will be on the table directly.'

Danny raced out of the back door, yelling, 'Dad, Gran says tea's nearly ready! Can Huw have tea with us as well?'

Ruth found the two men in the yard, facing one another in the sunlight; Connor in vest and trousers—Huw Pritchard stripped to the waist, wearing boxing-gloves, shorts and plimsolls.

Danny ran to Huw, jumping up and down with excitement, and begging: 'You will stay for tea, won't you? Please?'

Huw laughed. 'I think that's up to your father.'

Connor gave one of his rare, crooked grins. 'Since you've already been invited, I can hardly say no!'

When they saw Ruth, both men looked slightly abashed, like a pair of overgrown schoolboys, and Connor explained: 'This young man wants to learn the rudiments of sparring, so I said I'd give him a few pointers. Here, let's get those gloves off you.'

'Thanks.' Huw held out both hands, and Con unlaced the gloves expertly.

'Are you taking up boxing as a hobby?' Ruth asked.

'Not exactly, though I've always been interested, since I was a kid.' Ruth noticed that he stammered slightly, and appeared to be embarrassed by her presence. 'Of course, I never thought I'd have a coach as good as Mr O'Dell, but he kindly suggested I should call in on a Saturday afternoon, while the pub was shut...'

As soon as his hands were free, Huw ducked

away, retrieving a shirt and jersey that had been flung down on a pile of beer-crates, saying over his shoulder: 'Look, I'd better be pushing off. You don't want me barging in when you're having a meal.'

'Oh, you mustn't rush away—we'll be glad of your company, won't we?' Ruth turned to Danny. 'And now I look at you, my lad, a good wash before tea wouldn't come amiss either.'

'Can I sit next to Huw at the table, Mum?' Danny asked eagerly, as they went back indoors.

Since the day of Rosie's wedding reception, Huw had been a regular visitor at the Watermen, though Connor never told Ruth about the attempted assault on the young man by the Brotherhood's Punishment Squad.

Thanks to Connor's intervention, he had escaped comparatively lightly. For a few days there was a period of uncertainty, as Huw waited to see if the Brotherhood were planning another attack upon him—and the Inner Circle of the Guild waited to see if any steps would be taken by the Dockers' Union, or by the police, in defence of the young man.

When nothing happened, the Brotherhood decided that Huw could not have lodged a formal complaint about their treatment of him, so—with some relief, and a certain amount of grudging respect—they let the matter drop. When Huw reappeared, having lain low for several days, his scars and bruises were beginning to fade and nothing more was said on either side.

All the same, Connor suggested to him

143

privately that it might not be a bad idea for him to learn something about the art of self-defence, and offered to give him some lessons.

'It's good of you to give up your time like this.' Huw's voice was muffled, then his face reappeared through the neck of his jersey. 'You know I appreciate it.'

'My pleasure,' said Connor. 'To be honest, I enjoy it. It reminds me of days long gone!'

'I still think it was a black day for British boxing when you left the ring,' said Huw. 'You'd have been up there with the best of them by now.'

'Oh, there were good times and bad times,' said Connor, adding reminiscently, 'Did I ever tell you of the night I stood up to Jack Johnson?'

'The World Heavyweight Champion?' Huw goggled at him—then his face creased into laughter. 'You're having me on... That couldn't have happened, could it?'

Connor looked at him for a moment, then joined in the laughter. 'No, I don't suppose it could... I must have dreamed it.' And he led the way into the pub.

Ruth heard him laughing, and her heart leaped up. It was a long while since she had heard Con laugh like that; lately, he never seemed to find much to laugh at. For the first year of their marriage, they had both been so happy—enjoying every day to the full and sharing every precious moment; living, and loving—and laughing—together.

Then, gradually, a change had come over him.

Ruth loved him as much as ever, and hoped against hope that he still felt the same way about her, but somehow, something had been lost. It was as if a light had been extinguished; the colours which were once so bright and clear had grown blurred and faded.

She had tried to talk to him about it. She forced herself to ask, 'Con, is everything all right? What's the matter? Really?'

But her questions provoked nothing but conventional answers: 'Everything's all right. Nothing's the matter. Really.'

And the one question she wanted to put to him, she dared not ask: 'Do you still love me?'

That afternoon, when she found him giving Huw Pritchard a boxing-lesson, she caught a glimpse of the old Connor—the man she loved, the man she had married. All that evening, she watched the clock, counting the hours until closing-time, longing for the moment when he would come upstairs to their bedroom, as happy and as loving as ever.

She put on her prettiest nightdress, and took longer than usual to brush her hair; she put a dab of perfume behind her ears—on her neck—between her breasts. Then she got into bed and lay there, waiting.

She waited a long time; so long, she must have fallen asleep, for the next thing she knew the room was in darkness, and Connor was in bed beside her. She listened to the rhythm of his

145

breathing, unsure if he were awake or asleep.

Putting out a hand, she touched the firm muscles across his shoulders; he was lying on his side, with his back to her.

'Con?' she whispered.

'Mmm?' So he wasn't asleep.

'You were a long time coming to bed.'

'Was I? Yes, well, I had things to think about and some work to finish in the office. I was making up next month's order for the Brewery; it'll save time in the morning.'

'Oh, yes.' She stroked his back gently, waiting for him to roll over and face her, but he did not move.

'Con?' She tried again. 'Can I ask you something?'

'Ask me what? What d'you mean?'

She tried to think how to phrase the question, then said hesitantly: 'You would tell me, wouldn't you, if there was—something wrong?'

'Of course there's nothing wrong. It's just I'm a bit tired tonight, that's all.'

'I see... Well, I hope you have a good night's sleep,' she said.

'I hope you sleep well, too,' he said. 'Good night, Ruth.'

'Good night, Con.'

Almost six weeks later, something took place which was to have a lasting effect upon the Judge family; and it happened quite unexpectedly, without any warning. Looking back afterwards, Florrie found it hard to believe that such a

146

tragedy could have arisen from such trivial, everyday circumstances.

It began when she decided she needed new curtains for her front room.

The house in Jubilee Street was looking very drab, and the curtains in the parlour window—Nottingham lace, with a pattern of entwined leaves and flowers—had turned quite yellow with age, despite rigorous washing. Florrie made up her mind: she must buy some material and make a new set of curtains.

She discussed the idea with her sister-in-law Mabel, and asked her if she would like to come along to help choose some suitable fabric.

'Go shopping—together?' Mabel looked astonished; any event in her life, no matter how mundane, always came to her as a great surprise. 'Oh, do you think we could? Of course, I'd have to be back by four, on account of making tea for the boys when they get in from school.'

Florrie persuaded her that this would not be a problem. Fired with enthusiasm, she went on to say that she intended to go to Wickhams, the East End's own department store, in the Mile End Road.

'They've got a summer sale on till the end of June,' she explained. 'And we can get there and back on the bus.'

Still amazed, Mabel considered the possibility, and began to smile. 'I suppose we could,' she said. 'And while I'm there, I could buy some winter vests for the boys as well—and Josh needs a new shirt for best... Ooh yes, what a good idea! When shall we go?'

They settled upon the last Friday in June, and began to make their preparations. They would meet in the morning at Mabel's house, and have a cup of tea and a biscuit before setting out to fortify them for the journey. It was beginning to take on the aspect of a full-scale expedition, and both women were looking forward to it immensely.

When they got to Wickhams, they were determined to enjoy themselves. They started in the Fabric Hall, and spent a long time fingering various swathes of cloth. Florrie had decided she didn't want lace this time—a nice heavy woollen material would last so much better, looped back with crocheted bows on either side, and an under-curtain of plain net, to stop the neighbours prying.

After long deliberation, they settled on a dark bottle-green, and the elderly assistant measured off the required length, pulling yards of cloth from the bale and running it down the length of the counter, measuring it against a fixed brass rule.

Then Mabel took charge, leading the way to the Men and Boys' Outfitting on the first floor, where they took an equally long time comparing styles and prices of undervests, and shirts with detachable collars and cuffs.

But that wasn't the end of it; they had made up their minds to sample every diversion that Wickhams had to offer, and went on to explore the entire store, from Haberdashery, where Mabel bought some knicker-elastic, to Hardware, where Florrie could not resist a patent vegetable slicer which was being demonstrated by a lady in a snowy white apron, who showed them how the little gadget peeled apples, chipped potatoes, sliced onions and generally made itself invaluable to the busy housewife.

After that, Mabel got carried away and bought some china cups—on sale at bargain prices, because they had lost their matching saucers—and Florrie bought a cobweb brush with a special extending cane handle, for getting up into those awkward corners of the ceiling.

Flushed and triumphant after this orgy of extravagance, they left the store at last, keeping an eye on the time because Mabel mustn't be late with the boys' tea whatever happened—and then they had a long, annoying wait at the bus-stop. Mabel began to get anxious; why was the bus taking such a time?

Another woman in the queue said gloomily, 'It's the Whitechapel market what does it. Takes over half the road, it does—the traffic gets held up.'

Eventually the open-topped bus appeared in the distance, and they rushed to get on board. As they were about to go inside—for although it was a pleasant summer day, it was always likely to be windy on top, and their hats might blow away—Florrie exclaimed in sudden panic: 'Oh, good gracious! I've left my cobweb brush propped up against the bus-stop. Whatever shall I do?'

The conductor had just rung the bell, and the driver let in the clutch. The bus lurched forward as Mabel called out: 'Just a minute—my friend's left something behind. Stop the bus!'

She was nearly ten years younger than Florrie, and rather more agile. Without a moment's hesitation she jumped down from the platform of the bus, as the driver slammed on the brakes, swearing: 'Make up yer bleeding mind, for Gawd's sake!'

The bus rocked and skidded to a halt; a horse-drawn delivery van close behind them swerved violently—the horse reared, its front hooves lashing wildly in thin air—someone screamed, the frightened horse whinnied and plunged—and Mabel, struck down by flying hooves, lay motionless upon the roadway as one wheel of the van ran over her breast, and her life's blood dribbled away into the gutter. Her eyes were wide open, and upon her face was an expression of absolute astonishment.

Marcus and Joshua were working at their desks in the Guild Office when Florrie came in, later that afternoon. The two men put down their pens and stared at her; no woman ever set foot within the dockyard gates.

'What are you doing here?' asked Marcus crossly. 'Who let you in, may I ask?'

Joshua saw that she was trembling violently. 'What is it, Florrie? What's the matter?'

Her lips worked, but she could not speak. Exhausted, mentally and physically, she was on the point of collapse. Josh sprang up and helped her into a chair.

'What's wrong? Are you ill?'

She shook her head. 'Not me—Mabel. She...'

Florrie could not go on.

'Mabel's been taken ill? Where is she?'

With an enormous effort, she managed to blurt out the words: 'Accident... Knocked down—in the street. Ambulance came—took us to the London Hospital—only just along the road... But—she was dead when we got there.'

As best she could, she told her story. By the end, she was crying so hard they could hardly make out what she said. With tears running down her face, she blamed herself bitterly.

'My fault—all my fault. She only went back because of me... I'd left it behind, you see, at the bus-stop—my cobweb brush. And now she's dead, and it's all my fault...'

Marcus knitted his brows. 'What are you saying? What's that about a brush? Do you understand her, Joshua?'

But Joshua wasn't listening. He was already on his way to the door, muttering, 'The London Hospital—I must go to her.'

On the threshold he turned, as another thought struck him: 'The boys—what about the boys? They'll be coming home by now.'

'They'll be wanting their tea.' Florrie dabbed her eyes and wiped her nose. 'I'll see to that. I'll look after them...it's the least I can do.'

When Ruth arrived at the Rope Walk on Monday morning, she felt as if she were stepping back in time. It was a long while since she had visited her old home, and longer still since she had lived there as a girl. Yet nothing had changed. The street looked much the same—a cul-de-sac, with a brick wall at the

151

far end, closing the road; and above the wall, towering above the slate-roofed houses, a ship rode at anchor in the Jubilee Dock, its masts and funnels silhouetted against the sky. Ruth felt small and insecure, as if she were a child again.

The feeling was stronger still when Louisa opened the front door; the smell of steam, of soapsuds and wet sheets was unmistakable.

'I should have remembered—Monday's wash-day,' said Ruth, kissing her mother on the cheek. 'Nothing changes, does it?'

Even as she uttered the words, she realised how false they were. So much had changed within the Judge family. Her mother's hair was now completely white, her shoulders bent under the load of time, her face deeply etched by years of trial... And now—another blow had struck the family.

'You heard about Mabel, I suppose?' Louisa asked, leading the way back to the scullery.

Ruth nodded. 'That's why I came. Someone was talking about the accident last night in the saloon—word soon gets round on the Island. But I still don't know exactly how it happened.'

Her mother told her—not that there was much to tell. Standing by the old boiler, stirring the seething mass of laundry with a copper-stick, she explained about the accident in the Mile End Road.

'It's been very hard on Florrie. You see, it was her shopping Mabel went back for, so she feels responsible. Nobody's blaming her, of course, but she still feels bad about it.'

'Poor Florrie. It must be dreadful for her, but a hundred times worse for Josh. However will he manage without Mabel?'

'I don't know. He doesn't know himself—I don't think he's really taken it in yet. The funeral's on Wednesday; perhaps when that's over, he'll begin to pull himself together.' Louisa got out her scrubbing-board. Her hands kept busy as she glanced across at her daughter and said: 'I don't suppose you'll be coming to the Chapel, will you?'

Ruth shook her head. 'I can't. Besides, you know what Father's like.'

Louisa sighed, her red knuckles pummelling one of Marcus's shirts on the ribbed board, driving the soapy water in, squeezing the grime out.

'Oh, yes, I know what he's like. He can be very stubborn about his principles. Last night, we went round to Josh—I was making supper for the boys, and your father came with me. Afterwards, when the boys had gone up to bed, he told Josh that Mabel's death was an act of retribution on the part of Almighty God.'

'That's a terrible thing to say!' Ruth repeated the word: 'Retribution—what did he mean by it?'

'He's never forgiven Josh for Ebbie dying the way he did. And last night, instead of trying to comfort him for his loss, he told him it was God's vengeance upon him. "The Lord will repay"—that's what he said.'

For a minute or two there was no sound in the scullery except the heaving and bubbling in

153

the boiler, and the rhythm of Louisa's knuckles upon the scrubbing-board. At last Ruth asked: 'And is that what you believe, too?'

'No.' Her mother spoke so quietly, Ruth could hardly hear her. 'I don't believe Our Lord would do a thing like that. When we got home, I tried to say as much, but Father wouldn't listen to me. I'm sure he meant it for the best—I always told you, he means well—but I have to admit, he's not an easy man to talk to. That's where you're lucky—you and Connor. You can talk to your husband.'

There was another long silence, and then Ruth said: 'Shall I put the kettle on? I think we could do with a cup of tea.'

Later, they sat facing one another across the red chenille tablecloth, the teacups in their hands, and Louisa said with the ghost of a smile, 'It's good to see you, Ruth. Thanks for coming round here—it does help.'

'I wish I could do more. I'd like to go and see Josh, too—do you think he'd mind?'

'I'm sure he'd like to see you. You'll find him at home; he wasn't fit to go to work today. Father's gone in to mind the office.'

On her way back to the pub, Ruth called at the house, which had all the curtains drawn as a sign of mourning. Florrie opened the door to her.

'Ruth, come in. Did you want to see Josh? He's in the front parlour. I've given him the newspaper to read—I thought it might take his mind off things.'

As a rule, nobody ever sat in the parlour; it

154

was kept for show rather than for use, like the clock on the mantelpiece, under its glass dome. No one had bothered to wind it for a long time; the two hands were clasped together as if in prayer, pointing eternally upwards—either to heaven or to twelve o'clock.

Josh had the newspaper spread out in front of him on the table, but Ruth felt sure that he had not been reading it; she doubted if he even knew it was there. It took a moment or two before he registered who she was, then he said heavily, 'Good of you to look in like this, Ruth. Much appreciated, I'm sure.' He leaned forward and asked her confidentially: 'What am I going to do now, old girl—can you tell me that? What's going to become of me and the boys, eh?'

She tried to sound calm and reassuring, but he turned away before she had finished speaking, as if her words meant nothing to him. After a while she gave up, and left him sitting there, staring blindly into an unimaginable future. She went to find Florrie, who was busy in the kitchen, peeling potatoes and putting some cold meat through a mincer.

'It's the left-overs from yesterday's joint—I thought I'd make a shepherd's pie for supper. Josh doesn't have much of an appetite at present, but I expect the boys will be hungry when they get home from school.'

'Yes. He seems very anxious about the boys. I suppose he feels he can't look after them properly on his own.'

'Of course not. How could he, once he goes

155

back to work? But I've told him he needn't worry about that. I shall come in every day to clean up and cook for them. Emily and Maudie can mind the shop quite well without me, so I can look after Josh and the boys. After all, now Tommy's in America and Ebbie's been gathered, I've nobody else to care for. I was wondering last night if it might be the hand of fate. I mean, it almost seems as if things were meant to turn out like this—what do you think?'

During the days that followed, Ruth often remembered her mother's words: *'You can talk to your husband'...* If only she could have done so—but Con seemed to be further away from her than ever.

He was not unkind or thoughtless; he spoke to her gently and pleasantly, but his mind was elsewhere. One afternoon at the beginning of July, when the pub was closed for a few hours, she suggested they might take little Lil out for an airing.

'It's a lovely afternoon—the sunshine will do her good.'

'I don't think I'll bother. I'm a bit tired, to be honest; I'm going to get my head down for a while. Why don't you take Mam with you, if you want company?'

So the two women took turns, wheeling the pushchair to Island Gardens. Ruth's sense of uneasiness was stronger than ever; it was the first time she had ever heard Connor say he felt tired. She longed to ask Mary if she knew what was wrong with her son, but there was no point in worrying her unnecessarily and she kept her anxiety to herself. When they got back, Ruth put Lil into the cot for her afternoon nap and then went into the bedroom, to see how Connor was feeling.

He wasn't asleep. In shirt and trousers, he lay upon the big brass bedstead, his hands under his head, staring at the ceiling. When she spoke, he turned his head slowly, gazing at her as if she were a stranger.

'Hello there!' he said with an effort. 'Where have you been?'

'Down to the Gardens and back. It's really warm out; you should have come with us—you'd have enjoyed it. There were lots of people out for a stroll. I'll tell you who we saw—do you remember Gladys Harker, who used to run the pie-shop?'

Her voice trailed off as she realised he was not listening to her. She couldn't help remembering the way Josh had looked, that afternoon in the front parlour, so wrapped up in his own misery she couldn't reach him. With a stab of fear, she recognised the same lack of focus in Connor's eyes, as if he were looking inwards instead of seeing the world about him. She tried to speak lightly.

'Penny for them,' she said.

'Do what?' Again, he forced himself out of his reverie. 'What did you say?'

'A penny for your thoughts. What are you pondering so deeply?'

'Nothing at all. Just resting.'

157

'Oh... I thought you seemed, I don't know, rather unhappy.'

He smiled gently. 'What have I got to be unhappy about?'

I wish I knew she thought. Oh, how I wish I knew...

As she moved to the door, he called after her: 'Wait! There was something I had to tell you—what was it, now? Oh, to be sure, while you were out Ernest Kleiber telephoned.'

'About Rosie?' Ruth turned back quickly; she knew that the Kleibers' baby was overdue. 'What's happened? Is she all right?'

'He says she's fine. He was calling from the Lying-In Hospital; the baby was born a couple of hours ago. He thought we'd like to know.'

'Oh, thank God!' Ruth was overjoyed. 'What did she have? A boy or a girl?'

'Damned if I remember. I'm pretty sure he told me a boy, I think. Yes, I'm almost sure it was a boy.'

'Con, you can be so aggravating sometimes! We must go down and tell your mam, or she'll never forgive us. How long are they going to keep Rosie in?'

'Ernest didn't say, but he promised he'd look in some time soon, so you can ask him yourself.'

In a sudden rush of happiness, Ruth dropped to her knees beside the bed, hugging her husband. 'Oh, I'm so glad for them. Rosie hoped it would be a boy—isn't it wonderful she got what she wanted?'

Connor did not respond to her affectionate

embrace. A shadow she could not interpret crossed his face, as he said, 'Sometimes people don't know what they want—until they've lost it.'

She searched his face. 'What's that supposed to mean?'

Suddenly he sat up, shaking his head as if to throw off all troublesome thoughts, and managed a smile. 'I don't know what I mean. I'm talking rubbish—take no notice.'

Rosie had to stay in hospital for ten days, but on the first Monday morning after they let her out, she came round to visit the family.

Ruth was scrubbing the linoleum in the saloon when Rosie arrived, carrying a bundle wrapped in a shawl, and she scrambled to her feet, exclaiming: 'Show me! Let me see him—what's his name?'

'Abram. Ernest says he's going to be a leader of men!'

He did not look much like the leader of anything, for he was fast asleep; very tiny, with a shock of glossy black hair, and a wrinkled red face. Ruth thought he looked rather like a baby monkey, but she assured Rosie that her son was the most handsome child she had ever seen.

'We've all been longing to see him. Con's in the office, sorting out some business, but he won't be long. Let's go and find Mam, and I'll make some coffee.'

They were about to go through to the back-kitchen when the door behind the bar opened, and Connor came out with a large, pink-faced gentleman.

'Oh, I expect you'd both like some coffee too.' Ruth began the introductions. 'This is Connor's sister Rosie and her son Abram. Rosie, this is Con's solicitor.'

'We've already met,' said Rosie, smiling. 'We're old friends, aren't we, Mr Hardiman?'

The solicitor glared at her over the top of his spectacles, unamused.

'How do you do, Mrs Kleiber? You must forgive me, Mrs O'Dell, I fear I cannot stay for coffee—I have many other calls upon my time. I wish you all a very good morning.'

He seemed larger than ever under the low ceiling, and when he strode out through the street door, the saloon bar seemed quite empty without him.

'Well! He was in a hurry!' said Rosie. 'Fancy him being your solicitor—I'd no idea. It's a small world and no mistake.'

Then they went into the kitchen, where Patrick and Mary made the acquaintance of their latest grandchild, and spent an enjoyable half-hour drinking coffee, all talking at once.

When it was time for Rosie to leave, Ruth walked with her as far as the corner of the street. Abram was awake by then, and he stared up at his Auntie Ruth with dark lustrous eyes. For such a small person, he had a very solemn and penetrating look.

'You must tell your mum to bring you for another visit very soon,' Ruth told him.

'Oh, we'll come again, don't you worry,' said Rosie. Then, impulsively, she squeezed Ruth's hand, adding: 'I know Mr Hardiman made us swear we'd never try to find out where the money came from, but—well, now we've found out by accident, so that doesn't count, does it? And I just want to say thank you, to you and Con. Thanks a thousand times—I don't know what we'd have done without your help.'

Ruth was completely at a loss. 'I haven't the faintest idea what you're thanking us for.'

'Oh, come on now, you don't have to pretend! I'm very, very grateful. I can't wait to tell Ernest that you and Con were our anonymous benefactors all along.'

'You mean you think *we* lent you the money to start the business? But we didn't! You're making a mistake.'

Rosie laughed. 'Are you trying to tell me that old Hardiman is Con's solicitor—and that he's also acting for our mystery man? That it's nothing but a coincidence? Get away with you!'

That night, when the pub was shut and the last customer had left, Ruth went round with Connor, helping him to lock up. Alone together, she told him what Rosie had said.

'...so now she's absolutely convinced that we're the anonymous benefactors—isn't that silly? I couldn't persuade her we're not.'

Connor had his back to her, stretching up then stooping down to slide the bolts home at the top and bottom of the front door, but he said nothing.

Slowly, a strange thought occurred to Ruth. She remembered how close Connor and Rosie used to be; he had always been very fond of his half-sister—there was no doubt about that.

'I suppose it *wasn't* you, was it?' she asked.

When he turned to face her, he seemed quite annoyed.

'Where would I find the money to pour hundreds of pounds into their blessed shop?' he retorted irritably. 'You're talking nonsense—of course it wasn't me!'

'No, of course it wasn't. That's what I told her,' said Ruth. 'But hasn't Mr Hardiman ever mentioned Rosie to you at all? Hasn't he ever let slip any little hint about who it might have been?'

'No, he has not,' said Connor flatly, and his eyes slid away, unable to meet her gaze. 'Come on, let's go up to bed.'

She followed him slowly up the stairs, and her heart dragged her down like a leaden weight. She had known Connor O'Dell for nearly ten years now—she knew him better than anyone in the world—and tonight, she knew without any shadow of doubt that he was lying to her.

6

'I'm not going to school today, am I, Mum?' said Danny.

'No, love, not today,' Ruth told her son. 'School doesn't start till tomorrow.'

The new school year was about to begin on 5 September at the Catholic Infants in Willow

Row, and now Danny was five years old, he would have to attend it every day.

'Will I like it?' he asked doubtfully.

'Of course you will. You'll have lots of other boys and girls to play with, and lots of toys—it's going to be fun!'

Skipping along beside Ruth, holding her hand, he enquired: 'Where are we going today, then?'

'To buy you some plimsolls. They like you to change into indoor shoes at school,' she told him. 'And they don't sell plimsolls in Manchester Road, so we're going to Poplar High Street instead.'

Danny cheered up. Going to Poplar was far more exciting than the boring, familiar shops near the pub.

'Can we look in the toy-shop as well?' he said.

'If we have time.'

But when they turned the corner into Poplar High Street, she realised with dismay that they would never get near the shops. The streets surrounding the Town Hall were jammed with people; all traffic had stopped, for a crowd of two or three thousand had spilled across the roadway, making any progress impossible.

Danny jumped up and down impatiently. 'What's happening, Mum?'

'I don't know,' she began, and an elderly man standing nearby supplied an answer.

'They're going to lock them young women up!' he told her. 'We've come out to watch them being took off to jail!'

163

'No such thing,' chimed in an old lady who might have been his wife. 'We're here to put a stop to it! We won't let them take our girls to prison!'

'Which girls? Why are they being sent to prison?' Ruth wanted to know, but so many people were shouting, it was hard to hear what was going on. At different points, men and women were standing up on boxes, or hanging on to lamp-posts, haranguing the crowd.

'Release George Lansbury!'—*'Down with the Rating Scheme!'*—*'Stop unemployment now!'*

To add to the general hubbub, a fife-and-drum band was on the march, trying to make its way through the close-packed throng.

'Lift me up, Mum!' Danny tugged urgently at Ruth's arm. 'I can't see. Is it a procession?'

So Ruth picked him up, anxious that he shouldn't get trampled underfoot in this mass of swaying bodies, but Danny was a growing lad and she wasn't sure how long she could carry him. She was thankful she had left Lil at home with her grandma—she could never have managed the pushchair in this mob.

'Here, let me help you,' said a familiar voice, and a strong pair of hands took Danny from her.

She was about to protest, but the boy exclaimed with delight, 'It's Huw! Look, Mum, it's Huw!'

The young Welshman hoisted Danny high above his head and settled him upon his shoulders, where he would have a splendid view.

'Good morning, Mrs O'Dell. What are you

164

doing here?' he asked.

'I was trying to do some shopping, but that seems to be hopeless,' she replied. 'I still don't know what's going on.'

'Haven't you heard?' Huw explained. 'It's the Rate Equalisation scheme; they say Poplar's going to have to pay nearly twelve shillings in the pound—more than average for all the rest of London! The Labour Councillors refused to levy the new rates; George Lansbury and the other men have been sent to Brixton already, and now the police are going to arrest the women Councillors, too. Look—there's one of 'em now. That's Sue Lawrence...'

On the steps of the Town Hall, a young woman was speaking through a megaphone, trying to make herself heard. Her words were blurred and indistinct, but their meaning was clear.

'Don't try to rescue us—it'll only make us look like cowards... Let them send us to jail, like the men—we want to make our protest!'

'Good for you, girl!' shrieked the old lady, amid roars of approval.

As the five women Councillors were led to the waiting police cars, the crowd surged forward and Ruth lost her balance, thrown heavily against Huw.

'Oh—excuse me!'

Keeping Daniel steady with one hand, he put his free arm around Ruth's shoulders, saying, 'This is no place for you. Let's get you both out of here before anyone gets hurt. Isn't Mr O'Dell with you?'

'No, he had to go and see his solicitor this morning, on some business or other.' Ruth's voice changed, and Huw threw her a sidelong glance.

'In that case I'll see you get home safely,' he told her, and refused to listen to any arguments.

At last she gave up, saying, 'Well, if you're sure you don't mind. Shopping's obviously out of the question. You'll just have to manage without plimsolls tomorrow, Danny.'

Huw steered a skilful course through the mass of people, and as soon as they left the High Street Ruth offered to take Danny, but the boy hung on tightly, saying, 'Let Huw give me a carry, Mum. He wants to—he said so!'

Huw grinned, and carried Danny shoulder-high all the way back to the pub. When they arrived, Ruth insisted on inviting him in to have some coffee. In Connor's absence, his parents were helping behind the bar, and when Danny went out to play in the yard, baby Lil—who always wanted to copy everything her big brother did—toddled off in pursuit. For the first time, Ruth found herself alone with Huw Pritchard.

'You're not working at the docks today, then?' she asked. 'Weren't there enough jobs to go round?'

'I don't know. I didn't go to the call-over this morning,' he replied. 'I heard there was likely to be some trouble in Poplar—Labour Party members were asked to go along and support our Councillors.'

'They won't be best pleased at Jubilee Wharf,

166

will they, if they find out you took time off to go to a political rally?'

Huw shrugged. 'They're not best pleased with me anyhow. I've made my views known about them and their blessed Brotherhood before now. Honest, they're nothing but a pack of reactionary old—' Then he stopped, and a slow flush crept across his cheeks.

'Sorry, I shouldn't say that,' he mumbled. 'I was forgetting—you're related to the Judge family, aren't you?'

'I used to be,' said Ruth. 'But don't worry—we've not been on very good terms since I left home and got married. By this time, the Brotherhood are pretty well acquainted with my views, Mr Pritchard!'

They both laughed, and then Huw blurted out: 'It seems a bit daft, you calling me that, when Danny calls me by my first name. So, couldn't you... I mean, unless you've any objection?'

'Why not?' she said, smiling. 'From now on, we'll be Huw—and Ruth.'

As she said it, she could not understand the sensation of relief that swept through her; then, looking into his cheerful, friendly face, she realised what it meant. She was talking openly and easily with a young man—enjoying his company, laughing with him. Once upon a time she had known this same lightness of spirit when she was with her husband, but so long ago, she had almost forgotten what it was like. For one glorious moment, she had stopped feeling lonely.

The moment passed all too soon. Out in the yard, she heard a shrill wail of grief and frustration, and Danny called to her: 'Mum! Lil's fallen over again!'

With a sigh, Ruth pushed back her chair and stood up.

'You'll have to excuse me, Huw—I'm wanted,' she said, and went out to resume her duty as a mother. The brief interlude was over.

That night, when Jimmy and Bertie had gone to bed and the house was quiet, Josh walked into the scullery where Florrie was drying the last of the dishes.

'That was a tasty supper,' he said. 'Thanks, Florrie—I don't know how we'd manage without you.'

Modestly, Florrie lowered her eyes. 'I'm glad to be able to help,' she said.

'Well, we're very grateful, but we mustn't keep you so late another time. Did you know it's nearly half-past nine?'

'Is it? That doesn't bother me. After all, I've nothing to get back to but an empty house. My time's my own.'

She took the tray of clean plates, cups and saucers, and went through to the kitchen, where she began to set them out on the dresser. Josh followed her, saying, 'Matter of fact, I was thinking I might go for a stroll myself, to get a breath of air. We could walk along together, if you like.'

Florrie nearly dropped the plate she was holding, and said with a nervous smile: 'Are

168

you going to see me home, Josh? That's nice.'

Taken aback, Josh demurred, 'Well, no, I wasn't exactly thinking of that. I just meant, we could walk part of the way—as far as West Ferry Road, that's all. I thought I'd go down to the Ferry House for half an hour—have a glass of ale, meet some of my pals. You know...'

'Yes, I know.' But Florrie's smile had vanished. 'Do you really think you should? You know what your father would say.'

'Father can mind his own damn business!' snapped Josh. When she winced and turned away, he added gruffly, 'Sorry, didn't mean to bite your head off, only I'm sick and tired of him treating me like a schoolkid. I suppose you don't approve of me taking a drink either, do you?'

'It's not up to me, is it? It's your life—I wouldn't dream of criticising,' said Florrie, with her back to him. 'I was only going to say, perhaps I ought to stay here till you get back. You don't want to leave the boys alone, do you? Suppose the house was to catch fire?'

'That's not very likely.' Josh indicated the fireplace, with a fan of pleated paper in the empty grate, for the summer weather had stretched into September. 'Besides, they're fast asleep by now. They can't come to any harm.'

'No, truly, I don't mind. You go—I can get on with some darning while you're gone; you three all wear your socks out at such a rate!'

'It might be late by the time I get back. You don't want to have to walk home in the dark, when the pubs are turning out.'

'Well, if it's that late, p'raps I could make up a bed on the parlour sofa...' When Florrie put the last cup back in place, she did not turn round but stood absently tracing the line of ornamental beading along the edge of the shelf. 'In fact, I was only thinking the other day that it might be a good idea if I was to stay here—all the time. It would save me going to and fro every day, wouldn't it?'

'Stay here?' Josh repeated hoarsely, and cleared his throat. 'But, I mean, we haven't got a spare bedroom.'

'I suppose the boys could move in together, couldn't they? Then I could have Jimmy's room. I wouldn't intrude or anything—I'd be more of a housekeeper, like.' She forced herself to turn her head, and looked at him enquiringly, with a tremulous smile. 'It might be more convenient all round in the long run, don't you think?'

Josh felt himself breaking out in a cold sweat, and cleared his throat again, trying to think what to say to her. At once, she was full of concern.

'Oh dear, you're not catching a cold, are you? I thought you sounded a bit throaty—shall I make you a hot lemon drink?'

'No—no, really.' But he seized the excuse she was offering him. 'Now you mention it, I think I'll stay in and have an early night. I won't go out again this evening, after all. Thanks all the same, Florrie. You pop off home—I'll be all right.'

She tried to argue, but he swept aside her protests, fetching her bonnet and shawl. When

170

she finally left, telling him to take good care of himself and wrap up well, promising to return bright and early in the morning, he shut the front door behind her, mopping his brow.

He was still wrestling with the problem of Florrie the following day when he went to work, and later in the morning he tried to explain the awkward situation to his father.

'She's been a tower of strength since Mabel passed away—no question about that. But now she's beginning to—well, to dig herself in, as you might say. She's talking about moving into the house, turning Jimmy out of his bedroom. She says he can share with Bertie... She sees herself becoming a permanent fixture, so to speak.'

Marcus's eyes were heavy with disapproval under his beetling brows. 'A widow and a single man—under the same roof She must see that is out of the question. What can she be thinking of?'

Josh murmured uncomfortably, 'I'm afraid she may be thinking along matrimonial lines. Planning a second marriage, perhaps.'

'Marriage?' Marcus's growl was like the rumble of an approaching storm. 'Have you taken leave of your senses? Turn to the Book of Prayer—consult the Tables of Affinity—a man may not marry his brother's wife!'

'I think that's been changed now, Father. Don't you know? They passed an Act of Parliament a few years before the war, allowing a man to marry his deceased wife's sister. I suppose that means he could marry his deceased brother's widow, as well?'

'I am not concerned with Acts of Parliament—I am speaking of the Laws of God!' The storm broke in a thunderclap, and Marcus's eyes were lightning-flashes. 'The Almighty is not mocked. He has laid down His everlasting commandments!'

'Yes, all right, Father, I'm not arguing about that. I don't *want* Florrie moving in. For a start, she's older than I am, and even when she was a girl she was no oil-painting... But I'm in a very awkward situation. There's no denying she's made herself useful, and I can't run the house without some help—so what am I to do?'

For several moments, Marcus clasped his hands as if in prayer. At last he raised his head slowly, and said, 'The answer is perfectly simple. You may not marry your sister-in-law but that is no reason why you should not seek a wife elsewhere. Find some suitable young woman, and bind yourself to her in holy matrimony. Remember the words of St Paul—*"It is better to marry than to burn."* Obey the will of Almighty God, and take unto thyself a wife.'

The next time Gloria came to give Ruth a shampoo and set, she asked, 'How's Danny getting on at school?'

'Oh, not too bad. I thought we were going to have a problem with him the first day, when he came home and said: "All right, I've been to school but I won't bother to go any more, because I know about it now." But then he started making friends, thank goodness, so he's

172

beginning to enjoy it.'

Gloria whisked a towel round Ruth's shoulders and fixed it in place, saying, 'Oh yes, thank goodness for friends—they're so important, aren't they? I remember when poor old Saul was taken, the loneliness was the worst part. Having nobody at home to talk to.'

'Yes, that's the worst part,' said Ruth, then corrected herself 'I mean—it must be.'

Bleakly, she studied her reflection in the washstand mirror, while Gloria laid out the tools of her trade, asking, 'How do you want it today? Curls? Or straight? How about a fringe? What has the Lord and Master decreed this time?'

'If you mean Connor, to be honest I don't think he'd notice if I had it dyed bright red.'

Gloria looked at her sharply. 'What makes you say that?'

'Oh, nothing. It's just that he's been in a funny mood lately. We don't seem to talk to each other these days.'

'Well, what do you expect? You're both busy people—you with the two kids to look after, and him with the pub to run. It's a shame you can't get away for a little holiday, just the two of you. Couldn't his mum and dad manage the pub for a few days?'

'What—and leave them to look after the children as well?' Ruth shook her head. 'I couldn't do that. Besides, I don't suppose Connor would want to go away—not with me, anyhow.'

'What do you mean?' Gloria threw her a

173

quick, searching glance. 'You don't mean to say he's chasing after somebody else? Honestly, doesn't it make you sick?'

Ruth hastened to correct the misunderstanding. 'Oh no, it's nothing like that. At least, I don't think so. But he has been acting very strangely these last few months.'

She knew she shouldn't gossip about Connor to her cousin, yet she felt that if she didn't get it off her chest sooner or later she would explode. As simply as possible, she told Gloria about Rosie and Connor and Mr Hardiman and the 'mysterious benefactor', concluding, 'When I asked Con straight out, he said "No"—but I knew right away that he wasn't telling the truth.'

'Why should he lie about a thing like that?' Gloria was completely out of her depth. 'Rosie's his half-sister, isn't she? Why shouldn't he give her and Ernest a helping hand if he wants to?'

'No reason at all—except he made such a secret out of it. Why didn't he tell me the truth when I asked him? It's as if he felt guilty about it.'

'That's the part I don't understand. Why should he feel guilty?'

'I can only think of one reason. One day when we were talking about something else, he said: *"Some people don't know what they want—until they've lost it..."* and he looked so unhappy, my heart turned over.'

Gloria was still floundering. 'What's that got to do with—'

'Don't you see? Years ago, before Rosie and Con found out they were half-brother and sister, he used to go around with her. He was her "steady", as you might say.'

'Don't be so soft. You know very well that wasn't anything serious—just boy-and-girl stuff.'

'Was it? Suppose it was more serious than we knew? Suppose it only stopped because he found out they had the same father? Suppose he's always loved her—and *that's* why he put money into the shop? And that's why he could never tell me about it?'

Now she had said it all. With part of her mind, she hated herself for confiding in Gloria, but at the same time it was such a relief to be able to voice the black suspicion which had haunted her for so long...

Then, in the mirror, she saw a strange look on Gloria's face—troubled, unhappy—but determined.

'No, Ruth,' Gloria said quietly. 'You're wrong there... It's nothing to do with Rosie—it's not her.'

She came closer and put both hands on Ruth's shoulders, holding her tightly.

'I wasn't going to tell you,' she went on. 'I promised myself I'd never breathe a word about this. Then I thought you must have heard the gossip already, when you were talking about him growing tired of you—and I didn't know whether to say anything or not...'

'What are you talking about? What gossip?'

'But when you started on that cock-and-bull

175

tale about Rosie—well, I knew then I'd got to put you straight. I heard it from one of my other clients—you know how they gossip when they're having their hair done. She couldn't wait to tell me, knowing I was your cousin, of course!'

She hesitated, trying to find the right words. Agonised, Ruth burst out: 'You can't stop now—tell me!'

Gloria took a deep breath. 'According to what I heard, Connor's taken up with another woman. They've been seen about together, more than once. I'm ever so sorry.'

Ruth's face was completely blank; her lips felt stiff as she whispered, 'What other woman? Who is she?'

'Couldn't say—it's nobody we know. But from what they told me, she's smartly dressed—a coat with a fur collar, and a hat with a veil. But whoever it is, it's not Rosie.'

Late one October afternoon, Josh was on his way home from the docks.

The long summer had come to an end at last; it was clammy and cold now, and mist thickened the fading daylight. He sniffed the air, with its mixture of dank river fog and soot from a thousand chimneys. It was going to be a raw night and he would have to turn out again presently, for there was to be a meeting of the Brotherhood's Inner Circle, to discuss the Guild's finances; rising wage-demands and reduced profits from the Wharf posed a serious problem.

He shivered, looking forward to the warm kitchen and the hearty supper that awaited him. Florrie was still coming in every day to make a meal for the family, but ever since he'd told her that his father flatly refused to consider the idea of her moving in, she had not mentioned it again. Florrie knew better than to go against Marcus Judge's wishes.

Josh could imagine how she would be when he got home—a melancholy figure with a sacking apron over her mourning black, her shoulders bent to her tasks as she stirred the pans or mashed the potatoes. She did not talk to him as much as she used to; in some ways that was a relief, but her reproachful silence cast a gloom over the household.

What with her air of martyrdom, and Father's critical eye upon him, Josh wasn't getting much pleasure out of life these days. He had a sudden urge to call in at the Ferry House for a quick one before the meeting, to cheer himself up—but he would have to be careful. If Father smelt whisky on his breath, he would certainly launch into another lecture on the demon drink.

Passing a little newspaper and confectionery shop, he decided to go in and buy some peppermints, to be on the safe side.

When he entered the shop, his first reaction was one of irritation. There were already two customers between him and the counter—a young woman and a small boy—and they were both in tears.

The shopkeeper, a disagreeable old man called

Spinks, had to raise his voice to make himself heard.

'It's no good you carrying on like that—I tell you, I'm going to call the police! I won't have no thieving in this shop, and it ain't the first time, neither... That boy needs to be taught a lesson!'

The boy, who could not have been more than six years old, was not a handsome child; his pudgy face looked even less attractive because it was blubbered with tears, and his nose was running.

His mother was sobbing: 'Please, Mr Spinks, don't do it, don't call the police. I swear to you he won't ever do such a thing again, will you, Trev?'

The name struck a chord in Josh, and he looked at her more closely. Of course—she was the young woman who worked at Aunt Emily's shop and lived above it with her son. She was his Cousin Arnold's widow, Maudie.

'Hello!' he exclaimed. 'What's going on here?'

They all looked round, and when Maudie recognised him, she pulled out a handkerchief and began to dry her eyes, ashamed to be caught in such a humiliating situation.

'Oh, Mr Judge—fancy seeing you,' she began. 'Such a dreadful thing. We came in to get some cough-lozenges for your auntie, 'cos she's got a nasty cold on her chest, and Trev must have taken a bar of chocolate off the counter when I wasn't looking. He's too young to understand about paying for things, you see.'

178

'He understands all right!' interrupted Mr Spinks. 'That boy's been up to his tricks before now—and he nearly got away with it this time, and all. Halfway out the door they were, when I spotted there was a bar of milk-chocolate missing off the counter!'

'We've already said we're sorry,' Maudie threw in desperately. 'That's why Trev's crying—he's sorry for being a naughty boy.'

Josh was not so sure about that. It seemed to him that Trevor's howls were provoked by anger and frustration when the chocolate-bar had been taken away from him.

'She told me I'd made a mistake!' stormed Mr Spinks, righteously indignant. 'So I got hold of the little perisher and went through his pockets. Blow me if he didn't have the chocolate in one pocket, and a handful of gobstoppers in the other!'

'I've said I'll pay for them,' Maudie pleaded, 'only I haven't got enough on me at the moment. I only had enough in my purse for the cough-lozenges. If you'll let me go home, I can fetch some more money!'

'Oh, no—that's not good enough!' Adamant, Mr Spinks folded his arms. 'I'm not letting that boy off so light. I'll have him took up at the juvenile Court, I will—we'll see how he likes that!'

'No, please. Don't.' Maudie was beginning to weep again. 'Whatever would people say? He's only a child—can't you give him another chance?'

Josh had heard enough. He raised his hand

for silence, cutting through the argument in the voice that had quelled so many disagreements at Brotherhood meetings.

'That's enough. Be quiet the lot of you!' He fumbled in his pocket, then slapped a handful of coins on the counter. 'Will that be enough to settle the matter, Mr Spinks?'

The money was more than enough—ten times more—but Spinks still grumbled, 'That's not the point, is it? That kid should be took up, as an example to others. There's too much shoplifting these days and it's my duty as a citizen to take a firm stand.'

'It's your duty as a Christian to love thy neighbour, and forgive him his trespasses,' said Josh, uncomfortably aware he was echoing his father's sonorous tones.

'That's as may be, but—'

'I think you know me, Mr Spinks? And I'm well acquainted with your son, who works for us at Jubilee Wharf from time to time. He's a useful member of the Guild, and we think very highly of him.'

'Oh, ah—good of you to say so, I'm sure...' With the wind taken out of his sails, Spinks subsided. 'Well, seeing it's you, Mr Judge, I'll overlook it this time but I'm warning you, the very next time I catch that young scoundrel pinching stuff from my shop—'

'You can rest assured it won't happen again,' said Josh, putting his hand on Trevor's head, 'because if it did, he'd have me to answer to. Isn't that right, Trevor?'

He opened the shop door and offered Maudie

180

his arm; they went into the street together.

'Oh, Mr Judge, I don't know how to thank you,' gasped Maudie, when they were safely outside. 'The idea of little Trev being arrested—it would have broken your auntie's heart.'

'Well, it's over and done with now.' Josh smiled at the young widow. 'I'm sure Trevor will be a good boy in future, so let's say no more about it.'

Oddly enough, although crying had disfigured Trevor, tears were quite becoming to his mother; her big violet eyes glistened, and her lips were moist and trembling. She gave Josh a look of such gratitude and admiration, he could not help warming towards Maudie.

He accompanied them as far as the corner grocery, and she invited him in for a cup of tea, but he explained that he must be getting back, as supper would be on the table.

Well—another time, perhaps?' she said shyly.

'Certainly, another time,' he agreed. 'I'll look forward to that.'

And he continued on his way home. It wasn't until he was putting his key into the front door that he realised that in all the fuss and commotion he had forgotten to buy any peppermints.

'Well, never mind,' he told himself. 'Perhaps I won't need them.'

Perhaps he would not need a drink to cheer him up before the meeting, after all. To his surprise, he found that he was feeling quite cheerful already.

On another afternoon, at the end of the month, three young women were taking tea together: Sarah Kleiber, Maudie Judge and Ruth O'Dell.

Maudie had carried out her intention to keep in touch with Sarah, after their first meeting at the photographic shop, but today their sons were not with them, for Trevor and Benjamin were both at school. Danny O'Dell, too, was at Willow Row Infants, but Ruth had brought her baby daughter with her.

They were sitting round the scrubbed wooden table in the kitchen of the Kleibers' old house, while little Lil sat on the floor, painstakingly trying to make a tower out of wooden cubes with letters painted on the sides.

'Ben never plays with building bricks now,' said Sarah, watching her at work. 'Now he can read, he thinks he's much too grown-up... I suppose I should have given them away, really, but they belonged to Izzy when he was little, and somehow I couldn't let them go.'

'I don't believe we've got any of Arnie's toys,' said Maudie. 'I wish we had; it would be nice to think Trev could share something with his dad.'

Ruth listened to the conversation, but took no part in it. She was thinking how strange it was; like her companions, she had been a widow—unlike them, she had married again. Yet although she had a husband, she too felt bereaved.

182

It was not grief, or despair; it was not the sense of tragic loss they must have known when they heard their husbands had been killed in action.

When Gloria told her that Connor was going with another woman, Ruth felt as if she had become a different person. Of course, Sean had been unfaithful to her—that had hurt her at first, but she gradually realised that was the way he was—nothing would ever change him. But Connor... She had believed that Connor would love her for ever, and when she realised he might be deceiving her, the whole world turned upside-down—everything she believed in seemed to fall apart, and nothing made sense. She would never trust anyone again—she could not even trust herself; the face she saw reflected in the washstand mirror that day was the face of a stranger.

Outwardly, of course, things hadn't changed. She went through her daily routine automatically —she helped in the pub, she cooked and cleaned and washed up, she took Danny to school, she bathed and dressed Lil—she even found herself talking to Connor quite easily, chatting about the weather, or the price of coal, or the headlines in the daily paper... And it all meant nothing at all.

She was keeping up appearances from sheer force of habit, but the heart had gone out of her. She wasn't unhappy, or angry, or disillusioned. She didn't feel like raging against her husband, saying: 'How dare you deceive me? How dare you love another woman?'

She couldn't even remember what love felt like any more—or grief, or hatred, or pain... She felt nothing but a cold, paralysing numbness.

And the strangest part of all was that no one else had even noticed.

Of course, Gloria was solicitous and sympathetic, wanting to talk over the situation, offering comfort and advice—but Ruth told her coolly that she didn't want to discuss it.

'It's not worth talking about,' she said. 'As a matter of fact, I don't believe it. It's a mistake—it must have been two other people. Connor isn't like that.'

Originally, she had said it without thinking, putting it up as a barrier to ward off any more talk—a shield against the pain. But there didn't seem to be any pain and, as the days and nights passed, she began to ask herself: perhaps after all it really was a mistake? Perhaps Con hadn't gone off to some other woman?

But deep down, she never really doubted it. In his heart, Con had left her long ago; in her heart, she had known it all along.

With conscious effort, she put these thoughts from her, and tried to concentrate on what the others were saying.

'Yes, he did. He asked me to go out to supper with him,' Sarah admitted, with a touch of pride and a little embarrassment too.

Maudie looked quite shocked. 'Well, you are a dark horse!'

'Do you think it was wrong of me?' Sarah turned from Maudie. 'What do you think, Ruth?'

184

Ruth apologised. 'I'm sorry, I was miles away. What did you say?'

'Sarah was telling me,' Maudie chimed in, 'that one of her lodgers took her out to supper the other night—imagine that!'

'He's a commercial traveller for a pharmaceutical company in Frankfurt. He comes to London regularly on business,' Sarah explained. 'And he took me to a German restaurant he knows in Whitechapel... His name's Klaus Brendel—he's really very nice.'

'But weren't you nervous about going out with a stranger?' Maudie asked. 'I'd never dare! Suppose he tried to—well, you know what I mean.'

'Klaus isn't a stranger, he's stayed here several times before. He's also very correct—he'd never do anything that was not polite. And Frau Hoffmann offered to look after Benjamin until we came back, which made a nice change. I really enjoyed the evening.'

'Yes, but all the same...' Maudie shook her head. 'I'm sure I couldn't have done it, could you, Ruth?'

'It's different for Ruth,' Sarah pointed out. 'I don't suppose she can imagine what it's like now, not to have a husband.'

'No, I can't imagine it,' said Ruth, and looked at her watch. 'Maudie, we must go. We mustn't be late—our sons would never forgive us if we're not at the playground gates.'

The three boys went to different schools, and when their mothers parted, promising to meet again very soon, they all set off in different

185

directions. Willow Row was in Limehouse, so Ruth caught a bus along the East India Dock Road.

It was another foggy day, and the bus crawled through a thick, pea-green shroud. The street-lamps had been alight all day—their yellow globes shimmered unsteadily within the fog, which would lift occasionally for a few yards, and then close in again.

Ruth gazed out of the window, straining her eyes to try and identify some familiar landmarks. Lil was asleep on her lap, undisturbed by the crashing of gears as the bus slowed down to walking-pace. At one point they pulled up beside a jellied-eel stall, illuminated by naphtha flares; further on, the swirling vapours thinned for a moment, just long enough to reveal a taxi-cab drawn up at the opposite pavement, and a broad-shouldered man in a greatcoat helping a lady in. She turned back to say goodbye, leaning towards him from the open door of the cab as he embraced her.

Then the fog returned, blotting out the scene once more, and the bus groaned on; but in that instant, Ruth saw that the lady had a coat with a fur collar, and a hat with a veil—and she knew that the man was Connor O'Dell.

Moments later, the bus braked sharply and baby Lil awoke with a start. Bewildered, she looked up for reassurance, and was dismayed by the sight of the tears rolling down Ruth's face. It was the first time she had seen her mother cry.

Ruth was remembering, at last, what pain felt like.

7

Out of the darkness, tiny trails of light appeared, surging upwards, chasing one another. Then there was nothing but deep, velvety black—and a moment later the miracle happened.

Gigantic chrysanthemums appeared from nowhere, hanging in the night sky, throwing out petals of gold and silver, brilliant blossoms that floated earthwards as the onlookers exclaimed with one voice: *'Aaaaaaah...!'*

'Look, Mum—look!' shouted Danny, beside himself with delight. In his excitement, he bounced upon Huw's shoulders and drummed his heels against the young man's chest until Ruth put out a hand to restrain him.

'Careful, you'll hurt him!'

'That's all right,' said Huw cheerfully. 'I'll let you know when he cracks a rib.'

They had joined the crowds at Poplar Recreation Ground on Guy Fawkes night; a thousand men, women and children, their faces lifted to the night sky, watching the firework display.

Overhead, more rockets soared up, exploding in firebursts of crimson, of green and blue—and then a dazzling magnesium glare illuminated the whole scene. For a few seconds, night turned into day, and they stared at one another, magically transfigured.

Huw looked at Ruth, and saw her expression of wonder, her lips parted in amazement, and the soft bloom upon her cheek; at the same moment she turned to Huw, and saw his youthful passion, his sincere devotion. Then the light died, and the darkness swallowed them once more. Ruth found that she was trembling.

'You're shivering,' he said, putting a hand on her arm. 'You mustn't catch cold.'

'No, I'm all right, really I am,' she said breathlessly. In that shining moment, she had seen the look in Huw's eyes, and she felt ashamed.

Danny heaved a sigh of regret. 'I wish Dad had come too...'

'Your dad couldn't help it,' Huw told him. 'He's got to do his work, hasn't he?'

Saturday nights were the busiest time of the week at the pub and Connor had explained to Danny that, although he would have liked to come to the Rec and see the fireworks, he had to stay and manage the saloon bar. But Mum would go with him—and Huw had kindly offered to take them and bring them back afterwards.

'Still, it is a shame,' said Ruth.

A shame... She was hoping the darkness would continue for a little longer so that Huw would not see that she was blushing; that sudden, unexpected brilliance had revealed too much already. She knew now, without a shadow of doubt, that Huw was in love with her.

During the past week, life would have been

intolerable for Ruth without Huw's company. The fragile threads of love that held her and Connor together had frayed and broken. By day, in the rough-and-tumble of the pub, they kept up appearances well enough; no one else, overhearing their snatches of random conversation, would have dreamt that they were two strangers, imprisoned in a marriage that had become hollow and meaningless.

Eight days earlier, Ruth had seen her husband embrace another woman as he helped her into a cab; since then there had been nothing between them but a superficial pretence.

She wondered if Connor was aware of it, too. Didn't he even notice that his wife no longer touched him, or kissed him? One night he had asked if she was upset about something and she had replied: 'Of course not. What makes you think so?'

That was the moment when she should have challenged him, asked him outright about the other woman...but she did not have the courage. Either he would lie to her—which would be unbearable—or he would tell her the truth—and that would be the end of everything.

So she had kept up this empty charade, playing a part, and in her loneliness she had found some comfort in Huw Pritchard's company.

Of course Huw was totally ignorant of all this, yet he seemed to be almost intuitive, as if he sensed that his kindness and attentiveness were making life a little easier for Ruth. In her heart of hearts, she had already guessed something of his feelings, but refused to acknowledge them.

Now, in a shining moment of clarity, she knew that he loved her, and she was overwhelmed with shame. How could she have been so selfish, and so cruel?

'It's getting late,' she said. 'I think we ought to be getting back.'

'Oh no, Mum—we can't go yet!' Danny was indignant. 'The fireworks haven't finished!'

'All the same, it's long past your bedtime,' she told him. 'If you don't mind, Huw, I think we should be making a move.'

'Whatever you say.'

He turned and began to pick his way through the crowd, clearing a path for her.

Still perched upon Huw's shoulders, Danny let out a furious cry. 'I won't go! I want to see the fireworks—it's not fair!'

No, it wasn't fair... Ruth felt another pang of guilt. Unhappiness spread so quickly, like an infection. Retreating from her own misery over Connor, she had unwittingly involved Huw, and now she was running away from the consequences of her lack of judgment and spoiling her son's treat.

'No tantrums, young feller-me-lad!' said Huw firmly. 'You heard what your mum said, we've got to go. Cheer up—you won't miss the rockets. Keep looking up, and you'll see them lighting us on our way home.'

With that, Danny had to be content, and their journey was accompanied by further explosions and flashes of colour punching holes in the night sky.

By the time they reached the Watermen,

Danny had recovered his good temper. When Ruth opened the side door, he rushed off along the kitchen passage, impatient to tell his grandma of the wonders he had seen. Ruth turned to Huw, raising her voice a little above the clatter and chatter from the bar.

'Thank you,' she said. 'I hope you weren't too disappointed we didn't stay to the end, but it is rather late for Danny.'

'Don't worry, I had a grand time anyway,' Huw told her. 'I tell you what, it's Sunday tomorrow. If it's a fine afternoon, will you be taking the children to the Island Gardens? Maybe I could come along with you, and help give young Daniel a push on the swings?'

'Oh, I'm not sure,' she began.

In the saloon, someone was playing the piano, and the customers were joining in:

You are my honey-honeysuckle,
I am the bee...

'Hello—you're back already?' The bead curtain rattled as Connor appeared in the archway that led to the bar. 'Were the fireworks any good?'

'They were wonderful,' Ruth explained, 'only we decided not to stay till the end, because it was getting a bit late. Danny was rather cross.'

'Oh well, he can't have everything his own way.'

There was an awkward pause. They all stood and looked at one another, as the singing continued.

191

I'd like to sip the honey sweet
From those red lips, you see...

Huw broke in: 'I was just saying, perhaps if I was to give him a go on the swings at the Gardens tomorrow afternoon, we might make it up to him.' He turned to Ruth. 'That is, if you feel like another outing?'

'It all depends what Connor's got planned for tomorrow,' said Ruth.

I love you truly, truly—
And I want you to love me...

Connor stood in the archway, drying his hands on a glass-cloth and looking at his beautiful wife, who had grown so far away from him lately—and the red-headed Welsh boy, in the full flower of his youth and manhood.

'Sunday afternoon? I've no plans at all,' he said.

The singers in the bar worked up to a crescendo.

You are my honey-honeysuckle,
I am the bee...

Anger exploded within Connor like a rocket; he felt a sudden urge to smash his fist into that handsome young face and then, like a rocket, the impulse faded and died... These past few months, he'd had so many other things on his mind, small wonder if Ruth turned elsewhere

192

for company, to someone less preoccupied, less beset by problems—and ten years his junior.

Forcing his lips into a half-smile, he concluded, 'Sunday afternoon? I'll be happy to take things easy, put my feet up for an hour or so and study the sporting papers. Yes, why not take the kids to the playground. You'll enjoy that.'

He went back to the saloon, as the pianist began another old favourite.

Daisy, Daisy, give me your answer, do.
I'm half crazy, all for the love of you...

Huw turned happily to Ruth. 'Right, until tomorrow then. I'll look forward to it.'

Week after week, the long winter dragged on. Ruth tried to avoid Huw as much as possible, but it wasn't easy, since Danny kept begging her to invite him to tea and Connor told the young man, 'You know you're welcome whenever you've a mind to drop in. The lad's adopted you as an honorary uncle, so you're practically one of the family!'

At Christmas, Huw brought Danny a clockwork motorcar, and a fluffy rabbit for Lil—then, a little sheepishly, produced a bunch of golden chrysanthemums for Ruth, with the compliments of the season.

She knew she shouldn't encourage him, but she didn't want to hurt his feelings and, despite herself, she could not help finding some consolation in his company.

Connor's Christmas present to Ruth was a

brooch in silver filigree. The name printed upon the box showed that it came from an expensive shop near the Mansion House, and she couldn't help asking how he had managed to buy it, without her knowing.

He shrugged away from a direct answer. 'Oh, one day when I had to go up to town on business... I don't tell you everything, you know!' he teased her.

'No, I suppose not. Thank you—it's beautiful.'

'Glad you like it. Mind, I'd no idea what to buy, but a lady in the shop helped me choose it.'

'Oh, yes.' Ruth wondered who the lady in the shop might have been, but did not ask any more questions. 'It's too good to wear every day; I shall put it away for safety, and take it out for special occasions.'

Special occasions were few and far between that winter; it remained in a drawer of her dressing-table for months, untouched.

On a cold January night, Ernest and Rosie stood outside the old house in Poplar, a raw east wind nipping their ears, waiting for Sarah to open the front door.

'Ring again,' said Rosie. 'Perhaps she didn't hear the bell. We'll catch our death if we hang about out here.'

As Ernest put his hand to the bell, the door opened and Sarah stood in the hallway, pink and flustered in the lamplight.

'I'm sorry if I kept you. I was just doing my hair,' she said.

194

They followed her in, a little surprised. Instead of her usual plain dress and apron, Sarah was wearing her best clothes—a white silk blouse over a plum-coloured skirt, set off by a necklace of amethysts.

'Oh, I do like your beads!' exclaimed Rosie. 'They're new, aren't they? Where did you get them?'

'They were a Christmas present. Come in, let me take your coats.' She ushered them into the dining-room. The long trestle-table had vanished, and a small round table was set up in its place, laid for four.

'What's all this?' Ernest asked. 'What's happened to the lodgers?'

'I gave them their tea early tonight, and then we—I cleared the big table away. It's cosier like this, don't you think?'

Rosie was puzzled. 'Yes, but four places? Who else is coming?'

'He's here already. Klaus—come and say hello.'

A man in early middle-age emerged from the kitchen—fair-haired and trim, with a marked German accent. He introduced himself as they shook hands.

'Klaus Brendel... I am most pleased to meet you both.'

'Oh!' Rosie was beginning to understand. 'You're the one who took Sarah out to supper! How do you do?'

Now she had a shrewd idea where the amethyst necklace had come from. Sarah dished up the meal; she had gone to a lot of trouble, and

195

Herr Brendel contributed a bottle of excellent Moselle.

'I believe Sarah told me you were a traveller for a chemical firm in Germany?' said Rosie.

'A pharmaceutical company,' he corrected her politely. 'I was, but no longer. I am now employed by a similar company here in London.'

He went on to explain. 'The present economic state of Germany is very bad. The Deutschmark keeps falling; at present, the exchange rate is thirty-two thousand marks to one pound sterling. Over the past year, the cost of living in Frankfurt has almost doubled. Fortunately, I have always taken an interest in economics and I foresaw what would happen. I took certain steps to protect myself against such a disaster.'

'I don't understand. How could you protect yourself?' asked Ernest.

'I have been gradually transferring capital to this country, and at last I resigned from my post in Frankfurt and applied for work here instead.'

'But surely there are rules and regulations?'

Klaus wiped his lips delicately upon his table-napkin. 'Rules can be broken, provided one knows the right people and I have always taken care to know the right people. I have many friends in this country, in my own line of business; it was not difficult for me to obtain suitable employment. At this moment I am about to take a lease on an apartment in North London—a ground-floor flat with a garden, in West Hampstead.'

'So you won't be living in Poplar any more?'
Ernest turned to Sarah. 'You'll be sorry to lose
such a good lodger.'

Klaus and Sarah glanced at one another, and
he smiled.

'The plan is that Sarah should accompany
me to the new apartment,' explained Klaus.
'That is why I have been anxious to make your
acquaintance, Herr Kleiber. I am hoping you
will give us your permission to be married.'

Amazed, Ernest put down his knife and fork,
and turned to Sarah.

'Well! You have taken me completely by
surprise...but if that is what you wish, you do
not have to ask my permission. I am not your
guardian.'

'No, Ernest, but I would never take such
a step without your approval. You are my
brother-in-law—you are Benjamin's uncle—the
only relative I have left in the world.'

Rosie broke in: 'Have you talked to Ben
about this?'

'Ben and Klaus have become good friends
already. I am sure he will be happy to have
Klaus as his stepfather.'

'In that case, what objection could I possibly
have?' Ernest stood up, holding out his hand
across the table. 'I congratulate you, Herr
Brendel. You have chosen an excellent wife.'

Klaus rose to his feet and the two men shook
hands again, as if they were sealing a contract.
When they resumed their seats, Sarah added,
'There is something else I must ask you. Since
I shall not be able to continue looking after the

lodgers here, would you like me to find you another housekeeper?'

Ernest shook his head. 'That won't be necessary. Rosie and I have no intention of living here; we shall give the present lodgers notice to look for other accommodation. When the house is empty, I shall put it up for sale.'

The next time Ruth and Maudie came to tea with Sarah, there was a 'For Sale' board outside the house, and as she cut slices of cake, Sarah told them of the latest developments.

'Miss Hoffmann is the only one left here now, and she has found a nice room in a house at Bethnal Green. Klaus and I are to be married in three weeks' time. Benjamin has already been with me to visit our home; it will be good for him to have a garden to play in—he looks forward to it so much.'

'Where are you getting married?' Ruth asked. 'Here in Poplar? Or does Herr Brendel attend a synagogue in Hampstead?'

'Like Ernest, we are to be married at a registry office,' replied Sarah. 'Klaus is not Jewish; he does not practise any religion—but he is a good man, and that is all that matters, isn't it?'

Ruth was not quite sure how to reply. She herself had crossed over from one form of Christian belief to another, and she had not criticised Rosie when she talked of a possible conversion to Judaism, but she found it hard to imagine a life without a religious faith of any kind.

'Well, I'm sure you'll both be very happy,' she said, and kissed Sarah. 'The only sad part is that you're moving so far away. We shall miss our tea-parties, won't we, Maudie?'

Maudie nodded her agreement, and Sarah exclaimed: 'Hampstead's not so very far—and there are the buses. When the weather is warmer, you shall come and visit our new home. We can write to one another—we must keep in touch.'

They promised to remain close friends—but they knew they were not likely to meet very often. The Isle of Dogs was a little world of its own; to venture outside it as far as Poplar or Stepney was an effort—to go into the heart of the City was an achievement—but the thought of travelling right across London, to a remote outer suburb they had never seen, was like the prospect of a trip to the moon.

On their way home, Ruth said to Maudie, 'We shall miss her. Is that why you were so quiet this afternoon? You hardly said a word.'

Maudie bit her lip, then blurted out: 'I couldn't say it, but I think it's awful—her getting married again.'

'You mean because they're going to have a civil wedding?'

'No, it isn't that.' Maudie's words, which she had kept bottled up, poured out in a rush. 'She loved her first husband, didn't she? How can she even think of another man? You don't stop loving somebody just 'cos they've gone... That's like breaking a promise.'

'You still feel like that about Arnold, after all this time?' asked Ruth. 'You must have loved him very much.'

Maudie lowered her eyes, flushed and embarrassed. 'Oh, well. It's something I don't like to talk about,' she said, and changed the subject.

She went on to collect Trevor from school, and walked home with him tugging at her hand, cajoling and pleading.

'Norman Glen's got a cap-pistol, Mum, and he's not as old as me... Why can't I have a cap-pistol, Mum? Could I buy a cap-pistol if I was to save up all my pocket-money? If I help at home with the washing-up and go on errands for you, could I have some extra pocket-money, Mum? Please?'

Maudie said vaguely, 'We'll see. If you're a good boy—we'll see.'

But she wasn't really listening. Of course she had never loved Arnie like that. Oh, he had been kind enough in his way, and he had given her a son—but it was never love. Nowadays she tried not to think so much about Tommy, but alone in bed, on the borders of waking and sleeping, it was hard to put him out of her thoughts. She tried to keep her mind on other things; if she let herself remember Tommy, thinking of him so deeply and missing him so much, she always finished up crying for him all over again.

She despised Sarah, who was able to forget her first love and find another—yet at the same time she envied her too, more than a little.

When they reached the shop, she found her mother-in-law busy with a customer, scooping split peas into a brown-paper bag.

'Six ounces exactly, Mrs Higgins,' said Emily Judge, and turned to greet her beloved grandson.

'Did you have a nice day at school, Trevor?'

'It was all right,' he said impatiently. 'Gran, can I have a cap-pistol for my birthday?'

'Oh, good gracious, your birthday's a long way off—not till midsummer,' she told him.

'If I had a cap-pistol now, you wouldn't have to give me anything on my birthday,' he suggested hopefully.

'Well, we'll have to think about that, won't we?' she said. 'Run along now and wash your hands before tea, there's a good boy. Oh, Maudie...' she lowered her voice. 'There's a visitor waiting to see you in the kitchen.'

Trevor ran through to the back room, to see who the visitor might be, and when Maudie followed, she found him scrambling on to Joshua's lap, gazing up into his face and wheedling: 'Uncle Josh—if I'm a good boy, will you give me a cap-pistol?'

'You mustn't keep asking for things, Trev,' his mother reproved him. 'And don't call him "Uncle"—he's not your uncle, I've told you that before. Now get down and go and wash, like your gran said.'

Unwillingly, Trev trudged off to the scullery, and Josh stood up to greet Maudie.

'I thought I'd drop in on the off-chance,' he began. 'Did you know there's a moving-picture show at the Emmanuel Hall this evening?'

'Yes, they announced it last Sunday,' she replied. 'It's about the missionaries in Africa, isn't it?'

'So I understand. Native customs in the jungle, life among the pygmy tribes—that sort of thing. Anyhow, I've got two tickets. I wondered if you might like to come along?'

Maudie hesitated; she had been out with Joshua twice already—once to a recital of the Messiah at the Chapel, and once to the Christmas bazaar. Each time he had behaved very properly, and she had enjoyed the evening out, but she didn't want it to become a habit. 'It's difficult, really. I mean, there's Trev—I've got to put him to bed, and—'

'I took the liberty of asking Emily and she says she wouldn't mind looking after Trevor, that is—if the idea appeals to you?'

Having seen her customer out, Emily followed Maudie into the kitchen, saying, 'Do go, if you'd like to. I'm always happy to stay with my little cherub, you know that.'

So Maudie had no excuse; and she had to admit it would make a change. 'All right, then. Yes, I'd like to.'

Josh beamed. 'The picture starts at seven, so I'll pick you up about twenty to—all right?'

When he had gone, Maudie said: 'I hope I'm doing the right thing.'

'Of course you are! Why shouldn't you go to see a missionary show?'

'I mean, because of him... I wouldn't want him to get the wrong idea.'

'What a thing to say!' Emily glanced at the scullery door, in case Trevor might be listening. 'Josh must be so lonely these days, he just needs a bit of company, that's all. It will do you both good to get out.'

'Well, if you really think so.'

Maudie took off her hat and coat, glancing at herself in the looking-glass over the mantelpiece, and patting her hair. A gold chain glinted at her throat, and she tucked the heart-shaped pendant under the neckline of her dress, repeating under her breath: 'Just a bit of company—that's all.'

Rosie was making scrambled eggs for breakfast. It was one of Ernest's favourites, but she didn't make it very often. She hated scrubbing out the saucepan afterwards, and it was hard to judge when to start cooking it so that the egg and the toast were both ready when he came into the kitchen.

She had heard him whistling to himself as he shaved, and the sound of the water running out of the bathroom sink, so he shouldn't be long now.

In his high-chair, baby Abram banged his spoon, demanding attention.

'You'll get some—don't worry,' she told him. 'I'm only waiting for Dadda.'

This time she had judged it exactly; as Ernest took his place at the breakfast-table, she set his plate in front of him.

'Scrambled egg?' He rubbed his hands. 'What's this in aid of?'

'No special reason,' she said. This wasn't entirely true; she had to break some unwelcome news and she wanted him to be in a good mood. 'Oh, by the way,' she added, 'the post's come. He was early this morning.' She put three envelopes in front of him.

Ernest put on his spectacles, saying gloomily,

'More bills, I suppose?'

He was in no hurry to open them, for he did not want his breakfast to get cold. As she took her place beside Abram, he glanced across and asked: 'Aren't you having some?'

'Abram's having mine.' She spooned some egg into Abram's open mouth; it was like feeding a baby bird. 'I'm not very hungry this morning.'

He studied her more closely. 'There are shadows under your eyes. Did the gales keep you awake last night?'

'That must be what it was. I don't know how Abram managed to sleep through it—the windows rattled so loud, they woke me up.'

'The windows didn't come to any harm, but I'm not so sure about the roof I thought I heard some slates come down.'

'The postman told me it was like a hurricane, along the river. He said it did a lot of damage to some of the boats.'

'Never mind the boats—it's the roof I'm worried about,' said Ernest, with his mouth full. 'Let's hope we don't have to call in the builders again. If we need new tiles, it's going to cost a pretty penny.'

He began to tear open the envelopes, and Rosie's heart sank.

'Hello—we've got a letter from the estate agents,' he said. 'I wonder what the excuse is this time?'

The house at Poplar had been on the market for a couple of months now, but so far they had not had any firm offers.

Rosie took her courage in both hands; it was

better to get it over as soon as possible, before the morning mail depressed him still further.

'I've got something to tell you,' she began bravely. 'I'm afraid I—'

Then she broke off, because Ernest was smiling. He looked up, saying, 'I've got something to tell you, too! They've managed to sell the house, thank God! And for a very decent price. Some woman wants to open a dancing-school—she's going to turn the old workshop at the back into a classroom... She must have more money than sense.'

'That's nice,' said Rosie, without enthusiasm. 'Now can I tell you my news?'

'I'm sorry, I interrupted you. What is it?'

'I'm afraid you won't be very pleased, but I think—well, I'm practically certain—I'm pregnant again.'

For a moment his face was completely blank, then he said slowly, 'I don't believe it...it's so soon. Abram's not yet a year old.'

'It's true, all the same,' she said flatly. 'I'm very sorry.'

Suddenly he gave a shout of laughter. 'What do you have to be sorry about?' He turned to his small son. 'Do you hear that, Abram? You're going to have a baby brother, and your mama tells us she's sorry!'

'I thought you'd be angry.'

'Because God sends us another miracle, I should be angry?' He left his chair, and came round the table to embrace her. 'This is great news!'

'But children cost money, and I know you're

205

anxious about the shop.'

'Who cares? All right, so the shop hasn't done so well lately—that's not surprising, people don't want photographs in the winter. But just wait till the sun comes out, then you'll see; this is going to be the best year we've ever had. Besides, we've sold that sad old house at last! We'll have some money in the bank—we can pay off our debts.'

A sudden thought struck him, and he hugged her again. 'Who knows? Maybe we can pay back our anonymous benefactor. We shall be truly independent at last!'

One Sunday at the end of May, Trevor was being particularly difficult. At breakfast, Emily watched him overturn the milk-jug, and felt almost sure that he had done it on purpose. Then he refused to eat his porridge, and when Maudie told him he had to finish it all up or he couldn't go to Chapel, he announced that he didn't want to go to nasty old Chapel anyhow—he was fed up with Chapel—it was horrible! Then he shoved the plate of porridge away so violently, it fell off the edge of the table and smashed on the lino.

Mistakenly, Emily tried to restore his good humour by saying, *'That's* not my dear little Trevor—that's Naughty Norman! I don't like Naughty Norman—I want my good little Trevor to come back to his Gan-gan...'

Trevor's only response was to stick his tongue out, jump down from his chair and run upstairs to his bedroom. Maudie went up after him and

206

gave him a stern talking-to, warning him that if he didn't behave himself and apologise to poor Grandma that very minute, she would give him a big smack.

Trevor did not behave himself, nor did he apologise to his grandmother but Maudie, who could not bear to hurt her son, failed to smack him and went downstairs again, telling Emily that he was in one of his moods.

They agreed that they should leave him alone until he was in a better temper; there was no question of taking him to Chapel. So Emily went by herself, and Maudie stayed at home to look after her son. By dinner-time he was feeling rather peckish, and when Emily returned, he told her he was very sorry and promised never to be naughty again—so she kissed him, and said he could have some apple-pie for being such a good boy.

From Trevor's point of view, it had been a highly satisfactory morning.

Since Maudie had not gone to morning service, Emily offered to put Trevor to bed so she could attend evening service instead; and at six o'clock she set off to the Emmanuel Chapel.

It felt very odd, going to Chapel in the evening. She was used to sitting in the same place in the same pew every Sunday morning, surrounded by familiar faces. Now a stranger was in her usual seat, and she had to find a place further back. As the service began, she was aware of someone moving into the pew beside her, and when they struck up the first hymn, a voice said in her ear: 'Do you mind if I share your book?'

Startled, she looked up, and found Joshua next to her.

'Yes. I mean, no. I mean, I don't mind,' she whispered in confusion, and they held the hymnal between them, as Joshua sang in a rich baritone:

'In every clime, by every tongue,
Be God's surpassing glory sung:
Still let mankind His blessings prove—
Spirit of mercy, truth and love...'

She found it extremely hard to concentrate on the sermon; even when she knelt to pray, she was very conscious of his nearness. When his elbow brushed against hers, she moved a little further away.

Afterwards, they left the Chapel together, shaking hands with the Reverend Mr Evans who was saying good night to his faithful flock.

In the street, Josh fell into step at Maudie's side. Searching for some topic of conversation, she remarked, 'I didn't expect to see you here. You generally go to morning service.'

'Yes, I've been once today. I noticed Emily was on her own, and I said I hoped you weren't ill. She told me you'd had a bit of trouble with your boy—she said you'd probably come tonight.'

'Yes, Trev was a real little pickle this morning. I don't know what got into him...' Then she took in the full meaning of his words, and asked,

'But if you went to Chapel this morning, why did you come tonight?'

'I wanted to see you,' he replied easily, without embarrassment. 'I'd been hoping for a chance to talk to you on your own.'

She looked at him warily. 'What did you want to talk about?'

'Oh, this and that.' He gazed around, and unfastened the top button of his black Sunday jacket. 'It's a fine evening, almost like summer. A good evening for a walk, don't you think?'

Maudie hesitated. 'I don't know. I ought to be getting back.'

'We needn't stay out long; the sun will be going down presently. But there's somewhere I'd like to take you... Have you ever seen over the docks?'

She shook her head. 'They don't let women in, do they?'

'Not as a rule. But being as it's a Sunday, there's not likely to be many people about.'

'Won't the gates be locked?'

'I have my own key. I thought you might find it interesting.'

It seemed easier to go along with his plan than to dredge up improbable excuses for not going. And she couldn't help being rather intrigued by the idea; she had often wondered what Jubilee Wharf looked like.

It was only a short walk to the main entrance; Joshua pulled a bunch of keys from his pocket, and unlocked the heavy iron gates. Then he turned, and offered her his arm.

He was right; it was a good evening for

a walk. Although the sun was going down over the rooftops to the west, it still shone brightly on the ships at anchor, and the waters of the dock sparkled in the evening breeze. They walked through the Wharf, and Maudie gazed in wonder at the giant cranes, the vast warehouses, the packing-cases piled in towers on top of one another. It was like a strange new world, and they were the only people in it.

'Where is everybody?' she asked. 'Isn't there anyone on the boats?'

'The crews will be having a night ashore, before they go off to sea again. There'll be one chap left aboard each ship, on watch...'

A Lascar seaman, stripped to the waist, had appeared on deck, carrying a bucket of potato-peelings and dirty water which he tipped over the rail. A flock of gulls flew down to see if there might be any interesting pickings, then screamed indignantly and spread their wings, soaring off into the sunset..The seaman yawned and stretched, his muscles flexing under olive-green skin, and disappeared into the galley.

'That freighter's in from Calcutta with a load of jute,' Josh told Maudie. 'She'll be off again first thing, on the morning tide.'

'Fancy...' she sighed, then added, 'It must be wonderful, travelling round the world like that. I dream about going abroad, sometimes.'

'Do you?' He laughed shortly. 'You know what they say—"East, west, home's best". I've no wish to go travelling, myself.'

'I've always wanted to go to America,' said Maudie wistfully.

'America? Whatever for?' Josh stared at her, then grinned. 'I suppose you've seen it at the Kinema—the Wild West, and so on. That's the trouble with those film-shows, they put ideas in people's heads. We're better off where we are, in my opinion.'

He looked round the Wharf proudly, and continued in a more serious tone: 'I've done pretty well here, wouldn't you say? I've got a good job, running the Guild; Father mostly leaves things to me now. I take home a fair old wage-packet each week, you know.' He spoke slowly, picking his way from one sentence to the next like a man crossing a torrential river on stepping-stones. 'I admit I'm no spring chicken. I'm thirty-seven, but I've got my health and strength. And I've no wish to go on living without a wife. I've taken a real fancy to you, Maudie—you must know that. That's why I thought as how I should ask you—how would you feel about marrying me?'

She felt her cheeks flaming, and put her hands to her face. 'I—I couldn't do that, Joshua. I'm sorry—I don't love you.'

He put his arm round her shoulders; his touch was gentle, but very firm. 'Don't say that. You may not love me now—it's early days yet; we're still getting to know one another. But don't you think, if we were to take things nice and easy-like, we might find we *could* love another, presently? I'm sure I could... In fact, I believe I might—already.'

She shook her head, unable to speak, unable to look into his face.

He drew her a little closer, and she felt his warm breath on the nape of her neck as he murmured: 'You don't have to decide yet, you know. Just think it over, that's all I ask. Take your time, but promise me you'll think it over.'

They walked on slowly, and for a long while neither of them said a word. When they left the Wharf, he locked the gates behind them and they began to talk of other things. He escorted her back to the grocery shop, saying, 'I won't come in—not tonight. But I hope you'll think on what I said. Turn it over in your mind. There's no hurry.'

When she entered the back-kitchen, she found that Emily had a visitor; Florrie was sitting at the other side of the fireplace. They both looked up as she came in, and Florrie said, 'Good evening, Maudie. I saw you weren't at Chapel this morning; I was afraid you might be poorly.'

Maudie took off her straw hat and shook out her hair, saying, 'No, I'm quite well, thanks.'

'You look a little flushed, dear,' said Emily. 'Is it still warm out?'

'Not now the sun's gone down.'

'I was getting rather worried, because you're so late. The service must have finished long ago—wherever have you been?'

Suddenly Maudie faced them. She wanted to tell someone what had happened—she needed reassurance.

'Joshua was at Chapel again this evening. He came specially to see me, and afterwards we went for a walk. He took me all round the Wharf and showed me the boats and the warehouses and then—then he asked me to marry him.'

Emily gasped, 'Oh, good gracious!' but for a moment Florrie said nothing. Her eyes narrowed, and she leaned forward, gazing intently at Maudie.

'And what did you say to him?' she asked in a dry, toneless voice.

'I said I couldn't.'

'That's right.' Florrie relaxed slightly. 'It wouldn't do, would it, what with you and him being related by marriage.'

'Oh, that wasn't the reason. We're not blood-relatives anyway, so it wasn't that. But I had to tell him—I don't love him.'

Emily nodded sympathetically. 'Of course, dear, I know how you must be feeling. You think it's still too soon.'

'Yes, much too soon,' Maudie replied without thinking. 'It's not four years since—' She caught her breath, and stopped short.

Emily frowned. 'Whatever do you mean? It's nearly seven years since poor Arnie was taken.'

'Oh yes, of course, that's what I meant,' she corrected herself quickly. 'Seven years...'

Seven years since Arnold was killed in Flanders; but six years since she and Tommy made love for the first time, upstairs in the top bedroom—and only three and a half years since he went off to America, on one of those cargo steamers... And in all that time, she had never stopped thinking of him, and loving him, and praying that he would come back.

'Well, anyhow,' Florrie pursued, 'you refused Joshua, did you?'

'I tried to but he told me to take my time. He made me promise I'd think it over.'

Ruth was cleaning the ash-trays in the saloon at the end of the afternoon. It had been a perfect August day—hot, but not too hot, with a light breeze off the river to freshen the air. She had collected Danny from Willow Row School as usual and now he and little Lil were having their tea under Mary O'Dell's watchful eye, while Ruth got the bar ready for opening-time.

They were all well; the pub was doing good business—warm weather always gave the customers an extra thirst—and Con had seemed a little less remote lately.

As he came in through the front door, with a copy of the *Evening Star*, he pointed out a late news-item to her.

'Look at this—things in Germany are going from bad to worse, by the looks of it,' he said. 'The Deutschmark's dropped like a stone. Of course, it's been sinking for months, but they say it's halved its value in the last ten days... God knows what's going to happen there.'

'Sarah's husband saw it coming, and he got out just in time,' Ruth said. 'He was one of the lucky ones.'

Connor nodded, and walked through to the little office, where he would sit and read the newspaper for a while until the pub got busy.

Ruth went on wiping the ash-trays, thinking

of Sarah and Klaus. Yes, they were lucky—and not only in terms of money. She remembered the way Klaus smiled when he looked at Sarah. Of course, she and Connor had been lucky, too, They had a wonderful family and a prosperous business and she knew she should be thankful...but she could not remember the last time Connor had smiled at her like that.

When the first two customers came in, she greeted them automatically, talking her place behind the bar. The young man was a mechanic at the local garage; he ordered half a pint of mild and a port-and-lemon for his companion, a pretty girl who worked on the greengrocery stall in the street market.

They took their drinks to a table for two, as far as possible from the bar so they could talk without being overheard. Ruth saw them whispering to one another, laughing softly; they looked very young, and very happy.

A shadow fell across the polished floor as another customer arrived; a large man, who seemed to fill the narrow doorway. He doffed his hat as he entered, uncovering a shining pink dome surrounded by a fringe of silver hair.

'Good evening, Mr Hardiman,' said Ruth. 'We don't often have the pleasure of seeing you this time of day—what can I get you?'

'Good evening, Mrs O'Dell. Unfortunately I am here on business; I cannot spare the time to partake of refreshment. I hope your husband is on the premises?'

'Yes, he's—'

'He's in his office, no doubt—quite so.

Perhaps you'll be good enough to inform him that I am here?'

Ruth opened the office door and Con emerged, folding his newspaper.

'Mr Hardiman! I wasn't expecting—'

'I am sure you were not; I had not expected to find myself here, but as I was about to leave my office, a certain matter cropped up which necessitated that I should consult you without delay. As it happened, I already had an evening appointment across the river, so I was coming this way, and it occurred to me that I might kill two birds with one stone, to coin a phrase... I wonder if you could spare a few moments of your valuable time?'

'Of course. What's it all about?' asked Connor. 'Is something wrong?'

'Not exactly *wrong*—I would hesitate to use so definite a term—but perhaps it would not be inappropriate to call it a slight *complication*. It is, however, what one might describe as...' he threw a suspicious look at the young couple, who continued to gaze into each other's eyes, quite unaware of him '...as a private and confidential matter. Perhaps we could retire to somewhere more secluded?'

Ruth saw Connor's face change; he did not even glance in her direction, but she knew that there was some secret understanding between the two men—a secret she would not be allowed to share.

'Certainly, sir, come this way,' said Connor. 'My office is a bit cramped, but we shan't be disturbed.'

They disappeared into the office, and Connor shut the door. Ruth wondered how Mr Hardiman would manage to squeeze his great bulk into the single small chair. She wondered even more what they had to discuss—but the door fitted snugly and she could hear nothing but a faint murmur of voices.

A few moments later, the young couple finished their drinks and walked out, hand in hand. Ruth called 'Good evening!' after them, but they did not hear her.

As soon as the saloon was empty, she moved swiftly, placing herself very close to the office door. She hated herself for eavesdropping on her husband, but a desperate curiosity drove her on.

The men's voices were still indistinct, and then she caught some isolated phrases in Mr Hardiman's booming tones.

'The lady insists on seeing you. I tried to dissuade her, but... Unless you agree to meet her again, she says she will never...'

His next words were inaudible, and Ruth clenched her fists, her nails digging into her palms as he continued: 'Tomorrow morning... My office... Eleven o'clock.'

There was a flurry of movement and she retreated just in time before the door opened again and the men reappeared.

'Good night to you, Mrs O'Dell. I trust you will forgive my intrusion.' Mr Hardiman bowed formally, putting on his hat. His gold-rimmed spectacles flashed in the evening sunlight as he strode out of the pub.

Connor turned to Ruth. 'I've got to go and see him tomorrow.'

'Oh? What's it all about?'

He grimaced. 'Spot of bother over the licensing laws. You know what the local magistrates are like—a lot of fuss about nothing, I dare say. Still, I suppose it has to be sorted out.'

His eyes slid away, and she knew he was lying to her again.

The following morning, he put on his blue serge suit and his best shirt and tie; Ruth told him he looked very smart. At half-past ten, he set off for Stepney and the offices of Homer & Hardiman.

Ten minutes later, Ruth put on her hat and coat and went into the kitchen, where Mary O'Dell was making fish-cakes for dinner. Through the open back door, she could see her father-in-law sunning himself in the yard, smoking his pipe and keeping an eye on his granddaughter. Lil had undressed her dolls, and was telling them they had to go into the washtub, because it was bath-time.

Without any preamble, Ruth said to Mary, 'I've got to go out.'

Mary stared at her. 'I thought Con was going out on business?'

'Yes, he did—and now I must go too,' said Ruth. 'It's all to do with the same thing... I don't know how long I'll be gone so would you mind looking after the pub till I get back?'

'Very well.' Puzzled, Mary began to wipe her hands. 'I can finish the dinner later.' She went to the back door, and called to her husband: 'Patrick, will you come in now and help me in the bar? Ruth has to go out to—where is it you're going?' But when she turned back to ask her, Ruth had already vanished.

By the time she reached the solicitor's office, it was twenty past eleven; Ruth hoped she was not too late.

'Yes?' In the outer office, the female dragon looked up from her desk. 'What do you want?'

'My name is O'Dell—Mrs Ruth O'Dell. I don't know if you remember me, but I understand my husband has an appointment with Mr Hardiman?'

The dragon pursed her lips. 'You'll have to wait, madam. Mr Hardiman is engaged with clients. Kindly take a seat.'

'I'm sorry—I can't wait. I'm going in now.'

Ruth moved towards the inner office, and the dragon scrambled to her feet, catching her arm. 'I told you—you must wait. Sit down, please!'

Ruth managed to pull free. 'I'm sorry—this is very important to me.'

She took another step, and again the woman grabbed her. 'This is most irregular! Mr Hardiman is in consultation with—'

'I know—with my husband, and another woman. I have a right to know what's going on!'

Ruth pushed the dragon away; she staggered back against her desk, gobbling, 'How dare you! Infamous conduct—a clear case of assault!'

Ignoring her, Ruth reached the door and threw it open.

Interrupted in mid-sentence, Mr Hardiman was dumb-struck, and took off his glasses as if he could not believe the evidence of his eyes. Connor swung round towards the door; the lady sitting next to him turned and raised her veil to see what was going on.

'Hello, Ruth.' Moira Marriner smiled, a little sadly. 'It's been a long time..'

8

'How very peculiar that you should run into each other like that, the other day,' said Henry Marriner.

Ruth and Moira began to speak at the same time.

'Yes, wasn't it odd?'

'It's a small world, after all.'

They apologised, laughing, and Ruth was able to say with perfect truth, 'It took us both completely by surprise, didn't it?'

Moira agreed. 'You were the last person I expected to see...'

'It was a very lucky coincidence.' Mr Marriner flicked a crumb of sponge-cake from his watered-silk waistcoat. 'It's been far too long since you last visited us, Mrs O'Dell. I've always thought it a great pity that Moira lost touch with her family...' He turned to his wife. 'I never really understood why you and your sister fell out.'

'Henry, please! I don't think we need to go

into that now,' Moira told him firmly, throwing a warning glance at little Daniel, who was sitting on the edge of a garden bench, swinging his legs and looking bored.

'Ah, quite so, beg pardon—*harrumph!*' Henry Marriner cleared his throat loudly. 'I suppose, as a mere man, I shouldn't even try to question the whys and wherefores of the fair sex, eh? All I know is, you and Mary O'Dell drifted apart—so that's all the more reason for a little celebration. I was thinking I might open a bottle of bubbly—what do you say, old girl?'

'Henry, I've asked you a thousand times not to call me "old girl"!' said Moira sharply. 'And we certainly don't want champagne. Goodness, we've only just had our tea!'

They were sitting out in the garden of their house at Greenwich; the fluted teacups, patterned with violets, were still on the wrought-iron table in front of them.

'Oh, very well.' Henry tucked his double chins into his collar and subsided with a hangdog air.

There was an awkward silence, broken by the twittering of sparrows prospecting for crumbs, and the contented gurgle of Lil, picking daisies on the lawn. Ruth searched for another topic of conversation, but could come up with nothing better than, 'You have a lovely garden. Isn't it beautiful, Danny?'

Daniel looked about him. There was a formal rose-bed, enjoying its second flowering of the summer, and a tiny ornamental pond with goldfish, shaded by a weeping willow with trailing leaves that swept the grass; at the far end of the lawn Alexandra roses climbed over a rustic arbour. Though Danny had never been in such a splendid garden—on the Isle of Dogs, people thought themselves lucky to have a window-box or a pot of geraniums in the backyard—he was not particularly impressed.

'It hasn't got swings,' he remarked judicially.

'That's not very polite,' Ruth began, but Moira broke in.

'No, he's quite right, it's a boring garden for a small boy. But he's given me an idea... Henry, why don't you take Daniel up to Greenwich Park for half an hour? He can go on the swings and the slide, and run about and play—and you can leave the "fair sex" to exchange a lot of feminine gossip!'

'Whatever you say, dear.' With some difficulty, Henry levered himself up from his deck-chair. 'Come along, old chap—better do as we're told.'

And he set off, with Danny trotting obediently beside him. As soon as they were out of earshot, Moira said, 'I know what you're thinking—Henry's put on weight since you last saw him. Well, the walk will do him good. He's got a lot older, hasn't he?'

Ruth had been thinking that they had both aged a good deal, but at least Moira had kept her figure. Evading a direct reply, she said, 'I was trying to remember when we last met. It must have been the second year of the war so that makes it seven years ago. I came to tell you Rosie had left the Island.'

'When she went off to get a job in a department store? I was so worried about her...and after that I heard no more at all.'

'Neither did we; we thought we'd lost her for good. And during the war things were so difficult. Sean and Connor went into the army, and I was managing the pub. There seemed to be no time for anything but work and sleep.'

'I often thought of you, and wondered what was happening, but I couldn't come to the Watermen. Mary and Patrick made it clear I wasn't welcome.' As Moira's smile faded, she looked every day of her forty-seven years, and Ruth reflected yet again how foolish she had been. Seeing her expression, Moira asked, 'What is it? What have I said?'

Ruth shrugged. 'Nothing. I was just remembering last Friday, when I opened the door and found you in Mr Hardiman's office.'

After the first shock, she was overwhelmed with relief. So the smart, well-dressed woman that Connor had been meeting was his Aunt Moira.

There had been some moments of confusion, while the dragon secretary complained loudly that she had been physically assaulted, Mr Hardiman tried to pacify her and polish his spectacles at the same time, and Connor asked what the hell Ruth was doing there.

Then Moira had surprised them all by announcing: 'I'm *glad* you're here, Ruth. I shouldn't have tried to keep it from you, of all people.'

Diplomatically, Mr Hardiman took his secretary into the outer office, leaving the three of them to talk. Little by little, Ruth pieced the story together.

It had begun two years ago—and that time it was a genuinely accidental meeting. Moira Marriner was on her way to join her husband for lunch at his office in the City. Having some time to spare, she had gone for a walk round St Paul's—and had collided with Connor, who was not looking where he was going after a stormy meeting with the Brewery's Area Manager about rent increases.

He insisted on taking his aunt for a drink in a little sherry-bar he knew off Ludgate Hill, and they caught up with the family news.

'Of course, Aunt Moira didn't even know poor old Sean had gone. I had to explain that you and I were married,' Connor told Ruth.

'I wasn't altogether surprised to hear it,' Moira admitted, with a half-smile. 'Perhaps it was the way you two used to fight like cat and dog in the old days! Anyhow, I was delighted for you both.'

Inevitably, she asked Connor for news of Rosie.

Now, in the peaceful setting of the garden, with nothing to disturb them but the hum of insects and Lil, clucking over her fistful of daisies, Ruth asked suddenly: 'But why didn't you ask *me* about Rosie? I could have told you—'

'How would I get in touch with you, when you were living under the same roof as Mary and Patrick?' Moira shook her head. 'I couldn't risk it... And I knew how close you were—almost like another daughter. I was afraid you might feel disloyal, keeping secrets from them. But when Connor told me Rosie and her husband hadn't enough money to set up shop again, I decided I should help my daughter.'

The secret had to be kept from Henry, too, so Moira could not make the necessary arrangements through the Marriners' own solicitor. Connor put her in touch with Mr Hardiman, and acted as her go-between. They impressed upon him that the transaction must be confidential, and he promised not to say a word to anyone. Not even to Ruth.

Moira had insisted on that. Knowing how close Ruth and Rosie had been, she was afraid Ruth's kind heart would get the better of her—she could so easily have dropped one small hint which could have ruined everything.

Connor agreed, foreseeing no difficulties. It all seemed simple enough, but as the negotiations dragged on, and he had to make frequent trips between the solicitor's office and the house in Greenwich, the lies began to multiply.

At first Ruth had concealed her suspicions so well, it was some time before Con realised she was worried, and when he did, he felt bound by his promise. When Connor O'Dell gave his word to anyone, that word was set in iron; he could not break it. Then, as Ruth's unhappiness became more obvious, he changed his mind. Fearing that his own marriage might be at risk, on the day of the final meeting at the solicitor's office, he had gone in to demand that Moira must release him from the promise... And that was the meeting which Ruth had interrupted.

'I'm sorry I made Connor lie to you,' said Moira. 'I'd no idea it would upset things—I hope you'll forgive me.'

Matters had come to a head when Ernest sold the house at Poplar and insisted on repaying the loan.

'I couldn't imagine what had happened,' Moira continued. 'I was afraid they must have found out the truth. I thought they had decided to bankrupt themselves out of sheer pride, rather than accept a penny from me. That's why I said I wouldn't accept their money until I'd talked to Connor and found out what was going on... When he explained, I was very relieved, but in a way I was sorry, too. It used to be a comfort to me, thinking I'd been able to help my daughter—even if she never knew it.'

'I think she ought to know it,' said Ruth. 'Surely she has a right to know what you did for her?'

Moira looked away. 'She might resent it. She might say I'd been meddling.'

'I don't think so. She's very happy now—she has a happy marriage and, did Connor tell you? She's expecting another baby soon.'

'Yes, he did. I was very pleased...though it's strange to think of having grandchildren I shall never see.'

Ruth reached out and took Moira's hand. 'That's why I'd like to tell Rosie; she might be pleased to know the truth. Not yet, not till the baby is born but afterwards, if everything goes well and I can find the right way to break it to her—would you let me try?'

Moira thought for a moment, then squeezed Ruth's hand. 'When you think the moment is right—yes, I would like you to try.'

Two nights had passed since Ruth burst into Mr Hardiman's office, and although it had cleared the air, so that she and Connor were able to talk to each other again without any pretence or reservation, they had only talked about Rosie and Moira, and never touched upon their own relationship.

Even now Connor did not make any real demonstration of affection. On Friday and Saturday night, when he lowered the bedroom lamp, he kissed her on the cheek and said, 'Good night,' before turning over and settling down to sleep.

Sunday was a busy evening in the pub, and it was quite late before they locked up and went to bed. Lying in the darkness, Ruth said, 'The saloon kept us on the go tonight. Are you very tired?'

'Not specially—why?'

'We haven't had a proper chance to talk to each other. I wanted to tell you about my visit to Greenwich.'

'Yes—how did it go?'

She told him as much as she could remember, finishing with her intention to try and reconcile Moira and her daughter.

Connor sounded doubtful. 'I don't want to pour cold water on your hopes, but don't expect too much, will you? Rosie can be very unpredictable; you never know which way she's going to jump.'

'It must be a family failing,' said Ruth lightly.

'And what's that supposed to mean?' Connor asked.

'I never know what sort of mood you'll be in, from one day to the next!' Having ventured this far, she decided to take the plunge. 'Sometimes it's been like living with a stranger...not knowing what was going on in your head.'

He tried to laugh it off. 'Most of the time—probably not much!'

'I'm serious. These last few months, you've been so far away I couldn't get near you.'

He tried to wind up the conversation. 'I've been close beside you all the time, like I am now.' He demonstrated a yawn. 'Anyhow—as you say, it's been a busy night. I expect we're both tired...' He made a move as if he were about to turn away from her, but she put out her hand and stopped him.

'Con, you're doing it again—don't shut me out.' He remained silent, and she continued quietly, 'I can't help feeling there's still some barrier between us. Perhaps you don't need me any more, is that it?'

At last he said in a low voice: 'I thought maybe you'd no need of me. Let's face it—I'm a dull, ordinary sort of chap. When I married you, I thought I might have something to offer—a dash of excitement, maybe—but look at me now. The landlord of a small public-house, heading for middle-age, with nothing to look forward to but pulling pints for the rest of my days. If it wasn't for walking the dog every morning, I'd probably be putting on weight by now.'

She tightened her hand upon his shoulder. 'Don't talk about yourself like that.'

'Isn't it God's truth? I wouldn't blame you for growing tired of me. I've seen the way your face lights up every time Huw Pritchard walks into the bar. He still has the right idea in his head—the fun, the excitement—and more brains than I ever had.'

Gently, Ruth began to caress him. 'Huw's a good man, and he was a good friend when I felt all alone, but there's a big difference between the two of you. I don't love Huw Pritchard—I love Connor O'Dell.'

Her fingertips explored his body; every touch was a declaration of her feelings. Slowly, he drew her to him, his arms enfolding her.

'I thought I'd lost you,' he told her.

'I thought you were tired of me,' she whispered.

His mouth found hers, and he kissed her at last—a real kiss, full of the passion and the power and the tenderness of love; and they set out upon a long journey together.

Sometimes it was like walking through a garden, enjoying the scent of the flowers and the colour of the blossoms, the delight of perfect peace and tranquillity. Sometimes it was like listening to music; the sweetness of shared harmonies, the deep vibrations stirring their minds and bodies, and the fierce crescendo as the rhythm mounted, sweeping them along. And at last it was like a spring of fresh water, bubbling up from a hidden source—becoming a stream, then a river, then a flood, carrying them along with it, into a boundless and eternal sea...

Their journey was over; together they had travelled a very long way—and they had come home.

By the end of the summer holidays, the Island children were growing restless, running out of things to do.

On the last day of August 1922, when Maudie was helping Emily in the shop as usual, Trevor was being more than usually difficult. He didn't want to stay indoors like a good boy, and get out his toy fort and his soldiers, or colour a picture-book with his crayons—he wanted to go and play in the street.

His mother and his grandma said that was far too dangerous—suppose a car should come round the corner suddenly, and knock him down? They told him he could only go outdoors if he had a grown-up with him. Trevor thought this was silly, and said so—repeatedly.

When Gloria came in to buy some rashers of bacon, she exclaimed: 'Give us a rest, duck, for Gawd's sake—we can't hear ourselves think!' Then she added to Maudie, 'If I was you, I'd let him go out, sooner than have him under your feet all day. I leave young Matt on his own when I'm working. He generally goes to

230

play with the kids next door, and they're always running in and out—nobody seems to bother.'

But Maudie said she wouldn't have a moment's peace if her son went out by himself, so Gloria had another idea.

'Why don't I take Trev back with me this afternoon? Him and Matt will be company for each other. Give us a bottle of pop and a packet of biscuits, that'll keep them out of mischief.'

Trevor jumped up and down with excitement, pleading, 'Can I, Mum? Can I, please?' until Maudie gave permission.

Gloria had to wait while he washed his face and hands and put on his best clothes, because Emily wouldn't dream of letting her grandson go out to tea unless he was neat and tidy. But at last he was ready, and Gloria took him back to Cyclops Wharf.

She did not tell Maudie she had an elderly client coming at three o'clock. The old lady lived in a cheap lodging-house, with no toilet facilities except a communal outside lavatory and a cold-water tap on the landing, so she came to Gloria to have her hair done.

That meant Gloria would not be able to keep an eye on the boys for half an hour or so, but she knew they'd be happy enough playing with the kids next door, and she didn't want to worry Maudie.

As it happened, the next-door children were already outside. At low tide, the river had receded from its banks, uncovering a stretch of grey mud-flats broken by tiny tributaries and shining puddles.

'You'd better take your shoes and socks off,'
Gloria told Trevor as they set off to join the
neighbourhood gang. 'If you go home with mud
on you, I'll never hear the last of it—so mind
you take care!'

Barefoot, Trevor and Matt climbed over the
embankment wall and down a flight of wooden
steps on to thick, oozing mud. The next-door
children were playing further out, where mud
gave way to black, oily water, and the river-bed
shelved suddenly into a deeper channel.

'What are they doing out there?' Trevor
asked.

Matt dug in his pocket and pulled out a
folding device of two lenses set in sliding metal
grooves; he opened it up, and it became a
spy-glass. When he demonstrated it, Trevor
was fascinated; through the twin circles of
glass, he could see the opposite bank in sharp
detail, the rowing-boats high and dry on their
sides, waiting for the turn of the tide to lift
them off again—all so clear and so close, he
felt as if he could stretch out his hand and
touch them—and he yearned to possess this
marvellous toy.

'That's not half bad,' he said enviously.
'Where d'you get it?'

'It belonged to my dad,' said Matt. 'Ma gave
it me.' He held out his hand, but Trevor was
reluctant to part with it.

'I'll swap you for it,' he suggested. 'What
d'you want for it?'

'Nuffink. It's not for swaps—I told you, it
was my dad's.'

232

'He won't care,' said Trevor reasonably. 'He's dead, ain't he?'

'Yeah, but I still want to keep it. Give it here!' Matt wrested it from Trevor's hands, and stuffed it into his pocket.

'You didn't let me have a proper go!' complained Trevor. 'I want to see what those boys are doing, down by the water. They're digging in the mud—have they lost something?'

'Garn!' Matt curled his lip. 'Aincher seen mudlarking before? They're hunting for treasure; you'd be surprised what they turn up when the tide's out—a penknife—a pocket-watch. The watch didn't go no more, but some geezer gave 'em half a crown for it. And money as well; pennies mostly—shillings sometimes. Once they found a golden guinea!'

Trevor brightened up immediately. 'Can we go and look?'

They set out across the flats, the soft mud squelching between their toes. As they went further out, it became almost liquid, and they began to sink up to their ankles. Then Trevor lost his balance and slipped, landing flat on his back in a shower of water and slime.

The other children laughed and jeered. Furiously, he picked himself up, yelling at them: 'Don't you laugh at me. Stop it, d'you hear? Stop laughing—or I'll kill you!'

They laughed all the more, and Matt tried to calm him down. 'You'd best get out of them wet clothes, or Ma's going to give us what for. When the mud dries, it'll soon brush off.'

The idea of undressing on such a warm day appealed to everyone. With one accord, the boys all raced to the embankment, where they stripped off their clothes, leaving them spread out on the wooden stairs, Naked, they scampered back to the cool grey-green Thames, dipping in and out of the water, shouting and splashing to their hearts' content.

When Gloria came out half an hour later, she found the boys sprawled at the bottom of the steps, drying off in the sun.

'You little devils!' she exclaimed. 'Just look at you—covered in mud! Come indoors, the pair of you, and let's try and get you cleaned up.'

Despite her efforts, when Maudie came to fetch Trevor at the end of the afternoon, he was still looking very disreputable.

'Oh, Trev—in your best clothes, too!' she wailed, and turned to Gloria. 'You let them play in the water, all on their own? They might have been drowned!'

'Matt's a regular water-baby. He's been in and out of the river ever since he could crawl—takes after his dad.' Gloria tried to look on the bright side. 'Besides, Trev didn't come to any harm, did he? Give him a good wash when you get him home, and pop his clothes in the boiler, and he'll be none the worse.'

That evening, when Maudie was putting her son to bed, Joshua called in at the grocery shop.

Emily offered him a pot of tea, explaining that Maudie would be down in a minute. Pouring out two cups, she went on: 'You're quite a stranger. We haven't seen you round here lately.'

'No—well, I thought I should leave Maudie to think things over. Last time we met, I asked her a particular question—perhaps she told you?'

'Yes, she did.' A little flustered, Emily stirred her tea.

'And what did you think of the idea?'

'It's not up to me, is it? That's for Maudie to say.'

'But if she was to ask your opinion you wouldn't advise her against it, I hope?'

As Emily opened her mouth to reply, they heard a step on the stairs and Maudie came into the room, looking pale and anxious.

'Do you know what I found?' Then she broke off, seeing Josh. 'Oh—I'm sorry, I didn't hear you come in. I was putting Trev to bed.'

'Would you like some tea, dear? I can squeeze out another cup.'

'Thank you.'

When she lifted her cup, her hands were shaking; a few drops spilled on to the tablecloth.

'I'm sorry!' she gasped. 'Clumsy of me. Oh dear...'

'What's the matter?' asked Joshua.

'It's so difficult—I don't know what to do. I was picking up Trev's dirty clothes to go in the wash—he'd got himself in such a mess, playing by the river—and when I went through his pockets, I found this.'

She produced the spy-glass from her apron, and put it on the table. 'I asked him where it came from, and he said he found it in the mud when the tide was out.'

'Well, that was lucky, wasn't it?' Emily couldn't understand why Maudie was upset. 'Finders keepers—isn't that what they say?'

'The trouble is, I'm not sure if he's telling the truth,' said Maudie.

'May I see that?' Josh held out his hand for the glass. After a moment he said, 'I'm afraid you're right. I've seen this before; it belonged to my Cousin Saul.'

'And Trev was playing with Matt this afternoon...' Maudie bent her head, crushed by this news. 'What am I going to say to him?'

Josh scratched his chin. 'Would you like me to have a word with him? Is he still awake?'

'I expect so. He was, when I came downstairs.'

'Then I'll go up. We'll soon have this sorted out—don't worry.'

He climbed the stairs to the top floor; the door of the attic bedroom was ajar, lit by the dim glow of the gas-lamp on the stairs. He groped his way to the narrow bed and sat on the edge of it. Trevor did not stir, and Josh was pretty sure he was holding his breath, feigning sleep.

'Your mum showed me the spy-glass you brought home,' he began. 'Very nice too—but you'll have to give it back, you know.'

'Why should I?' The boy let out his breath in a rush. 'It's mine, I found it.'

'Finding it doesn't make it yours, does it? You see, I know where it came from. It used to belong to Matt's father. I expect it belongs to Matt now.'

236

'No, it doesn't. I found it,' Trevor repeated stubbornly. 'I picked it up—it was in the mud.'

'Well, we can find out easily enough. We'll just have to take it to Matt and ask him, won't we?'

'No, you mustn't!' Trevor sat up in bed. 'He'll take it back!'

'Take it *back?* So it does belong to him?'

Trevor said nothing, but began to sniff miserably. After a moment, Josh went on: 'I think you knew that, really. I think you wanted that spy-glass so badly you just took it—right?'

Between sniffles, Trevor whimpered, 'When I went back to get dressed, Matt's clothes were next to mine and I sort of found it. I'm sorry.'

'I see.' Joshua sighed, patting the boy's shoulder. 'It was a silly thing to do, but we all do silly things sometimes—things we're ashamed of after. Now, I'm going to take that glass back and say it was all a mistake. But next time you get in any trouble like that, come and talk to me about it, will you? I might be able to help.'

When he went down to the kitchen, Maudie asked anxiously: 'What happened?'

'I'll explain to Gloria, don't worry. Trevor and me had a bit of a talk. He's a good lad really, I'm sure. It's just that—well, I dare say he needs a father.'

For a long time, nobody spoke. Then Emily broke the silence, saying in a small voice:

'Maudie, dear, I think perhaps Joshua's right. There's no denying—a boy does need a father.'

At the beginning of September, the children went back to school and life on the Island resumed its usual pattern.

Little Lil, who admired her brother and tried to imitate him in everything, objected to the fact that Danny was allowed to go to school, and she was not. Ruth tried to explain that one day she too would go to Willow Row, but that didn't satisfy Lil. She had a quick, enquiring mind, and Ruth was hard put to it to keep her amused and interested.

When they went shopping in the market, Lil sometimes carried the basket, and Ruth let her hand over the money when they made their purchases.

'Fourpence ha'penny change, my darlin'...' The old woman at the fishmonger's stall counted it into the small hand, a coin at a time. 'One, two, three, four pennies and half a penny for your ma—and another ha'penny to buy yourself some sweeties.'

'Oh, that's very kind. Say thank you, Lil,' prompted Ruth.

Lil looked up, with solemn eyes. 'Thank you. I'll get sherbet suckers. They're two for a ha'penny, so that's one for me, and one for Danny.'

The old woman chuckled. 'By the time that one goes to school, she'll learn the teachers a thing or two!'

They moved on between the stalls, with Lil

leading the way; wherever they went, she always knew the short cuts. Following more slowly, Ruth was hailed by a familiar voice.

'Hey, Ruth! Hang on a minute!'

It was Huw Pritchard, buying a pound of apples from the greengrocer. Ruth waited while he paid for them, then he joined her, holding out the paper bag. 'Have an apple. Best food in the world.'

Ruth took one, and bit into it. 'Who says so?'

'Your husband—and he ought to know. He said he used to eat apples all the time when he was in training.'

'Perhaps he did; I didn't know him very well in those days.'

'Mum, come on!' Lil had returned to see what was delaying her. Then she grinned, her cheeks dimpling. 'Uncle Huw!'

He picked the child up and whirled her through the air, then set her down again and offered her an apple.

'Present for you, Lilian. To make you grow up strong and well—and beautiful, like your mum.'

'No, thanks.' Lil rejected his offer politely. 'I'm going to have a sherbet sucker. Mum, are you coming?'

'You go on; I'll catch you up. Just to the end of the road, and wait at the corner. Whatever you do, don't cross over till I get there!'

Lil trotted off happily, and Ruth turned back to Huw. 'This is a nice surprise—where have you been hiding?'

'I called in at the pub a few times, but you were always busy in the saloon, so I went into the public—I didn't want to bother you.'

'You could have said hello.'

'There were too many people around. I wanted to see you on your own.'

'Why was that?'

'Oh, you can't talk in a crowd... I used to enjoy our talks.'

'So did I. Very much.'

He gave her a searching look, and said hesitantly: 'Sometimes, I got a sort of notion that you weren't particularly happy... It wasn't anything you said, more the way you looked. I'm sorry—now you can tell me to mind my own business.'

'I'd never tell you that,' said Ruth. 'It's true, I was going through a bad time—but not any more. Things are much better now.'

'I can see that,' he said.

They stood looking at one another, alone together in the middle of the market—and then Ruth heard her name called again.

'Ruth—I have been looking for you!'

It was Ernest Kleiber. He had just called at the Watermen, where Connor told him Ruth was out shopping.

'I had to find you—Rosie sent me with a message. We had another addition to the family yesterday morning: a little girl, weighing six pounds, three ounces—a sister for Abram—Miss Sharon Miriam Kleiber.'

'I'm so glad! Is Rosie in hospital? Can I come and visit her?'

240

'She'll be delighted, but she had the baby at home this time. We've a nurse who calls in each day, that's why I was able to come out.' Then he remembered Ruth was not alone, and apologised: 'Forgive me, I am interrupting your conversation.'

Ruth introduced him to Huw, and the two men shook hands.

'You weren't interrupting,' Huw told him. 'I was just going, anyhow. We'd said all there was to say.'

But at that moment they were interrupted once more. Between the hardware stall and the greengrocery, a small accusing figure looked up at her mother.

'You *said* we could buy sherbet suckers,' Lil reminded her sternly. 'Aren't you ever going to stop talking?'

The following afternoon, Ruth visited the photographic shop in Silmour Street, carrying a bunch of flowers.

'Michaelmas daisies! Look, Ernest, aren't they lovely?' Rosie buried her face in the mauve petals. 'Mmmm, they smell like autumn.'

'Mary and Patrick send their fondest love. They wanted to come and see the new arrival, but I persuaded them to stay at home and look after Lil. They'll come on Sunday, instead, if the weather's fine.'

'That's good—but I wish you'd brought Lil with you. Wouldn't she be interested to see her new cousin?'

'She'd be so interested, no one else would get a word in edgeways!' Ruth laughed. 'There'll be plenty of time for Lil and Sharon to meet, another day. Am I allowed to hold her?'

'Of course you are. Go to your Auntie Ruth, there's a good girl.' Rosie handed Ruth the tiny bundle, wrapped in a white shawl. 'Well? What do you think of her?'

'She's a beauty.' It was not an exaggeration; some newborn babies are red-faced and furious, some look like pixies—but Sharon Miriam Kleiber was a beauty, there was no doubt about that. 'You must be so proud.'

'Yes, we are.' Rosie smiled up at her husband, sitting by the head of the bed. 'First Abram, and now Sharon—if I was any happier, I'd burst.'

Ernest agreed. 'We have been very lucky.'

Looking at them, Ruth decided that this was the moment. This was the reason she had not brought anyone with her; what she had to say was for their ears alone.

'You've been luckier than you know,' she said.

They were still smiling, though a little puzzled, as she began to explain. As simply as possible, she told them how she had accidentally discovered who their benefactor was. When she reached the end of the story, Ernest said quietly, 'I'm glad you told us; I should always have wondered.' He turned to Rosie. 'Now we know, I suppose I should write to your mother and—'

'She's not my mother. She never wanted me; she gave me away when I was born.' Rosie was no longer smiling. 'At first I thought it was Connor who lent us the money and I wish to

242

God it had been. I don't want anything to do with her.'

'All the same, this was a kindness on her part. I should write to thank her, at least.'

'No, Ernest!' She spoke sharply; in Ruth's arms, the baby stirred. 'We don't owe her anything. Our debt was paid off when you sold the house in Poplar, and she has no claim on us at all. I don't want anything to do with her—not now, not ever.'

Ruth had hoped to persuade her to change her mind. She had planned what she would say, the arguments she would put forward, the picture she would paint of an unhappy woman who regretted her mistake and longed to put it right.

But she heard the steely determination in Rosie's voice, and she knew it would be a waste of time.

Disturbed by the sudden tension, the baby opened her mouth and began to cry.

At once Rosie's face changed. She held out her arms, speaking softly and fondly.

'Ah, my little love—what's the matter? Come to your mama... There's nothing to cry about, darling, nothing at all. Let Mama make it better.'

On Friday evening, Joshua arrived at the corner grocery to take Maudie out to supper. Emily had helped her to get ready and Gloria had called in during the afternoon to give her a shampoo and set, so she would be looking her very best. They all knew that this was to be a special occasion.

When he came in, Josh looked at Maudie with undisguised admiration, but could think of nothing to say except, 'My word, you do look smart!'

She was wearing her best dress, of white broderie anglaise with pink ribbons laced through the holes at the neck. It was a summer dress and the material was very light, so Emily had lent her a crocheted stole in soft grey wool, warning her not to get a chill on this crisp autumn evening.

'No fear of that,' said Joshua. 'I've ordered a taxi to take us there and bring us back. Nothing but the best tonight—eh, Maudie?'

Emily was overawed; this was the height of luxury. She stood in the shop doorway, watching them drive off—a little sadly, remembering poor Arnie—but in her heart she knew this was the best thing for Trevor, and possibly for Maudie as well.

The taxi took them to an old-established eating-house in Bow Road. Joshua had been taken to lunch there by the Wharfmaster once or twice, when there were knotty problems over the dockers' wage-settlements to be discussed. At mid-day, it was very popular with the prosperous local businessmen.

This evening, it was almost empty; there were more waiters than customers—lounging about, leaning against the dark oak panelling, picking their teeth and stifling their yawns. The tables were separated by high-backed settles, upholstered in red plush, reminding Maudie of her one and only trip in a railway train, when she went to Margate on the choir outing.

She felt very self-conscious, almost speechless with nerves, but Josh tried to put her at her ease, keeping up a steady, one-sided conversation.

Looking back on the evening afterwards, she couldn't remember anything he had talked about; nothing stayed in her memory except the menu. She had never been taken to a restaurant before, and it was all so wonderful—the tomato soup, the lamb cutlets, the sherry trifle, the Stilton and celery, and the black coffee in little doll's-house cups... The whole evening was like a fairy tale, and as the waiter refilled her wine glass from time to time, she gradually forgot to be nervous.

At last the headwaiter glanced at his watch, and placed the bill reverently upon the table, but Josh waved it away.

'Not yet—we want some more coffee. You'll have another cup, my dear?'

Maudie smiled dreamily. 'Yes, if you like. I don't mind.'

While another pot was brewing, Josh leant across the table, taking one of her hands in both of his, and saying: 'Now I want to ask you a question... I think you know what it is.'

His eyes seemed to be extraordinarily large —warm and brown and liquid, and they seemed to be growing larger every minute; she felt she could fall into those eyes, and drown.

'I want you to be my wife,' he continued. 'I'll try to be a good husband to you and a good father to your lad, just as I know you'll be a good mother to my boys. So I'm asking you, Maudie—will you marry me?'

Hypnotised by those huge brown eyes, and still under the spell of so much good food and wine, she almost said again: *'Yes, if you like. I don't mind'*—but she was vaguely aware that this was not the reply he expected. Pulling herself together, she concentrated hard, and managed to say: 'Yes, Josh, I think I'd like that. And thanks for asking.'

He smiled, and fumbled in his waistcoat pocket, producing a little square box covered in purple velvet. Opening the box with some difficulty, she took out a ring; a tiny cluster of seedpearls set in silver-gilt, which he slipped on to her finger.

'Now we're engaged,' he told her.

'Thank you,' she said again. 'That's very nice.'

When they returned to West Ferry Road, Joshua kissed her on the lips, before they alighted from the cab; and that was very nice too. He was good-natured and easy-going—she would never feel afraid of him, as she had sometimes been afraid of Arnold.

He paid off the taxi, and they went in to break the news to Emily.

Emily's reaction was predictable; she congratulated Joshua, she admired the engagement ring—and then offered to make them a pot of tea. Joshua was in high spirits, already planning ahead. He wanted to get married as soon as possible, and suggested a wedding in early December.

Reluctant to awaken from her happy dream,

246

Maudie said wistfully, 'Couldn't we leave it till after Christmas? Some time early next year—Easter might be nice, don't you think?'

Joshua smiled, patting her hand. 'I'm a patient sort of chap, but I can't wait that long.'

So they were to be married in December; by Christmas Maudie would be settled in her new house, to look after her husband, her son and two stepsons.

Josh kissed her again before he left—on the forehead, because Emily was watching—then he kissed Emily too, said good night and departed.

'Well, that's done,' said Maudie, and went up to her room.

She examined the engagement ring, turning her hand this way and that, admiring the pearls that gleamed in the lamplight. She thought she would enjoy being married to Joshua; he was a kind man. Her only regret was that he wanted the wedding before Christmas. She wished it could have been after 26 December... Boxing Day, four years ago, was the last time she had seen Tommy Judge. Since then, she had waited for him—three years, nine months and eighteen days—but he had never come back to her, nor sent any message. She had to accept that she would never see him again.

In front of the dressing-table, she began to undress. She took off the engagement ring, and hung it on the ring-stand. Next she took the plain gold band from the fourth finger of her left hand, adding that to the ring-stand as well. Lastly, she undid the clasp of the fine

247

silver chain around her neck, pulling the heart-shaped pendant from its hiding-place between her breasts, and she put the little keepsake away carefully in the smallest drawer of the dressing-table.

Downstairs, Emily turned out the wall-brackets, leaving a single lamp burning above the kitchen table. She knew now what she had to do.

Today was Friday the thirteenth; as soon as she woke up, she had felt sure that something terrible was going to happen. When the letter arrived by the first post, before Maudie was up, she was certain of it. This time, Emily scarcely glanced at the American stamp or the USA postmark; she knew the handwriting at once.

Turning it over, she found Tommy had written his address across the flap of the envelope—*1092 Providence Boulevard, Yonkers, New York, USA.*

Marcus had destroyed his last letter without a moment's hesitation, but Emily could not be quite as ruthless. She had carried it about all day, burning a hole in her pocket; although Joshua's intention had been plain enough, she could not be sure of Maudie's reply. Well, now she had accepted him, and that was probably for the best. Now the die was cast, and Emily could only hope that they would both live happily ever after.

With trembling fingers, the old lady took the envelope from her pocket and smoothed it out. She fetched her pen and inkwell from the sideboard; sitting down at the table, she scored

248

a line through Maudie's name and address and in shaky block letters she penned the words: RETURN TO SENDER—NOT KNOWN AT THIS ADDRESS—GONE AWAY.

Then she put on her coat and her bonnet and, leaving the front door on the latch, hurried over the road to the pillar-box on the opposite corner and posted the letter once more. It would go off first thing tomorrow morning—and that would be the end of that.

9

So time went by, and the river ran on, rising and falling as life itself flowed on—never changing, ever-changing.

By the end of 1922 Maudie had acquired a new identity. As Mrs Joshua Judge, she moved into Josh's house and became a housewife—to all intents and purposes for the first time, for at the corner-shop there had always been Emily and sometimes Louisa as well to share the household chores. She also became the stepmother of two strapping adolescent boys—to Trevor's intense indignation.

Josh was a good husband to her, as she always knew he would be; he was slow and patient in his wooing, and when at last he made love to her upon the old-fashioned brass bed, he approached her tenderly, with some understanding of her feelings, and she was grateful to him.

In time, she came to enjoy their love-making, and almost forgot she had ever been another man's wife. Arnold was no more than a dim memory now, far away in the past. But she could never forget that Tommy had been her lover—the only real love of her life—and though she told herself that he had gone for ever, and sometimes managed to put him from her mind, she could never put him entirely out of her heart.

One spring morning in 1926 when she had been Josh's wife for nearly three and a half years, she awoke in the double bed to find Josh caressing her and trying to rouse her; his hands were urgent and inquisitive, exploring her body. He did not kiss her on the lips—that was not his way—but his mouth was on her breasts, nuzzling her greedily.

'What time is it?' she asked sleepily.

'Early yet,' he mumbled. 'Plenty of time before the boys wake.'

'I can see the light through the curtains,' she whispered. 'Look at your watch—it must be nearly time for breakfast.'

'It's only the street-lamp—the sun's not up yet,' he told her, rolling on top of her and slipping his hand between her legs. 'I want you, Maudie... I want you now.'

Still half-asleep, she was not prepared for his importunate advances, but her body responded to his and she found herself becoming excited.

'Not so fast! Slowly...' she gasped, as he tried to enter her. She wanted him too, but not like this; she had to be ready for him.

Maudie shut her eyes and tried to dream again, to dream of Tommy—to imagine it was Tommy she held in her arms, young and slender, his skin electric against hers. That made it better—swifter, easier—even though she knew she was deceiving herself. Josh's forty-year-old body was heavy and clumsy, and he smelled of last night's stale beer and tobacco. But for a moment she was able to remember her love, and she received him joyfully.

Then there was a sudden knocking on the bedroom door, making her jump, and Jimmy Judge's voice calling out:

'Has your watch stopped, Dad? It's nearly seven o'clock!'

'I told you, Josh. Stop! No, we must get up,' she pleaded, but nothing could stop him now.

'Nearly there—in a minute.' He tightened his grip upon her, groaning, 'Give it to me now, yes, *now!*'

Moments later, triumphantly satisfied, he rolled off and lay panting, getting his breath back. Fretful and unsatisfied, Maudie scrambled out of bed and hurried to the washstand, splashing cold water from the ewer into the basin. Another day had begun.

Although he only ate a hasty breakfast, Josh was late when he arrived for work at the Guild Office. He found his father there waiting for him, glowering.

'What time do you call this?' Marcus asked, with a metallic edge to his voice. 'The Wharfmaster's sent a message. He wants to see us both, as soon as possible. You may keep

251

me waiting, if you choose—but I shouldn't advise you to do the same to him.'

Father and son crossed the yard to the Head Office, and found three men in black suits sitting at a table, talking in low tones and looking extremely serious. It was the Wharfmaster himself, together with two colleagues from the Port Authority.

'You've heard the latest, I suppose?' the Wharfmaster addressed them without any preamble. 'This is a fine kettle of fish, and no mistake!'

Trouble had been slowly brewing for more than a month, ever since the Royal Commission on the Coal Industry, in an effort to economise, had tried to withdraw from their previous industrial agreement by making cuts in the men's wages and putting other restrictions on their working practices. The Miners' Federation refused to accept these drastic measures, and the coalfields had come to a standstill. At the pithead gates, picketing workers chanted their slogan: *'Not a penny off the pay, not a minute on the day!'*

Negotiations had gone back and forth, but by the end of April they were no nearer a settlement. The employers made a final offer, which was not acceptable to the workers; they appealed to the Trade Union movement for support, and now the TUC had voted to back the miners.

'Of course, the *Daily Mail* has put the tin lid on it!' grumbled the Wharfmaster. 'The Editor wrote a leading article denouncing the

TUC—and the printers refused to set it up in type. The men walked out—and now there's to be a General Strike. The Government's declared a State of Emergency.'

'What's that mean, exactly?' Josh's brain was still fuddled. 'Closing the docks as well?'

'That's what the Unions want, but it's our business to keep the Jubilee operating as best we can. It's up to you, gentlemen—you and the Brotherhood. You're not going to let the Unions put you out of work, I hope?'

Marcus turned to his son, saying balefully, 'Now perhaps you see that I was right all along. I told you from the start we should never have allowed any of our members to join the Union. I said it would lead to trouble, and so it has.'

'We had no choice, Father,' muttered Josh. 'What you don't seem to realise is that the dockworkers have grown powerful. If we'd refused to accept them, they'd have called their members out on strike—they'd have smashed the Guild.'

'If you let them call your men out now, they'll smash us all,' said the Wharfmaster. 'We look to you to keep the dock running. You can carry on the work with non-Union labour, can't you?'

Joshua tried to cudgel his brains; he had a difficult decision to make. At last he said wearily, 'We'll do our best. I can't say fairer than that, can I?'

'Good man. And for our part, we'll do all we can to make things run smoothly. You may tell your members that during the emergency we'll offer every man who continues to do his

253

job an extra shilling a day on his wages. That should help them to see which side their bread's buttered... And of course the Government will play its part—they're already making plans to send in a volunteer force to help us unload the ships.'

The news spread round the Island like wildfire. By mid-morning, everyone knew that the Jubilee Wharf was determined to break the strike.

When Connor O'Dell opened the pub, Huw Pritchard was the first man to enter the public bar.

'Do you know what those bastards are trying to do?' he burst out.

'Watch your language,' Connor reproved him mildly.

Too late, Huw noticed Ruth getting up from her knees behind the counter, where she had been mopping some spilled beer, and he turned brick-red.

'I'm sorry, I didn't see you,' he stammered lamely.

'Don't apologise,' she smiled. 'What's the trouble this time?'

'The blessed Brotherhood—I wish to God I'd never joined it, I can tell you,' he said. 'They're calling all non-Union men to carry on working, trying to break the strike by offering an extra shilling a day. It's blood money!'

'When will they learn?' Connor shook his head. 'They tried that two years back, during the last dock strike. An extra bob for the blacklegs—what was it Ernest Bevin called it? *"A shilling for Judas"!'*

'Judas must have put his rates down,' said Huw bitterly. 'As I remember, he used to get thirty pieces of silver when he betrayed his friends. Seemingly, betrayal comes cheaper nowadays.'

'I dare say you won't be enjoying the extra money yourself?' Connor rolled up his sleeves, preparing to pull the beer-handles. 'What can I get you? A pint of our very best?'

'Not today, thanks, I'm not stopping. I only came in to tell you the news—I'm going back on duty now. We're keeping a picket-line at the dock-gate, day and night, till this is sorted out. And if any man's fool enough to try and cross that line, he'll get more than a shilling for his trouble, I promise you that!'

'Huw.' Ruth was no longer smiling. 'Take care, won't you? Don't go looking for trouble, you might get hurt.'

'If there's going to be any trouble, I'll not run away from it,' said Huw stubbornly. 'It's them as began the trouble, anyhow, not us.'

'No, you must be sensible. It's not worth getting into a fight,' Ruth persisted.

'I'm sorry, I have to disagree with you there. I think this is worth fighting for.' Huw turned to Connor for support. 'What do you say?'

'I think you're right,' Connor nodded. 'And I wish you well. Come back when you can, and let us know how things are going. There'll be a drink waiting for you, when you want one.'

A small voice piped up, 'What's happening, Dad? What's Huw fighting about?'

Cross-legged under the shadow of the counter,

Daniel had been listening to every word. Ruth pounced on him quickly.

'And what do you think you're doing, my lad? I thought I told you to stay with your sister?'

'Lil's playing with her dolls—it's girlie stuff,' complained Danny. 'Is there going to be a boxing-match? Can I watch?'

'No, there's not—and no, you can't.' Ruth turned her son round and gave him a good-natured smack on the bottom. 'You know very well you're not allowed in here during opening-time, now run along.'

She turned to Huw and explained, 'We couldn't send them off to school today, so of course Danny's under our feet all the time, wanting to know what's going on. How do you explain a General Strike to a ten-year-old boy?'

'It shouldn't be too difficult,' said Huw. 'It's only the difference between right and wrong, that's all.'

When he had gone, Ruth sighed, saying to Connor, 'If only it was as simple as that.'

Connor lifted the counter-flap and walked over to the open door, replying, 'It is that simple—for someone like Huw.'

Standing in the doorway, he watched the young Welshman walking briskly down the street, eager to reach the dock-gates impatient to be in the thick of the baffle, and he added quietly, 'Fifteen years ago, I'd have been there with him.'

'Two, four, six, eight—no, I think it's seven. Oh dear...'

Emily Judge and her sister were stock-taking in the cellar store-room, trying to count the packets of tea on the shelves, but Emily kept getting muddled and having to start all over again.

'Could you hold the candle a little nearer, Lou? It's so dark down here, I can hardly see.'

Ever since Maudie married and moved out, Louisa had been coming in to the shop every day, to help serve behind the counter, for she knew Emily couldn't manage all by herself. Marcus had never approved of his wife going out to work, but Louisa told him firmly that the shop was a family concern, and that if Emily was to keep it going, she would need all the help they could give her—and although he might resent it, Marcus had to put up with the situation.

Emily had never had a head for business, so Louisa kept a close eye on her, making sure that the shop did not run short of regular supplies and that the till was cashed up properly each evening and the day's takings entered in the account-book.

Now, for the first time, the store-room was half empty, and the accounts reflected the loss in profits. The wavering candle-flame revealed many vacant spaces on the shelves, and Emily said at last: 'We do need a good many items—tea, coffee, rice and flour. Never mind, the wholesalers will be sending the new delivery first thing Monday morning.'

'I'm afraid they won't, dear,' Louisa pointed

out. 'Not as long as this strike goes on.'

'Oh, but they must send food supplies. The Government wouldn't let people starve!' Emily was very shocked. 'That would never do!'

'The Government will do its best, but unless they can get the supplies through the docks, and unless they can find some kind of transport to deliver them to the shops, we're just going to have to tighten our belts and make the best of a bad job.'

They were interrupted by the ping of the shop-bell from the floor above.

'There now, we've got customers,' said Emily thankfully, relieved that things appeared to be going on as usual, despite her sister's dire warning. 'We'd better go up and see what they want.'

In the shop, Gloria was looking round the shelves. When the old ladies joined her, she greeted them.

'Hello, Ma, hello, Auntie Lou. I must say, you seem to be running very low on groceries, don't you?'

'It can't be helped, Glory,' said Emily. 'Your auntie was just explaining to me that it's all because of this dreadful strike.'

'They say there's boats full of stuff, standing in the docks waiting to be unloaded.' Gloria tossed her head. 'It's not right—somebody ought to *do* something!'

'I'm sure you're right, dear. And where's my precious nephew this morning?' Emily peered over the counter short-sightedly. 'Didn't you bring Matt with you? He can't have gone to school today, surely?'

'No, the school's shut too, it's a perishing nuisance,' said Gloria. 'And I've got my work to do—three hair appointments. I couldn't drag the kid round with me all day, could I, so I had a bright idea. I took him round and left him at Josh's house. Well, Maudie's a lady of leisure these days; she can look after him, she's got nothing better to do. Besides, he'll have Trevor to play with—they'll keep each other out of mischief.'

'Oh, yes, that's nice. And I suppose Josh's two boys must be at home as well, if there's no work at the docks?'

As soon as they had reached the magic age of fourteen and were able to leave school, first Jimmy and two years later Bertie had followed in their father's footsteps and joined the Brotherhood.

'They weren't at home when I called in. Maudie said they'd gone to work as usual, but she must have made a mistake as there's nothing doing at the Wharf today. I know that, 'cos when I went past the dock-gates, there was men standing outside with placards. They're not letting anyone in.'

'Well, I don't know, I'm sure.' Emily turned to her sister. 'Lou, you'll know better than anybody else. Is the dockyard shut or not? What did Marcus say about it?'

Louisa looked troubled, unwilling to commit herself, but finally said, 'I'm not really certain. You know how Marcus is, he always keeps things to himself. But I do believe some of the

259

dockers may be working, for the extra money. After all, most of them have wives and families to think of. It's all very difficult.'

'But if there's a picket at the gates, how do they get in?' Gloria wanted to know.

'I couldn't say, I'm sure.' Lousia changed the subject. 'But we mustn't keep you talking when you're so busy, Gloria. What can we do for you this morning?'

'I want some sugar, please. I was just going to get half a pound, but if you're running short, I'll take two pounds while you've still got some left. Matt's got a sweet tooth; he takes after me that way.'

Obediently, Emily took down a big two-pound bag from the shelf, but Louisa stopped her.

'Just half a pound, I think, dear. I'm sorry, Gloria, but we must be sensible, mustn't we? If we gave everybody two pounds, there'd be none left by the end of the day, and goodness only knows when we'll be getting any more. Much better share it out equally all round—half a pound for each customer—that's the only fair way to do it.'

'Oh, come on, Auntie Lou—you can give us a bit extra, can't you? We're *family!*' exclaimed Gloria.

'I'm sorry, dear. The Government's warned us not to encourage hoarding. It wouldn't be right.'

On that point at least, Louisa felt she could stand firm.

On Friday, Connor got up early, as he did every morning, to take the dog out for a run. As he was unbolting the side door, he heard a patter of feet and Danny came running down the stairs.

'Please, Dad, can I come with you?'

Connor frowned. 'What's all this? Up and dressed already?'

'I get fed up staying at home all day. I heard you get up, and I thought if I was quick, I could catch you. I got dressed real fast!'

'Your mum will be worried sick when she finds you've gone missing. She won't know where you've gone.'

'That's all right. Lil's awake—she'll tell Mum I'm with you.'

At Connor's feet, Barker the dog whimpered impatiently, his nails scrabbling on the linoleum. Connor looked down at them both—two pairs of pleading brown eyes gazed up at him—and gave in.

'Well, all right.' Then he added suspiciously, 'I'll lay odds you haven't washed your hands and face, or cleaned your teeth, or brushed your hair—right?'

'I'll do all that when we get back,' Danny promised. 'Come on, Dad, let's go!'

Though the calendar said it was spring, it was a raw, misty morning, but the sun was trying to break through a bank of low cloud, throwing a pearly glow over the rooftops. They stepped out briskly along the quiet streets.

Danny took two strides to every one of his father's, and still found enough breath to keep up a continuous flow of chatter.

261

'Lil was real cross when I told her I was going with you. She wanted to come too, but I said she couldn't 'cos she's a girl.'

'That's not very fair, is it? What's wrong with being a girl?'

'Oh, *Dad!*' Danny was scornful. 'She'd have kept us waiting for hours. She never gets ready in time and she always keeps stopping to look in shop windows. Girls are horrible.' As they turned a corner, he asked hopefully,' Are we going to the docks?'

'I suppose so. I generally go that way when I take Barker for his run. Why?'

'Will we see the men outside the gates? Will Huw be there? Will there be a fight?'

'I don't know about Huw but there'll be no fighting, I promise you that.'

It was a long walk, and a great deal of it was rather dull; they followed the curve of a wall that seemed to go on forever—much too high for anyone to see over the top. Danny skipped up and down with impatience, knowing that just the other side of that high, blank wall there was the deep-water dock, and big ships moored up alongside Jubilee Wharf. All he could see were the tops of the cranes; he'd often watched them before, moving like lumbering giants, advancing and retiring, dipping their heads to each other in a solemn ritual, but today they stood idle and motionless.

When they got near the gates, Barker pricked up his ears and sniffed the air; the line of men standing guard in the street was unfamiliar and somehow threatening. He uttered a low growl,

262

deep in his throat, and the hairs on his neck bristled.

'Heel, Barker! Stay close. Heel, I say!'

But if Barker scented trouble ahead, Danny was cheerfully welcoming. 'Look, Dad, there's Huw! He's seen us!'

He began to wave, and Huw responded, wagging a painted placard at them. Carefully and correctly, Danny spelled out the slogan: *'No shillings for Judas'*...that's what you said yesterday. What does it mean, Dad?'

Connor gave a half-smile. 'Huw's telling the bosses what they can do with their dirty money.'

Most of the men on the picket-line knew Connor as the Watermen landlord, and they gathered round, hailing him as a friend and ally. Huw asked, 'What's this, then? Two more recruits come to join us?'

'Not today,' said Connor. 'Just exercising our thoroughbred.' Barker lifted his head proudly, and gave several loud yelps. From the opposite corner, two policemen looked across with interest. 'Under observation, are you?' Connor went on. 'Do they stay there all the time?'

'They come and go—different chaps at different times of day. They're not a bad bunch; just doing their job, I suppose.'

Behind the picket-line, the iron gates were standing open, but there was no sign of life within the yard.

'And you've not seen anyone go through?' Connor asked. 'Not even the office staff?'

'Haven't seen a soul up to now. Mind, they've

263

stuck up a notice—they must still be hopeful they'll drag in a few recruits.'

He indicated a hastily printed poster, inviting men to report for duty, promising: *Special reward payments for volunteers.* Underneath, an unknown hand had scrawled: *We all know the value of this Government's promises.*

Huw grinned. 'Don't worry. None of our chaps are stupid enough to fall for that rubbish.'

But Danny tugged at his sleeve. 'There's someone going in now,' he said.

'What? Where?' Huw turned sharply. While their attention had been diverted by the early-morning visitors, another newcomer was taking the opportunity to dodge behind the picket and slip in through the gates. Only Danny, on the edge of the group, had noticed him.

'Hey, you! Where d'you think you're going?' shouted Huw.

The man redoubled his pace. He was a small, shifty-looking character with a cap pulled down over his ears and a muffler hiding the lower part of his face. Huw thrust his placard into Connor's hands, saying, 'Hold this, will you?' and raced after him at top speed.

He caught the man just before he disappeared round the corner of the office block, and collared him, saying,'Well! If it isn't my old friend George Parkin. And where are you off to in such a hurry, brother?'

'I—I was just having a look inside—just to see what's going on.' Very scared, Parkin choked on the words. 'I ain't done nothing wrong. Let go of me!'

'Why weren't you on the picket-line with us, George? Don't you want to stand up for your mates?'

Huw frog-marched him out through the gates, as the policemen strolled across the road. The senior constable began heavily, 'Now then, you heard what he said. Let him go.'

'I'm just explaining to brother Parkin,' said Huw. 'He ought to know better than to cross a picket-line.'

'That's up to him, not you. Take your hands off him.'

Unwillingly, Huw obeyed. As soon as he was released, George Parkin ran off as fast as his legs would carry him, the clatter of his boots echoing between the high walls.

'You know you're not allowed to exercise violence. You have a legal right to make a peaceful demonstration, without aggression. I suggest you nip off home sharpish—we don't want any trouble here, do we? The rest of you can stay, provided you just stand there with your banners and don't try any funny business. But as for you, Taffy, you'd better sling your hook—all right?'

'Damnation. Now we'll be one man short,' said Huw, moving reluctantly away.

Connor said suddenly, 'I'll take your place —for an hour or two, anyhow.'

'Just a minute. You're not a member of the Dockworkers' Guild, are you, sir?' asked the police constable.

'I used to be, a while ago. And I'm declaring my solidarity with the workers,' said Connor pleasantly. 'Any objection to that?'

The two policeman retired to a discreet distance and conferred. A few moments later they remembered a previous appointment elsewhere, and fell into step, walking away up the road with great dignity.

Connor shouldered his placard, and winked at Huw. 'Take the lad home, and explain to his mother. Say I'll be along presently, and tell her to keep the kettle on the stove. I'll be ready for a cup of tea by the time I get home.'

The mists closed in again during the day, and the sun gave up the struggle. When evening fell, it grew dark earlier than usual. In a dingy basement room, lit by a single candle—for the tenants could not afford to pay for gas—a skinny woman nursed a baby and nagged her husband.

'How are we going to manage, if you don't bring home your wages? Tell me that, George Parkin! What am I supposed to do, eh? Sit and watch our kids starving to death? I can't bring up a family on the money I get taking in washing, so don't you think it! You're supposed to be the breadwinner here—it's up to you to provide for us!'

'How can I?' Parkin tried to defend himself. 'I wanted to go and sign on for work this morning, you know I did.'

'So you say. For all I know, you might have been off playing pitch-and-toss with the rest of the Weary Willies. Mum was right, she told me I should never have married you.'

266

A knock at the street door interrupted her; they looked at one another.

'Who's that?' he asked.

'How should I know? You'd better go and find out, unless you're too bone-idle to shift yourself off of that chair.'

Defeated, George Parkin climbed the basement stairs and opened the front door. Two young men were waiting for him on the step.

'Lucky we found you in,' said Jimmy Judge, with a sly smile. 'Having a quiet evening at home, were you?'

'We want a word with you,' added his brother Bertie. 'If you wouldn't mind stepping outside for a minute?'

'Sorry, not now, can't leave the missus and the kids,' began Parkin. He drew back, about to shut the door, but Jimmy planted his boot on the step.

'Not so fast,' he said. 'If you know what's good for you, you'll listen to what we've got to say.'

'We're here on business—official-like.' Bertie's chest swelled with pride; he was enjoying an unaccustomed feeling of importance. 'Guild business, this is.'

George Parkin eyed the two boys. He knew their ages, eighteen and sixteen, and he was older than both of them put together. But they were big, beefy lads, and they were the sons of Joshua Judge—and Marcus Judge's grandsons. He did not dare to cross them.

Slowly, he stepped out on to the pavement. They moved in closer, one on each side, gripping his arms above the elbow and edging him a little further away from the house.

'That's better,' said Jimmy, still wearing the same gloating smile. 'Nobody will be eavesdropping on us out here.'

Bertie chimed in like an echo, 'This is private and confidential, see?'

'What's it all about? What's up?' George Parkin tried to swallow, but his mouth was dry.

'The Guild's very disappointed in you, Mr Parkin,' said Jimmy softly. 'We looked for you to report for duty this morning.'

'I wanted to. I did try, but the picket caught me going through and I got chucked out,' Parkin explained. 'It weren't my fault!'

'You should've been a bit quicker off the mark,' said Bertie. 'The Guild's relying on you, brother.'

'I tell you, I done me best—honest to God!'

'You'll have to do better'n that tomorrow,' said Jimmy. 'There's special arrangements been made. Every man's expected to turn up on time and put in a full day's work. Dad says he's counting on you, Mr Parkin.'

'I dunno. It's too risky—if I get caught again—'

'If you don't turn up tomorrow, it'll be the worse for you.' Bertie lowered his voice to a whisper. 'Your name's on the list already, for letting them down today. If you don't turn up tomorrow, you'll be turned over to the Punishment Squad...'

He laughed suddenly, sounding even younger

than his sixteen years, but that childish giggle had a note of cruelty that made George Parkin's blood run cold. He had never had to face the Punishment Squad, but like every member of the Brotherhood, he knew what he could expect at their hands.

'I'll try. I swear I'll try,' he gasped. 'But if the picket's still outside the dock-gates tomorrow, how will I get in?'

'You won't be going through the gates tomorrow.' Jimmy drew him closer still, his fist gripping George's arm like a vice. 'I told you, there's other arrangements been made—very special arrangements.'

The following day, the mists were still hanging low upon the Island, shielding the curve of the river like a woman concealing a secret under her shawl.

When Connor took Barker for his early-morning run, he turned a deaf ear to Daniel's pleading, and left the boy at home. Some sixth sense told him there would be trouble today. If there were to be any ugly scenes, he didn't want his son to witness them.

This morning, the strikers had lashed the dockgates together with a length of rope, and Connor found the picket sitting in a miserable group upon the kerbstones, huddled together for warmth with their placards propped up against the wall.

'No sign of any blacklegs today?' he asked.

They shook their heads and yawned, stretching and scratching themselves.

'Been dead quiet all night,' said one man.

269

'Might as well have stayed at home in our beds.'

Connor glanced round. 'Where's Huw Pritchard?'

'He's taking the day-shift—he'll be along later.'

So far, so good. Everything was quiet—unnaturally quiet, Connor thought. Even the two watchful policemen had not put in an appearance this morning. But there was nothing to be gained by hanging about. He whistled for Barker, who came bounding up, his tail wagging, then man and dog disappeared together into the damp morning mists.

Nobody in the East End had any idea what was happening 'up West'. No one knew about the huge convoy of lorries that was turning out of Hyde Park at that moment, heading for the City, for the Tower and for the Pool of London...

Hyde Park had been turned into a storage depot for food and fuel supplies. A village of tents had sprung up, and mobile canteens serving refreshments for the volunteers, trying to keep the essential services going. But they would not be able to provide for London very much longer, unless new supplies could be brought in from the docks.

When Ruth went out shopping with the children, she saw the long line of vehicles moving steadily down West Ferry Road. There were a hundred motor-lorries, each one manned by a couple of khaki-clad soldiers with the badge of the Welsh Guards in their caps. The convoy

270

was protected at its head, on both flanks and in the rear, by armoured cars driven by men of the Royal Tank Corps. She could guess where they were heading, and her heart sank.

'Come along—time to go home,' she told the children briskly.

'Can't we stay and watch the soldiers?' Danny asked.

'I told Dad we'd be back by opening-time. Come on now—quick march!'

Still half-asleep, the men on the picket-line struggled to their feet as they saw the armoured cars approaching. They tried to confer, to decide what they should do, but everything happened so fast, there was no time to think.

Some of them snatched up their placards and walked out into the road, facing the oncoming vehicles, but it was clear that nothing would stop the convoy, and as the leading cars accelerated, the strikers broke ranks and leaped on to the pavement, dodging left and right.

The gates, fastened together with rope, burst apart under the impact of the leading car; two uniformed men jumped down and hauled the gates wide open, then sprang on to the running-board again and continued their triumphant invasion of the dockyard.

When the day-shift arrived to take on their turn of duty, Huw Pritchard turned on his workmates angrily.

'Didn't any of you try to stop them? Didn't you even say anything?'

'It was all over in minutes. Nobody said a word—they never even slowed down.'

'So they're all in there now, on the Wharf? They've got the army unloading the ships?'

'They won't get much done; there weren't more'n a couple of blokes in each lorry. Besides, they won't know how to set about it. It's skilled work, that is. They don't realise...'

But the soldiers were not the only men on the docks that morning. It had all been carefully organised; the lorries were drawn up along the Wharf in parallel lines, backed up three at a time to the unloading chutes, where volunteers were already at work.

The army had been reinforced by civilians, picked up by lighters further upstream and brought down the river before dawn, slipping quietly into the docks to await the convoy. Men of all kinds were there. Many of them were youngsters down from the universities, out for a lark, and there were medical students from the teaching hospitals, clerks from city offices, bricklayers and dustmen, engineers and shop-keepers... And among them all, a sprinkling of skilled, knowledgeable men—a small corps of dockers who needed to support their families and cared more for the extra wages than for the solidarity of the strikers.

By midmorning, Huw and his mates could not stand helplessly outside the gates another minute. They had to know what was going on.

Stealthily, they walked through the gates and made their way to the Jubilee Wharf—then stopped short, staring in dismay at the scene of activity along the waterfront.

Some of the volunteers had stopped for a breather, taking a break and enjoying refreshments—mugs of tea or coffee and doorsteps of bread and jam, doled out by the Port Authority from a tin hut. And there, in among the crowd, was George Parkin.

That was when Huw lost his temper. He felt as if his head would explode from the force of the rage burning within him, and he lowered his head, charging into the crowd like a young bull.

Parkin saw him coming and tried to escape, but Huw was on to him in a moment. He did not waste words. His fury erupted into action and he threw himself upon the frightened man, raining blows upon him. Parkin fell upon the slippery cobbles, with Huw on top of him. Some of the other workers went to his rescue, and a dozen hands dragged the two men apart. Dazed and injured, with blood trickling from a cut above his eye where he had hit his face upon the stones, Parkin took to his heels, ducking between the parked vehicles, dodging and weaving, heading for the gates—running for his life.

A heavy lorry laden with flour, with one of the Welsh guardsmen perched on top of the bulging sacks, backed slowly out, about to begin its return journey to Hyde Park. Pinned behind it, Huw could only clench his fists in frustration, venting his anger upon his fellow-countryman. 'You bloody traitor!' he yelled, falling into his mother-tongue for the first time for years. 'How can you betray your brothers?' As the soldier stared at him, he reverted to English, spitting out the worst abuse he could think of 'Blackleg—scab—Judas!'

Then the lorry moved off, and he began to run once more in pursuit of his enemy, George Parkin.

By now Parkin had several hundred yards' start on him, but Huw was not going to give up. His legs working like pistons, he raced on. At the end of the long, narrow road, Parkin vanished round the curve of the wall and Huw forced himself to increase his speed. When he reached the street market, he did not slow up for an instant, but tore through the crowd, darting between the stalls while angry costermongers yelled after him—but he scarcely heard them.

In the distance, he could just see the open doors of the Three Jolly Watermen—and he caught a glimpse of Parkin's back as he fled into the public bar.

A few moments later, Huw followed him in, breathless but determined.

There was no sign of Parkin; nobody but Patrick O'Dell in his favourite chair by the fireplace, two old men playing dominoes at a corner table and Connor behind the bar.

'Where did he go?' Huw panted thickly.

Connor frowned. 'Ruth took him through to the kitchen. What the hell's going on?'

Huw did not stop to reply. Without asking permission, he shouldered through the archway into the passage beyond, and opened the kitchen door. George Parkin, his complexion greenish-white, marbled with streaks of blood, sat in his shirtsleeves; his clothes filthy with mud, his chest heaving, too far gone to speak.

Beside him, Ruth was wringing out a facecloth in a basin of warm water, tending to his cuts and bruises.

George looked at Huw, and his eyes were blank with terror.

When Ruth turned and saw Huw, for a moment she could say nothing. Shock, incredulity and then contempt—these emotions chased one another across her face. Huw stared at her; he could only think that he had never seen her looking so angry, nor so beautiful.

'*You* did this?' she said at last.

'I—I came to find him. You don't understand —he's a blackleg!'

'No, I don't understand you. Not any more... Please get out of my house,' she said, and each word was a knife-thrust.

At a loss, Huw looked about him. Suddenly he dreaded that he might find the children there, and she interpreted his thoughts immediately.

'Don't worry, they're not here. Their grandmother took them out to the Gardens,' she told him. 'If Danny saw what you'd done, I think it would have broken his heart.'

Behind Huw, in the doorway, Connor asked, 'What in God's name have you been up to?'

Huw turned, desperate for his support. 'Parkin's supposed to be a member of the Guild. He took their damn shilling to work with the army—unloading our ships, breaking the strike.'

Ruth cut in: 'I don't want to hear any more.'

275

She dried Parkin's face with a towel, then helped him into his jacket. Ignoring Huw, she addressed her husband. 'Connor, this man needs to rest. You'll have to take him home—see that he gets there safely. I'll mind the pub till you get back. Will you do that, please?'

Connor nodded, and helped the frightened man to his feet. On their way out, as he passed Huw, Parkin flinched away.

For what seemed to be an eternity, there was silence in the kitchen. Huw and Ruth faced one another like strangers. At last, Huw struggled to explain himself once again.

'He was a blackleg. Don't you see, it's because of men like that—'

But she would not listen to him. 'He's a human being, and you behaved like an animal. I would never have believed it of you.'

He stood looking at her, and all his secret hopes and dreams turned to dust. 'I loved you,' he said brokenly. 'I thought—I believed—you felt something, too.'

She turned away from him, taking the basin of water out to the scullery, and saying over her shoulder, 'Then you were mistaken. Now, just go. Leave me alone.'

She would not look at him again. As she poured the dirty water down the sink, she heard the sound of the kitchen door closing. When she turned round, the room was empty.

On Sunday morning, a second army convoy entered the docks. Again, the strikers did not attempt to put up any resistance; they knew

276

they had been outmanoeuvred.

Gradually, the leaders of the Trade Union Congress realised that they had allowed themselves to be jockeyed into an untenable position: opposing the Government's authority without either the will or the means to do so.

The following Wednesday, the TUC Chairman and Secretary went to Downing Street for a last discussion with the Prime Minister, and by midday, the General Strike had been called off, unconditionally.

10

The winter of 1927–8 was cold and hard, and for weeks the Island was in the iron grip of ice and snow, but after the turn of the year, a thaw set in and snow melted into rain—heavy, continuous rain, which seemed as if it would never end.

When Emily called at Marcus's house with the account-book from the shop, she was wet and shivering. Louisa pulled her chair closer to the kitchen range, spread her coat over the fireguard to dry, and poured her a hot cup of tea.

'Drink up, dear. This will soon warm you through.'

Privately, she wondered if her sister was shivering with cold or with fear, for the moment she arrived, Emily had asked nervously, 'Is Marcus at home?'

'No, he's not back from the Wharf yet. Why?'

'Oh, nothing. I just wondered.'

Now, as she sipped her tea, Emily kept stealing uneasy glances at the cloth-bound account-book on the table, and at last Louisa asked her, 'What are you so anxious about, Em? Is it the book-keeping again?'

A mouthful of tea went down the wrong way, and Emily spluttered a little before replying, 'Well, yes. I'm afraid Marcus will be very cross with me. The shop's made a loss again this month—rather a heavy loss.'

'But I thought business had been picking up? You were so busy, the week before Christmas.'

'The rest of the month was ever so slow, and then there was all that trouble over the windows.'

The shop was double-fronted, and some time during Boxing Day, when the streets were deserted and blanketed by snow, not just one but both of the big plate-glass windows were shattered. A half-brick had been chucked through each of them.

When Marcus arrived home, he too was soaked to the skin and not in the best of tempers. Louisa hung his topcoat near the stove and suggested that he might like to go up and change into dry clothes while she laid the table for tea. He pooh-poohed this, telling her not to fuss. He had better things to occupy his mind than a pair of wet socks.

So she carried on getting the tea ready, while Marcus began to study the grocery shop accounts.

When he had checked Emily's arithmetic, and corrected it in several places, he slammed the book shut with a crack like a pistol-shot, which made Emily jump. He turned on her immediately, saying, 'I suppose you know what this means?'

'No, Marcus. What does it mean?'

'It means, Emily, that you have been throwing your business away, playing ducks and drakes with all the capital I have invested in you over the years. Letting it pour away like rainwater down the drain...' Marcus's eyes flashed. 'It means that it's time to put up the shutters. Time to sell the shop.'

Louisa and Emily stared at him, and Emily began to cry. 'Oh, no! Don't say that!'

'But I do say it! You can't expect me to go on throwing good money after bad. My resources are not a boundless supply of wealth which you can draw upon indefinitely. I've reached the end of my patience, Emily. The shop must go.'

Louisa tried to intervene. 'Surely it can't be as bad as that? Couldn't we help Emily tide things over for a while, just until she gets through this difficult patch?'

Marcus turned to his wife, and his expression was as stern and unyielding as before. 'You heard what I said. I cannot squander my life-savings upon your sister any longer.'

'Just for a few months, dear. When the spring comes and the weather improves, business will pick up again.'

'I said no, Louisa! This is not a question of business falling off; the costs of running that

279

shop are outweighing the profits. Outgoings this past month are the highest I ever remember.'

'That's because of the broken windows.' Emily dabbed her eyes with her lace handkerchief. 'It was so expensive having them both repaired, but that wasn't my fault. There have been so many windows smashed in the district just lately. It's happened to lots of people.'

'I don't wish to hear any excuses, Emily. Stop snivelling, blow your nose, and try to face the facts. I have made up my mind—the shop is to be put up for sale.'

Louisa walked across to her husband, saying quietly, 'And where is Emily to live? That shop is her home as well as her business. You can't be so unfeeling—you must have some consideration.'

Marcus rose to his feet, pushing back his chair, and thundering: *'You will not tell me what I must do!* The shop belongs to me, the property belongs to me. Am I not master in my own house?'

Bravely, Louisa faced him. 'When you do something wrong, it's my duty to tell you so. Because if I don't, nobody else will.'

His face became mottled with anger; his square-cut beard bristled. 'I take my orders from Our Father in Heaven! God Almighty tells me where my duty lies; I will listen to no other voice but His!' He pushed past his wife, grabbed up his coat which was still wet and steaming, and began to pull it on.

Louisa tried to stop him. 'Where do you think you're going? You're wet through already, and

280

you've had nothing to eat!'

He brushed her aside and picked up a worn, black leather satchel from the sideboard, saying, 'In case it has slipped your mind, today is Friday. Had you forgotten that I collect the rents from our tenants every Friday night?'

'There'll be time for that later. Stay and have some tea first...'

'I do not need food or drink! I do not need foolish women telling me how to manage my business! I do not need your interference, Louisa, nor do I need Emily weeping and wailing. I do not need you at all!'

When he swept out of the house, the slam of the front door made the china on the dresser rattle and shiver. Louisa said nothing, but put her arm round her sister, patting her on the shoulder and trying to stop her crying.

In another narrow street, not much more than a hundred yards away, Joshua came home from work a little later than his father. He too found a family crisis awaiting him.

Even before he had finished peeling off his dripping waterproof, Maudie greeted him with a tear-stained face.

'Josh, there's been some trouble. Trevor's been naughty...'

Joshua shook his mackintosh out in the scullery and hung it up to dry, then came back into the kitchen, where the twelve-year-old boy sat curled up in the armchair, staring sulkily into the fire.

'What have you been up to, my lad?' Josh asked, not unkindly.

Trevor would not look at him. 'Nothing much. I broke a window, that's all. It was an accident.'

'Oh, yes? And how did that happen?'

'I was playing in the street, throwing a ball. It sort of slipped out of my hand and went through a window. I couldn't help it.'

Josh knew at once that the boy was lying. 'Playing ball in the street?' he said. 'In this weather?'

Trevor looked up quickly, the picture of injured innocence. 'Yes. I was on my way home from school, bouncing the ball in the puddles just for fun—you know, making them splash. That's how it happened, honest, isn't that right, Mum?' He threw his mother a meaning look, encouraging her to support him, but she turned away.

'Never mind, Maudie,' said Josh. 'It doesn't sound very serious, after all. Accidents will happen, and if it's just a question of paying for a broken window—'

Maudie still looked unhappy, lowering her eyes. 'No, it wasn't like that. You must tell Dad the truth, Trevor.'

'He's not my dad!' Trevor leapt at the opportunity to change the subject. 'Why do you call him my dad when you know he isn't? My dad got killed in the war. He was a hero!'

'Sssh, Trevor, don't start that again. He's been as good as a father to you—better than

282

most, I dare say. So you mustn't tell him lies, and you mustn't expect me to, either.'

'Oh, *Mum.*' Trevor gazed at her with big, reproachful eyes.

'So what really happened?' Josh persisted.

Haltingly, Maudie explained. 'It wasn't a ball, it was a half-brick he threw at the window—on purpose. And the man who lives there came out and caught him, and brought him home. He was talking about going to the police, as you know there's been a lot of broken windows round here recently. He says Trev's the one that's been doing it.'

Joshua stared at her, then at the boy. 'Is this true? You're responsible for all of them? Even the grocery shop windows—your own grandma's shop?'

Trevor's lower lip quivered, and he began to sniff. 'I didn't want to do it,' he said in a small voice. '*He* made me. Mr Otley—he made me do it.'

'What are you talking about?' Now Josh was completely lost. 'Who's this chap Otley?'

Maudie explained. 'Sid Otley. He's the man you see going round the streets with panes of glass on a barrow—the one who puts new windows in.'

'That's right.' Trevor nodded vigorously. 'He's wicked, he is. He said he'd give me a penny for each one I broke—threepence for shop windows.'

Joshua managed to keep a straight face as he said, 'I thought we had an arrangement, Trev. I said if you ever got into any trouble, you were to come and talk to me about it. Why didn't you do that?'

'I couldn't.' The boy hung his head. 'I didn't want to do what he said, only he bullied me. He twisted my arm and he did things to me—bad things. He *made* me do it.'

Joshua sighed. This wasn't going to be as easy as he had thought. 'Very well. Tell me where I can find him. I'd better have a word with Mister Sidney Otley.'

After tea he set out again, the collar of his mackintosh turned up, his chin tucked in, and his head well down against the driving rain. He found the glazier's workshop without much difficulty. Sid Otley had straggling grey hair and a wispy beard, and contrived to look both relieved and apprehensive at the same time.

'So you're the boy's father, are you?' he said, gasping for breath. 'You'll have to excuse me coughing and spluttering, but this rain plays me up something shocking. Chronic bronchitis I've got, and the wet weather makes it worse. You want to give that boy of yours a good talking-to. He's artful as a waggonload of monkeys, and cunning with it.'

'What do you mean by that?'

'Well, wouldn't you call it cunning? Coming to me with a scheme like that all worked out? He was to go round breaking windows, and I was to give him a share of the money I made for replacing them.'

'Are you telling me it was *his* idea?'

'Straight up—true as I'm standing here.' Otley wheezed, and thumped his chest. 'You don't

284

think I'd dream it up on my own, do you?'

'But you went along with the scheme? You let him talk you into it?'

'I didn't fancy it, but he—he said if I didn't, he'd tell everybody bad things about me. He's got a strange mind, for a boy of his age.'

'Bad things? What sort of bad things?'

'He said...' The old man hesitated. His hands were shaking, and he began coughing and hawking again, spitting into a filthy handkerchief, playing for time. 'He said he'd tell people I'd done dirty things. Interfering with him—you know.'

Joshua took a long breath. 'But it wasn't true?'

'As God's my witness. May He strike me dead if I ever laid a finger on the boy!' Otley shuffled, and wiped his nose with the back of his hand, then admitted grudgingly, 'Look, there was some trouble a few years ago now. People said things behind me back—you know how they like to gossip—just 'cos I ain't never been married, nor nothing. But there was never anything proved, see—only a lot of nasty talk. I dare say your boy must've picked up the story somehow, and that's what give him the idea. But I can tell you now—I'm glad you found out. I'm really glad you come round to talk to me, so I could get it off me chest, see?'

Underlining his words, he pounded his chest again, wheezing, 'I'm glad to be shot of the boy. I don't want no more to do with him.'

When Josh left the workshop, he walked into a cloudburst. The rain was coming down like stair-rods but it didn't bother him now. He lifted his head, welcoming the water that streamed over his face. After what he had been told, he needed a good wash.

Gloria's son Matt was nine months younger than Trevor; he wouldn't be twelve until February. But in some ways he was old for his years—perhaps because for so long he had been the only man in the household—so when he called his mother down from the kitchen, she knew she must take him seriously.

'Come and see this!' he shouted up the stairs. 'It looks like we're in for trouble!'

Gloria had been slicing onions to fry up with some sausages for their supper, but she wiped her hands and went down the rickety old staircase. The warehouse on Cyclops Wharf had always been a cold, draughty place at the best of times and tonight, as she lit her way downstairs by candle-light, the flame guttered, threatening to go out. Shielding it with her hand, she said, 'Sounds as if it's blowing up a gale out there.'

'Wind and water—they're both fierce tonight. See for yourself.' Matt led his mother to the ground-floor window, looking on to the river. The rain attacked the panes with such force, it was hard to see through them, but Gloria knew at a glance that something was wrong.

'The lights on the boats, bobbing about— they're too high up,' she said.

'We've had some high tides lately, but this

286

one beats the lot and it won't start going down for another hour or two, so there'll be worse to come.'

'What are you talking about? I don't understand.'

'Take another look.' Matt pointed. 'The river's up to the top of the embankment wall already. Every time the wind drives one of them big waves this way, it spills over—see? There's six inches of water slopping across the path already, and it ain't high tide yet.'

'You mean it's going to get deeper? It might flood the house?'

A gust of wind took her by surprise and the candle went out, leaving them in darkness. Cold fear clutched her suddenly, and she fumbled for the boy's hand.

'Matt—I don't like it. What are we going to do?'

'Keep out of the way of it, I suppose. Is there anything down here you want to carry upstairs, before the water rises?'

She tried to think. 'No. There's nothing down here but that dirty old junk your father left in the shop—when it was still a shop, I mean. It's not worth anything now, just a load of old rubbish. Leave it where it is and let's go upstairs. We'll be able to keep out of the wet up there, won't we?'

'I should hope so.' The boy thought for a moment, then added: 'Unless... Maybe we ought to leave here and go somewhere else, further from the river.'

'But what about the neighbours—the people

287

next door?' asked Gloria. 'Shouldn't we go and tell them?'

Matt's voice had not yet broken, but in the darkness he sounded oddly tough and ruthless—and she was reminded of her husband.

'Never mind about them, they can take care of themselves,' he said. 'I think we ought to get out right now, while the going's good.'

When Josh returned home, he did not waste words. Pulling off his wet coat, he began to roll up his shirtsleeves, saying curtly, 'Trevor—go to your room. I'll be there in a minute.'

Trevor opened his mouth to argue, but something in Josh's expression silenced him, and he went upstairs quickly. Maudie looked blankly at Josh.

'What are you going to say to him?'

'Not much. Where's the stick?'

He went back into the hallway, where he hung up his coat and began to rummage in the umbrella-stand. He had never been a harsh father to his own sons, but he had sometimes had to give them a good hiding when he felt they had earned it, and he kept a rattan cane for that purpose.

Maudie followed him into the hall, her face chalk-white. 'Oh no, Josh, you can't. You mustn't hurt him!'

'It's the only way to knock some sense into the boy. I'm sorry. I've tried to be lenient for your sake, but he has to be taught a lesson.'

'For breaking a few windows? That's all he's done, and that old man Otley put him up to it—you heard what he said.'

'I've heard what Otley had to say as well, and it's not fit for your ears. Leave him to me please, Maudie.'

As he went upstairs, she called after him, 'I don't know how you can be so cruel. I'll never forgive you!'

Firmly, Josh shut the door of Trevor's room and addressed the boy: 'Unfasten your belt and drop your trousers. Bend over that chair.'

Trevor did not argue; he knew he would only be wasting his breath. He was very frightened, but he had not quite given up hope.

With his trousers round his ankles, he bent over obediently. Then, as Josh flexed the cane, he turned his head and looked back over his shoulder, smiling up under his long lashes—a smile so provocative and knowing, Josh caught his breath and almost dropped the cane.

Pulling himself together, he slapped Trevor hard across the face with the back of his hand, grabbed him by the scruff of the neck, forcing his head down, then lifted the cane and gave him the punishment he deserved.

Downstairs, Maudie sobbed her heart out and put her hands over her ears, trying to blot out her son's cries. None of them noticed the sound of the wind and rain outside, beating upon the window-panes.

The Watermen was always crowded on a Friday, because the regulars had received their weekly pay-packet, but tonight the saloon was particularly busy. Ruth and Connor worked as a team, side by side behind the bar, while more and more customers pushed through the street door—cold and wet, grateful for warmth and shelter.

Kept on the go, Ruth and Connor hardly had a chance to exchange more than a few words, but as she waited for him to finish drawing a pint, she remarked, 'They say the tide's breaking over the embankment, down West Ferry Road. I hope Gloria's all right. That old warehouse is right on top of the river.'

'Maybe I'll take a walk that way after closing-time, to make sure they've not come to any harm,' said Connor.

'On a night like this? You'll do no such thing!' Ruth scolded him. 'If Gloria needs any help, she knows where to find us.'

The words were hardly out of her mouth when the door opened again, and a young man came in, brushing the rain from his face. He was wearing glasses, which steamed up immediately, and he had to wipe the lenses before he could see.

'Mrs O'Dell—is she here?' he asked. 'She's wanted...'

A hush fell, and the crowd drew aside, leaving enough space for him to get to the bar.

'It's my cousin, isn't it?' said Ruth, guiltily. 'Gloria Judge. I knew it—there's been an accident!'

'No, missus, it ain't her. It's the old gentleman—your dad. Me and my mate was on our way to the bakery, going on the night-shift, see, and we found him.' As he unbuttoned his wet coat, Ruth saw that he was dressed in the white jacket and trousers which all the bakery staff had to wear. 'He was lying in the gutter, down along Manchester Road. Been knocked about, he has. God only knows how long he'd been there when we picked him up—soaking wet, he was. My mate knows him by sight. He used to work on the Wharf, before he chucked it in and went into bakery instead.'

'Never mind that,' Connor broke in. 'Where's Mr Judge now?'

'I left my mate with him. He's proper dazed-like, don't seem to know what happened to him. We was going to try and carry him home, but then my mate remembered as how your missus was his daughter so we come here instead, 'cos it was nearer.'

'Where is he now? Why didn't you bring him with you?' Connor demanded.

'We tried that. We got him as far as the corner, but then he wouldn't come no further... Very cussed, the old gent is.'

Connor and Ruth exchanged glances, and Ruth said, 'I'd better go and see to him. You stay here.'

'No, I'll get Mam to mind the bar. Fetch your hat and coat.'

In less than a minute they were out in the pouring rain. The young baker directed them to the end of the street, where they found Marcus Judge sitting on a dustbin, slumped against a wall, supported by the other young baker.

Ruth dropped to her knees on the wet pavement and took her father's hands, which were like ice. His eyes were closed, and she wasn't sure if he was still conscious.

'Father, it's me—Ruth,' she said. 'Don't you know me? I'm your daughter.'

Slowly, Marcus opened his eyes, focussing upon her with difficulty. 'I have no daughter,' he said, forcing the words out one at a time. 'You went away. Rejected your family...'

Connor was about to lift the old man on to his feet, but the second baker warned him: 'Careful! I think he's broken his arm.'

'What's happened to him, for God's sake?'

Marcus glared up at Connor. 'Do not—take the name—of the Almighty—in vain,' he said. 'God is not mocked.'

'But what are you doing out here, at this time of night?' began Ruth, and then she remembered. 'It's Friday night. Of course, you were rent-collecting, weren't you?'

He nodded. 'Rents, every Friday. Where's the bag? Someone's taken my bag.'

They looked about, but there was no sign of the ancient black leather satchel.

'So that's it,' said Connor. 'Somebody knocked him down, took the money and left him lying in the road. Come on, let's get him indoors.'

Suddenly galvanised into life, Marcus drew back his head and glared at Connor.

'Into your public-house? I would not set foot in the place. I wish to go to my own home.'

'That's what he said to us,' said the first bakery man. 'We tried to shift him, but he wouldn't have it. Very strong-minded, he is.'

'Very well. Help me get him up on his feet, and put his good arm round my shoulders,' Connor instructed them. 'We'll get him home somehow, between us.'

The bakery men hesitated awkwardly. 'Trouble is—we're late already. If we don't report on time, they dock our wages, see?'

'Don't worry then, I can manage on my own. You can walk, can't you, Mr Judge? If you put your weight on me?'

They got the old man to stand upright, then Connor began to help him along the street. Ruth offered to lend a hand. 'He can lean on me, too.'

'No, I can manage,' said Connor. 'Don't forget, he's been robbed—you need to report that. Go in and telephone the police and call a doctor, too. Tell them they'll find your dad at home in fifteen minutes or so... And you'd better help Mam in the saloon till I get back.'

Ruth watched them go. Connor was taking most of Marcus's weight, half-steering, half-carrying the old man, and they made slow progress. She thanked the bakery men, then went back to the pub to start telephoning.

When Louisa opened the door to find Connor supporting her husband on the front step, she was very shocked, but as soon as they were inside the house, and she recognised her son-in-law in the dim light of the hall gas-lamp, she felt somehow reassured.

Con brought the old man through to the kitchen. Looking round the room, he asked:

'Is there anyone here to help you, or are you all by yourself?'

Louisa shook her head. 'My sister was here earlier on, but she's gone home now. But I can manage, if you'd be kind enough to help me get him up to bed.'

By that time Connor was very tired, but he squared his shoulders and with some difficulty carried Marcus up the narrow staircase. Between them, they undressed the old man, taking off his sodden clothes and putting him into a flannel nightshirt which had been warming by the kitchen fire.

Marcus was shivering, and he did not seem to understand what was happening. Louisa tried to give him a drink of hot cocoa, but his teeth chattered against the rim of the cup, and he could not swallow it. He was only half-conscious, and could barely speak; he struggled to utter a few words, but they made no sense.

Connor told Louisa as much as he knew, and she sighed. 'He's so silly,' she said gently. 'Just a silly, stubborn old man. He won't be told...'

As they watched, he drowsed off into a feverish sleep. When they heard a knock at the front door, they left him to rest and went downstairs.

A young policeman had arrived in response to Ruth's phone-call and once again Connor had to explain what had happened, as well as he could.

'I looked about for the money-bag on the way over—a black leather satchel, my wife said—but I couldn't see it anywhere. What's the chances of it being picked up? D'you think you'll get the villain who stole it?'

The policeman shrugged. 'Hard to say, Mr O'Dell. We'll do our best, but I can't hold out much hope.'

Connor turned to his mother-in-law. 'How much do you reckon he'd have had in that bag of his? If he'd collected all the week's rents?'

Louisa rubbed her eyes; she was looking exhausted. 'I'm not sure. I could work it out, if you like—he'll have all the figures written in his bank-book. He writes everything down.'

Then she lifted her head, listening. They heard Marcus's voice calling feebly from upstairs: 'Louisa, where are you? What's happened?'

His voice was almost unrecognisable; he sounded so much older. Louisa went up to him, calling out, 'It's all right, Marcus. I'm just coming.'

The young policeman threw Connor a sidelong glance, saying, 'I don't think there's any more I can do here for the moment, sir. I might as well be pushing off. You did say there's a doctor on the way?'

'My wife was going to phone the doctor; he shouldn't be long now.'

'That's all right, then.' But the constable seemed unwilling to leave. He fumbled in an inside pocket and produced his wallet. To Connor's surprise, he pulled out a five-pound note and handed it to him.

'What's this?' he asked, bewildered.

'Payment of a debt, Mr O'Dell. I should have repaid it before now—eight years this has been hanging over me. Well, better late than never, isn't that what they say?'

'Eight years?' Connor stared at him; something in the young policeman's face seemed vaguely familiar. 'You'd not have been much more than a boy, then?'

'Fourteen, I was. We came in to the Watermen late one night, me and my dad. He's passed away now—he hadn't been well, not for a long while. When I left school I was lucky enough to get taken on as a police cadet. Burns is the name—Mike Burns.'

Then it all came back: the midnight break-in, the half-starved, desperate burglar and his young son, and the fiver Connor pushed into the boy's hand before he let them go.

'I've never forgotten that—I'll always be grateful. And I'm glad to have had this chance of telling you so. Good night, sir.'

As they walked along the hall, Connor heard someone coming up the steps to the front door.

'That'll be the doctor now,' he said.

But it wasn't. Another policeman appeared from the drenching darkness, looking for PC Burns and saying, 'I've been sent to find you—there's an emergency call out. Every man's been pulled in to help, on or off-duty. We've got to go to every house on the Island, with a flood warning. The river's burst its banks.'

Emily stood in the middle of the grocery shop, too confused and too scared to decide what she should do. Gloria and Matt had arrived soon after she got home, with a frightening story about the river breaking over the embankment at Cyclops Wharf, so she told them they were welcome to stay the night. She was glad to have them here; if she'd been on her own, she would have been terrified out of her wits.

Gloria and Matt pulled up the roller-blind at the shop door, pressing their faces to the glass and peering out into the blackness.

'You can't see the road no more, or the pavements neither,' said Matt. 'There's nothing there but water.'

Emily drew closer, hovering behind them. She had been getting ready for bed when they arrived, and was still wearing her old carpet-slippers. Suddenly her toes felt ice-cold and wet; looking down, she gave a little cry of alarm. A puddle of water was creeping under the door, advancing steadily across the floor and lapping over her feet.

'Quick! Fetch some towels—old rags—any-thing you can spare, to wedge in the crack under the door,' began Gloria.

'That's no good,' Matt told his mother. 'You'd need sandbags to keep the water out. And if it's got in here, it'll be pouring into the basement by now.'

'The cellar—the stock-room!' gasped Emily. Her face was working, and her fingers flew to her quivering lips. 'All the stores are kept down there—whatever shall we do?'

'We must carry everything upstairs,' said Gloria. 'Come on!'

Emily produced a candle, but her hands were

297

shaking too much to strike the match. Gloria did it for her, and led the way down the cellar steps with her mother and son close behind her. Then she stopped short.

'Too late,' she said. 'We can't go down there.'

The candle did not throw much light, but there was enough to show them the black, swirling water at the foot of the steps, more than a foot deep. Sacks of flour and rice and dried fruit were already half-submerged, and cardboard cartons of food were floating upon the flood. There was a dreadful sucking and gurgling noise as the drains spewed still more water into the cellar.

'We can't do anything about it,' said Gloria. 'We must go back upstairs out of the way.'

Emily found it hard to climb the steps; her legs felt as if they would collapse under her, and she was terrified of falling into that awful black pool and drowning.

Between them, Gloria and Matt managed to help her up the cellar steps, but by the time they reached the ground floor, the shop was awash.

'Don't worry, Ma. Keep going up the stairs—we'll be safe in the bedroom.' As they passed through the back-kitchen, Gloria added, 'P'raps we ought to take the valuables up with us, just in case—silver and cutlery and that, and your handbag. Where's your handbag, Ma?'

Of course Emily had no idea where she had it last, and while they were searching for the bag, they suddenly heard an extraordinary noise, getting louder and louder. Emily put her hand

298

to her heart, moaning, 'Oh, my dear Lord! Whatever's that?'

It sounded like a series of explosions, like frequent bursts of gunfire or a mad percussionist beating a bass drum, and it was coming from the street outside, and getting nearer all the time.

Emily began to sob, 'It's the Germans. They're dropping bombs again. They've declared war!'

Gloria put her arms round the old lady, saying fiercely, 'Don't be so daft, it's nothing of the sort. It's probably just a thunderstorm.'

Matt ran back into the shop, splashing ankle-deep through the water to his vantage-point by the front door.

'It's oil-drums!' he called out. 'A load of empty oil-drums, like they have on the Wharf. They've come loose and floated down on the water. They're banging together and bashing against the walls—that's why they're making such a racket.'

'Can't somebody stop it? Can't anybody do anything?' Emily clutched her daughter, crying helplessly. 'We're all going to die. We're going to be drowned, I know we are...'

In Silmour Street, Rosie had gone upstairs to the children. The noise outside had disturbed them. Five-year-old Sharon was whimpering fretfully while Abram, a year older, stared at his mother with huge dark eyes:

'Is it the end of the world?' he asked.

'Of course not—what an idea!' Rosie cuddled each of the children in turn, trying to calm them and soothe them back to sleep. 'Everything's all right. It's just very bad weather, that's all. Papa's gone down to fetch some things; he'll be up in a minute.'

Luckily the Kleibers used a spare bedroom as their photographic store-room, so most of their stock was safely out of danger on the first floor, but Ernest had gone to retrieve all the cameras and rolls of film from the shop, and bring them upstairs.

'Has the rain got in yet?' Rosie asked, when he appeared on the landing, carrying a box of valuable equipment.

'Not yet, but it could happen at any time.'

Ernest coughed and Rosie suggested, 'Let me go down for the rest of the stuff. The doctor said you mustn't strain yourself.'

'Nonsense! There's only one more load and it's not heavy,' he told her, and went back downstairs.

Somewhere in the street, he could hear a man shouting urgently. He unlocked the shop door, looking out into the night. By the light of a street-lamp, he could see a policeman running towards him, banging on every door along the road.

'The river's up!' he was calling out. 'Take precautions—go up to the top floor. It's coming this way!'

Seeing Ernest in the doorway, he zigzagged across the street, asking breathlessly, 'Are you all right? D'you need any help?'

'No, everything's fine. My wife and children are upstairs.'

'Better go up with them, sir.' The young

constable wiped the raindrops from his face and pointed in the direction of the river. 'The tide's that high, the boats on the waterfront look like they're up above the rooftops...'

Then, as he was speaking, they saw a terrifying spectacle. At the end of Silmour Street, across the Manchester Road, was a ten-foot wall; beyond it were some warehouses and a few old cottages. Now, before their eyes, the entire wall bowed, buckled and collapsed. They could hear nothing through the lashing of wind and water and the continuous drumming of the rain, but they saw a gigantic wave crashing through the buildings—hundreds of tons of water plunging towards them under a crest of white foam, like a line of galloping horses.

'Dear God!' exclaimed Ernest.

'Get inside—upstairs—fast!' said the constable.

'How about you? Come in and take cover.'

'I can't, I've got to report back.' And PC Mike Burns set off the way he had come, still shouting to anyone who might be able to hear him: 'The river's up, heading this way! The river's up!'

Ernest saw him disappear into the night, pursued by the flood-tide, and retreated into the shop. The first gush of water raced in under the door, but he locked and bolted it anyway, then hurried upstairs.

The children had fallen asleep. In a hasty undertone, he told Rosie what was happening.

'Do you suppose the rest of the family are safe, at the pub? Shouldn't we ring through and warn them?' she said.

Ernest had installed a telephone a few months earlier, so he went back to the shop once more and lifted the receiver. Halfway down the stairs, Rosie stood and watched as he jiggled the receiver-rest.

'Nothing,' he said, hanging up again. 'The line's dead; the wires must be down. There's nothing more we can do.'

'Come back, come upstairs.' Rosie held out her hands to him. 'Please, Ernest, hurry!'

Already the water was up to his ankles. He waded through it and went up to his wife, putting his arms round her. As they reached the half-landing, the electric lights went out, leaving them in total darkness.

Rosie clutched him tightly. 'What is it? Is it the fusebox?'

They groped their way to the upper floor, and Ernest went to the front window.

'No. The street-lamps are out—there are no lights anywhere. The power station must be flooded. It's a good job we got a torch for this sort of emergency. Now, where did we put it?'

But neither of them could remember.

Throughout the Island, the hours of darkness were a waking nightmare.

Maudie and Trevor were alone on the attic floor of Joshua's house, with only a small, uncertain night-light to cheer them. Josh and his sons had been called out several hours before, along with every able-bodied man who worked on the docks.

'We must pray.' Maudie closed her eyes. 'We must pray that God will protect them and keep them safe.'

Trevor said nothing, but he had a prayer in his heart too. He prayed that his stepfather and stepbrothers would all be swept away in the flood and drowned, so he could have his mother all to himself, for ever and ever.

At the Watermen, Ruth lit candles and tried to reassure her in-laws; Mary and Patrick sat up in bed, huddled together for comfort, looking old and fragile.

'How are the children?' Mary wanted to know. 'Are they all right?'

'I've just been in to make sure and, would you believe it, they're both sound asleep! How they can sleep through this racket I don't know, but they've managed it somehow. Would you both like a cup of tea? I thought I'd go down and put the kettle on.'

'Oh, you mustn't go downstairs!' Mary exclaimed. 'The kitchen's under water.'

'It's not too bad. I'll take off my shoes and stockings and paddle.'

Ruth tried to make light of it, but she did not enjoy wading through the brown, smelly water. However, there was still a fire burning in the kitchen range, and she was able to fill the kettle and warm the teapot.

Connor had gone to inspect the cellar; she could hear him banging about down below and cursing so she knew he was safe, but she did wish he would hurry.

By the time he reappeared, she had a cup of

303

tea ready and waiting, and he looked as if he needed it.

'Con, you're wet through! What have you been doing?'

He turned in the open doorway and Barker, almost unrecognisable with wet fur plastered to his body, sidled into the kitchen, picking his way miserably through the water.

'This fool of an animal came down after me. The steps were wet and slippery and he fell in! Then he started to panic, swimming for dear life in the dark. I'd only the torch with me, and the battery's near dead by now. In the end I had to jump in and haul him out... God, I'm frozen to the marrow!'

Barker, with an expression that could only be described as hangdog, scrambled up on to the armchair before they could stop him, shaking himself vigorously and showering them both.

For a moment Ruth thought Connor was about to explode with rage then, unexpectedly, he started to laugh. Splashing across the kitchen, he began to tear off his wet clothes, standing near the grate for warmth and chuckling.

'But what's it like down there?' Ruth asked. 'Is the water very deep?'

'Three feet at least. Some of the barrels are floating and bumping about. It's going to be hell's delight clearing up the mess when the water goes down. Still, we must think ourselves lucky. God knows, there will be plenty of poor souls worse off than us this night.'

As he stood there, with the glow of the red coals gleaming on his half-naked body, Ruth thought she had never loved him so much.

On Jubilee Wharf, men were working in the wind and rain, hour after hour, desperately trying to move the cargoes before they were ruined by the floodwater. Hundreds of bales, barrels, crates and boxes were being hoisted to places of safety, but merchandise worth thousands of pounds had already been swept away and lost for ever.

Two barges, heavily laden with timber, were waterlogged and sank; as the planks came loose and floated away, they crashed in all directions, creating an extra hazard for the stevedores. Tonight there was no question of men who needed work being turned off; every man who arrived on the scene was welcome, whether he were a member of the Brotherhood or not.

Among the crowd, Jimmy and Bertie Judge laboured on through the night without stopping; as each load was cleared, they moved immediately to the next. At one moment, Huw Pritchard found himself working beside Joshua Judge, and they shifted crates together. There was no love lost between the two men, but tonight they worked like partners. Josh shouldered his load like all the rest. It was a long time since he had left his office desk and taken a turn at moving cargo, but in this crisis there was nothing to choose between one man and the next.

So the dark hours rolled on, and at last the rain began to ease off and the first streaks of dawn brightened the eastern sky.

The new day brought a new challenge, the

weary business of clearing up the debris and estimating the damage.

Amazingly, although many men and women on the Island had been injured, none had lost their lives, but daylight revealed a scene of terrible devastation.

As soon as she could leave the children, Ruth set out to find her parents and make sure they were safe. As she picked her way through streets she had known all her life, she felt completely lost; everything looked so different.

The flood-tide had receded, but it had left a trail of destruction in its wake. There was not one house which did not bear a high-watermark of mud and slime. Gates had been dragged from their hinges, walls and fences carried away and pathetic heaps of broken furniture lay washed up at street corners.

Though there was no loss of human life, the animals were less fortunate; in one house after another, Ruth heard mothers trying to console weeping children whose pet rabbits had been trapped in their hutches, or poultry drowned in the chicken-runs.

It was a relief when Louisa opened her front door and greeted her. 'You're all safe? So are we, thank God. Come in, dear. Your Aunt Emily's here too.'

Emily was in the kitchen, a little tremulous after her gruelling experience, but very eager to tell her story.

'You mustn't look at me, I'm a perfect fright, I know I am—but I'd left all my clean clothes downstairs in the airing cupboard, and everything was soaked, so when the rescue-party carried me out of the shop, through all that water, I was still in my night-attire—so dreadfully embarrassing... It was very kind of Lou to lend me this blouse and skirt, though of course she is a size bigger than me but there, beggars can't be choosers, can they?' She rattled on, explaining that Gloria and Matt had gone out to see what they could salvage at Cyclops Wharf.

Louisa chimed in, 'I've told them they must come and stay here until they get settled, like Emily. After last night, of course, your aunt will have to shut the shop, but at least she was covered by insurance, so that's some comfort.'

'You're going to have a houseful,' said Ruth, wondering how her father would react. 'And how is Father this morning? What did the doctor have to say?'

Louisa sighed. 'The doctor couldn't get through last night, but he came first thing after breakfast. I'm afraid your father's not at all well. We still don't know how long he was lying out there in the cold and wet. The trouble is, it's not just his arm. The doctor says he's developed pleurisy. He talked about sending him to the Infirmary, but of course your father wouldn't hear of it. It's a good job I shall have Emily to help look after him.'

Louisa turned to her sister and a strange, wistful smile passed between them.

'He's going to need careful nursing,' Emily said. 'But there—sometimes it's rather nice to feel you're needed, isn't it?'

PART TWO

THE THIRTIES

11

Monday, 14 April, 1930

'Oh!' Lil uttered an agonised cry. 'Oh, Mum.'

Ruth stopped ironing immediately. 'What is it?'

'The sky's run off the edge, and it's made Tiger Tim's face all blue,' wailed Lil. 'I've spoiled it now.'

Ruth looked over her daughter's shoulder. The *Rainbow Annual* had been a present for her tenth birthday six weeks ago, and was much loved. By now Lil knew all the stories by heart, but not all the pages had the luxury of coloured illustrations, so she was repairing this omission by painstakingly filling in the outlines of black-and-white drawings with all the care of a medieval monk illuminating a sacred manuscript.

'It's only a tiny scrap of blue. Paint some yellow over it when it's dry and perhaps that will cover it up,' Ruth suggested.

'It won't, it'll just make Tiger Tim green,' Lil objected.

'It will be better than black and white,' Ruth told her. 'Your trouble is, you always want everything to be perfect, and this isn't a perfect world.'

'You never spoke a truer word,' remarked

Mary O'Dell from the chimney corner. 'And if you leave that hot iron resting on Con's shirt, *that* won't be perfect either!'

Hastily, Ruth snatched up the flat-iron —luckily it hadn't left a scorch-mark—but at that moment she was interrupted again by a knock at the side door. Mary glanced at the clock on the dresser.

'That'll be the Welsh feller,' she said. 'He's early—it's not opening-time yet.'

'Is it Huw already?' Lil's face lit up, Tiger Tim's problem instantly forgotten. 'Can I let him in?'

'And you in your nightie? You'll catch your death,' said Ruth. 'You can make yourself useful taking this shirt up to your dad. He's waiting for it.' The girl pulled a face, but did as she was told. As Lil skipped up the stairs, Ruth went along the passage and unlocked the side door.

Huw nodded to her politely. 'Evening, Ruth. How are you?'

'I'm well, thank you, and how are you?'

'Mustn't grumble.'

It was four years since their quarrel at the time of the General Strike. Huw had avoided the Watermen for months after that, and Ruth wondered if they would ever speak to one another again, but then Connor had run across him in the street and told him not to make himself a stranger. He knew that Ruth and Huw had fallen out about the blackleg, but that was all over and done with now, surely? He insisted on bringing Huw back to the saloon and standing him a drink, and when Ruth came into

312

the bar and found Huw there, she had greeted the young man civilly enough.

Since then, on the surface at least the rift seemed to have mended, but they were never quite at ease with one another. Whenever Huw dropped in, he tended to remain in the saloon talking with Connor. He never sought Ruth's company.

The two men continued to have a good deal in common; they shared a mutual interest in boxing, which was why Huw had called in this evening.

'Con's upstairs. He'll be down in a minute,' Ruth explained. 'You're a few minutes early, aren't you? Would you like to come into the kitchen while you're waiting?'

'Thanks all the same but I won't disturb you.' Huw pulled an afternoon edition of the *Star* out of his jacket pocket. 'You carry on. I'll sit in the bar and catch up on the news.'

'Suit yourself.'

Ruth left him in the saloon and returned to the kitchen, where Mary was peering at herself in the glass, patting her hair into place.

'Do I look presentable enough to face the customers?' she asked. 'This blouse was clean on at tea-time, and it looks as if the dog had slept on it already.'

'You look fine,' Ruth told her. 'You're sure you don't mind helping out in the public this evening?'

'Why would I mind? I'm glad I can make myself useful. And I'll have the potman to help me if I'm rushed off me feet. Besides, it's good

313

for Con to take a night off now and then. You know the old saying—all work and no play...'

Connor and Ruth did not take regular time off from the pub, but if Ruth wanted an evening out, Mary was always happy to step in and take a turn behind the bar, and whenever the local amateur boxing championships were on, Connor had got into the habit of going along with Huw, to cast a professional eye over the rising generation. This evening, Daniel was being allowed to go with them as a special treat.

At first, Ruth hadn't been too keen on the idea. She remembered her own mixed feelings when she saw Connor sparring in the boxing-booth at the fairground, long before they were married—her excitement, her fear, her sickening dismay as she heard the cruel thudding of gloved fists and saw the trickle of blood on naked flesh... But she knew she must not keep her son tied to her apron-strings.

'He's fourteen now,' Con had reminded her, 'and he's busting to be a grown-up man, going to prizefights like his da. Let him come along with me and Huw. It'll be an education for him.'

Now Connor and Danny came running down the stairs, the boy hard upon his father's heels, both of them in best suits and shirts with stiff white collars. Looking at them, Ruth could not help feeling proud of her menfolk. Danny was growing taller every day. He'd inherited Sean's handsome regular features, his blue eyes and ready smile, but he had acquired something

314

of Connor, too—a warmth, a depth—that Sean had never known.

'You look very smart, the pair of you,' she said, then addressed herself to Connor alone. 'Don't keep the boy out too late, he's got school tomorrow. And don't lead him astray, d'you hear?'

'At the Public Baths? It's hardly a den of vice,' Con remarked, kissing her lightly. 'We'll be back before closing-time. Where's Huw?'

'Waiting for you in the saloon.' The kitchen clock began to strike, and Ruth added, 'Off you go now, and let me get to work. It's time we were open for business.'

When the little group left and Ruth was unbolting the street doors, Lil hung around behind the saloon bar, saying enviously, 'It's not fair. Why does Danny get to go out with Dad? Why do boys have all the fun?'

'For a start, you're not old enough and anyhow, it's not the kind of thing girls enjoy. You wouldn't like it.'

'How do you know I wouldn't? I can do everything Danny can do. I can whistle, and I can run as fast as him, and I can box—'

'*Watching* a boxing-match is different. I went to one a long while ago, when Dad was fighting. That was enough for me—never again,' said Ruth firmly. 'Now get out of here before anyone sees you—you'll have me shot! Half an hour more to finish your painting and then it's bedtime for you, young lady.'

315

'Silence...' muttered Marcus Judge, but nobody listened to him.

'I just noticed your cushion-covers—haven't they faded?' Emily was saying to her sister. 'This last year or two, since I've been here, they've lost all their colour. Such a nice bright pink they used to be, too.'

'Silence,' he repeated under his breath. 'Silence...'

'It's because they get the afternoon sun on them from the back window,' agreed Louisa. 'That always takes the colour out. Still, we've had them for donkeys' years—we could really do with a new set of cushion-covers.'

Marcus drew a harsh breath, uttering the word more sharply: 'Silence!'

'If you get a nice piece of material, I could help run them up on the sewing-machine,' Emily offered. 'Last time I was in Wickhams, they had some lovely remnants. Ever so reasonable, they were.'

Marcus lifted his head, howling like a wolf. *'Silence!'*

The two old ladies stopped talking and looked across the kitchen in surprise.

'What is it, dear?' Louisa asked. 'Did you want something?'

'I want silence—I want peace in this house!' he complained. 'Must I listen to the everlasting babble of women all the days of my life?'

'I'm sorry, Marcus.' Emily was apologetic. 'Were we talking too much?'

He lay back in his chair, his legs up on a little stool and a rug across his knees, rolling

316

his head from side to side in frustration.

'Am I never to be master in my own house again?' he asked. 'You speak as if I were not here. You gossip about trivial domestic details until my brain feels as if it will split!'

'I thought you liked coming down to sit by the fire,' Louisa reminded him. 'You used to say you felt as if you were in prison, up in the bedroom all the time. Ever since the doctor said you were strong enough to come down here, you've seemed more cheerful.'

It had been a slow and painful convalescence for Marcus Judge. The pleurisy had been very severe, and for a long time his life hung by a thread; and then his broken arm had mended awkwardly, the fracture knitting together in the wrong way, so it had to be re-broken and set all over again.

But he was still a man of great strength—there was no doubt of that. His doctor had told him he would be permanently bedridden, and Marcus was determined to prove that diagnosis wrong. By sheer willpower he had finally got back on to his feet, and at last, with an enormous effort, had managed to cross the bedroom on two walking-sticks, handing himself laboriously down the stairs, clinging on to the rail for all the world, as Josh remarked later, like an old parrot clawing its way around its cage.

During all the time Marcus was marooned in bed, Emily had been helping Louisa to run the house. Driven out of her flat above the shop by a combination of flood-damage and insolvency, she had been grateful to take refuge in her sister's house, and Marcus had suffered torments listening to her light shrill conversation from the floor below, never able to distinguish the words, never knowing quite what she was talking about.

When he first came downstairs, he thought it would be well worth the pain and stress of the journey to be restored to the heart of the household, at the centre of things...only to discover that he was now regarded as a helpless invalid, tolerated when he was not ignored, continually trying to break into the flow of chatter, struggling to reassert himself.

'I will speak my mind!' Marcus ground his teeth. 'I will be heard!'

'Yes, dear, of course you will,' Louisa soothed him. 'What was it you wanted to say?'

'I...' He gasped for breath. By now, he had forgotten what had been in his mind. 'It is time for our nightly reading,' he concluded lamely. 'Pass me the Good Book.'

Louisa got up and took the Bible from the sideboard. It was not their old, original family Bible—that had passed into Ruth's hands long ago—but another volume, a little smaller and a little less weighty.

'Why can't we have our own Bible again?' he complained, turning the pages and screwing up his eyes. 'This print is too small. Tell the girl she must bring it back, d'you hear? Tell her I order her to return it!'

'Don't you worry yourself about our old Bible,' Louisa told him. 'It's safe enough where it is. Ruth will look after it until her children grow up, and then she can pass it on to them, so it will be handed down through the family.'

'They are not our family!' The veins on his forehead were beginning to stand out. 'They are papists, godless idolaters!'

'What a thing to say about your own grandchildren!' Louisa leaned forward. 'Let me find the place for you. Which Book do you want to read tonight? Which chapter and verse?'

'The Book of Judges, of course. Chapter sixteen, verse nineteen.'

'That's one of your favourites, isn't it, Marcus?' said Emily. 'I'm sure I've heard you reading it before.'

Louisa turned the pages, and sighed. 'He comes back to it again and again. There you are, dear—would you like the gas a little brighter?'

Although she gave him as much light as she could, he still found it hard to distinguish the words, as he began in the sonorous boom that had rocked the Emmanuel Chapel for so many years: '...*And she made him sleep upon her knees; and she called for a man, and she caused him to shave off the seven locks of his head, and she began to afflict him, and his strength went from him...*'

Marcus rubbed his eyes, then continued. He lost his place and began a little further down the page.

'...*But the Philistines took him and put out his eyes, and brought him down to Gaza, and bound him with fetters of brass; and he did grind in the prison-house...*'

The front-door knocker beat a brisk tattoo,

and Emily scrambled to her feet, saying, 'There now, whoever can that be? Would you like me to go?'

'*Our God hath delivered into our hands our enemy, and the destroyer of our country, which slew many of us...*'

Emily scurried along the hallway and opened the front door.

'Oh, Glory dear, what a lovely surprise! Do come in. Louisa, you'll never guess—here's Glory come to see us!'

'*And it came to pass, when their hearts were merry...*' The print blurred and swam in a red mist, but Marcus would not give up. He continued from memory as best he could: '*And Samson called upon the Lord, and said, O Lord God*—will you stop that everlasting twittering?—*remember me, I pray Thee, and strengthen me that I may be avenged*'.

Louisa stood up to greet her niece. 'Gloria, come in and sit down. Can I get you a cup of tea?'

'*And Samson took hold of the two middle pillars upon which the house stood. And Samson said, 'Let me die with the Philistines—and he bowed himself with all his might...*'

'What's going on?' asked Gloria. 'Is it a prayer meeting?'

'*And the house fell upon the lords, and upon all the people that were therein...*' Marcus took a long, shuddering breath and invented a conclusion of his own: '*And they were all destroyed...including the women.*'

'Well, that's a cheery sort of welcome, I must

say!' Gloria took off her hat and sat down. 'Evening, Uncle. Keeping well, I hope?'

Marcus put his hand over his eyes. Speechlessly, he shook his head.

'He keeps losing the place, dear,' explained Emily in a stage whisper. 'The doctor says he really needs glasses, but of course he won't hear of it.'

Louisa replaced the Bible on the sideboard, and began to set out cups and saucers.

'And to what do we owe the pleasure of this visit, dear?' Emily asked her daughter, when they were sipping tea. 'Where's Matt? You haven't brought him with you this evening.'

'No, I left him at Josh and Maudie's. Trevor said something about them going out for a walk and, well, it's a nice evening for it. Quite mild for the time of year.'

Marcus gulped his tea noisily, then enquired with heavy irony, 'And is that why you've come to call upon us? To discuss the weather?'

'No, it's not. The fact is, Uncle, you're the one I really came to see. I've got a business proposition to put to you. Well, you and Ma.'

For the first time that evening, Marcus's eyes revealed a gleam of interest. 'How do you mean, business? What sort of business would that be?'

'It's about the old grocery shop,' replied Gloria. 'Ma's old shop.'

Marcus corrected her promptly: '*My* shop.'

'It's been a sort of joint ownership,' Louisa tried to intervene tactfully. 'Your mother put a lot of hard work into it, and Uncle Marcus put in the capital.'

321

'Well, whoever it belongs to, you've had that For Sale board stuck up outside for nearly two years, and never a sniff of an offer so far as I know,' Gloria continued.

'No firm offers as such,' Marcus conceded grudgingly. 'At least, none worth considering. But the property market is very slow at present.'

'Stands to reason. There isn't the money about, what with people going broke and the unemployment figures going up and up—it's something shocking, it really is. That's why I thought we might do a deal, you and me. I'm prepared to make you an offer for that shop.'

'*You?*' Marcus's eyes narrowed and he tried to focus upon Gloria's plump, powdered face. 'You are proposing to buy the corner-shop?'

'Not buy it, rent it. You could let it to me at a fair rent—the shop and the living quarters up above. How much d'you want for it?'

Marcus scowled. 'I wouldn't consider letting. I want an outright sale—I want to recover my capital. And I'm prepared to wait until the right purchaser comes along.'

'In that case you could be waiting from here to kingdom come! Look—I'll play fair with you. As it happens, I've got a little money to lay out. I've just found a buyer for Cyclops Wharf, thank God...' She added quickly, seeing her uncle's face convulse, 'And before you say anything, I'm not swearing. I mean it—I thank God on my bended knees for taking that tumbledown old scrap-heap off my hands, believe you me! Not that I got much for it, mind. The house isn't worth anything, only some prospective builder's got his eye on that stretch of foreshore, for development, see. Anyhow, now I'm looking for somewhere else. I could pay you a small deposit and a reasonable rental, so much a month... What sort of figure would you have in mind?'

Marcus was chewing his whiskers. 'I don't know about that. I'd prefer an outright sale.'

'What do you want the shop for, Gloria?' asked Louisa. 'You're not thinking of going into the grocery trade, are you?'

'Don't make me laugh! I'm going to open a hairdressing shop, my own salon at last. I've done pretty well over the last few years and I've not been a fool with my money, neither—I've managed to put some by. I've got plenty of regular clients and I'm sure I can make a go of it. There's the flat upstairs for me and Matt to live in, and,' glancing across at her mother, Glory saw the wistful look in her eye and added impulsively, 'if you feel like moving back to your old home, Ma, I can only say you'll be very welcome.'

Emily burst into tears immediately, but they were tears of joy.

Marcus continued to grumble. 'I don't know. A hairdressing parlour—it sounds a fly-by-night proposition to me. I wouldn't wish to be involved in anything that—'

'Well, I think it's a splendid idea,' Louisa broke in. 'And Emily can move back to her old place. I can't think of anything nicer.'

Later, when Gloria had left and Marcus had been helped laboriously up the stairs and into bed, he was still complaining.

'No good will come of this, you mark my words. That young woman's little better than a painted Jezebel. I only wish you'd allowed me to speak my mind for once, Louisa.'

'Try not to upset yourself, dear.' She settled him comfortably, tucking in the bedclothes. 'Gloria has done very well with that hairdressing business and I'm sure the new shop will be a success. And besides, it will be nice for Emily, living in her own home again.'

'Yes.' Marcus relaxed against the pillows, and his expression softened infinitesimally. 'That's the only reason I did not oppose the scheme outright. I thought it might be more convenient for Emily and—possibly—not only for Emily...'

They exchanged glances, and Louisa's lips twitched.

'Yes, Marcus,' she said. 'I thought that's what you thought.'

It was very late when Connor and Ruth went up to bed. She sat at the dressing-table, brushing her hair, and in the mirror she could see Con sitting on the edge of the bed in his drawers and undervest. His face was still a little flushed, still exhilarated from the evening's sport.

'You enjoyed yourself, then?' Her hair hung loose and she brushed it with long, slow strokes.

'It wasn't half bad.' He smiled reminiscently. 'And the boy enjoyed it too. I had to hold him down; he kept jumping on to his feet, and the fellers behind us couldn't see the ring.'

'I hope nobody was badly hurt?' Ruth asked.

'No serious injuries?'

'A few black eyes, cuts and bruises—what do you expect at a boxing-match? Huw got quite carried away. For two pins, I believe he'd chuck in his job at the Wharf and try his luck as a fighter.'

'I hope he wouldn't do anything so silly,' said Ruth, turning her head this way and that. 'Con, do you think I should have my hair cut?'

'Between you and me and the gatepost, he'll never get far. He's not got the weight behind him, nor the power in his fists.' Con frowned. 'What was that about cutting your hair?'

'I've had it done like this as long as you've known me. It looks so old-fashioned for nineteen-thirty. The new styles are all short—perhaps I might have it shingled. What do you think?'

He stood up. 'You'll do no such thing. I like your hair the way it is—I've no wish to see it changed. These modern fashions are a passing fancy, no more than that. Don't you know a woman's hair is her crowning glory?'

'Well, if you say so.'

Satisfied, Con moved away and stood before the long narrow mirror set into the wardrobe door.

'Huw's not got what it takes to be a pro,' he resumed in a quieter tone, almost as if he were talking to himself. 'Either you've got it, or you haven't. When I was his age I'd got it, sure enough.'

Ruth put down the brush and turned to her husband; he was studying his body in the glass.

The vest and drawers were not so very different from the outfit she had seen him wearing that night in the prizefight booth at the fairground, and his expression was strange and far away.

'I had the world at my feet—that's what he said.'

'Who said?'

'Mr Cassidy, remember? The American promoter, Leopold Cassidy. He said he could make me into a World Champion. Then the war came and—things turned out different.'

'And now you regret the chance you missed.' Another memory fell into Ruth's mind. 'Of course. A long time ago, you said to me, *"Some people don't know what they want until they've lost it"*. And that's what you wanted, isn't it? The chance to be a World Champion.'

He ran his hands over his chest, breathing deeply, feeling the firm, hard pectorals rise and fall; then he turned away from his reflection.

'No use crying over spilt milk. But like I said the war put a stop to that.'

'No it didn't,' she said.

'What?' He spun round eagerly to face her. 'What d'you mean?'

'It wasn't just the war. When the war finished and you came home, Cassidy offered you a contract then, but you turned it down. You turned it down in order to take on this pub and marry me.' She moved to him swiftly, her hands upon his shoulders, her eyes searching his face. 'Is that the barrier that came between us, Con? Is that what you regret?'

He gripped her wrists, and his voice was

almost savage. 'Don't be so foolish, of course I don't regret marrying you. This place, the family—you're everything in the world to me, you know that.'

He pulled her to him, bringing his lips down to hers, stopping her mouth with a kiss—and his kiss was hard and passionate. But when at last he broke from her and climbed into bed, he still had that strange, faraway look, and although he smiled at her, she had a feeling that he did not really see her at all.

The next morning, Danny and Lil set off to school, with Danny leading the way and Lil following, lingering to gaze in all the shop windows. As they turned into West Ferry Road, Danny hailed his cousin, Matt Judge, and the two boys fell into step.

They were the same age, within a month or two, and though they were not close friends, they were in the same class and often met in the mornings as they dawdled to school, or in the afternoons on the way home, when their pace was quicker.

Today, they had plenty to talk about. Matt was full of news. His mum had come to an arrangement with Grandfather Judge last night, and they were going to move in over the empty shop at Millwall Road as soon as possible.

Danny had news of his own. His head was still whirling after the excitement of the previous evening and he launched upon a highly coloured account of the boxing-bouts at the Baths, but Matt wasn't very interested.

'You should've been with us,' he said. 'Me and Trev—we had a bit of fun last night. We went all the way to Mile End.'

'What's the fun in walking to Mile End and back?' Danny wanted to know.

'Don't be stupid! It wasn't just a walk...Trev's in with this gang, see, and he said 'cos I'm his cousin, I could go along with them.'

Danny wrinkled his brow. 'Hold on! I'm Trev's cousin, too. He never said I could go!'

'You weren't there, were you? You was at the boxing. We did our own fighting—it was a proper lark. You missed a treat.'

'What d'you mean, fighting?'

Matt looked round. Lil had caught up with them, and was hanging on every word.

'If you split on me, I'll pull your tongue out, I will!' he threatened darkly. 'Promise you won't tell nobody? See this wet, see this dry—cut your throat and hope to die?'

Dutifully, Danny and Lil repeated the words and gestures of this dreadful oath.

'All right, then. Trev and his mates took me up to a place called Eric Street, off Mile End Road—it's where a lot of Jew-boys live. Trev's gang had collected a load of bricks and when we got there, we started pelting their houses and smashing all the windows, see? Course, all the yids come jumping out, so then we had a pitched battle—us one end of the street, and them down the other, all chucking bricks. It was a proper beano, believe you me!'

He began to laugh until Danny, rather mystified, asked: 'But what was it all about?

328

What had the Jews done?'

'They hadn't *done* nothing—they're yids, ain't they? Foreigners. I told you, it was just a bit of a lark.'

He laughed again, until Lil chimed in, 'We've got cousins that are Jews, haven't we, Danny? Auntie Rosie's Abram and little Sharon. They're Jews, but we like them all right.'

Matt looked offended. 'You mustn't ever *like* them. Jews are your enemy. You ought to know that—you go to church and all that stuff, don't you?'

'Of course. What's that go to do with it?'

'Well, stands to reason. It's the Jews what murdered Jesus, ain't it? I tell you, they're foreigners—and there's too many bloomin' foreigners round these parts. You can see that for yourselves!'

They had reached Limehouse by this time, and in a sweeping gesture Matt indicated the unreadable ideograms above the chop-suey shops and the yellow faces and pigtails of the passers-by.

'See what I mean? They all live down the Causeway, hundreds of the bleeders...smoking opium pipes and gambling. Trev says the police ought to put a stop to it.'

'Sssh! They'll hear you!' Lil protested. 'Anyway, there's nothing wrong in being Chinese.'

'Gambling's wrong.' Matt went into details. 'They play a game called Puck-a-Poo. You give 'em sixpence, and you get a bit of paper with squares on it and numbers, an' if your squares have got the right numbers, you can win hundreds of pounds back. Something like that, anyhow.'

'Puck-a-Poo?' Lil's interest was aroused. 'Could I play? Are ten-year-olds allowed?'

'You haven't got sixpence,' Danny pointed out. 'And there goes your school-bell. Better run or you'll be late—go on, scoot!'

He delivered her at the entrance of the Junior and Mixed Infants and then, as he went on with Matt into the Senior playground, he started to describe his own exciting night out at the Baths. But another bell began to clang and a teacher blew a whistle, and they all had to fall into line and go into Assembly for morning prayers.

Easter 1930 came and went, and spring brought its own resurrection to the grey terraces of the Island; fresh green leaves broke through black twigs and stunted privet-hedges, and bright dots of colour appeared in flowerpots and window-boxes.

During the next six weeks, the legal details involved with Gloria's move to Millwall Road were completed. On the last Saturday in June, she borrowed a hand-cart from a neighbour and with Matt's assistance began a series of trips from Cyclops Wharf, ferrying their possessions—the sticks of furniture, the clothes, the pots and pans that were the sum total of their worldly goods—and installing them in the flat above the corner-shop.

Emily had been looking forward to the move but she could not tackle such an upheaval all by herself, so Ruth brought Danny and Lil to lend a hand, and between them they helped the old lady to pack. Marcus Judge remained in bed, safely out of the way, while the O'Dell family invaded his domain. He heard their voices and rolled over, burying his head in the pillows—he expressed no desire to acknowledge his grandchildren's existence.

They transported Aunt Emily, bag and baggage, to her old home. It took a long time to get her settled, and tears of joy ran down her cheeks as she took possession of her own dear bedroom once more.

Once that had been accomplished, they turned their attention to the ground floor and began to spring-clean the shop. The shelves were empty and covered in dust, and everything had to be scrubbed. Glory directed operations; she knew how she wanted her salon to look—bright, light and spotlessly clean. She had spent most of her nest-egg on some up-to-date hairdressing equipment, and the workmen would be starting on Monday morning, installing a pair of washbasins and plumbing in running water.

By the end of Saturday, they were tired but triumphant; at least the worst of the donkeywork was over. The shop was empty, but as Glory said, 'You could eat your dinner off the floor'—and she couldn't wait to transform the place with fresh paint and wallpaper.

Ruth collected her children and prepared to leave, saying, 'Come on, time to go home for tea. Dad will be wondering what's become of us.'

Emily, who had just unfolded her best lace tablecloth, looked quite crestfallen. 'Won't you stay and have a bite with us? I'm afraid it's only bought cake—I haven't had time to do any baking—but you're very welcome, and the kettle won't take a minute to boil.'

'No, really, we must be on our way. Thanks all the same.'

'Well, we're very grateful to you for all your help, aren't we, Glory?' Emily rummaged in her handbag. 'And the children have been as good as gold, running up and down, fetching and carrying. They deserve a special present!' She found her purse and doled out sixpence apiece—one to Matt, one to Danny and one to Lil.

On their way back to the pub, Danny discussed various ways of laying out this unexpected windfall. By careful management, sixpence could be made to go a long way—a second-hand comic, a stick of liquorice, an all-day sucker—but he'd also been saving his pocket-money to buy an old gramophone he'd seen in the window of the local rag-and-bone shop. It was hard to decide the best thing to do.

'And how are you going to spend your sixpence, Lil?' Ruth asked.

'I don't know yet,' said the little girl. 'I'll think of something.' She went on thinking about it all through Sunday, and by Monday she had made up her mind, but she was not going to confide in anyone—not even Danny.

On the way to school, they fell in with Matt

as usual. The two boys were counting the days until the end of term, for now they were fourteen and would soon be leaving school for good, and looking for a job.

Trevor, a year older, had already put his schooldays behind him. Joshua had found him a post as a clerk in the Guild Office, so Trevor was following in his late father's footsteps—sitting behind a desk on a high stool and learning the mysteries of double-entry book-keeping. Matt and Danny were in agreement; they didn't fancy that kind of work at all.

'I wouldn't want to push a pen all day,' said Matt. 'Trev says it drives him potty, adding up figures, and they tick him off if he gets the answers wrong or makes a blot. Worse'n being at bloody school!'

Danny glanced back to see if Lil were listening. There was always the danger that she might report an overheard swear-word at home, and then there would be trouble...but Lil was wandering along the pavement's edge with a remote, secret smile on her face, and seemed to be lost in a little world of her own.

Lost... The word came back to him, setting up uncomfortable echoes, when he returned home at the end of the afternoon.

As a rule, the junior school-day ended half an hour before the Senior's, so by the time Danny left the playground, Lil had gone on ahead with some of her classmates who lived in the same area; he never expected to see her on the homeward journey.

Today, when he reached the pub and pushed

open the side door, his mother was standing in the passage.

'Where's Lil?' she asked immediately, and her face was drawn and pale. 'Have you seen her?'

'No, why? Isn't she here?'

Ruth exclaimed impatiently, 'If she was here, I wouldn't be asking, would I? No, she's not here. She should have been home half an hour ago. I telephoned the school; they say she left at the usual time.'

'Perhaps she went to tea with one of her friends,' began Danny.

'Without asking us first?' Ruth shook her head. 'Your dad's gone out to ask around some of the neighbours but I told him she'd never do that without letting us know. Whatever can have happened to her? Can you think of anywhere else she might have gone?'

Suddenly, Danny remembered the sixpence Aunt Emily had given Lil—and then he knew.

12

Danny told his mother vaguely that he had a sort of idea where Lil might be. He was vague because he didn't want to burden her with any additional fears; he said he would go and look for his sister, and that he would come back as quickly as he could.

Ruth wanted to go with him, but he dissuaded her. Suppose Lil should return while they were out? Besides, he could go much faster on his own.

He ran all the way, at first as if he were going back to school, but as soon as he reached Limehouse he struck out in a new direction by Three Colt Street, making for the Chinese Causeway that Matt had told them about. He knew where to find it, though he had never been along the Causeway on his own; it had a sinister reputation throughout the East End.

It was a long, narrow street, so narrow that the sun hardly ever touched it; even on the brightest day, it was dark with shadows. The roadway was made up of big cobblestones, laid at odd angles as if to set traps for the unwary pedestrian. You had to be on your guard in the Causeway. There was not enough room for two people to walk abreast on the thin strip of pavement, and stepping off it was to risk life and limb, for a single horse and cart would take up the entire width of the street, its wheels scraping against the kerbstones on either side.

It hadn't always been known as the Chinese Causeway; the terrace of houses had been lived in by English tenants at one time, but whenever one of them died or moved away, leaving a property vacant, one of the Chinese would move in. By 1930, there was hardly an Englishman left there; only a fishmonger who cured his own kippers and haddocks in the smoke-hole at the side of the shop.

All the other establishments were Chinese —food shops and eating-houses, along with some more mysterious premises with their windows boarded up. Danny had heard rumours that these anonymous frontages concealed gambling-dens.

Halfway along, there was a vacant site where an old building had been torn down, leaving a hole like a missing tooth. On the tiny patch of wasteland and rubble, half a dozen young Chinamen stood in a circle, amusing themselves by playing a game. They were passing a shuttlecock between them, to and fro across the circle, without using their hands; they kept the shuttlecock in the air with the sides of their feet, in a series of deft back-kicks. The object of the exercise seemed to be that it must never touch the ground.

They were dapper young men, in smart well-cut suits, with Western-style collars and ties, and they all wore straw boaters, fixed to their lapels with silk cords to keep them from blowing away. Their only concession to a more traditional appearance was their hair, pomaded and shining, combed tightly into a V-shape at the back, and finished off with a neat pigtail.

Danny would have liked to stay and watch, but he knew he must get on—he had to find Lil. Nerving himself up, he addressed the youngest boy in the group. 'Excuse me. I'm looking for my sister, Lilian O'Dell. Have you seen her?'

The game stopped; the shuttlecock fell to the ground and was ignored. They stared at Danny in silence, then the youngest boy smiled politely.

'Yes, please?' he said.

'My sister—have you seen her?' repeated

336

Danny. 'Her name's Lilian, she's ten years old.'

They looked at one another, and the boy spoke quickly; his words sounded liquid and bell-like, as if they were the call of some strange exotic bird. Two or three of the men replied in similar tones, and then the boy spoke to Danny again. 'Your sister is ten years old? An English girl?'

Danny nodded. 'She's never run away like this before. My mother is very worried.'

More swift, unintelligible Cantonese, and then the boy resumed: 'You come with me, please.' Holding out his hand, he took Danny by the arm.

Danny did not feel at all afraid, although when he looked back on it afterwards, he never understood how he could have been so reckless as to go off with a total stranger, into a house he had never seen before... And yet it seemed perfectly natural at the time.

The boy led him a little further along the road, and turned aside, pushing open a shabby door. It was one of those featureless, boarded-up houses, and at that moment Danny did feel a stab of fear—but he could not turn back now.

They went down a dingy staircase, and the darkness came up to meet them. It was warm and scented, sweetly pungent and flowery. The boy pushed open a door and drew Danny inside.

It was a basement room, with the windows shuttered and curtained, lit only by a dozen tall wax candles in an elaborate centrepiece of red and gold wood, carved in the shape of a dragon bearing a branched tree upon its back.

A low circular table of polished brass stood in the centre of the room, and seated at the table was a very old couple—an ancient gentleman in an ornate silk robe, intricately embroidered with scrolls and flowers, and a still more ancient lady in a shining black gown, her white hair coiled in an elaborate bun upon the top of her head. They both sat on the floor, cross-legged on cushions, surrounded by a dozen children of all ages—from solemn, watchful boys and girls of ten or twelve down to fat, cheerful toddlers in padded jackets and trousers—and among all these people, looking completely at her ease, as if she had been living in a Chinese household all her life, was Lilian.

She looked up, mildly surprised to see her brother. 'Hello, Danny,' she said. 'What are you doing here?'

For a moment he felt very angry. How dare she be so casual and unconcerned, when her family was frantic with worry? However, he controlled himself and replied, 'I've come to take you home. Mum and Dad have been anxious.'

At first she didn't want to go, but the elderly couple understood at once that Lil had to return to her own family, and they rose to their feet, bowing courteously and saying goodbye to her. She had to say goodbye to each of the little children in turn, and they showered gifts upon her—paper flowers, a fan, a toy boat and lots of sticky, glutinous sweets wrapped in cones of brightly coloured paper. Last of all, the old man pressed a sixpenny piece into her hands. She tried to argue, but he insisted that she must keep it, explaining in his halting English that it would bring her good luck.

All the way home, Lil poured out her story, and when they got back to the Watermen, she had to go through it all over again for the benefit of her parents.

As Danny guessed, she had gone to the Causeway because she wanted to play Puck-a-Poo. She had asked every Chinaman she met; some of them did not understand her at all while others told her she was too young, it was not a game for children—but at last she was directed to the basement room, where she had received a warm welcome.

The Chinese have always been very fond of children, and the old couple introduced her to their grandchildren and their great-grandchildren. The old gentleman had taken the sixpence she offered him, giving her in exchange a sheet of Puck-a-Poo numbers; after one cursory glance at it, he told her that she was very fortunate, and that she had won a prize—not just one, but many prizes—toys and sweets of every kind. They gave her some little rice cakes to eat and sweet, sharp-tasting sherbet to drink, and encouraged the children to teach her some of their games.

At the end of the afternoon, the old gentleman explained that it was against the law for a child to take part in a gambling game, but that did not matter since he was going to return her stake-money.

Lil still felt rather guilty about that, as if she had won her prizes under false pretences, but she had had a wonderful afternoon and made some new friends.

'That's all very well,' exclaimed her father when she finally paused for breath, 'but what you don't seem to realise—'

'All right, Con, leave this to me,' said Ruth. 'I'm going to take her up to bed and we'll have a long talk. Come along, Lilian.'

Lil hung her head; when she was called by her full name, things must be serious indeed.

As soon as mother and daughter were out of the room, Con turned to his son. 'Well—no bones broken, anyhow, that's some comfort. When you think what might have happened...'

'The Chinese people were very nice,' Danny tried to explain. 'They'd taken good care of her.'

'That's not the point!' Con burst out angrily, then pulled himself up. 'Sorry, I mustn't take it out on you. You're a good boy, so you are, going and rescuing her like that.'

Then he looked at Danny again, and threw him a half-smile. 'But you'll not be a boy much longer. Practically a young man these days, eh?'

'Yes, Dad. I'll be finished with school in a couple of weeks...and looking for a job.'

Connor cocked his head on one side, doubtfully. 'Are you sure that's what you want? You don't have to leave school yet,

340

you know. You could study some more—make something of yourself. I'm not a rich man, but if you're wanting to stay on and take some examinations—'

'No, Dad. I want to get a job—earn my own living. You left school when you were my age, didn't you?'

'That's different entirely. I never had the choice.'

Danny broke in. 'Mum told me once that the first job you ever had was working on the docks, like Huw. That's what I want to do.'

Later that night, in bed at the end of a long, difficult day, Connor told Ruth what Danny had said. She turned to him in the dark.

'Couldn't you persuade him to change his mind? He's so intelligent. If he sticks at his lessons, he could go a long way. Haven't you any ambition for him?'

'Certainly I have. My ambition is for him to grow up a happy man, with a good wife and family, like myself. He says he wants to follow in my footsteps—how could I advise him otherwise?'

'It's not just you he's following. He wants a job on the docks because of Huw Pritchard,' Ruth said bitterly. 'Huw can do no wrong as far as Danny's concerned. You should have talked him out of it!'

'Huw's a good lad. I know he has some wild political notions in his head, but his heart's in the right place. If Danny wants to take him as an example, he could do a lot worse... Besides, the boy's still young, with his whole life before him.

There's plenty of time for him to take another tack later on, if he fancies going in a different direction. Right now, with unemployment the way it is, he'll be lucky to get any job at all... Do you think you can pull some strings to get him accepted into the Brotherhood?'

Ruth felt an old, familiar sensation of fear, like an icy hand gripping her heart.

'Oh, no—not the Brotherhood, Con. Never that...'

'Why not? Huw will be able to keep an eye on the boy.'

'You know what I feel about the Brotherhood. My father—my brothers—you should know better than anyone what it means to work for them. Have you forgotten the night I met you, all those years ago? After they discovered you were a Catholic, and threw you out? How I found you lying in the street—beaten up, bruised and bloody, and helped get you home?'

Con drew her close to him; the warmth of his body was helping to thaw the chill within her. He put his lips to her ear, murmuring, 'D'you really think I'd forget such a thing as that? If it hadn't been for the Judge family and their black, Bible-thumping Rules and Regulations, I might never have met you at all. That's why I'm grateful to them and their damned Brotherhood—and I always will be.'

His breath tickled her ear, making her squirm. She nestled in his arms, melting under his touch. 'I know, but seriously, Con, you can't want to see Danny in their hands?'

'The Brotherhood's altered a good deal since

342

those days. Your father's not in charge any longer and from all I hear your brother Joshua is a changed man now. It's a hard life on the docks, but it's a healthy life—a year or two of that won't do young Daniel any harm. That's why I thought you could put in a good word for him, with your family. Will you do that, for the boy's sake? For my sake?'

She could not resist; when he kissed and caressed her like that, she felt as if she were a young girl again, helpless in his arms, giving herself to him completely.

'How can I refuse you anything?' she whispered.

'First-class kippers,' said Josh, with his mouth full.

'I'm glad you like them,' said Louisa.

'You know I always enjoy a bit of smoked fish,' said her son, washing down the last morsel with a gulp of tea.

It had become a regular ritual now. Every Friday evening, Josh called on his parents after work, and Louisa gave him his tea before he went out rent-collecting for his father. Ever since Marcus had been attacked and robbed, Josh had taken over this task—as he had gradually taken over so many of his father's duties—and Louisa said the least she could do in return was to cook a meal for him before he set out on his rounds.

'I bought those kippers from the fishmonger in the Causeway; he's got his own smoke-house,' she continued. 'Quite tasty, aren't they? Don't

343

you think so, Marcus?'

'They're well enough.' Marcus picked at his food without enthusiasm. 'Why did you go so far afield to buy kippers? Don't they sell fish round the corner any more?'

'None as good as those,' Louisa told him. 'Besides, I was curious to take a look at the Causeway again. It's true, they're nearly all Chinese living there now. That's where Lilian ran off the other day, silly girl,' she continued artlessly. 'It's a mercy Daniel was able to find her and bring her home safe and sound.'

'Ruth's kids?' Josh looked up, surprised. The O'Dell children were not often mentioned at his father's table. 'What was that all about?'

Marcus put down his knife and fork with a clatter. 'Must we waste our breath, discussing strangers?' he asked.

'What a thing to say! How can you call your grandchildren strangers?' Placidly, Louisa reached out for Marcus's teacup. 'You'd both like second cups, I expect?'

As she poured the tea, she explained. 'I happened to see Ruth the other morning in the market, and we had a chat. She told me what an upset they had. Young Lilian ran off on her way home from school and finished up with some Chinese people.'

She did not fill in all the details, and refrained from mentioning Lilian's attempt to become a gambler. Marcus broke in impatiently. 'I'm sure Joshua is not interested. What those children do is no concern of ours.'

'But it might be, dear, that's why I mentioned

344

it,' said Louisa. 'I was just about to say, Daniel's such a bright boy—he's got a good head on his shoulders, by all accounts—and he'll be leaving school very soon. Ruth tells me he's set his heart on finding work at the docks.'

'Rubbish,' said Marcus crossly. 'It's out of the question.'

'I don't see why. Trevor got a job with the Guild, not so long ago.'

Joshua looked uncomfortable, trying to avert an argument. 'What Father means is that there aren't any more vacancies. We're fully staffed in the Office.'

'Oh, Daniel doesn't want a clerking job. He's keen to work as a docker and wants to join the Brotherhood, like Jimmy and Bertie.'

'Is that a fact?' Josh was taken aback. 'Does he realise how hard the work is? Dockers need plenty of muscle.'

'Daniel's very strong. I've watched him growing up, over the years—he's tall and well-built.'

Marcus was becoming increasingly restive. 'You've been seeing this boy? Meeting Ruth's family in secret, behind my back?'

'Don't be silly, Marcus. I get out and about—I often run into Ruth and the children when I'm shopping. Whether you like it or not, they're still our flesh and blood, and since Daniel's so eager to join the Brotherhood, I—'

'I tell you it's impossible!' Marcus struck the table with his clenched fist, and his cup of tea slopped into the saucer. 'Isn't the boy a practising Roman? Isn't that why his father was expelled from the Guild?'

'You mean his stepfather,' Louisa corrected him. 'Connor O'Dell is Daniel's stepfather.'

'I am well aware of that! She married her deceased husband's brother, against the ruling laid down in the Tables of Kindred and Affinity!'

'I told you, that law's been changed, Father,' Joshua tried to remind him. 'It's perfectly legal for a widow to marry her brother-in-law.'

'I am not concerned with the law of the land. I respect one law, and that is the law of Almighty God!' Marcus's face was becoming mottled, with ugly purple blotches upon his cheeks. 'In any case, the Rules of the Guild are clear enough: members of the Roman Church may not be accepted for membership. That boy is not eligible to join—let that be an end to it!'

Louisa stood up, saying quietly to Joshua, 'I'm afraid Father's overtaxed his strength; he should lie down. Will you help me get him upstairs, dear? He needs to rest.'

Some time later, when Marcus was safely tucked up in bed, Joshua pulled on his hat and coat and prepared to set out on his rounds.

Before he opened the front door, Louisa put her arms round him, saying, 'Thank you for your help, dear. You do so much for us, and I'm truly grateful. Will you think over what I said about young Daniel?'

Joshua sighed. 'You heard Father—he'll never agree.'

Louisa held him a moment longer. 'The worst

thing that ever happened to us was when Ruth walked out of this house. I pray every night that some day her family—our family—will be reconciled. If Daniel were allowed to join the Brotherhood, that might be a step in the right direction.'

'Even though the O'Dells are Roman Catholics?'

'Sssh!' Louisa reached up and put her finger upon her son's lips. 'Your father isn't in charge of the Guild now, and rules can be changed. I'm only asking you to think about it, that's all.'

The following week, Connor was in the saloon when Huw Pritchard called in for a pint. After he had taken his first long swig, he wiped his mouth and said, 'That's better! My tongue's hanging out. It was like a furnace on the Wharf this afternoon.'

'I dare say it was; the thermometer's up in the eighties.'

'And it's due to stay like this for the rest of the week at least. To make matters worse, we were unloading jute. When you're sweating, those damn fibres get inside your clothes and stick to you—I'm itching all over. When the whistle blew, I had half a mind to jump into the water, to cool off!'

Then he pulled a copy of the evening Star from the pocket of his overalls. 'Here, I almost forgot. Have you seen this?' He folded it back to the sports reports, and handed it across the bar. It was not a major news item, just a short paragraph to fill a column.

*American boxing promoter in England... Mr
Leopold Cassidy from Pennsylvania, at one time
manager of black World Heavy-weight Champion
Jack Johnson, arrived in London yesterday at the
start of a European tour, searching for talented
young pugilists. Mr Cassidy is staying at the Royal
Park Hotel, and looks forward to meeting old friends
and colleagues among the boxing fraternity.*

'Isn't that the chap who gave you your big
chance?' Huw asked.

'He wanted to, only my life turned out
different.' As Connor stared at the newsprint,
he saw again the face of the smart American
businessman. 'Leo Cassidy—well, well.'

'You ought to get in touch with him.'

'Think so?' Connor smiled reminiscently.
'He's probably forgotten me by this time.'

'It says he looks forward to seeing old friends.
Why not drop him a line?'

'Maybe I will. Yes, why not?'

Next morning, Connor shut himself in the
office behind the bar, while Ruth was scrubbing
the lino on the floor of the saloon. When she
straightened up, her back aching, the office door
flew open and Con called, 'Ruth, can you spare
a minute? I've been writing a letter. I've had
two or three goes at it, but before I send it off
I'd like you to cast your eye over the spelling.
I don't want to make a fool of myself.'

She read it through; it was brief and to the
point, and she could see that he had taken
great pains with it. His handwriting was careful,
with the words spaced evenly upon the ruled
notepaper. There was not a single smudge, and

the spelling was absolutely correct.

Dear Mr Cassidy, I do not know if you will remember me after this long while, but you were good enough at one time to give me some training, and you told me you had hopes of turning me into a champion. As you know, I did not pursue a career in the ring, and have remained at the above address, managing the public-house, getting married, and raising a family. If you should ever happen to be in this part of town, you will always be very welcome to our hospitality, such as it is. I hope you are keeping well, and that your travels in Europe will be successful. With all good wishes and many happy memories of the old days, I remain your obedient servant, Connor O'Dell.

'Well? What do you think?' he wanted to know.

' "Obedient servant"? That's a bit strong, isn't it?' she objected. 'You're nobody's servant, Con!'

'Oh, that doesn't mean anything. It's only a form of words,' he assured her. 'Anyhow, I've spent long enough writing it. I'm not going to go through it again—not unless I've made a mess of the spelling.'

'The spelling's fine, but what's the point of writing at all? You've nothing to say to the man now, surely?'

'Well—you know, since he's in London... Huw suggested I should make myself known to him.'

'Oh, it was Huw's idea, was it?' Ruth shrugged. 'Well, it's up to you.'

She said no more about it. Connor addressed

the envelope and sealed it, stuck on a stamp and took it to the postbox at the corner, while she went off to scrub the wooden floor in the public bar, and put down fresh sawdust.

The heatwave continued, and after school on Thursday, Daniel was going to the swimming-baths with some of his friends. When Lil heard this, she demanded to be allowed to go as well, but Ruth said that it wasn't fair to saddle Danny with the responsibility of a ten-year-old sister, and refused flatly to allow her to go by herself. Finally they reached a compromise; Ruth would go to the Baths with Lil, watch her while she was in the water, and bring her home again afterwards.

Lil complained that she was being treated like a baby, but was forced to submit to this indignity.

It was another sweltering afternoon. Ruth wished she had sufficient confidence to accompany Lil into the water, but she hadn't gone swimming since she was married, and felt much too self-conscious to hire a costume.

She sat on the steps at the side of the Baths, with the strong smell of chlorine in her nostrils and the endless, echoing roar reverberating under the high glass roof, and felt that time had turned back and that she was a gawky schoolgirl once more. It seemed unimaginable that the slim child splashing in the shallows could be her daughter, and even more incredible that the tall, muscular youth diving into the deep end could be her son...

Then she noticed Danny was treading water,

spluttering and laughing with some of his pals, and among them she saw a face she thought she recognised. The red-haired young man glanced over in her direction and waved; she waved back automatically, only realising a moment later as he scrambled out on to the surrounding tiles that it was Huw Pritchard.

He wandered across and greeted her cheerfully. 'Hello, how are you?' The water ran off his body in silver rivulets, making a puddle round his feet; he was dressed in nothing but a pair of navy-blue woollen trunks which clung to him wetly, outlining every detail of his anatomy. She fixed her eyes upon his face, knowing that she was blushing and feeling very stupid.

'The children wanted to go swimming—I thought I'd keep them company,' she explained lamely.

'That's nice,' he said, 'but you should go in as well. Don't you like swimming?'

'I used to, once upon a time. I've given it up now.' She thanked her lucky stars that she had not been tempted into the water; she could not have faced him if she had been wearing a bathing-suit.

'That's a pity,' he remarked. 'Specially on a day like this.'

'I expect it's one of those things you grow out of.' Frantically, she cast about for another topic of conversation and heard herself say abruptly, 'Like boxing—Connor gave that up years ago. As a matter of fact, I've been meaning to speak to you about that.'

He stared at her. 'I don't understand.'

She had never felt so aware of his physical presence. Struggling to appear calm and composed, she continued, 'He told me you suggested he should write to that American. I wish you hadn't. It only unsettles him, remembering the old days, thinking back to the time when he was a prizefighter. It makes him restless and—well, I just wish you wouldn't encourage him, that's all.'

Now it was Huw's turn to be embarrassed. A slow flush spread across his face as he said stiffly, 'I'm sorry, I didn't realise. We're both keen on boxing—I enjoy hearing about his days in the ring. But of course, if you'd rather we didn't talk about such things...' For the first time, he seemed to be aware of his near-nakedness, and clasped his hands together as if to cover himself. 'Perhaps you'd sooner I didn't come to the pub at all, is that it?'

'No, I didn't say that. I didn't mean—'

'It's all right—I don't .go where I'm not wanted. I'll stay away in future.'

Goaded into action, he turned and dived headlong into the deep water, making his escape.

The heatwave dragged on, week after week, until even those people who had enjoyed the warm weather at first were beginning to grumble, saying it was high time they had some rain to clear the air and wash down the streets.

Huw did not return to the Waterman. Connor was puzzled by his absence, and joked to Ruth that the young Welshman must have found the beer cheaper somewhere else. She looked away, and said nothing.

But the hot summer was good for business, and the pub was packed with customers. As always, the weekends were the busiest time, and one Saturday night, when Con was trying to deal with half a dozen different orders at once, an unexpected visitor dropped in.

'Hi there, Con. How's the world treating you, my friend?'

The American accent was unmistakable. Although Leo Cassidy had aged in the past ten years, he looked as smart as ever in an elegant suit of soft, dove-grey material, which showed off his plum-coloured velvet waistcoat. His hair was silver now, and his sunburned face deeply lined, but he was still every inch the man-about-town.

'Mr Cassidy—this is a real pleasure!' exclaimed Con. 'Take a seat—if you can find one, and allow me to give you a drink. What will it be?'

'I don't suppose you carry bourbon? No, never mind, scotch will do me just fine.'

'Let me call my wife in to take over the bar, so I can come and talk to you,' Connor went on.

'Ah, I was hoping I might meet your good lady. I trust she's keeping well?'

When Con returned with Ruth, Cassidy was as charming as ever, bowing over her hand, telling her she looked even younger and lovelier than he remembered, enquiring after the rest of the family with fervent sincerity—and she didn't believe a word of it. She had never liked or trusted Leopold Cassidy, and saw no reason to change her opinion of him.

But she took Con's place behind the bar with good grace, watching from a distance as the two men settled at a corner table, deep in conversation. As they talked, a strange transformation took place. She saw Con become a young man again. He straightened his shoulders and there was a new light in his eyes, a new vigour in his gestures.

After half an hour, Leo Cassidy pulled out a gold fob-watch and said, 'Time certainly flies when you're in good company—I'd no notion it was so late. But now I've found you again, we'll certainly keep in touch. Next time we might even discuss a little business, maybe? I've an idea at the back of my mind that might appeal to you.'

He said good night to Ruth and kissed her hand, before disappearing in search of a taxi-cab.

'Discuss a little business...' Con turned to Ruth. 'What do you suppose he meant by that?'

'Probably nothing at all. He's a great talker—but I wouldn't take too much notice if I were you,' she advised him.

'Don't be like that!' said Con. 'He's always been straight with me. If he says a thing, he means it.' Then he broke off. 'Hello! Looks like we've another visitor..'

Joshua Judge had just walked through the door. When he saw Con and Ruth behind the bar, he made his way through the crowded saloon.

'Evening, Ruth—Mr O'Dell. Good to see you,' he said, and ordered a pint of bitter.

'On the house, Mr Judge,' said Connor. 'Seeing you're one of the family.'

'That's good of you—it's a family matter I've come about. I thought perhaps I should have a word with your lad—Daniel, isn't it? Is he here?'

'Danny's in the kitchen,' Ruth told him. 'Would you mind coming through? He's still too young to be allowed in the bar.'

'But not too young to be applying for work, I hear?' Josh smiled. 'Thanks, Ruth, I'd like to meet the boy.'

So Ruth took her brother into the kitchen, and introduced him to her mother-in-law and to Danny. They exchanged polite conversation for a few moments, and then Josh said, 'Well, young man, they tell me you're hoping to get a job on the Wharf, working on the ships. Is that right?'

'Yes, sir.'

'I'm glad to hear it. We need bright young chaps like you, and it's a good life if you're not afraid of hard work. My own boys are dockers now, and they've not come to any harm. I don't see why you shouldn't join them.'

'Thanks very much, sir. I won't let you down.'

'You'd better not! You can start on Monday week. Report to my office first thing in the morning—seven-thirty on the dot—and don't be late!'

The following week, Connor received a letter. It was on headed paper, embossed with the crest of the Royal Park Hotel; typewritten, but signed in a flowing hand.

Dear Connor, it was good to see you again. I was especially glad to note that you have kept yourself in trim; I could see at a glance that you still have an excellent physique which many a younger man would be proud of. That was, in part, what helped me to decide to put a certain business proposition to you.

Will you be good enough to come and see me on Monday next? I hope twelve noon would be a convenient time, then we might take a bite of lunch together. I look forward to seeing you again, and will say no more at this stage except to add that you may expect to hear something to your advantage. Yours, with every good wish, Leo Cassidy.

Con showed the letter to Ruth. He could hardly wait for her to finish reading it before he burst out, 'Didn't I tell you he's a man of his word? What do you think he has in mind for me? What do you suppose it is, this business proposition?'

'I really don't know,' she said flatly.

'You don't seem very pleased about it.' His smile dimmed slightly. 'I thought you'd be happy for me.'

'I don't know whether I'm pleased or not—that depends on what he has to say, doesn't it? I suppose you are going to meet him on Monday?'

He stared at her, and laughed. 'I should say

so! You don't imagine I'd refuse an opportunity like this? I turned down Leo Cassidy once before—I'll not make that mistake again.'

He took the letter from her, and his eyes were dancing. Ruth had not the heart to dash his hopes. Even if she had expressed her doubts, she did not think it would have made any difference; his mind was absolutely set upon the forthcoming appointment. For Con, there was only one cloud on the horizon.

'I wonder if Huw will be coming in tonight. We haven't seen him lately, and I'd like to show him this letter. I mean, if it hadn't been for Huw, I'd never have known Cassidy was in London.'

'That's true.' Ruth turned away. 'If there's nothing else I'd better go up and make a start on the bedrooms.'

As she left the room, Connor added under his breath, 'Maybe I'll send the lad a note, and ask him to drop in some time. He'll be pleased about it—I'm sure of that.'

Daniel too was looking forward to Monday. He couldn't wait to start his new life; next week, he would not be a schoolboy any more, but a grown man.

He was grateful to his mother, who had put in a good word for him, and he was grateful to his Uncle Joshua for inviting him to join the Brotherhood. But there was someone else who must have been involved in the decision: the head of the Judge family—the founder of the Guild—his grandfather.

Marcus Judge was not much more than a name to Danny; he was a shadowy figure, scarcely ever mentioned in the O'Dell household. There had been some rift between his grandfather and his mother—he knew she had left home to get married against her father's wishes, and they had never been on good terms since. In the past, Danny had occasionally caught a glimpse of the old man from a distance. Other boys had told him: 'That's old man Judge, see? A proper terror, he is. That's your Grandad.'

He knew that the old gentleman was a semi-invalid now, who never left the house. All the more reason, he thought, why he should make the effort to go and thank him.

He did not tell anyone else what he planned to do; now the school holidays had begun, he had plenty of time on his hands. Nobody asked him where he was going when he left the pub on Friday afternoon and made his way to his grandparents' house. He was a little apprehensive, but his mind was made up. It was only right that he should thank the old man in person.

He was not nervous about meeting his grandmother; he had spoken to her several times, and she had always been kind and affectionate. He looked forward to seeing her again.

Unfortunately for Danny, when he arrived at the house, Louisa had gone out. She had been about to make a cake, and when she cracked an egg into the mixing-bowl, she knew at once that it was stale. It would not take her five minutes

358

to go and buy another, so she told Marcus she wouldn't be long, put on her hat and slipped out, leaving the door on the latch.

As a result, when Danny knocked at Number 26, the Rope Walk, he got no response. He banged the knocker a second time, then heard a faint voice calling inside the house: 'Push the door—it's not locked.'

He tried the door. It swung open, and he walked in. When he entered the kitchen, his heart sank. There was no sign of his grandmother, only the bearded old man, propped up among the cushions of his armchair and glaring at him under beetling brows.

'Well?' Marcus addressed him hoarsely. 'What is it? What do you want?'

Danny took a deep breath. 'I—I've come to say thank you, Grandfather.'

'Eh? What's that? Come closer, boy—who are you?'

Danny took a few steps towards the awesome figure, whose red-rimmed, glittering eyes seemed to see right through him.

'My name's Daniel O'Dell, sir,' he said. 'My mother is your daughter. I want to thank you for letting me join the Brotherhood.'

The old man sat motionless, as if he were carved in stone; the only sound in the room was the laboured rasping each time he drew breath. At last he managed to croak, 'Who told you that, may I ask?'

'Uncle Joshua, sir. Your son.'

Another long silence—and then the old man exhaled a deep sigh. 'Ah, so that's it. Thank you for the information, Daniel O'Dell. You may leave me now.'

Danny didn't need telling twice. Blurting out, 'Good afternoon,' he turned and fled, and did not stop running until he reached the pub. His mother did not ask where he had been, and he did not tell her.

When Louisa got home with a fresh egg and carried on with her baking, she noticed Marcus was unusually silent, but put it down to the weather. It was hotter than ever now, close and sultry, with a crackle of electricity in the air. She could feel a headache developing behind her eyes.

'Must be thunder about,' she remarked, stirring the cake-mixture, but Marcus did not reply.

Although it was a Friday, which meant that Josh would be coming in for tea later, Louisa thought he might prefer some cold meat and salad on such an oppressive day, with a slice of newly baked fruitcake to follow.

Throughout the afternoon, Marcus said nothing at all. Louisa knew something was wrong, but if he did not choose to confide in her, it would be a waste of breath to ask what was the matter. Perhaps he would tell her in his own good time—and if he did not, she would let sleeping dogs lie.

She thought Josh's arrival might stir the old man out of his brooding silence, but Marcus did not seem to notice his son, or return his casual greeting.

Josh took off his jacket, and loosened his

collar and tie. 'It's a scorcher, all right,' he announced. 'You could fry an egg on the pavement.'

'I thought you wouldn't mind a cold supper for once,' said Louisa. 'Just a salad—but there's a nice piece of cold gammon.'

For the first time, Marcus spoke. Without looking up he said softly, 'I'm surprised at you, offering Joshua meat on a Friday, Louisa. He might feel compelled to eat fish instead, out of respect for his Roman friends.'

'What are you talking about, Father?' Joshua was completely at a loss. 'What Roman friends?'

'Friends—or conspirators. I'm referring to your sister and her papist family. Friends of yours, but not of mine.' Slowly, he raised his head. 'Answer me one question, if you please. Did you or did you not agree to let a Catholic become a member of the Guild?'

Joshua found that he was sweating again; he pulled out his handkerchief and mopped his brow.

'If you mean Daniel O'Dell—yes, I said he could join the Brotherhood. After all, Father, he is a member of our family!'

'Do not presume to call me Father—you are no son of mine. I disown you, do you understand?'

Louisa tried to interrupt, but by now he was working himself into a rage and there was no stopping him. At first Marcus's tone was quiet and measured, but as he continued to speak, his words grew louder and louder until they boomed like the tolling of a bell.

'You talk of a family—but I have no family. I have a heavenly Father, and in His infinite wisdom, He has chosen to burden me with all the sorrows known to mankind—trials even greater than those He inflicted upon Job. I have been tested in the fiery furnace, and destroyed in order that I may rise again and ascend to my everlasting reward...I have been struck down by my enemies, and robbed. Those I have tried to help have turned against me, wasting my substance in their foolishness and extravagance. My firstborn son was taken from me by death. My daughter forsook the path of righteousness and scorned her parents' love, removing herself to a place of drunkenness and debauchery, living with two godless men, bearing them pagan children... And now, to crown my misfortunes—to add the cruellest blow of all—I find my one remaining son, the prop and stay of my old age, has turned traitor. We did wrong to christen you Joshua. Your name should be Judas...'

With every word he uttered, his voice gathered power until it rang through the house. He seemed to draw upon mysterious resources of strength; at the height of his passion, he pulled himself up until he stood erect, with no stick to lean upon, pointing a quivering finger at Joshua.

'In your pride and sinfulness, you choose to disobey your father, you break the solemn Rules of our Brotherhood, you strike me down with your faithless treachery. For this will I tear you out of my heart for ever. I will cast you from my sight and my curse shall be upon you, from

362

this day until the world's end!'

As he said these words, they saw a dreadful change come over him. His mouth began to work strangely, his complexion darkened until it was almost black, and a line of foam appeared upon his lips.

Louisa gasped, and put out her hands to him, but it was too late. Before their eyes, Marcus's face seemed to split into two halves; one side drawn up in a terrible rictus, the other side sagging down, one corner of his mouth gaping and slack—and he pitched forward, falling headlong across the tea-table.

Louisa rushed to help him, but Joshua was there before her, saying, 'He's had a stroke. Fetch a doctor... I'll take him up to bed.' Then he lifted the old man in his arms as if he weighed no more than a child, and carried him upstairs.

As Louisa ran through the darkening streets, the first drops of rain began to fall and the first great clap of thunder broke overhead. It was as if Marcus, in his anger, had called down a storm from heaven.

13

Monday should have been a great day for the O'Dell family. Danny was to join the Brotherhood and start work on the Wharf, while his father was going to have lunch with

Leopold Cassidy in order to learn 'something to his advantage'.

Inevitably, the weekend had been shadowed by the news of Ruth's father. The morning after Marcus suffered his stroke, Josh called at the pub to tell her what had happened.

'Have they taken him into the hospital this time?' she asked.

'No, the doctor said there was nothing they could do for him. He just needs to stay in bed and rest; they say there's every chance he'll recover, given time. We just have to hope for the best.'

'How did it happen? Do you know what brought it on?'

Josh's eyes slid away. 'We'd been having a bit of an argument and he got ratty about something I'd said. You know how he is. He worked himself up into a rage and that was it.'

'I'll go round to Mum right away. There might be something I can do,' began Ruth.

'She'll be glad to see you, I'm sure, but I doubt if there's much anyone can do at the moment. Aunt Emily's there to keep her company, and Maudie's going to be with them most of the day as well, in case Mum needs any help with lifting him or washing him—that kind of thing.'

'Well, I'll look in anyhow.'

Ruth did so, and she went again on Sunday morning after Mass—but on both occasions her mother seemed preoccupied, immersed in her own anxieties and the practical problems of caring for a helpless invalid.

On Monday morning, the O'Dells had an early breakfast together in the pub kitchen before Danny set off to work. They were all rather silent. Even Lil, who had nothing exciting to look forward to that day, seemed a little subdued.

Con glanced at Ruth's plate, where a single slice of toast remained almost untouched, and said, 'You've hardly eaten a thing. Are you still worrying about your dad?'

'Not so much about him. I'm more concerned for Mum, really.'

'I'm sure she'll manage. He'll pull through—you'll see.'

'How can you say that?' Ruth asked him irritably. 'You haven't seen him. He's just lying there, staring at the ceiling, with his face all twisted. He doesn't seem to know what's happened to him, or where he is, even.'

'Well, there's one thing I know for sure—your father's as tough as an old boot. He won't give in without a fight.'

Danny interrupted urgently. 'It's ten past seven—I ought to go.'

'You've plenty of time,' Connor assured him. 'You'll be there in ten minutes.'

'I think I'll make a start, just in case.'

Ruth had cut some sandwiches for Danny's midday meal. When she handed them over and said goodbye to her son, she stayed at the pub door and watched him hurrying off along the road, trying not to let anyone see how scared he was, and she sent up a heartfelt prayer.

In the kitchen, Connor was polishing off the last rasher of bacon. Ignoring him, she began to pour two more cups of tea, addressing her daughter: 'Lil—if you've had all you want, you can take these up to Grandma and Grandad.'

Nowadays, Mary and Patrick liked to have a bit of a lie-in every morning. As soon as Lil left the room, carefully carrying the tea-tray, Ruth turned to her husband.

'I don't know. There's so much to do, so much going on, and you sit there as if nothing was happening at all!'

'If you're fretting about the boy now, he's going to be fine,' Connor said easily. 'So don't go upsetting yourself.'

'According to you, we're all going to be fine!'

'And why shouldn't we be?' He rose from the table and stretched his arms, flexing his muscles. 'This could be a new beginning for us all.'

'What do you mean by that?'

'Well, there's Danny starting work—and with any luck, I might be getting an offer as well, later today.'

Sudden anger flared up in Ruth. 'You're talking nonsense! What sort of an offer could that man Cassidy make to you?'

'How do I know? A job of some kind—that's most likely what he has in mind.'

'Con, you have a job already, managing this pub. Isn't that good enough for you?'

He didn't seem to take in what she was saying. His eyes were misty, as if he were focusing upon something else, far away.

'A job...' he repeated softly.' A job in the ring—that's what it will be. He told me I'd kept meself in good shape. He's no fool, he could see at a glance I'm as fit as ever I was.'

Ruth faced him, gripping his shoulders in both hands, forcing him to look at her. 'Do you know what you're saying?' she demanded. 'You've told me often enough that boxing is a young man's game. You don't really think Cassidy is going to make a World Champion of you, at your age?'

'Who said anything about World Champion?' he retorted defensively. 'I'm not exactly an eejit—I realise it's too late for that, but just put the gloves on me and I promise you, I can still give a good account of meself... Good enough to go round the country, taking on all comers. I'll surprise some of these young buckos, you see if I don't. Anyway, forty's no age at all—I'm in the prime of life!'

She let her hands drop to her side, in a gesture of despair. 'Is that really what you want?' she asked him. 'Is that the dream you've been hanging on to, all these years? To leave me, and the children, and go off gallivanting again? What about the pub? What about your family? Don't you think of us at all?'

'Of course I think of you! Don't you see I'll be making good money, enough money to keep you and the kids in luxury for the rest of our lives. And don't bother your head about the pub—we'll be able to afford a full-time manager. You can take things easy at last—it's no more than you deserve.'

'I don't want to take things easy,' she said in a low voice. She felt that she was talking to herself, but she had to say it anyway. 'I want you here—at home with me.'

'Don't you know I'll be coming back to you, every minute I'm free? But while I have the chance, I've got to prove myself, Ruth. Don't you understand?'

'No,' she said. 'I don't understand—and you don't understand me. After all these years, we don't seem to understand each other at all.'

Automatically, she began to clear the table, then went out to the scullery to make a start on the washing-up.

Danny sat in the outer room at the Guild Office, and waited to be summoned before the Inner Circle of the Brotherhood.

His heart was beating so loudly, he felt sure they would hear it too, and guess how frightened he was; and if they suspected that, they might tell him to run away, and come back to them when he was a man. He had to make a good impression upon them; he wished he had put on his best suit, which might have made him look more grown-up—but that would have been no good either, because if he were accepted he would be set to work right away. That was why he was wearing an old shirt and a shabby jacket, and a pair of trousers handed down by his dad, with patches on both knees and across the seat...

He could feel the cold sweat trickling down his spine, and he clenched his fists, digging the nails into the palms of his hands. He had to be strong and brave like Dad, and like Huw. He mustn't let them down; he had to get this job.

The inner door opened suddenly, making him jump and catch his breath. 'You may enter,' said a man he did not recognise.

The windows of the inner office were covered with dark green blinds, so the meeting should be private, hidden from prying eyes. As a result, the room was in a half-darkness.

Through the green gloom, Danny could make out a semi-circular table and behind it nine men who were all strangers to him, except for his Uncle Josh, who was seated at the centre of the line in a position of authority. Joshua looked up and spoke to him solemnly, but not unkindly.

'You may step forward. Come closer, boy.'

Danny licked his lips, swallowed hard, and did as he was told.

'What is your name?'

'Daniel O'Dell, sir.'

'Do you wish to become a member of our Brotherhood, Daniel O'Dell?'

'Yes, please, sir.'

'Are you prepared to abide by the Rules and Regulations of this Guild?'

'Yes, sir, I am.'

Joshua murmured something to the man next to him. Danny couldn't hear what he said, but the man rose and came towards him, carrying a large black book.

'Take the book in your hands, please.' Danny obeyed, and realised it was a Bible. 'Are you prepared to swear an oath of silence, vowing never to repeat to any other person anything you may learn within this Brotherhood?'

'Yes, sir.'

Very well. You will repeat after me—*I, Daniel O'Dell...*'

So the oath was administered, and Danny repeated the words as clearly and carefully as he could, finishing: *'If I should ever break these solemn promises, I shall be duly punished for my misdeeds, and in the last resort expelled from this Guild and cast into darkness, never again to be received within the Brotherhood. All this I swear by Almighty God... Amen.'*

Then Joshua stood up and walked towards him, taking the Bible from him and placing it upon the table, saying, 'Hold out your hands. Accept this tally, accept this claw—as the tools of your trade and the symbols of your membership.'

Danny looked at the two objects he had been given; a brass tally engraved with his Guild number, and a curved double spike with a wooden handle.

'Congratulations, Daniel.' Uncle Josh patted him on the shoulder. 'You have been admitted to our Guild. Now you can go to Number Seven Warehouse, to report for duty and start learning your trade. I'm putting you on one of the shipboard gangs, because you'll find your cousins Jimmy and Bertie there. I'm sure they'll give you all the help they can. Good luck.'

It was a red-letter day for Gloria, too.

'Well, Ruthie?' she said proudly. 'What do you think of it, eh?'

Ruth looked round the new hairdressing salon. Five weeks after Glory had moved in, the shop was open for business.

'Very nice,' she said. 'I wouldn't have known it was the same place.'

Gloria laughed. 'I should hope not, after all the work I've put into it—and the money! Up to last week, I thought the men would never get finished in time, but they managed it somehow, so you're going to be my very first customer.'

The shop had been transformed. Only a few of the old shelves remained, and they were painted in bright, cheerful colours and stocked with bottles of shampoo and setting lotion, packets of hairpins and hair-nets. Two cubicles had been created, each one curtained off between plywood partitions, each with its own basin and mirror and a shiny new chair for customers. There was some gleaming new equipment for hair-drying and permanent-waving.

With a flourish, Gloria shook out a floral wrapper, putting on a very refined voice: 'Would moddom care to take a seat?'

Ruth sat in front of one of the basins. The wrapper was tucked deftly around her and Glory set to work, unpinning Ruth's hair, mixing hot and cold water until she had achieved the correct temperature, and preparing the shampoo.

'You really do like it?' she continued anxiously. 'You're not just saying that?'

'Of course I like it—it's very smart.'

'Oh, good. Only I thought you seemed a

371

bit down in the mouth. I wondered what was wrong.'

Ruth sighed. 'I called in to see Mum on my way, that's all.'

'Oh, lor'. Uncle Marcus hasn't taken a turn for the worse, has he?'

'He's no worse—and no better either. Much the same, according to Mum. I didn't go up to see him. I wanted to, but she said I'd better not. The doctor told her they mustn't do anything that might upset him, and well, we all know how he feels about me...'

Their eyes met in the glass, and Gloria smiled sympathetically. 'It's not your fault he's a cussed old devil—always was, always will be.'

'In a way it is my fault. I stirred things up when I asked them to let Danny join the Brotherhood. Seemingly Father got to hear about it and that's what set him off.'

'It's no good you blaming yourself. If it hadn't been that, it'd have been something else.' Gloria urged her to lean forward over the basin, and began to wash her hair. Changing the subject, she chattered on. 'I thought you'd be sure to bring Lil with you today, seeing she's on holiday. Didn't she want to come and see my new salon?'

'Not today.' Ruth's voice was muffled. 'She's helping her grandma make gingerbread men. She likes putting in the currants for the eyes and buttons down the front.'

'Oh, I can remember doing that when I was a nipper. And what's Danny up to?'

'It's his first day at work. Of course, he thinks

he's a grown-up man now.'

'Bless him. And how's Connor?'

Ruth hesitated for a moment before replying bitterly, 'Connor's on top of the world. He's going up West this morning to meet Mr Cassidy, the boxing promoter. They've having lunch together at some posh hotel.'

When the lathering and rinsing was finished, she raised her dripping head, looking critically at her reflection.

'It's funny, when you come to think about it. Con, Danny, Lil—all of them doing whatever they want to, this morning.' She turned her head this way and that, watching the long strands of wet hair clinging to her like brown seaweed, then added abruptly: 'It's about time I did something I want to do, as well. You can cut my hair today, Glory—I'm sick to death of looking so old-fashioned. Cut it off short, and give me a new style.'

It had been a long, strenuous morning at Number Seven Warehouse.

A timber-ship from Sweden was berthed alongside, and the working gang was divided into two groups: four 'outsiders', unloading on the quayside, and the rest 'inside men'—Danny and eight others—who worked on board the ship, down below in the hold. There were two derricks in use; one above the open hatchway, the other over the ship's side, and as each 'set' of timber was made up, it was hoisted, swung out and lowered on to the Wharf, where it would be transferred to a fleet of waiting lorries.

The hatchwayman was in charge, and under his instruction Danny learned the mysteries of making up a 'set'—piling lengths of timber on to a 'bolster', binding them into a neat load, then hooking it on to a chain attached to the derrick overhead.

Danny found the work hard and uncomfortable. More times than he could count, his fingers were pinched between the heavy timbers, and though he had been given thick leather gauntlets to wear, some splinters still got through. By the time the whistle blew to announce the dinner-break, his hands were bruised and bleeding.

Jimmy and Bertie Judge had thrown him a sullen acknowledgment when they began, then ignored him for the rest of the morning. Huw Pritchard had been more welcoming, but he was one of the 'outsiders' on shore, so Danny had not seen or spoken to him since. He was hoping he might have a chance to talk to Huw during the break.

They all returned to the quayside and Danny went to join Huw, opening the packet of sandwiches his mother had made, but before they could exchange half a dozen words, they were interrupted.

'O'Dell, you're wanted,' said Jimmy Judge.

'Oh? What for?' Danny looked up at his two cousins. They were grinning, as if they shared a private joke.

'You'll find out,' said Bertie, with a knowing wink. 'Come on.'

Danny turned to Huw doubtfully. 'What's it all about?'

Huw frowned at Jimmy. 'Aren't you getting a bit old for kids' games?'

'It's not a game. He's got to be properly initiated into the Brotherhood—we've all gone through it,' said Jimmy. 'We're going to make a man of you, O'Dell.'

They grabbed him by both arms and marched him away, around the corner of the warehouse. Some of the older men in the gang watched them go, guffawing among themselves. Huw shook his head; he knew it was no more than a stupid joke, but there was something about the Judge brothers he didn't care for.

At the back of the warehouse a gang of young stevedores, all in their teens and early twenties, were waiting for Danny.

'Here's the new boy,' said Jimmy. 'All right, lads—get to work!'

They gathered round him immediately, and Danny felt the leaden weight of fear at the pit of his stomach. He remembered his early days at school, and the group of bullies who had set on him in the playground.

He tried to defend himself as they fell upon him, but he never stood a chance. They threw him to the ground and began to tear off his clothes, shouting with laughter and jeering as they exposed his nakedness. Despite his struggles, they stripped and held him down, daubing him all over with a foul-smelling mixture of engine-grease, bilgewater and sawdust.

'Now we're going to give you what for!' yelled Bertie. 'A hundred whacks for good luck!'

375

They rolled him on to his face, spread-eagled upon the cold stones, then took it in turns to strike him—with their fists, their boots, with any stick or stone they could lay hands on, keeping up a singsong count as each blow fell:

'One—two—three—four—'

At first each of the blows was a sharp, searing pain for Danny, but as they went on, the separate pains began to flow together into one continuous pain, until he felt that there was nothing in the world but pain—pain that would never end...

'Twenty-three—twenty-four—twenty-five—'

And then, cutting through the mindless chanting, he heard Huw's voice. 'Stop that! What the hell are you doing?'

The blows ceased, but the pain still went on; Danny lay where he was, shuddering and sobbing for breath under the relentless punishment.

'It's the initiation ceremony,' began Bertie, panting with excitement.

'That's no initiation! What are you trying to do—kill him?'

'If he wants to be in the Brotherhood, he's got to take his medicine,' said Jimmy Judge heavily. 'He'd no right to join in the first place—Grandfather said so. But now he has, he's got to be taught a lesson.'

'Don't be a fool. You're like mad dogs, the lot of you. Get out of here, and think yourselves lucky I stopped you in time. Go on—get out!'

Grumbling among themselves, the gang drifted away and Huw dropped to his knees beside Danny. 'You'll be all right now,' he said

376

quietly. 'Come on, let's clean you up and get some clothes on you.'

When Danny was half-dressed, Huw helped him back to the Office and asked for the primitive first-aid box, applying stinging iodine and plasters to his cuts and grazes. One of the clerks produced a mug of hot sweet tea, and between sips Danny asked Huw, 'What's going to happen to me now? Will I lose my job?'

'Of course you won't. We'll just report it as "superficial injuries incurred during an accident in the course of duty"—and that'll be the end of it. You don't want to put in a complaint and set off more trouble, do you?'

'No, but—they'll have it in for me after this.'

'I don't think so. They know I'm watching them now, and if they try any more of their tricks, I'll have the Union down on them. I don't care whose sons they are!'

At the same moment, slightly less than seven miles to the west, Connor O'Dell was being introduced to the pleasures of the restaurant in a hotel overlooking Hyde Park.

'What do you fancy?' asked Leopold Cassidy. 'Soup, smoked salmon, oysters?'

They were studying the menus; menus so large, with so many different items, Connor had not the faintest idea where to begin.

'I'll have whatever you're having,' he said.

'Fine! I can tell you, I'm going to start with a dozen oysters. I hope you like oysters?'

'I do indeed, though to be honest I've not

tasted 'em more than once or twice in my life. We go in more for shrimps and cockles and jellied eels...but times change, don't they? They say in the old days oysters were so cheap, it was only the poor that used to eat them.'

'Is that so?' Leo Cassidy glanced at the waiter taking their order, embarrassed by the mention of the poor within the Royal Park Hotel. 'What do you recommend to follow, Luigi? Is the beef good today?'

'Very good beef, sir, but today's speciality is saddle of mutton with redcurrant jelly—if you are partial to mutton?'

'OK, we'll take the mutton. Now then, what are we going to drink?'

Luigi faded away and was replaced by the wine-waiter; a bottle of chablis was selected to go with the oysters, while a bottle of claret would accompany the mutton.

As they sat back and waited for the meal to arrive, Cassidy asked, 'Is this the first time you've been to the Royal Park? I always stay here whenever I'm in London. I reckon they do me pretty well.'

Connor looked around. Outside the window, a troop of cavalrymen were trotting their horses back to the barracks at Knightsbridge; inside, the dining-room was bathed in a warm glow of red and gold, with points of light throwing rainbows over the silver and crystal. Expensively dressed men and women sat and conversed in low, confident tones as waiters scurried to and fro to do their bidding. Taking in the scene, he gave a half-smile.

'Yes, I dare say they do,' he said.

Tucked away in an alcove at the far end of the room, a string trio struck up some discreet background music. Connor recognised the dance-tune that was the latest rage—something about *'directing your feet—to the sunny side of the street...'* There was no doubt about it, he was on the sunny side now, all right.

Turning to Cassidy, he asked, 'What was it you wanted to talk about, then? A business proposition, I think you said?'

Cassidy smiled, with the flash of a gold tooth. 'Plenty of time for that later. Never let business spoil your digestion.'

The wine-waiter filled their glasses and Cassidy quoted an old toast: 'Here's to us—who's like us?—damn few!'

He went on to talk in general terms about the leading figures in the boxing fraternity. Connor listened carefully, wanting to make an intelligent contribution to the conversation—which wasn't easy, since Cassidy had seen them all in action, and Connor had only read about them in the newspapers. At the same time, he tried to guess what bearing these sporting celebrities might have upon his own immediate future, but could not see any obvious connection.

The only time Cassidy's talk ceased to be general and became specific was when he broke off abruptly, leaning a little closer and muttering, 'Do you see those two guys that just came in? The older man—going bald—with the gardenia in his buttonhole? And the other one, with his hair slicked down with brilliantine?'

'I see them. The youngster's very light on his feet; from the way he moves, he could be a fighter himself'

'Well done!' Cassidy raised an approving eyebrow. 'You don't miss much, do you? That young man has just won the biggest amateur championship in South Africa, and he's come to Europe to try his luck as a pro. But it's the other guy I want you to take a look at. Study him closely. Memorise that face, so you'll know him another time.'

Rather puzzled, Connor did as he was told. It wouldn't be difficult; the balding man had a shining pink face, and a tiny rosebud mouth almost hidden between folds of fat.

'Yes, I've seen him—who is he?' he wanted to know.

'Never mind that now. Just pull your chair a little more this way, so you'll be hidden by the potted palms. I'd sooner he didn't get too close a look at you.'

Connor put two and two together. 'Would he be another fight promoter, by any chance? Is that why you don't want him to see me?'

Cassidy laughed. 'Now you're being too smart altogether! Like I said, we'll talk about that presently. Here come the oysters—let's eat.'

When the whistle blew for the last time, and Danny's first working day was over, Huw fell in beside him as they left the Wharf.

'I'll come back to the pub with you, if you've no objection,' he said.

'All right, but what am I going to say to Mum?' Danny touched the cut above his left eye, and the graze along his jaw. 'It's lucky she won't see the bruises on my back—but she'll want to know what's happened.'

'That's one of the reasons I'm coming with you. Between us, we'll cook up some kind of a story. And I'm hoping to have a few words with your dad while I'm there.'

Danny looked alarmed. 'You're not going to tell him?'

'I am not. From all I've heard, there's enough bad blood between the two sides of your family already. Least said, soonest mended.'

By the time they reached the Watermen, the pub was open for business. They went in through the side door, and met Ruth in the passage. Seeing Huw, she said awkwardly, 'Oh, it's you. Hello... Well, Danny? How did it go today?' Looking closer, she exclaimed, 'What have you done to your face?'

Danny cleared his throat. 'I had a bit of an accident at work.'

'Nothing serious,' Huw broke in quickly. 'Just a few cuts and bruises, but I thought I should explain...'

'You'd better come through to the kitchen.' Ruth led the way. 'Lil and her grandma went to the park and they're not back yet, and Grandad's upstairs having a rest before this evening, so we've got the place to ourselves.'

In the kitchen, she turned to her son. 'That's an ugly cut—how did it happen? Do you want me to put a dressing on it?'

'I'll be all right, Mum, don't fuss,' Danny told her.

'We've painted it with iodine; it'll soon heal up.' Huw came to Danny's rescue for the second time that day. 'He was packing up a set of timber in the hold when the chain slipped, and some of the planks fell on him. But he's fine now, aren't you?'

'Course I am. Is the boiler on, Mum? Is there enough hot water for a bath?'

'There should be. You'll find a clean towel in the airing cupboard.'

Danny nodded, and made his escape; they heard him running up the stairs.

'That's what he needs,' said Huw. He wouldn't look at Ruth, but kept his eyes fixed on the floor. 'The hot water will bring out the bruises—by tomorrow he'll be right as rain.'

'I'm glad to hear it,' she said coolly. 'Are you going to sit down? Do you want a cup of tea?'

'Please don't trouble yourself. I only looked in to ask if—isn't this the day Connor was going up to see Leopold Cassidy?'

'That's right. They were meeting for lunch, and I haven't seen or heard from him since. No doubt he's enjoying himself so much, he's not noticed the time. He wrote and told you all about it, did he?'

'He sent round a note the other day, asking me why I hadn't been in the pub lately. He sounded a bit put out. That's partly why I called in—I hope you don't mind.'

'It's nothing to do with me, is it? If you and

Connor want to sit round and discuss prizefights all day and all night, that's no business of mine.' Suddenly she burst out, 'Thanks to you, he's talking about taking it up again—going back into the ring! It's the last thing I want him to do, but he's made up his mind, so—'

'He's *what?*' For the first time, Huw looked her full in the face. 'But that's impossible. He's not a young man any more.'

'I tried to tell him that, but he won't listen to me. He says he knows he'll never be a World Champion, but he still thinks he can make a living as a fighter. He's set his heart on it—didn't you know that?'

'I did not. If I had, I'd have done my best to talk him out of it. He's too old to start that all over again—what the hell is Cassidy playing at?' Then Huw's face changed, and he added in a different tone, 'You've done something to your hair. It looks different.'

'I had it cut off. It looks terrible, doesn't it?'

'It looks beautiful. You look—beautiful. I'm sorry.'

'Sorry? For what?'

'For putting my foot in it. You know I love Connor—and I love you—and I want you both to be happy. But everything I do seems to make things worse. I'd better go.'

'No! Huw, wait a minute.'

He was about to leave and she started to follow him. When he turned to her, he found her very close to him, then all at once she was in his arms, and he kissed her—a long, desperate kiss that said more than any words.

When at last they drew apart, he tried to find a way of telling her what she meant to him, but they heard the side door open again, footsteps in the passage and Lil's voice calling, 'Mum! Dad! We're back!'

By the time Mary O'Dell and her granddaughter entered the kitchen, Huw was straightening his collar and Ruth was in the scullery, filling the kettle and saying over her shoulder, 'You're just in time for tea.'

'Oh, good!' Lil greeted Huw enthusiastically. 'Are you going to have tea with us? Where's Dad?'

'Your dad's not back yet, but he should be here any time now.' Huw sounded breathless. 'And I'm not staying for tea—I only dropped in for a minute. So long.'

Lunch at the Royal Park had dragged on for a very long time; they sat over coffee and brandy until they were nearly the last people to leave the restaurant. Then Cassidy said, 'We'll go upstairs now—we can talk there.'

Connor had already had a good deal to drink, and his memory of the next few minutes was a trifle hazy. He had a faint recollection of waiting for a lift, and the strange sensation of gliding upwards in a gilded cage, seeing the different floors falling away one after another, and then walking along a thickly carpeted corridor.

Leopold Cassidy did not have a bedroom; he had an entire suite. He led Connor round it, showing him the marble bathroom and toilet in case he might need it, the huge sitting-room, the balcony outside the french windows, looking out over the tops of trees far below. He demonstrated the very latest glass-and-chromium drinks cabinet, lit from inside when he opened the sliding doors to take out another bottle.

'How do you take your bourbon? Neat, with water, or on the rocks?'

By this time, Con's head was spinning. The Isle of Dogs seemed very far away, and he felt he should leave while he could still tackle the homeward journey. But he couldn't go without finding out what he had come for.

'No, thanks all the same, no more for me.' He waved the glass away. 'You said we were going to talk—why don't we do that?'

Cassidy's gold tooth flashed again as he smiled. 'Right,' he said. 'Let's get down to business. I'm offering you a job.'

Connor nodded sagely. 'I was hoping you might say that.'

'I have to tell you, this is no ordinary job. It needs someone pretty damn special to handle it. That's why I thought of you, my friend.'

A warm satisfaction began to spread through Connor's veins. This was the moment he had been waiting for. 'You're going to send me out on the road again, is that it?'

'On the road? No, what makes you say that? You don't have to go outside London.'

Better and better. Ruth would be pleased, he knew that. 'Fine—it's the London circuit, then? Place like—where was it you first saw me? South

385

Norwood, that's it. You want me to start off with the old demonstration bouts, then match me against the local sportsmen—' He stopped. Cassidy was still smiling, but he was shaking his head.

'You got me wrong. We're not talking about public appearances, we're on to something more private. More—confidential.'

Connor blinked at him, completely at sea.

'Remember that character I pointed out to you during lunch? Old Baldy? He's been giving me a few problems lately, like—there's this young flyweight of mine who's really going places, and that bastard's trying to double-cross me, offering my boy more money and—hell, I don't need to bother you with the details. I just want for you to persuade him he's stepped out of line.'

'But you said a job.' Connor still didn't understand. 'What kind of job would that be?'

'Let me explain. There's nobody else I can turn to—no one who isn't already known in this game. So when you wrote me the other day, it was like the answer to prayer. And when I came and saw you—still tough, still punchy—I knew then you were the only one who could pull it off.'

'What are you telling me?'

'Look, you saw the guy—you'll know him when you see him again, right? Here's what you do. I give you his address and tell you when you can find him at home. You hang around outside, and when he comes out, you grab him and give it to him good... Not too much, we don't want any trouble—just enough to scare the shit out of him, OK?'

'You want to hire me to beat him up?' The warm feeling had drained away; Connor felt very cold now—he began to shiver. 'I thought you were going to offer me a contract to go back in the ring.'

Cassidy settled back comfortably in his armchair and laughed: 'Do me a favour, my friend! Are you living in the past, or what? Those days are long gone, but you can still make yourself a little purse of gold if you do what I—'

That was when something snapped inside Connor. He did not stop to think about it; he acted immediately and instinctively. His first punch landed on the point of Cassidy's jaw, rocking him back and overturning the armchair. But he was still filled with anger; a black, bitter anger that left a taste in his mouth like vomit.

As Cassidy struggled to pick himself up from the floor, Connor grabbed him by the lapels, hauling him to his feet and hitting him again and again, until the man went limp; then he threw him down on the elegant, grey-velvet settee.

He lay there with his head back and his mouth gaping, grunting like a pig, unconscious but alive. Connor took the water-jug from the drinks cabinet and emptied it over his head.

'Maybe that'll bring you round,' he said thickly. 'But when you wake up, don't bother to call me. Sorry, I'm not interested.'

Then he left the luxury suite, making his way

slowly and carefully along the corridor, down
several flights of stairs, out of the hotel and into
the fresh air.

It was nearly eight o'clock by the time he got
back to the pub.

Ruth was serving in the saloon; the moment
he walked through the door, she knew he had
been in some trouble. He moved heavily towards
her, and leant on the counter.

'What happened?' she asked.

'I've got a bit of a headache.' He spaced the
words deliberately, one at a time. 'I need to go
upstairs for a while—and get my head down.'

Connor's father was at his usual place in the
corner; Ruth saw him frown and rise to his feet,
coming over to find out what was wrong.

'Go on up,' she said quickly. 'I'll be with you
as soon as I can.'

She managed to head Patrick off, telling him
Connor was very tired and asking him to stand
in for her behind the bar for a few minutes.
Then she followed her husband upstairs.

She found him sitting at the foot of the
bed, his shoulders sagging, looking down at his
hands, lacing and unlacing his fingers.

'Tell me,' she said.

He began to talk—disjointedly at first, then
gradually filling in the gaps, until she had pieced
the whole story together.

Listening to him she felt ashamed, as if she
were eavesdropping on a misery so intense and
so personal, it was wrong to intrude upon it.
For nearly twenty years, Connor had been the

strongest man she had ever known. Now, within the space of a few hours, he seemed to be falling apart before her eyes—his whole world collapsing in ruins about him.

'I've been a bloody fool,' he said hoarsely. 'I tried to lie to myself. I pretended I could have my life all over again, but even Cassidy knew better than that. He saw me for what I am—a worn-out old pug, good for nothing but a little grievous bodily harm. Today I saw myself through that man's eyes—and I didn't like what I saw.'

Ruth sat beside him on the bed, and put her arm around him. 'You mustn't say that,' she told him. 'You mustn't run yourself down. Cassidy's nothing but a crook, and you're well rid of him.'

'You're right there. I was thinking on my way home, thank God I never signed that contract with him when I left the army. It would have been the biggest mistake of my life.' He turned to her blindly. 'But you knew that all along. You tried to tell me, and I wouldn't listen. I've been drinking too much, as well—but I suppose you know that, too.'

'Do you want me to make some black coffee?'

'No, not yet.' He held her hand. 'Don't leave me for a minute.' Then he screwed up his eyes, peering at her. 'What have you done to your hair?'

'I had it cut off. I was so angry when you left this morning that I went and had my hair cut. You see? I'm as big a fool as you are. We're

389

as bad as one another.'

'No, not you.' As he looked at her, his face cleared and she saw the love shining in those bloodshot eyes. 'I've never seen you like this,' he said. 'You look ten years younger.'

Then he pulled her close to him, and whispered, 'I must have been crazy to think I could go off on my own. I wouldn't last five minutes without you, I know that... And you'd never leave me, would you?'

Her heart went out to him, and as she hugged him, the tears began to run down her cheeks.

'Of course I wouldn't,' she said. 'I'll never leave you.'

14

In October 1932 Poplar prepared to receive a visit from a member of the Royal Family.

Outside the Queen Victoria Seamen's Rest in Jeremiah Street, an excited crowd had gathered to welcome Queen Mary's son, Prince George, who was to make a gracious appearance at the headquarters of the Seamen's Mission.

Hundreds of schoolchildren had been given the afternoon off, and they lined the pavements, each one clutching a paper Union Jack on a stick. Behind them, men and women jostled for the best vantage-points, determined to get a good view of the illustrious visitor.

Not everyone shared these loyal emotions.

Mysteriously, when no one was looking, unwelcoming slogans had appeared, chalked on walls and hoardings. *Seamen are starving while Princes debauch* was one of the more eloquent examples. Nobody knew who was responsible; by the time the slogans were discovered, it was too late to do anything to obliterate them, so harassed officials urged the taller members of the crowd to stand in front of the most offensive messages.

Then the royal car appeared; a schoolteacher led the children through a shrill version of the National Anthem, and many people in the crowd sent up a cheer.

As the car slowed down, about to turn in through the open gates at the front of the Mission, there was a sudden uproar. A dozen men ran out into the road, surrounding the car and shouting: 'We want bread!'

Waving her little flag, twelve-year-old Lil stopped singing in the middle of 'Long to reign over us,' as she recognised one of the protesters.

'You've got motors while our people are starving!' yelled Huw Pritchard.

The disturbance did not last long. The police, already alert for possible trouble among the unemployed men in the district, had reinforcements standing by, and the demonstrators were quickly overwhelmed and dragged away. The royal car moved on, the iron gates closed behind them, and the last rebellious shouts were drowned by patriotic cheering.

The whole thing was over in a matter of minutes, and as the children were led away

391

again in neat crocodiles, two by two, Lil craned her neck, trying to see what had become of Huw—but he had disappeared.

The news of this disgraceful incident swept through the Island very quickly. When Florrie came round to have tea with Louisa, she was full of it.

'Just fancy, men shouting out at His Royal Highness like that! Shocking, isn't it? I don't know what things are coming to, I really don't.'

'The unemployment's shocking too,' Louisa reminded her, as she dished up sausage and mash on three plates. 'It's gone on getting worse and worse, and the Government doesn't seem to do anything about it.'

'I know there's not enough jobs to go round, but that's nobody's fault, is it? Except for all those Roman Catholics and foreigners—breeding like rabbits, they are.'

Louisa knew that this was a dig at the O'Dells, but she kept her mouth shut, refusing to rise to the bait. Thwarted, Florrie got up and took her place at the table, concluding, 'Anyhow, that's no excuse for people to insult the Royal Family, is it?'

From his armchair by the fire, Marcus croaked hoarsely: 'Change and decay in all around I see... These are the times we live in; the Day of judgment is at hand.'

Louisa went over and helped him to his feet. 'Yes, dear,' she said, 'but now it's supper-time. Won't you come and say grace?'

She guided him to his place at the head of the table, and he gripped the table-edge in both hands, his head thrust forward, his craggy face twisted with passion and his eyes blazing with ice and fire as he intoned: 'For what we are about to receive, may the Lord make us truly thankful—and may He strike down the godless, the heathen and the unrighteous, so they shall be destroyed and punished in eternal fire, for ever and ever, amen.'

Then he lowered himself into his chair and began to eat, taking no further interest in the conversation of his wife and daughter-in-law.

As soon as the meal was over, he heaved himself up and crossed the room with painful, stumbling steps, making for the hall.

Florrie leaned forward. 'Is he going out again?' she asked.

'Of course,' replied Louisa. 'Marcus goes out every evening, you know that.'

'It's not right,' Florrie protested, but she spoke quietly for she did not want him to hear. 'You oughtn't to let him do it, at his age. He'll go making himself ill again.'

'He is ill—he's been ill for a long time,' said Louisa. 'And I couldn't stop him, even if I wanted to.'

She went to help her husband into his raincoat, then tied a muffler carefully round his neck and put a battered felt hat on his head.

'The banner,' he mumbled irritably. 'Where's my banner?'

'Where it always is, dear—behind the door. Here you are.'

He took it from her, a wooden pole and crosspiece from which hung a piece of shiny American cloth, painted with seven words in ornate lettering: *The End of the World is Nigh.* She accompanied him as far as the front door, then kissed him on the cheek and watched him shuffle laboriously along the Rope Walk, holding the banner in one hand and supporting himself against the railings with the other.

'Don't stay out too late, Marcus—and don't stand about in a draught and catch cold!'

When he disappeared into the gathering shadows, she sighed and went back to the kitchen, where she began to clear the table. Florrie got up to lend a hand, but continued to grumble. 'He shouldn't be allowed. Suppose he had another of his nasty turns?'

Louisa took the kettle from the stove and filled the stone sink in the back-scullery, to start the washing-up.

'If you mean another stroke, that was two years ago and the doctor said he's made a very good recovery, considering. Oh, he walks slower than he used to and he's not as strong as he was, but that's only to be expected at his age. He'll be seventy-three next birthday, and if he wants to go out spreading the word of the Lord, who am I to say he shouldn't?'

Florrie clicked her tongue disapprovingly as she wielded a tea-cloth. 'I'm very sorry, I don't think it's right. It's not Marcus's job to go out preaching to people. There's a time and place for everything, and he should leave sermons to the Minister at the Chapel.'

'According to Marcus, our new Minister is too easy-going.' The ghost of a smile touched Louisa's lips. 'He doesn't take a strong line, like the Reverend Mr Evans used to, so Marcus feels it's his duty to keep up the old standards.'

'Well, I just wish he wouldn't do it in the streets!' Angrily, Florrie polished a plate. 'Everybody's talking about him—it's very embarrassing.'

'Never mind, dear. We all have our cross to bear.'

Florrie turned on her indignantly. 'It's easy to say that, but I've had more to bear than most! I lost my husband thanks to that terrible war, and my only son ran off to America in disgrace. I'm alone in the world, and as if that's not enough, my father-in-law has to go round making an exhibition of himself!'

'If you go on rubbing the plate like that,' said Louisa mildly, 'you'll scrub the pattern clean off...'

On Friday nights at the pub, those men who were fortunate enough to be in work usually celebrated the opening of their weekly pay-packets, and Ruth and Con were kept busy behind the bar.

'Sixpence and fourpence makes half-a-crown,' said Ruth, expertly counting out change, then turned to the next customer waiting to be served. 'Oh hello, Josh.'

'Evening, Ruth... Mr O'Dell.' Josh nodded at Connor. 'A pint of your best, please.'

Ruth pulled the beer-handle slowly and evenly,

taking care not to let too much foam climb up the side of the glass.

'You're quite a stranger,' she said. 'We don't often see you in the Watermen, do we?'

'It's a bit outside my usual territory,' he replied. He slurred his words, and she realised that he had taken a few drinks already. 'I was wondering if Huw Pritchard might be here,' he continued, looking around.

'I haven't seen him,' said Ruth. 'I believe he's working tonight. I know Danny is, and I think he said Huw would be on the late-shift with him.'

'That's right. We've three ships to load and get off before morning,' agreed Josh. 'A good few of our men are working double shifts today, but Pritchard turned down extra money for some reason. He didn't report for work this morning, either. I was wondering why that was.'

'I couldn't tell you, I'm afraid.' Rather tight-lipped, Ruth slid the brimming glass across the counter without spilling a drop.

'Thanks. I thought he might have gone to the Seamen's Mission.' Josh raised the beer to his lips. 'Your very good health! I hear there was a spot of bother there this afternoon—some troublemaker was arrested, they say.'

Ruth and Con looked at one another. When Lil came home at tea-time, she had given them a dramatic account of the incident, and Huw's part in it.

'We've been in all day,' Con said. 'We wouldn't know anything about that.'

396

'Ah, I see.' Joshua took his drink and moved away, finding a seat near the door.

Con said quietly to Ruth, 'You don't suppose it was Huw that got took up by the police?'

'How should I know?' she retorted. 'Anyway, it's nothing to do with us. What Huw Pritchard does is his business—and if he gets into hot water, it's his own look-out.' She tried to speak calmly, but the colour in her cheeks betrayed her.

'Why d'you say a thing like that?' Con reproached her gently. 'Talking of the lad as if he were a stranger. You know very well you're fond of him—we both are.'

Ruth bit her lip. Ever since that evening when Huw had kissed her, she had tried to put him from her mind. She was a happily married woman; she loved her husband and her children—she had everything in life a woman could ask for. Why should she want anything more?

And yet she could never quite forget that moment when Huw had taken her in his arms. Sometimes at night she dreamed of it, and awoke to find herself lying beside Con, guilty and oppressed under the weight of her secret.

Huw had continued to visit the pub from time to time, but he took care never to be left alone with Ruth. He realised that she and Connor were reunited, and that he could never be more than an observer—a friend, a supporter—but always an outsider.

Half an hour later, when the saloon was

bursting at the seams, he walked into the bar. As usual, he came up to the counter, throwing a polite smile at Ruth, but addressing Connor.

'I told Danny I'd meet him here. Is he ready to go?'

Ruth went and called her son. He was waiting in the kitchen, his donkey-jacket over his shoulders, his sandwich-tin and a flask of coffee in a canvas satchel. As soon as he came into the bar, he greeted Huw eagerly.

'You're all right, then? Lil said she saw you at the—'

Connor cut in quickly, 'Of course he's all right. Now be off the pair of you, before you're late for work.'

Huw threw him a grateful glance and headed for the door, but Josh stood up, barring their way.

'Evening, Pritchard,' he said. 'Do you mind telling me just what you've been up to this afternoon? You weren't with your Socialist cronies at Jeremiah Street, by any chance?'

Huw shrugged, smiling broadly. 'Don't you know I'm on the night-shift, Mr Judge? I'll need my wits about me for that. If I hadn't taken a few hours' shut-eye this afternoon, I'd be hard put to it to keep awake, wouldn't I? Come on, Danny-boy, let's go. Good night, Mr Judge.'

'Night, Uncle,' mumbled Danny, following Huw out.

His face darkening, Josh pushed through to the bar to have his pint mug refilled, saying: 'You shouldn't encourage the boy to make a friend of him. That young man's too sharp by half. He'll be cutting his own throat one of these days.' Out in the street, Danny was asking, 'Why did Uncle Josh want to know where you were?'

'The Brotherhood don't like its members to take an interest in politics,' said Huw. 'Leastways, not my kind of politics.'

'Your politics are no concern of his,' declared Danny. 'It's a free country, isn't it?'

'Not yet it isn't,' said Huw shortly.

'Anyhow, what did happen at Jeremiah Street?' Danny went on. 'Lil said she only saw you for a minute, then you vanished.'

'The coppers moved in, ten of them to each one of us, but I was too quick for 'em. One of my mates got clobbered—he'll be spending the night in the cells.'

'Suppose the police had got you as well?' Danny wanted to know. 'What would Uncle Josh have done? He couldn't kick you out of the Guild for a thing like that, could he?'

'The Brotherhood have their own ways and means. Didn't anyone ever tell you about the Punishment Squad? I'd have been chucked out all right—and beaten up into the bargain, most likely.'

They turned the corner and began the long walk around the dockyard wall. Behind them, a solitary figure in an old raincoat and battered felt hat emerged from the darkness, taking his place opposite the Watermen.

Inside the saloon, Josh drained his glass, wiping his mouth with the back of his hand. 'I'll say good night then,' he said to Ruth.

At that moment, there was a brief, inexplicable pause in the chatter and clatter of the pub, and Ruth remarked, 'Must be an angel flying overhead. Good night, Josh. Give my love to Maudie.'

He turned to the door, and in the comparative quiet they all heard a voice from the street, declaiming hoarsely: 'The end of the world is nigh. Repent ye, for the Day of judgment cometh, when sinners and drunkards and fornicators shall be cast upon the everlasting bonfire...'

A cheerful roar went up from the customers. They all knew that voice—by now Marcus had become a familiar figure throughout the Island, and his threats of damnation were a source of ribald amusement.

Ruth did not laugh; neither did Josh.

'He picks on us about once a week. We're one of his regular targets,' she said. 'Does he know you're here?'

'I hope not. How could he know?'

'Then he'd better not see you. I'll let you out by the side door, and you can slip off down the alley.'

'No.' Breathing deeply, Josh tried to clear his fuddled brain. 'Why shouldn't he see me? Do you think I'm afraid of my own father?' Setting his jaw, he walked out into the street.

When he saw Joshua, Marcus Judge hesitated for no more than a second in the middle of his diatribe, then continued in a harsh, penetrating voice.

'Wine is a mocker—strong drink is raging.

400

Woe to that man who doth not honour his father; it were better for him that he should have a millstone tied about his neck, and be flung into the deepest waters to drown in his sin and shame. Woe to the wine-bibber, woe to the ungrateful son—for he shall be condemned to perish in the eternal flames of hell...'

Crossing the road, Joshua ignored the outstretched, clawing fingers and passed by the old man, saying thickly, 'Thank you, Father...and the same to you.'

Some time after midnight, Danny was working with Huw, loading bales of wool on to a ship bound for Greenland. They made up sets—three huge bales at a time—running a chain round them and hooking them on to the crane that would hoist them inboard.

Each time they made up a new set, they had to wait for the crane to swing back and drop its hook again; for a moment they were able to talk.

'Will you be making any more protests, after today?' Danny asked.

'You don't suppose we're going to let it rest there, do you?' exclaimed Huw. 'There's a demonstration organised for Sunday afternoon, when we're marching from Poplar Town Hall right through the Island, over to Limehouse and back along East India Dock Road. Do you want to come with us?'

Danny's eyes lit up. 'Yes, I'll come,' he began, then his face fell. 'I've just remembered, I can't.

We've got to go out to tea on Sunday, to our relations.'

'Oh, you don't want to waste time at tea-parties,' Huw told him. 'You can get out of that, can't you?'

'I'd like to, but it's a bit special, people who are going abroad—we'll probably never see them again. Besides, I sort of promised Mum.'

'Oh, well, in that case. Some other time, perhaps.'

The crane clanked and rattled overhead, and they set to work again.

An hour later, when the whistle blew, they stopped to take their break. While Danny was eating his sandwiches, the foreman came by and looked over the gang as they sat around, perched on bales of wool.

'Gentlemen of leisure, eh?' he said. 'Well, I want a couple of lads to do a special errand for me right away. We just had word that the starboard light at the river-gate is out of fuel. I want two volunteers to carry some oil-cans—you and you!'

He pointed at Danny and another sixteen-year-old—a lanky youth called Cheshire, known to his mates as 'Cheesey'.

Danny swallowed a last mouthful and stood up, while Cheesey Cheshire hung back, whining, 'Do I have to? I only just started me supper.'

'It'll still be there when you get back. Come on, look alive—if that lamp's not alight in the next three minutes, there'll be hell to pay! Jump to it!'

The dock was fed from the river through

402

a pair of lock-gates, keeping the water at a permanent depth, whatever the state of the tide. When the gates were open, shipping was able to pass through, and for navigation after dark, the two pierheads were crowned with red and green lights respectively.

The boys set off, walking the length of the stone jetty, each boy carrying two large cans of oil.

Danny was not a particular friend of Cheesey's, but he did his best to be pleasant, chatting about this and that. Cheesey did not seem to be in a talkative mood, answering in curt monosyllables, and presently his pace slowed down to a crawl.

'What's up?' Danny asked. 'Got a stone in your shoe?'

'No.' Cheesey swallowed. 'Tell you what, I'll wait here. You go on to the lightkeeper, then come back for the other cans, all right?'

'What's the point of that? If we both go, we'll get the job done quicker.'

'Yes, but I'd sooner stop here. You can go.'

'But why?' Even in the darkness, Danny could see that Cheesey's face was pale. 'What's wrong with you?'

'I don't want to go along there,' Cheesey muttered. 'They say as how it's haunted, along the river-wall.'

'Get away!' laughed Danny. 'You don't believe that stuff, do you?'

'It's true. There was a man died, long ago...' Cheesey lowered his voice and moved closer. 'One of the dockers—murdered, he was.

Nobody knows who did it; he just disappeared, like. Weeks later they fished him out of the river, over that wall there—drowned dead. People say his ghost comes back sometimes, this time of night. I don't care what the bloody foreman says, I ain't going any further!'

'There's no such thing as ghosts, that's a load of nonsense,' Danny began, but when he realised that no argument would shift Cheesey, he finally capitulated. 'All right. I'll take my oil-cans, then come back for yours.'

He continued along the narrow stone jetty by himself. Of course there was no truth in those stupid stories. He wasn't a kid any longer, to be scared by bogey-men. All the same, it was very dark. After the noise and bustle of a working quayside, it seemed eerily silent by the river's edge, with no sound but the slip-slopping of water against the stone wall and the occasional moan of a ship's hooter, far away.

Then his skin crawled, and the hairs upon the backs of his hands pricked up, as he felt a weird sensation. It was like walking through spiders' webs, as if he were breaking innumerable cobwebs, clinging softly to his face... It was absurd, for how could there be cobwebs floating above the river? But the sensation was so vivid, he set down the oil-cans and brushed his face with his fingertips. There was nothing there...and yet there had been *something*...

He got to the end of the jetty at top speed and handed over his two cans to the old lightkeeper, who asked irritably what had taken him so long.

Danny said, 'There's two more to come—I'll be as quick as I can.' About to set off again, he added suddenly, 'Have you ever heard any tales about a ghost out on the river-wall?'

The man looked up sharply. 'Just seen something, have you? Out of the corner of your eye?'

'I've seen nothing—and heard nothing. But I had a strange feeling...'

'Ah.' The old man spat into the river, lapping below them in the darkness, then muttered, 'Between sundown and first light, just at the turn of the tide. If you ain't seen or heard nothing, you can think yourself lucky, boy. And don't ask no more questions.'

'Ruth! Come in—it's lovely to see you.'

On Sunday afternoon, Ruth took Lil and Danny to Silmour Street, at Rosie's invitation. She explained that Connor sent his apologies, as he had a prior engagement at the pub, but she did not go on to explain that she had left her husband with his feet up on the bed, keeping his weekly appointment with the sports pages of the News of the World. Tea-parties were not quite Con's style.

All the same, this was a special occasion.

Rose and Ernest welcomed the O'Dells, ushering them through the photographic shop and up the stairs to their sitting-room on the first floor, where the best china was laid out on the best tablecloth.

The Kleiber children—quiet, watchful Abram and pretty little Sharon—leaped to their feet to greet the visitors, but the guests of honour were the three members of the Brendel family—Sarah, her son and her husband.

'You remember Klaus Brendel, don't you?' Rosie prompted Ruth. 'And of course you know Ben.'

Correct as ever, Klaus bowed over Ruth's hand. At his shoulder, a tall young man of eighteen smiled shyly.

'Herr Brendel, how nice to see you again. It's been a long time,' said Ruth. 'And Benjamin! I must admit I wouldn't have known you, Ben. The last time I saw you, you were still a boy—and now you're a grown man.' Then she turned to Sarah, and the two women hugged one another, both talking at once.

'It's been too long—much too long,' Ruth continued. 'I'm ashamed that we've never been to see you since you moved to North London, but it's such a difficult journey.'

'I know, and I've been just as bad,' confessed Sarah. 'It's the thought of waiting about at bus-stops, and all those changes... Hampstead and the Isle of Dogs are such a long way apart.'

'And now you're going still further away?'

'Yes, we are to return to Frankfurt, my home-town,' said Klaus. 'We pack up and move to Germany on the first day of November.'

'I was very surprised when Rose told me,' Ruth said. 'I thought you had settled down so well in England.'

'I have been happy here, and I have prospered in my work,' agreed Klaus. 'But I have always kept in touch with my original employers, the pharmaceutical company in Germany. And because of the experience I have gained in London, they have now offered me an excellent post in their Overseas Marketing Department. I shall be in charge of selling the company's products throughout Great Britain and the United States of America. It was too good an offer for me to refuse.'

'Yes, I see, that's wonderful,' said Ruth as they took their places round the tea-table. 'Congratulations.'

'Naturally I am most happy to be returning to my own country, and my own people. Ten years ago, the economic situation in Germany was on the brink of disaster; now it is very different. The National Socialists are the biggest and most powerful party, and—'

'You mean the Nazis, don't you?' said Ernest quietly. 'You are a great admirer of Adolf Hitler, I believe.'

'How can anyone not admire such a man? Look at what he has already achieved. I tell you, very soon the whole of Germany will be united under his leadership.'

'He is not universally admired,' retorted Ernest. 'Many of the Jewish people are already making arrangements to leave Germany, just at the time you are going back there.'

Klaus smiled pleasantly. 'No doubt they have their reasons, but those reasons do not apply to me as I am not myself a Jew.'

'Perhaps not, but surely—' Ernest turned to Sarah who looked away, embarrassed.

'Sarah no longer practises her religion; she

and Benjamin have become Freethinkers, as I am,' said Klaus.

Rosie, who had been pouring cups of tea and trying to break into this conversation, seized her opportunity. 'That's enough politics. Let's see, who takes sugar? Sharon, pass round the bread-and-butter, will you? There's watercress and celery and shrimps; everybody's got to help themselves.'

They all began to eat, and the talk became general. Ernest, who was sitting next to Danny, asked, 'Tell me, how are you getting on these days, Daniel? Of course you have left school now. Have you managed to find any work? Perhaps you are helping your father at the Watermen?'

'No, I've got a job at Jubilee Wharf, working on the docks,' said Danny.

Ernest put down his knife and fork and stared at Danny as if he could not believe his ears.

'You mean to say you are working for that man Judge? You are a member of the Brotherhood?'

'Joshua Judge is my uncle,' Danny reminded him. 'I was lucky to be taken on, the way things are now. But Mum put in a word for me.'

'Did she indeed? I must say you surprise me.' It was as if a shutter had come down; Ernest's face was giving nothing away. 'I hope you are happy in your work.'

'Oh yes, I am.' Danny could not help adding, 'Excuse me for asking, but don't you approve of the Brotherhood?'

'I do not. If you must know, I would rather

you were employed anywhere else in the world, than you should work for such people. But that is only my personal opinion. You must do as you think best.'

He turned away and began to talk to Lil, who was sitting on his other side. For the rest of the meal he ignored Danny altogether.

When tea was over, Rosie began to clear the table. 'If we're going to have a lot of grown-up talk, it will be very boring for the children,' she said. 'Abram, Sharon—why don't you take your cousins up to the attic and show them the model trains?'

Uncertainly, Benjamin half-rose to his feet but Rosie gestured to him, urging him to sit down again. 'Oh no, Ben, I don't mean you! You must stay here and talk to us.'

Privately, Danny was rather hurt to be included among 'the children'. He was only two years younger than Ben, after all, but he said nothing and obediently followed the others up to the attic.

Ernest had put in a skylight and a loft-ladder, converting the whole attic floor into a playroom for his son and daughter. Abram swung the ladder down, and invited the visitors to climb it.

'I don't want to go into the attic,' Sharon announced suddenly. 'I'm tired of those rotten old trains. Lil, let's go into my room and I'll show you my new frock...'

Sharon was two years younger than Lil, but she took charge of the situation so firmly, Lil found herself doing what she was told. Ever since Sharon was old enough to make her wishes known, she had possessed the knack of getting her own way.

They went into her bedroom, and she explained, 'I've got the biggest room after Mumsie and Papa. Abram's room is tiny—it's just a box-room really, but he doesn't need much space, being a boy. I've got heaps of clothes, that's why I have to have this big cupboard.'

She flung open the wardrobe door and began to bring out her latest acquisitions, including a pair of silver shoes with diamanté buckles and metal plates on the soles and heels.

'These are my new tap-shoes,' she said. 'Aren't they gorgeous? I suppose you know Mum sends me to the Grosvenor Academy now?'

'No, I didn't know that. What's the Grosvenor Academy?'

'It's a dancing-school in the house where Papa's mother and father used to live in Poplar. Miss Ethel Grosvenor runs it. She used to be a professional once, dancing on the stage. She teaches tap and classical, and her sister Miss Hilda plays the piano. I go every Tuesday and Thursday evening. Miss Ethel says she's putting me in for my bronze medal this term, and I'm going to be in the Rosebud Ballet—would you like to see my costume?'

As she spoke, she was already throwing off her clothes. When she was down to her vest and knickers, she put on a net tutu in bright pink, with the bodice covered in artificial-silk petals. Then she pulled on her ballet shoes, lacing them and keeping up a running commentary at the same time.

'These are blocked shoes, so I can do point-work. Miss Ethel says I'll never be a prima ballerina now, and that's Mumsie's fault 'cos she didn't start me off at classes when I was little, but she says I've got a lot of talent, and if I practise hard she's almost sure she can get me into the Christmas panto at the Queens, as a Rosebud in the ballet and a Baby Snowflake in the Winter Wonderland finale...'

Lil sat and watched and listened, not understanding half Sharon was saying, but just letting it all wash over her, marvelling at her cousin's self-assurance. It must be wonderful, she thought, to be ten years old and so absolutely confident, knowing exactly what you wanted to do.

At twelve, there were so many things Lil would like to do; sometimes she wanted to go on an aeroplane and fly round the world—to explore darkest Africa, or die for her country—but those things would all be so much easier if she were a boy. Most of all, she wanted desperately to be like Danny...

Upstairs in the attic, Abram was demonstrating the model train circuit; it was his pride and joy, and a hobby that he shared with his father. On his knees beside the tracks, he asked Danny, 'Have you got a model railway at home?'

Danny shook his head. 'I never had a toy train.'

'I suppose you're a bit old to start now,' Abram said regretfully, 'though Papa often helps with the layout when he can spare the time. It's not just for kids, you know.'

'I'm sure it's not,' said Danny politely.

The gap that yawned between eleven and sixteen seemed very wide; he put on a show of interest, but as he watched the Hornby locomotives whirring round the rails—frequently overturning on the sharper bends and having to be carefully replaced on the track—he kept thinking of Huw on the protest march, and wishing he were out there with him, striding along, shoulder to shoulder.

Abram saw the look on his face and said, 'It's not much fun for you, is it? Mum shouldn't have packed you off with us. You're not "children"—you're grown-up now. I heard you talking to Papa over tea—you work at the docks, don't you?'

'That's right. Your father didn't seem too keen on the idea.'

'No, well—he's got special reasons for feeling badly about it.' Abram sat back on his heels with such a sad, thoughtful expression that Danny suddenly had the strange feeling that, at eleven, Abram was more grown-up than he was himself. 'It's because of his brother.'

'Whose brother?'

'Papa's brother—Izzy Kleiber. He worked in the docks, too. He was a member of the Brotherhood, like you. Didn't you know that?'

'No, I didn't.'

'Uncle Izzy was Benjamin's father. He was

412

Sarah's first husband, before she married Herr Brendel.'

'You keep saying "he was". What happened to him? Is he dead?'

'Oh, yes.' Abram looked up into Danny's face and went on. 'When I was old enough to understand, Papa told me how his brother died. He said he broke some Regulation—he talked about things that were going on, to people outside the Brotherhood.'

Surprised, Danny agreed. 'Yes, that's one of their strict Rules. You have to swear an oath of secrecy when you—' Then he realised that he was in danger of breaking the oath himself, and stopped.

'That's what Papa said. And he told me there's something called a Punishment Squad, isn't there? Well, when Izzy broke the Rules, he thought as long as he left the Brotherhood, they wouldn't be able to do anything, but they went after him all the same and one night—he just disappeared. He was missing for weeks; everybody was crazy with worry. Then the police found him. They fished him up out of the river—what was left of him. That's what the Brotherhood did to Uncle Izzy. That's why my papa doesn't like them much.'

It was twilight when they left Silmour Street. Since the clock had gone back a few weeks ago, the days were drawing in very early and the smoke of bonfires mingled with river-mist, thickening the fading light.

413

Turning into Manchester Road on their way back to the pub, the O'Dells heard the sound of music. Coming towards them, lit by flaming torches, they saw a small procession led by a scratch four-piece band—a trumpet, a pair of banjos and a concertina. Two men carried a banner stretched between two poles, bearing the slogan: *We Want Work!*

Ruth sighed. 'It reminds me of the ex-servicemen we used to see years ago, just after the war. Different men, but the message is the same.'

Danny wasn't listening; suddenly he tore off his cap, waving it frantically.

'It's Huw! Look, Mum—there's Huw! He asked me to go on the march, so I'll be able to go part of the way, anyhow. See you later!' And he took to his heels, racing up the road. Ruth called after him, but the cheerful music drowned her words.

Proudly, he took his place beside Huw at the back of the procession, and as they passed Ruth and Lil, the two young men threw them a mock salute. Huw turned to Danny.

'You've arrived at the right moment—my arms are aching. Here, you can carry this for a while,' and he handed Danny a banner proclaiming: *Communist Party of Great Britain—East London Branch.*

'Is that what you belong to?' Danny asked. 'Are you a Communist?'

'Of course. A fully paid-up member, that's me. Well, we've had a Labour Government, and they didn't do anything to stop the rot.

Communism's the only answer now.'

'Can I join, too?'

'When you're a bit older, why not?'

Holding his head high, Danny stepped out in time to the music—a very free version of *The Sun Has Got His Hat On.*

'"Hip-hip-hip-hooray...."' Huw swung along with the band, breaking off to interpolate: 'Of course the words are rubbish, but it's a good tune to march to.'

Under cover of the music, Danny said abruptly, 'Huw, I've got something to tell you.'

'Oh yes? And what's that?'

'You know what I said the other night, that story about the man who was drowned outside the river-wall?'

'Your ghost story?' Huw grinned. 'What about it?'

'I just found out there *was* a man drowned out there. And it was the Brotherhood that killed him—the Punishment Squad.'

'Keep your voice down, can't you?' Huw glanced round uneasily. 'Not so loud.'

Carefully and quietly, Danny repeated as much as he knew about Izzy Kleiber's death. When he had finished, Huw was silent.

'Well, what do you think?' Danny asked. 'Could it be true?'

Huw's face gleamed red in the flickering torchlight. When he spoke at last, his voice was low.

'I don't know, but I promise you one thing... I'm going to find out.'

415

15

It was late on Thursday afternoon, but the sun was shining so brightly and the air was so soft and warm, it seemed as if evening would never come.

Lil was walking across the Island on her way to Millwall Road, when a pleasant voice broke in on her thoughts.

'Hello, dear. It is Lilian, isn't it?'

It was her grandmother—her other grand-mother, whom she did not know very well, for they only met occasionally, like this, and at long intervals. Louisa kissed her, then looked her up and down approvingly.

'I do believe you're taller than ever, and you're filling out, too; you're quite a young lady. Let's see—how old are you now?'

'Thirteen, Grandma.'

'My goodness gracious, the older I get, the more the time flies.'

She was carrying a bulging shopping-bag, and Lil immediately offered to carry it for her. Gratefully, the old lady handed it over.

'That's good of you—it was beginning to get a little heavy. I've just been down to the market for some potatoes. As a rule I like to do all my shopping first thing, when I'm feeling fresh. I did go to the greengrocer's this morning, and I meant to get some then, but that's another thing about growing old—you forget things. It wasn't till I started to make your grandfather's tea that I realised there were no potatoes! And where are you off to, this time of day?'

'I'm going over to Auntie Glory. I go most evenings, as soon as I've finished my homework,' explained Lil. 'She's teaching me hairdressing. That's what I'm going to do next year, when I leave school.'

It was an arrangement that suited both parties very well. Gloria had a young assistant to help her from nine to five every day, but the salon stayed open in the evenings, too. Many of her clients had daytime jobs and could only have their hair done after work, so it had been agreed that Lil should go over to help Glory and learn the trade in her spare time.

At first Ruth had been against the idea. When she was Lil's age, she had had dreams of becoming a schoolteacher. Her headmistress told Marcus she wanted to put Ruth in for a scholarship, because she felt sure Ruth would win a place at a teacher-training college, but Marcus had refused his permission, and Ruth had never forgiven him. Instead, after she left school she had been sent to help Aunt Emily in the old corner grocery. Now the grocery shop was a hairdressing salon, and though Ruth and Con would have been proud and happy for their daughter to train as a teacher, it was Lil who couldn't wait to leave school. She was impatient to follow Danny's example and start to earn her own living.

'If that's what she wants,' Connor had said

finally, 'we can't stand in her way. And there's many worse things she could do. Face the facts—she's a pretty girl. I dare say in a few years she'll meet some young chap and chuck her job in to get married and start a family, so it'll all come to the same thing in the end. After all, what does it matter as long as she's happy?'

Reluctantly, Ruth had been forced to agree, so now Lil was earning a little extra pocket-money at the salon, shampooing the clients' hair, and then watching and learning as Glory expounded the mysteries of shingling and tinting and permanent-waving.

'So you go all the way to Millwall every afternoon, and back again every evening?' enquired Louisa, as they walked side by side. 'What time do you get home at night?'

'Different times. Eight o'clock—nearer nine, sometimes.'

'But it's dark by nine! I don't like to think of you walking all that way in the dark.' Suddenly Louisa's face brightened and she asked, 'You haven't got a bicycle, have you? Do you know how to ride one?'

'A lot of the girls at school have got bikes, and they let me have a go. I'm not very good at it, but I can ride without falling off.'

'Well, that's the main thing, isn't it? Can you spare five minutes to call in at our house on your way, or will it make you late?'

'I don't think five minutes will make any difference, but won't Grandfather be cross?

Mum says he doesn't like us going into his house.'

'That won't matter; he'll be upstairs having his afternoon rest. Come on—I've got a surprise for you.'

They went through the house, leaving the bag of potatoes on the kitchen table, then through the scullery and out into the backyard. Next to the outside privy was an old shed. Long ago, when Josh and Eb were boys, they had taken up carpentry, making rickety footstools, or a hutch to keep rabbits in, or a model boat with sails, and this shed had been their workshop. Nobody used it now. Louisa had to struggle to push the door open, for the hinges were stiff, and inside was a clutter of odds and ends: some woodwork tools, a set of blades for a fretsaw, a soapbox which Josh had once tried to turn into a doll's-house for Ruth, but due to some long-forgotten quarrel had never been finished and, hung up by two hooks in the back wall, an old bicycle.

Between them, they lifted it down and set it upright, and Louisa's face fell. 'Oh dear, I hadn't realised it had got into this state. Just look at it!'

It had no cross-bar, for it was a lady's bicycle, more than twenty years old. There was rust on the handlebars and the glass lens in the lamp was broken. Both tyres were flat and the pump was missing.

'It used to belong to your mother, She rode it to school and to choir-practice in the evenings—that's what reminded me. After she left home, she didn't need it any more, so it's been here ever since. But you can't possibly ride it like that.'

Lil said hopefully, 'I can try! Could I take it with me? I can wheel it home and I bet Danny would help me fix it up. It only needs cleaning, then it'll be as good as new.'

'Well, if you really think so. I'll give you a hand getting it through the house.'

With some difficulty they manoeuvred the bicycle through the scullery and into the kitchen.

'Mind how you go. Be careful of the wallpaper,' Louisa began.

Then they heard a strange, choking sound and they looked round. Marcus Judge had come downstairs, hanging on to the banisters; he was standing and swaying on the bottom step. He gazed at Lil wide-eyed, his mouth sagging. Pointing a shaky finger, he managed to force out the words: 'What are you doing here?'

'I invited her, Marcus, and she's just leaving. We mustn't keep you, dear. I don't want to make you late.' As quickly as she could, Louisa bustled Lil and the bicycle along the hall and out into the street.

'What's the matter with Grandfather?' Lil whispered. 'Why is he looking like that? Is he ill again?'

'Not really. He's been asleep and when he first wakes up, he gets confused. Don't worry about that—he'll be all right. Off you go. Give my regards to Gloria and my love to your mother.'

She watched Lil wheeling the bike along the street, then went back to see to her husband. Marcus had managed to get to his armchair and sat there, huddled up, staring at Louisa with haunted, fearful eyes.

'Who was that girl?' he asked.

'That's Lilian, your granddaughter. Didn't you recognise her?'

He took a long, shuddering breath and seemed to relax a little.

'I thought I was going off my head,' he said at last. 'I didn't know what was happening. Seeing her there like that with the bicycle, I thought she was Ruth—our Ruth—come back to us again...'

In a very similar house, just a few streets away, Maudie sat in the kitchen with a sewing-basket on her lap. Having to keep house for a husband, a son and two stepsons occupied all her time. When she wasn't cooking for them, or cleaning their rooms and making their beds, or doing their washing and ironing, there was always the mending waiting to be done. Four grown men took a lot of looking after. They were forever making holes in the toes of their socks, or wearing through the heels. There were always threadbare places in their vests and underpants which needed patching or darning—frayed collars or cuffs to be turned and replaced so the worn parts wouldn't show... The work was endless. It made her eyes ache and her fingers sore.

Tonight it seemed especially difficult. Maudie

found it hard to concentrate on her work, for Josh and Trev were sitting at the table with a draught-board between them, two glass tumblers, a bottle of scotch and a jug of water. She could smell the whisky right across the room; she had smelled it on Josh's breath often enough when he came to bed. Nearly always, it was the signal for a bout of clumsy, sweaty love-making, and the fumes from the bottle made her feel sick.

To make it worse, there was a smoky fug hanging in the air, for both men were puffing cigarettes. Josh never used to smoke in the house when she first married him. She knew he enjoyed a pipe of tobacco when he was out with his cronies or at the pub, but last year Trevor had taken up cigarettes, and soon Josh had acquired the habit, too.

She could hardly complain when it was her own son who had introduced cigarettes into the house. She wished Trev wouldn't smoke, but he was eighteen now and she couldn't treat him like a schoolboy any more. She didn't like him drinking either, but what could she say when he brought home a bottle and invited his stepfather to share it with him?

Of course she was glad they were getting on so much better these days. That was a great comfort, because for years Trev had been so difficult and sullen with Josh and now they had become almost like pals.

Lifting her head from her sewing, she saw Trev replenishing Josh's empty glass and saying, 'Drown your sorrows, guv'nor. I'm sorry to have to say it, but you've lost again. That's half-a-crown you owe me.' He made a swift series of moves, one white draught leapfrogging over Josh's black pieces, bringing the game to a sudden end.

'Well, damn and blast! How'd you manage that?' Josh scowled, and took another drink of scotch. 'We'll have to have another game—you must let me have my revenge.'

'Sorry, guv, not tonight. We're supposed to be going back to the Office, remember? If we don't get the books up to date for the annual audit next week, we'll have the accountants on our necks.'

Originally, Maudie had tried to persuade Trevor to call Joshua 'Dad', like the other boys, but he refused point-blank. In time he settled on 'guv'nor'. It was half-cheeky, half-respectful—and by now she rather liked it.

Josh pushed his chair back and struggled to his feet. 'You're right, as usual. Time to go back to the Office—work before pleasure,' he said solemnly, then spoiled the effect by losing his balance and falling back into the chair.

'That's all right, guv. You've had a long day—I expect you're tired. Look, why don't I go and finish off the paperwork tonight? Then all you've got to do is sign the accounts when you come in tomorrow.'

'Good idea, that's the answer.' Joshua beamed at Trevor and turned to Maudie. 'You should be proud of your boy; he's got a head on his shoulders.'

Trevor took his straw boater from the hall-stand and cocked it at a rakish angle.

'Good night, Ma!' he sang out. 'I've got my key. I might call on a few chums when I finish work, so don't wait up, will you?'

As he was going out, he met Jimmy and Bertie coming in. They grunted as they passed him in the hall, slamming the front door after him. Though Josh and Trevor were now on good terms, there was still no love lost between Josh's sons and their stepbrother.

Maudie put aside her mending and stood up. 'Shall I clear the table?' she asked. 'You'll be wanting your supper, I expect?'

'Later on,' said Jimmy. 'Not just now.'

'We got something to talk to Dad about,' chimed in Bertie. 'Something important.'

'Important—and private.' Jimmy continued. 'It's to do with the Brotherhood, so if you don't mind...'

'Oh, all right. You'd like me to go upstairs for a while, is that it?' Maudie picked up her sewing-basket. 'I'll take this to the bedroom, then I can get on with it while you talk business.'

As she climbed the stairs, she thought. When we were first married, Josh would never have let the boys speak to me like that. Now they treat me like a servant, and he doesn't even notice.

She tried to be patient, telling herself that one day things would come right for her and Josh. When he wasn't so worried about the Brotherhood, and about his father, he'd be able to enjoy life again. He wouldn't drink so much or smoke so much—he'd be in love with her, the way he used to be. And quite soon no doubt the boys would be getting married to some nice girls and setting up homes of their own. Even darling Trev would leave home one day, and though she'd miss him dreadfully, she knew that would be right for him, too. Then she and Josh would be on their own, with nothing to worry about—nothing to do but love one another, and be happy...

With a little sigh, she settled herself on the big double bed and began to darn one of Bertie's socks.

Downstairs, Jimmy and Bertie sat facing their father across the table. He took another mouthful of whisky, squinting a little as he tried to bring them into sharp focus.

'What's the trouble?' he asked.

'It's Pritchard again,' said Jimmy. 'Up to his old tricks.'

'He's not threatening to call the Union members out on strike again? Just let him try it; he'll be in for a big surprise,' said Josh quickly. 'We don't need him or his flaming Union. Let 'em stay off work if they want to—we've got enough members to keep the ships moving without them.'

'Dad, just a minute.' Jimmy tried to break in. 'Hold your horses, will you?'

'Who said anything about strikes?' demanded Bertie. 'He's been asking questions again.'

'What sort of questions?'

'Questions about the Guild. Remember last year, when he kept pestering everybody about the

425

Punishment Squad? Like—what the sentences were, who carried them out... You had to call him in and give him a warning.'

'Yes, well, that shut him up, didn't it?'

'For a while it did. Only now he's started again. Some stupid berk must have been talking too much; seems he's heard about the Discipline Register, and as soon as he found out there was a book somewhere with all the details in it, he got very interested. Wants to know where the Register's kept, who's in charge of it—all that.'

Bertie nodded, echoing his brother. 'All that... Stirring up trouble all over again. Will you give him another going-over, or kick him out of the Guild?'

Josh shut his eyes. 'You know damn well I can't do that. If we expel him without any reasonable cause, the Union will play merry hell.'

He tried to cudgel his brains. He knew something must be done, but just at the moment he was finding it hard to think straight. Rousing himself, he cradled his glass in his hands and stared into it, watching the brown liquid eddy in spinning circles...

'No use talking to him—I tried that,' he said.

'So what are you going to do?'

'I won't do anything, not this time.' Suddenly Josh felt supremely confident; master of the situation. 'This time, it's up to you boys. I'm leaving it in your hands. You can deal with him.'

Then he lifted his tumbler, and emptied it in one gulp.

Danny scrubbed away at the rusty handlebars and said, 'Tell me some more about the—what's it called? The something Register...'

'The Discipline Register,' said Huw. 'Chuck me that spanner, Lil, there's a good girl.'

They were sitting in the sun outside the back door of the Watermen on Saturday afternoon, surrounded by oil-cans, metal-polish and the contents of Huw's tool-kit. When Lil asked Danny to renovate the old bike, he had enlisted Huw's assistance.

In his shirtsleeves, Huw was struggling with the bicycle-chain, which had slipped its cogs. He was determined that the machine should be absolutely safe before he would let Lil take it out on the road.

She passed him the spanner, watching and listening with great interest. 'What's a Discipline Register?' she wanted to know.

Instead of answering her question, Huw countered: 'I'm busting for a cup of tea, aren't you, Danny? How about nipping indoors and putting the kettle on, Lil?'

'Oh, all right. But don't say anything important till I get back!' she told him, and vanished into the scullery.

'Better not talk about the Register while your sister's around,' Huw cautioned Danny under his breath.

'Why not? Because it's secret Brotherhood business?'

'Not only that,' said Huw. 'It's not exactly suitable for a young lady's ears.'

'What d'you mean? What sort of thing do they put into this Register?'

'Every time the Inner Circle sentence one of their members to be punished, they enter it in the Register—the date, the name of the offender, the nature of the offence, the type of punishment and the names of the chaps who carry it out—everything.'

'So you think there might be something about Izzy Kleiber, the night the Punishment Squad got him?'

'I should imagine so. And I'll do my best to find out.'

'But how? Do you know where the Register's kept?'

'Somewhere in the Guild Office—in Mr Judge's desk, probably.'

'Then you haven't got a hope of finding it. How would you ever get in there to look through his desk?'

'I've thought about that. Next Monday I'm on nights again, and I've noticed lately that Judge's stepson has been working in the evenings, on his own. If I call in there before I start work, with some query about my pay-packet, he'll leave me in the front office while he goes off to look up my file in Accounts. While he's busy, I'll nip into Mr Judge's room.'

'Suppose he comes back and catches you?'

'He won't...and if he does, I'll persuade him to keep his trap shut. He's a crooked little devil—he'll turn a blind eye if I slip him a quid.' Then he added, 'I suppose I shouldn't say that. He's one of your relations, isn't he?'

'Trevor? Yes, he's a sort of cousin—but you don't have to apologise. I can't stick him, either. All our Judge cousins are a bit peculiar.'

'Not all of them. Matt's not so bad,' said Lil, from the scullery door.

Huw looked up sharply. 'Hello—that was quick,' he said. 'How long have you been standing there?'

'Not long. I'm just waiting for the kettle to boil,' she told him.

'You shouldn't listen in on other people's conversations,' said Danny loftily. 'And what do you know about Matt, anyhow? You haven't seen him since he left school.'

'That's all you know, clever-dick. I see him every time I go over to help Auntie Glory, don't I? Sometimes he helps me sweep the salon afterwards, and clean the washbasins. It's funny, he never bothered to speak to me when we were all going to school together, but he's been quite friendly lately. I don't know why.'

Exasperated, Danny interrupted. 'You don't half talk rubbish sometimes. Go and keep an eye on that kettle, before it boils over.'

Tossing her head, she did as she was told and Danny turned back to Huw. 'So you're going to try and get a look at the Register? Suppose you do find out something about Izzy Kleiber, what will you do?'

'If I find any proof, there's only one thing I can do,' said Huw quietly. 'I'll have to go to the police.'

429

Unfortunately, things didn't work out quite the way he'd planned.

When he signed in for work on Monday evening, Huw went straight to the Guild headquarters and saw a light in the window. He knocked at the door of the Accounts Office, but got no reply, so he turned the handle and walked in.

There was no one there. Trevor was not at his desk, though there were some box-files on top of it and a couple of ledgers left open. Huw decided he must have slipped out for five minutes—fate was obviously on his side.

He made his way to Joshua Judge's private office. This time he did not bother to knock, but as soon as he opened the door, he knew he'd made a mistake. Joshua wasn't there either, but his sons were. There were more ledgers and more files spread over the big desk. Jimmy and Bertie, who had been studying them, looked up. Clearly they did not welcome the interruption.

'What are you doing here?' snapped Jimmy. 'What do you want?'

'Who gave you permission to come in?' asked Bertie.

'Nobody.' Huw thought fast. 'I was hoping to see someone in Accounts. I thought Trevor Judge might be working late, but there's nobody there.'

The two brothers looked at one another.

'Trying to find Trevor Judge, eh? You're not the only one,' said Bertie. 'What did you want him for?'

'Oh, I had one or two queries, that's all.' Huw's voice trailed off and he concluded lamely, 'It's not urgent—I'll see him tomorrow. Sorry to have troubled you.' He began to back out of the room, but Jimmy stopped him.

'You still haven't told us what you're doing here. This office is private, nobody comes in without permission.'

'Looking for something, perhaps?' Bertie suggested with a sneer. 'Poking and prying about—is that it?'

'Of course not! I told you, I—'

'We take a poor view of people who poke their noses in where they're not wanted,' said Jimmy. 'Aren't you supposed to be working on the late-shift?'

'Yes, I'm on the crew at Number Three Warehouse, loading the *Maria Theresa.*'

'That's been changed,' Bertie said abruptly. Jimmy looked at his brother in surprise as he went on, 'You're to go to West Quay Six instead. They're one man short, unloading the timber-ship. Tell them I sent you.'

'Right, I'll do that. So long.'

As soon as Huw left the Office, Jimmy asked: 'What the hell did you say that for?'

Bertie smiled. 'It seemed like a good idea. Perhaps it'll teach him to mind his own business. Now then—where's bloody Trevor got to? D'you suppose he'll be at home?'

'If he is, Dad will find him.'

When Joshua Judge entered his house, he slammed the front door so hard, the pictures rattled on the walls. Maudie shrank back as

431

he burst into the kitchen, snarling at her: 'All right, where is he? Where's that boy of yours?'

'Trevor's not here, Josh. Whatever's the matter?'

'Fraud's the matter. Falsifying the books —nearly seven hundred pounds gone missing— that's what the matter is!'

'I don't understand. Seven hundred pounds gone? Gone where?'

'That's what we'd all like to know. God, I've been a fool, letting that young blackguard pull the wool over my eyes. Getting round me with drinks and games of draughts—and robbing me on the sly all the time!'

'Oh, no, Josh—not Trevor!' She shook her head. 'You're making a mistake!'

'There's no mistake. He's never been straight with me—he's been lying and cheating ever since he was a kid. I thought I'd sorted him out. I thought if I trusted him, if I gave him some responsibility, it would set him on the right track. And all this while he's been plotting and scheming how to swindle me!'

'Don't say such things!' Maudie was pleading with her husband, clinging to him. 'He wouldn't do that—not Trev!'

Josh pushed her angrily aside, making for the staircase. 'I'll have it out with him—is he up in his room?'

'No, he hasn't come home yet. I thought he was still at work.'

'We haven't seen him since mid-morning. He went to the bank to pay in some cheques, and never came back. Then we found the petty cash had gone too, and we started checking up. He's been stealing for months—making false entries, lining his own pockets...'

Breathlessly, he ran up the stairs two at a time, with Maudie at his heels. They reached the top floor and entered Trevor's room.

At first glance, everything seemed to be as usual, and Maudie began: 'Everything's just how it was this morning, when I made his bed.' Then she went towards the washstand. 'Only, his washing-things have gone. His face-flannel, his toothbrush and razor—he must have taken them.'

'So he *did* come back during the day? I thought you said you hadn't seen him?' Furious, he grabbed her by the shoulders. 'If I find you've been lying to me, if you're trying to protect him—'

'No, I swear. Let go, you're hurting me!' He released her and she rubbed her arms. 'I tell you I haven't seen him since breakfast. He must have slipped in while I was out shopping, but I'm sure he'll be home soon. I'm sure he'll be able to explain...'

The words died on her lips as Joshua flung open the wardrobe door. It was empty. All Trevor's clothes had gone—and so had his suitcase.

Joshua turned to his wife and said bitterly, 'Explain? How much explanation do you want? He's gone for good.'

'This is my cousin, Sharon Kleiber,' said Lil,

introducing them. 'Sharon, this is my Auntie Gloria.'

'How do you do?' With great poise, the little girl extended her hand.

Rather surprised, Glory shook hands. 'Pleased to meet you, I'm sure.'

Lil went on to explain. 'I thought p'raps you wouldn't mind if—well, Sharon wants to have her hair done. And if you're too busy tonight, I said you might let me do it. Will that be all right?'

Gloria looked doubtfully at Sharon. 'Well yes, I suppose so, dear—though your hair looks very nice the way it is. What did you want doing, exactly?'

Without waiting to be asked, Sharon settled herself in one of the cubicles, gazing critically at the mirror over the basin, and tossing her ringlets.

'It's not too bad, I suppose. Mumsie puts it in curlers every night, but it's not very comfy to sleep on, and the curls don't stay in very long either. That's why I thought Lil could do me some permanent curls that would last.'

'I told her about the special rollers, and that chemical stuff you put on,' Lil explained.

'I don't know.' Glory shook her head. 'We don't use chemicals on children as a rule, and besides, what would your mother say?'

'Mumsie doesn't mind; she said so. You see, my hair's got to look really nice because I'm doing another concert next Saturday, in aid of the Sunshine Homes for Orphans... Two dance-scenes, and Miss Grosvenor's letting me

434

do my *Toy Soldier* tap-dance with the drum, to close the first half. That's why the curls are so important, for my stage-work. I can afford to pay for it, if that's what's worrying you. I've still got some pocket-money saved from the panto I did last winter.'

'I wasn't thinking about the money,' said Glory, 'but if your mother doesn't mind—well, all right. It'll be good practice for Lil and we'll only charge you half-price, on account of her being a trainee.'

'I hope she won't make a mess of it.' Now it was Sharon's turn to look dubious. 'I wouldn't want anything to go wrong.'

'Don't worry, we shan't send you home with green hair!' smiled Glory. 'Right-ho, Lil. You can start with the shampoo, as usual.'

Lil gave Sharon a very professional shampoo, then under Glory's supervision she applied the setting-lotion to each ringlet, rolled it round a cotton-wool pad and fastened it with a metal clip. She put ear-pads on her cousin so she shouldn't get burned, tied a hair-net over the top then wheeled the electric hair-drier into the cubicle and fixed it over her head.

And all the time, Sharon never stopped talking.

'Did you hear what happened at our shop last week? My papa's on a committee now—he's ever so important. Did Mumsie tell you?'

'No. What sort of committee?' Lil asked.

'It's the East London Anglo-Jewish Committee.' Sharon pronounced each word with great care. 'They called a meeting, asking

435

for people to support their fight against the Germans. Papa's one of the organisers.'

'Don't tell me they're starting another war!' Glory threw up her hands. 'Haven't we had enough fighting already?'

'Oh no, nothing like that, but the Germans are being horrible to Jewish people, so Papa and his friends are trying to get back at them by telling everybody not to buy things made in Germany. He had some posters printed as well, and put them in our shop window.'

'Oh? I went along Silmour Street on my bike yesterday afternoon,' said Lil, 'and I didn't see any posters.'

'No, they'd only been in the window a couple of days when a policeman came in and made him take them down.'

'Why was that?'

'I don't know. They said he mustn't go stirring up trouble—I didn't really understand it.' Sharon chattered on carelessly. 'Of course I didn't tell Papa, but actually I was quite glad. I mean, there's no need to go round letting everybody know we're Jewish, is there?'

Glory broke in. 'You're not ashamed of it, are you?'

Sharon bridled. 'Of course not! But we don't have to go on and on about it—people are funny about things like that. Besides, I'm only half-Jewish. When I go on the stage, I might change my name. "Sharon Kleiber" wouldn't look very good on the posters, would it?'

Gazing dreamily at her reflection under the gleaming metal helmet, she added, 'I was

436

thinking—I might go blonde, one of these days. How much would it cost? It's not very expensive, is it?'

Tactfully, Glory said, 'One thing at a time, eh? I'd have to talk it over with your mum before I could do anything like that.' Then the street door opened, and Sharon was left under the drier while Glory and Lil went to attend to another client.

Later, when they unfastened the clips and took out the cotton-wool pads, Sharon was delighted with the result, smiling at herself in the glass.

'Oh, that's lovely! Miss Grosvenor will be ever so pleased. You must let me know how much I owe you—I'll settle up next time 'cos I forgot to bring my purse. Will you be ready to go soon, Lil? Shall we walk back together, part of the way?'

Lil explained that she couldn't leave yet. She had to stay and tidy up after the shop was shut and in any case she would be riding home on her bike. Sharon didn't seem to mind and skipped off quite happily on her own into the purple dusk, as Glory murmured: 'She's a proper little madam, and no mistake! If I was her mother, I wouldn't let her out on her own—not this time of day.'

'I'm sure she knows her way home,' said Lil. 'She won't get lost.'

'I'm not talking about getting lost,' retorted Gloria. 'I'm thinking about men. There's some nasty characters about, nowadays.'

'Oh, Sharon wouldn't do anything silly,' Lil

437

assured her. 'They used to tell us at school about not talking to strangers.'

When the last client departed, Glory put the Closed sign on the door and turned out some of the lights, saying, 'I'm going to make some cocoa while you clear up. D'you fancy a cup?'

'Yes, please.'

As Glory went into the back-kitchen, Matt came downstairs wearing his cap and raincoat, and she exclaimed: 'And where do you think you're off to?'

'Out—what's it look like? Out to see some of me mates,' he replied.

'I hope you're not thinking of going to the pub, by any chance?' she said. 'I know you think you're a big strong man, but you're still not eighteen—and don't you forget it.'

'Oh, put a sock in it, Ma!' Matt snorted. 'I'm old enough to play a game of snooker, ain't I?'

She regarded him suspiciously. 'Well...if I catch you smelling of drink when you get home, I don't care how big and strong you are, I'll tan your backside for you!'

She disappeared into the kitchen, and Matt grinned sheepishly at Lil, who had already started to sweep drifts of hair-clippings from the floor.

'She don't mean half what she says. Here —d'you want me to give you a hand with that?'

'No, that's all right, I can manage. You don't want to be late.'

'Well, if you're sure. I'll push off, then...'

438

But he still lingered for a moment, as if he were about to say something more. His big, raw-boned body looked out of place in a ladies' hairdressing establishment, and he seemed embarrassed. Finally he blurted out: 'Come here a minute, will you?'

She put down the broom, and went over to him. 'What do you want?'

'Nothing. Only, how about a good-night kiss?'

With that, he pulled her roughly towards him. Caught off-balance, Lil fell into his arms. He clutched her tightly, his hands groping her thighs, her breasts. She was overwhelmed by the smell of him—a rank smell of sweat and tobacco and masculinity—and when his mouth found hers, the taste of him was strange and disturbing.

Lil had never been kissed by any man except her father and, very rarely, her brother. She didn't know if the sensation was pleasant or unpleasant—she only knew it excited her, and made her dizzy.

When at last he let her go, she held on to the door-post for support, staring at him.

'You're a grand kid,' he said huskily, then he hurried out into the darkness as if he were running away. When Lil got her breath back, she closed the street door and rested her burning face against the cool plate-glass, feeling her heart pounding.

She remembered what they had said earlier, when Sharon went home. Was this what the schoolteachers had tried to warn them about?

439

Was this what happened when you stopped and talked to a stranger?

No, of course not. She was breathing more deeply now, and her skin tingled like an electric shock. After all, Matt wasn't a stranger—he was family, wasn't he? So that made it all right, and she needn't worry about going to Confession...

The following day, around noon, Ruth and Con were in the saloon.

'It's quiet this morning,' said Ruth, polishing glasses behind the bar.

'It's early yet. Business will pick up soon, you wait and see.' Connor stood sunning himself in the doorway. Stripped down to dungarees and a singlet, he had been helping the delivery-men to roll barrels down the cellar-chute, and it had been warm work.

'Put a shirt on—make yourself respectable!' Ruth scolded him.

'All right, in a minute. I'm enjoying the sunshine,' he said. Then his voice altered. 'Hello—what's the boy doing home this time of day?'

'Which boy?' asked Ruth. 'Who are you talking about?'

'Danny. He's racing along the road, full-tilt, as if the devil himself were after him!' He moved aside as Danny ran headlong into the bar.

'I ran—all the way—from the docks,' he panted.

'They've not turned you off, halfway through the shift?' Con asked.

'No, I'm on my dinner-break. I had to come

440

home—and tell you...'

'Tell us what?' Ruth came out from behind the counter.

'I just heard. Huw was working last night —there was an accident.'

'Oh, God—what's happened? Is he all right?' The words were torn from Ruth in a cry of anguish.

Con put his arm round her shoulders, gripping her tightly. 'Easy, now, let the boy finish. Tell us, Danny.'

He tried to tell his story clearly and simply. 'Huw was unloading timber on West Quay Six. They'd just made up a set of logs and given the signal to heave away, over the side and on to the dock. He was underneath, on the quay. The crane-driver saw the chain start to slip, but he couldn't warn him in time. The whole set fell apart; the driver said it's a miracle Huw wasn't killed. He said that crane always wobbled when the arm was out to the furthest point—he'd reported it lots of times, 'cos it wasn't safe, but nothing was done about it. Anyhow, they called an ambulance and Huw was taken to hospital.'

Ruth's face was stiff. It was difficult to move her lips to ask, 'Where have they taken him?'

'The London Hospital. That's why I came home.' Danny turned to Con. 'Will you ring up and find out how he is? Please?'

Connor felt Ruth trembling under his hands, as he replied, 'Of course I will. If he's allowed visitors, I'll get Mam and Da to take over

441

for an hour; we can get a cab to take us to Whitechapel.'

Over the phone, the Ward Sister said that Mr Pritchard was doing as well as could be expected, and that visiting hours were from two to four. A little reassured, Danny went back to work and on the stroke of two, when the doors opened, Connor and Ruth went into Men's Casualty.

There was a cradle above Huw's bed; he had one leg in a plaster-cast, suspended from a tangle of wires and pulleys. He looked almost like a stranger. The pallor beneath his tan gave his skin a greenish tinge, and he had a bandage round his head, hiding his red hair. When he recognised his visitors, he managed a smile. Ruth sank into the chair by his bed, not knowing what to say.

'I'm sorry we didn't bring any flowers,' she began idiotically. 'There was no time...'

'What's the damage?' asked Connor. 'What have you done to your head?'

'Oh, that's nothing. I cracked my skull a bit, but that won't do any harm—it's solid bone, see, all the way through. And I'm black and blue all over, but that's only bruising. The real trouble is my leg—shattered in a dozen places, they tell me. It's going to take weeks to knit together again and then they say I'll have to walk with a stick. Seems like I'll be dot-and-carry-one for the rest of my life...'

Ruth made a small, inarticulate sound; she dared not speak, in case she broke down in tears.

'Dan told us the crane had been reported as unsafe, but nothing was done about it—is that right?' asked Connor.

'Seems so. I had the Branch Secretary from the Union in to see me this morning. They're putting in a claim for compensation against the Wharfmaster, for gross negligence. I suppose that's some comfort, but one thing's certain—I shan't be working as a docker any more.'

'Don't bother about that,' said Connor. 'Do you reckon you'll be able to stand up behind a bar and pull a beer-handle? As long as you can manage that, you've a job for life, my bucko—at the Watermen.'

Ruth turned and stared into Connor's eyes, shocked and silent, with the questions beating at her brain: How can he do this? How could he *not* do this? But—does he realise, does he understand what he's doing?

As if in reply to her unspoken thoughts, Connor nodded slightly and his lips twisted into that old, lopsided grin... And she knew that he understood everything.

16

'More crowns!' announced Ruth as she came out of the front door.

The pub presented a very patriotic appearance already, though it was soon after breakfast and Jubilee Day had only just begun. King George

443

the Fifth had been reigning over Great Britain for exactly twenty-five years, and his people were determined to celebrate this splendid achievement.

Today, Their Majesties would attend a service of thanks-giving at St Paul's, and a national holiday had been declared. The whole country was ablaze with red, white and blue flags, and the Three Jolly Watermen were not going to be left out of the festivities.

Up on a stepladder, Connor tied one end of a string of bunting to the Brewery's signboard; further along the pavement, Huw knotted the other end to a lamp-bracket, his walking-stick propped up against the bench beside the door.

Ruth and Lil had been busy making cardboard crowns covered in silver paper; now they would be attached to the decorated façade at strategic points.

'We've done six more,' she said, looking up at Connor and shielding her eyes against the morning sunlight. 'Will that be enough?'

'That'll be fine, he told her, tying a last knot. 'There, that's done.'

But he spoke too soon. Pulled tight, the string of bunting snapped in two, and dozens of miniature Union Jacks fluttered to the pavement.

Cursing, Connor climbed down the steps and said, 'We'll just have to tie the ends.'

This was easier said than done, for though the broken ends met, the tapes weren't long enough to knot together. Huw came to lend a hand, and between them they managed it at last—each man pulling one string taut, while Ruth made a reef-knot with the loose ends. For one moment three pairs of hands touched, and the job was done.

Ruth left the two men and went quickly back to the kitchen, where Patrick and Mary sat expectantly beside the Marconi set, waiting to hear the broadcast of the Jubilee procession. Lil was twiddling the knobs at the front of the bakelite cabinet, without much success.

'It keeps making these whistling noises,' she complained. 'Where's Huw? He's much better than me at tuning it in.'

'He'll be coming in presently, there's plenty of time,' Ruth told her. 'Don't be so impatient.'

'Ah, what would we do without Huw?' said Mary O'Dell fondly.

From the moment Huw had accepted Connor's offer of a job, he had proved to be invaluable. His lameness did not prevent him from being an efficient barman, though after standing behind the counter all the evening he often went home with his leg throbbing painfully; and he made himself useful in many other ways, too. He helped Ruth in the office, keeping the paperwork up to date, he helped Connor by putting in the Brewery orders and supervising the deliveries, checking full and empty barrels in and out, he carried out errands for Mary and kept Patrick company when everyone else was too busy to spare time for him—and he remained a friend and ally of both Danny and Lil.

He did not live in, for there were no vacant

rooms above the pub, but went home every night to his Welsh relatives at the dairy in Three Colt Street; but in every other way, over the past two years he had been accepted by the O'Dells as an additional member of the family.

Only Ruth felt uneasy about the situation. Once, soon after Huw first began to work for them, she had tried to talk to Connor about it.

'Doesn't it seem strange to you sometimes, having Huw here with us all day and every day?' she asked.

'No, what's strange about it?'

'You know what I mean. We're so close, the three of us.'

'I don't see it like that. What else could we have done? Left him high and dry, out of work and on the dole? You wouldn't have wanted that for the lad.'

'Of course I wouldn't and he isn't a lad any more.'

'No, he's a man—and a good friend. He's become like a young brother to both of us. I'd say we're very lucky to have someone so—close.'

She searched Con's eyes, trying to see into his heart, but she could not fathom those emerald-green depths. On one point she was sure that Connor was wrong; having had brothers of her own, Ruth knew about brotherly love—and her feelings for Huw were not quite like that.

Later, the whole family sat round the table, listening to the outside broadcast as the royal cavalcade passed through Trafalgar Square and along the Strand.

'Listen to those bells pealing,' said Mary. 'It makes you feel you're right there with them, doesn't it?'

Patrick cupped his ear with his hand, leaning forward. 'What's that?' he asked. 'I can't hear you, Mary—speak up!'

'I said it makes you feel you're really there, watching everything, listening to the bells.'

'It's no good.' He shook his head. 'I can't hear a word you're saying, for them bloody bells.'

Then the sound of the crowds changed, and they heard laughter mingled with the cheering as the voice from the loudspeaker explained: 'The most extraordinary thing... A little black and white dog, possibly a terrier of some sort though I rather suspect he's a mongrel, has just dashed out of the crowd and joined the procession. He's running along in front of the royal carriage...'

'Let's hope he doesn't frighten the horses,' remarked Connor.

'Oh dear, this could be awkward.' The rigidly controlled accents of the BBC commentator became almost lively. 'The police are running after the animal now, trying to catch him, but he's taken refuge underneath the moving carriage, and he's refusing to come out.'

At her elbow, Ruth heard a loud sniff and looked round to find her daughter beside her, trying not to cry.

'Lil, whatever's the matter?'

'It was him talking about the dog under the

447

carriage,' said Lil. 'I couldn't help remembering... Suppose he falls under the wheels?'

One evening last summer, when Danny was taking Barker out for a walk, the dog had slipped the leash and run out into the traffic on the Manchester Road. It was nobody's fault; the lorry-driver had jammed on his brakes, but he was too late.

'He was getting to be an old dog by then,' Ruth reminded Lil gently. 'The vet said Barker died instantly—he wouldn't have felt any pain.'

'Anyhow, I was the one who felt badly about it,' Danny pointed out. 'I was in charge of him, wasn't I? He was my dog!'

Lil turned on him. 'What difference does that make?' she said. 'When you love somebody, what does it matter who they belong to?'

Across the table, Huw and Ruth glanced at one another for an instant, then Huw looked away.

Sometimes he thought it might have been better if he worked somewhere else—if he could ever manage to get another job. In some ways it might even have been better on the dole. Being so near Ruth, seeing her every day, was a kind of torment—yet he had no choice. He knew he would never leave the Watermen now; he could never leave Ruth.

The commentator's voice continued: 'The royal carriage is now passing our vantage-point, giving us a splendid view of the King and Queen. His Majesty is wearing the scarlet uniform of a Field-Marshal. Beside him, Queen Mary is smiling and waving, acknowledging the cheers of the crowd. Her Majesty is all in white, with a white fur collar and a white toque, and a necklace of five rows of pearls...'

Maudie and Joshua were listening to these words on their own wireless; the joyful occasion had encouraged many people to purchase a radio receiver for the first time.

'Five rows of pearls,' Maudie repeated wistfully. 'Fancy that...'

She fingered the string of carved ivory beads at her throat, a present from Josh last Christmas. They must have cost a lot of money, and she was very touched that he had taken the trouble to choose them for her, even if they were a little old-fashioned.

Still, they went nicely with her new cream silk blouse and her cream linen skirt and jacket—also presents from Josh, for her birthday. Of course she had gone to choose them herself, at Wickhams; on her birthday morning, Josh had pulled out a wad of notes and thrust them into her hand, saying, 'Many happy returns, old dear. Go and buy yourself something pretty.'

He was a generous husband, no doubt about that. Since that awful day when Trev ran away from home, he had been especially kind and affectionate, knowing how miserable she was and trying to make it up to her. But that was two years ago, and things had changed since then.

What Trevor had done was very wrong; he had brought shame upon the family—she could not deny that. Josh had decided not to call in the police. He had preferred to hush things up,

449

making up the loss to the company from his own savings rather than face a public scandal.

It had been a dreadful shock for Aunt Emily. Trevor had always been her ewe-lamb, and she could not understand how he could have been such a naughty boy, running away from his own dear Gan-gan... Since then, Emily had not gone out very often, but preferred to spend most of her time in her room, nursing a headache and taking cat-naps throughout the day. She was two years younger than Louisa, but although both sisters were now in their seventies, Emily seemed the older of the two—frail, nervous and increasingly confused—while Louisa looked after a difficult, ailing husband, cooking and cleaning for him and managing the house as well as ever.

Maudie wondered if she would be as strong and capable as her mother-in-law when she was seventy-five. She couldn't really imagine being such an unthinkable age. Why, when she was seventy-five, Josh would be eighty-six...if he were still alive.

She glanced across the room; he was sitting at the table, listening to the wireless, and he had a bottle of whisky at his elbow. As she watched, he filled his glass to the brim and she saw that his hand was shaking already—that was a bad sign.

'Oh, Josh.' Before she could stop herself, she exclaimed plaintively, 'Do you think you should, so early in the day?'

He turned his head and smiled at her. 'A loyal toast, old dear—for a patriotic occasion,' he said, raising his glass. 'To our great and glorious Majesties, God bless 'em. And just for once perhaps you'd give me a rest from your everlasting whining, eh?'

She bit her lip; she should have known better than to criticise his drinking. He always turned nasty if she mentioned it.

He sat listening to the music of a military band which emerged from the loudspeaker, his free hand vaguely beating time, the same fixed, meaningless smile on his face—and she longed to go and dash the glass from his hand, to make him stop—but she knew that would do no good. She wanted to stand in front of him, forcing him to look at her, crying out: 'I am your wife—had you forgotten that? Can't you see me any more? Can't you see anything except that whisky bottle? If only you'd look at me, just for a minute, really look at me—you might see how unhappy I am.'

She could never tell anyone about the pain in her heart, like a wound that would never be healed; the unbearable loneliness she lived with, day after day, for the two only men she had ever really cared for—her son, her lover—had both run away and left her, without any warning, without even saying goodbye.

'Now the carriage draws up outside St Paul's. A red carpet has been laid upon the steps, and Their Majesties are alighting. They are about to enter the great Cathedral...'

The broadcaster's voice droned on, but Maudie did not hear it. She was looking at Josh, watching him smiling over the rim of

451

his glass. She recognised that smile. It meant that he had reached the point when the drink took control; he no longer knew what he was doing, or where he was—he no longer cared about anything except the next drink. He had become a stranger.

The celebrations went on, and the streets of East London continued to flaunt their decorations, for the King and Queen had a full calendar of events arranged, visiting different parts of London—on 25 May they were scheduled to take tea at Limehouse Town Hall.

But before that day arrived, they made an unscheduled visit.

The weekend after the Jubilee, Lil and Sharon spent Sunday afternoon together. It was a fine day, and they decided to go sightseeing and inspect the decorations in other parts of the East End. Lil was riding her bicycle, but Sharon had never bothered to learn to ride a bike ('I mustn't fall off, 'cos Mumsie says I bruise so easily') so she accompanied Lil on a pair of brand-new roller-skates.

'Skating's much better than silly old bikes,' she said grandly. 'Besides, Miss Grosvenor says the chorus often have skating numbers in shows nowadays, so I thought I might as well start practising now, just in case.'

'You're not thinking of getting a job as a chorus-girl?' Lil was rather taken aback: chorus-girls were popularly considered to be only one step away from street-walkers. 'Your mum and dad wouldn't let you, would they?'

'Lots of famous actresses started as chorus-girls,' Sharon explained. 'Anyway, I shan't stay in the chorus for long. Miss Grosvenor says I've got star quality.'

They went on, side by side. Lil had to ride quite slowly, in order to keep pace with Sharon's skates. They looked at the loyal tributes strung up in the streets of Stepney and Mile End, and told one another that they didn't hold a candle to the Isle of Dogs' superior display.

'Come on, let's turn round and go back,' Sharon said at last. 'I'm getting really bored with this old Jubilee.'

'We might as well go on to Whitechapel now we've come this far, and go back through Limehouse,' said Lil. 'I wonder if they've put Union Jacks out along Chinese Causeway.'

They passed one house which had gone to great lengths to outshine its neighbours; the owner had painted the entire front wall in red, white and blue stripes, and photos of the King and Queen, cut out of newspapers, had pride of place in every window.

'If you ask me, that sort of thing looks ever so common,' said Sharon loftily.

Lil smiled. 'What's the matter with you today? You've been in a bad mood all the afternoon. Did you get out of bed the wrong side, or what?'

'No, it's just—oh, everything's rotten these days!' Sharon exclaimed resentfully. 'And it's all 'cos I'm a girl—that's the unfair part. Abram's going to Germany with a school party at the end of term—why couldn't my school send me on an outing like that?'

'I know what you mean,' Lil sighed. 'Wouldn't it be lovely to go off on holiday? Just to go somewhere different—even for a few days—and get out of London for a while.'

But for both of them this was an impossible dream. Ernest Kleiber couldn't afford to shut his photographic shop and take his family to the seaside, and Connor O'Dell couldn't leave the pub in the hands of his elderly parents.

'P'raps one day we'll go away somewhere.' Lil tried to look on the bright side. 'When we're older, we might—*look out!*'

The last words burst out as a sudden urgent warning, for a large black Daimler had just turned the corner, bearing down upon them. Luckily it was moving slowly, and they had time to jump on to the pavement.

'Did you see that?' Sharon's eyes were like saucers. 'Did you see who it was?'

'Must be some real toffs,' Lil guessed. 'Nobody round these parts drives a car like that.'

'It's not toffs—it's *them!*' gasped Sharon. 'The King and Queen—I saw them!'

'Don't be silly, you couldn't have. What would the King and Queen be doing in a place like this?'

'They're coming to Limehouse, aren't they, Saturday week? I dare say they've come for a look round first, to give their driver a chance to find the way,' said Sharon.

As she spoke, a gang of children came tearing

454

round the corner, some on foot, some on push-bikes—one on a scooter—all chasing the royal limousine, laughing and shouting: 'God save the King! God save the Queen!'

'You see? It *was* them. Come on, let's catch up and have another look!' Sharon urged Lil.

They joined the unofficial cavalcade of twenty or thirty children, tearing down the street. At the junction of Burdett Road and Commercial Road, a set of traffic-lights had recently been installed, and now the lights turned red. The black car stopped obediently, waiting for the lights to change, and Lil said: 'I told you it can't be them. The King and Queen don't have to stop at traffic-lights!'

But Sharon redoubled her roller-skating pace, until they caught up with all the other children surrounding the Daimler.

Inside the car, Their Majesties gazed out at their excited entourage, smiling shyly and waving. Instantly, Sharon saw her chance.

'Give us a bit of room, can't you?' she demanded, with such authority that the other kids drew back to make a space for her.

There and then, she went into one of her solo ballet routines, on her skates—arms held high, head well back, her lips parted in a radiant smile—whirling in a tight circle and finishing with a perfect arabesque, just as the lights changed to amber and green; Miss Grosvenor would have been proud of her. Through the windows, they saw His Majesty beaming jovially and Her Majesty politely clapping white-gloved hands, then the car moved on and away, out of sight.

When they got back to the Watermen and told everyone, nobody believed them at first.

'The King and Queen wouldn't come here on a visit without letting anyone know,' objected Ruth.

'That's right,' agreed Connor. 'Not without a police escort to keep guard, either. They'd have cleared the roads and stopped the traffic.'

'But we *saw* them—we did, honest!' Lil persisted.

It was only when the surprise visit was mentioned later in the day during a wireless news-bulletin that everyone realised the girls had not imagined it, or invented it. Nobody ever knew why Their Majesties should have decided to visit East London without any prior warning to the local authorities, but it had happened, and for the rest of her life Sharon often boasted about it.

'When I was only twelve, I danced for the King and Queen of England—all by myself—and they gave me a round of applause!'

Next day, when Lil went back to work at the hairdressing salon, she told Gloria the whole story.

Glory laughed. 'Well, aren't you the lucky ones—getting a grandstand view of the Royal Family! And that Sharon, she's a real caution. Fancy her doing her dance...practically a Command Performance.'

As she polished the taps on the washbasins,

Lil added, 'I was ever so glad for her. She'd been a bit fed up till that happened.'

'What's she got to be fed up about?' asked Glory, putting out the clean towels, folding them and stacking them in a pile. 'Strikes me she gets everything she wants. Some people are never satisfied.'

'The only thing she wants now, she can't have,' said Lil. 'Abram's going to Germany with a school-party, and she's dying to go on holiday too, only she can't. They're like us. Mum and Dad can't ever take time off from work.'

'Same here.' Gloria stopped what she was doing and gazed out of the shop windows. Tiny white clouds raced over a bright blue sky, and at the end of the street she could just see the masts of a ship above the roofs and chimneys. 'I'd give anything to go down to Southend for a day or two. I haven't been there for years. Last time I went, the tide was that far out, I never even saw the sea! Nothing but miles and miles of mud...'

'Did you go to Southend when you were little?' asked Ruth.

'No such luck! Not till I was old enough to get took by—a gentleman-friend of mine.' Gloria pulled herself together and went on folding towels. 'We couldn't afford holidays when I was a kid. We used to go hopping once a year—that was the nearest thing we ever had to holidays. Still, it made a break.'

'Hopping? You mean hop-picking? We never even did that,' said Lil sadly. 'Dad and Mum were always too busy. I bet it was fun, wasn't it?'

457

'It was hard work, duck—believe you me. On the go all day, we were, but I must admit we had a few laughs and it was grand just to get into the country and smell some fresh air.' Then she paused again, as a thought struck her. 'I tell you what, why don't you and Sharon go hopping next September? It'd be better if there was two of you; you'd be company for one another.'

'We couldn't go on our own, could we?' Lil stared at her. 'Would you come with us?'

'I wish I could, but if I shut up shop, my regulars would all start looking for another hairdresser and I mightn't get 'em back. But I could manage without you for a week or two, and you deserve a break. I just remembered, your Aunt Florrie goes hopping every year with some of her neighbours. She earns herself a bit of pocket-money, and it makes a change. I expect if you was to ask her nicely, she'd take you along as well—you and Sharon. Course, you'll have to talk to your mum about it, but if she says yes, shall I have a word with Florrie?'

So it was all arranged, and Lil and Sharon began to look forward to their first excursion outside London, their first holiday away from their parents, their first steps into a strange new world...

Meanwhile, just before the end of term, Abram's school-party set off for Germany and ten days later they returned home, tumbling out of their charabanc, suntanned and cheerful.

Sharon still envied her brother, but then

she noticed that he was rather silent and uncommunicative about the whole experience, and she suspected he hadn't really enjoyed it much—so that made her feel a lot better.

'What was it like?' she wanted to know. 'Did you get homesick?'

'No, course I didn't! Well, not much. Most of the time, it was good fun. The Rhineland's beautiful; we went on a river-steamer from Koblenz and saw the rock where the Lorelei used to lure sailors to their death. I've brought back some postcards to show you.'

'Pictures of drowned sailors?' enquired Sharon.

Ignoring her, he opened his suitcase and took out a handful of coloured photographs of a blue river winding between high hills covered in vineyards—then he distributed some little packages, one for each member of the family.

Sharon got a carved wooden bear with moving limbs; Rosie's package contained a scarf from Bonn, printed with a portrait of Beethoven—and Ernest was given a meerschaum pipe with a carved stem and a metal lid on the bowl.

They all expressed their surprise and delight, and then Ernest asked, 'And you met your Aunt Sarah? Were you able to visit her while you were in Frankfurt, as we hoped?'

'Oh, yes. The teachers let me stay·the night with the Brendels. They sent you their love—Benjamin's not a boy any more, he's twenty-one now... They asked me to give you this photograph.'

It was only a small snapshot, of Klaus Brendel and Sarah, smiling into the camera.

They seemed to have got older and plumper in the three years since they left England. Benjamin was the tallest figure in the group, broad-shouldered and thick-set, wearing the traditional *lederhosen* and standing with his hands on his hips.

'We must put it into our family album,' said Rosie. 'It's nice to know Sarah and Ben have settled down so well out there.'

Later, when she went into Abram's room, she found him lying on the bed, reading; his suitcase was open on the bedside table.

'I thought I'd better collect your dirty clothes and put them in the wash,' she explained.

'Mmmm...' He did not take his eyes from his book; it looked unfamiliar, with an orange and white cover—the first paperback book Rosie had ever seen.

'What's that you're reading?' she asked.

'One of our teachers lent it to me to read on the boat, so I wouldn't get seasick. I hadn't finished it when we got home, but he said I could let him have it back next term.'

She tried to read the lettering, upside-down: 'Something about penguins, is it?'

'No, it's called *Tarka the Otter*—it's all about animals. "Penguin" is the kind of book; they're only sixpence each.'

'Sounds like a bargain.' Rosie went on sorting out Abram's laundry, and as she picked up one of his socks, a small metal object fell out, tinkling on to the floor. 'Hello, what's this?'

'Oh, I forgot...' He sat up, as she retrieved it from under the bed. It was a big badge

460

made of gun-metal, with a pin at the back, decorated with a laurel wreath that surrounded a swastika.

'How did you get hold of this?'

Red-faced, he took it quickly from her. 'Benjamin gave it to me the night I stayed at Auntie Sarah's. He took me out that evening; he helps to run this sort of club. There were lots of boys there about the same age as me. We played games and had a singsong and all that...'

He looked so unhappy, she sat beside him on the bed. 'What do you mean? What sort of club?'

'A bit like the Boy Scouts, only it's called the Hitlerjügend. They had armbands on, with swastikas, and they sang *My Bonny Lies Over the Ocean* in English, specially for me—so I joined in when they sang: *Deutschland Uber Alles*. At the end, we all had to salute and say "Heil Hitler". I meant to chuck the badge away as soon as I got out of Germany, but it was in the luggage and I couldn't get at it.' He looked at her anxiously. 'Don't tell Papa, will you? He'd be ashamed of me and I couldn't help it.'

'You were just being polite—he'd understand.'

'It wasn't only that.' Abram frowned at the silver-grey badge, turning it over and over. 'Before we went to the club, Ben warned me I mustn't tell anybody I was Jewish. He explained that it's sort of against the rules there.'

'But he's Jewish himself! So is Sarah.'

'That's what I said, and he looked at me as if I'd said something very shocking, then he sort

461

of whispered: "You must never say that—we are all Germans now... There will be no more Jews".'

He pushed the badge into her hands. 'Don't say anything to Papa, and don't show him this. Throw it in the dustbin, will you? I just want to forget about it.'

The summer wore on, and turned into autumn. In the middle of September, Lil and Sharon packed their bags and joined Auntie Florrie's hop-picking expedition.

They had to make an early start, for a local greengrocer had agreed to give them a lift in his van, on his way to Covent Garden, dropping them off at London Bridge to catch the 'Hoppers Special'—a train laid on at cut-price fares, which left before dawn and would take them to Tunbridge Wells. There they were to be met by a farm-lorry, to carry them on to their destination.

The girls sat on their suitcases in the back of the van, which smelled of cabbages, rattling and lurching through the darkened streets, thrilled and nervous at the same time, with no clear idea of where they were going or what to expect when they got there.

Lil had an additional private worry, which she could not share with anyone. At the last moment, Gloria's son had decided to join the hopping party. Since the evening when he had grabbed her and kissed her, Lil's relationship with Matt had become a problem. Several times after that he had offered to help clean up the

462

salon at the end of the evening, and as soon as his mother was out of the way, he had kissed her again. Each time, the attempt had become more reckless until he was fumbling inside her blouse and putting his hand up her skirt.

She knew then without any doubt that they were doing wrong, and that if she allowed him to continue, she would have to confess to the parish priest that she had been engaging in 'impure conduct'. So she held Matt off, telling him firmly that making love like that was sinful, and that they must never do it again.

After that, he seemed to lose interest in her and she hardly ever saw him at the salon; she was not sure whether to be relieved or disappointed. And now he had joined the hop-picking expedition... She wondered if he would begin to make advances all over again—and what she should do if he did.

She had enjoyed Matt's kisses and caresses, until he got too rough, but she knew that if she let him go on, she might find herself committing a mortal sin. The prospect was terrifying—and very exciting.

One afternoon, about ten days after the hoppers left London, a taxi drew up in Jubilee Street outside Florrie's house, and a man in a smart gaberdine raincoat and a snap-brim hat climbed out, saying, 'OK, cabbie—you don't have to wait.'

He spoke with an American accent and he pulled out an alligator-skin wallet to pay the fare.

The cab backed up the street—it was a cul-de-sac, not wide enough to turn round in—and with a grinding of gears vanished round the corner.

The stranger glanced up at the house and took a deep breath, then attacked the door-knocker. Nothing happened, so after a few moments he knocked again.

Next door, a sash-window on the first floor slid up, and a woman in a hair-net called out: 'Who d'you want?'

'Mrs Judge. Seems like she's out.'

'That's right, away for a fortnight, she is. Gone hopping.'

'Ah, hell,' said the stranger under his breath then, more loudly: 'Yeah—she would be. I should have known.'

He began to move away, and the woman shouted after him inquisitively, 'When she gets back, shall I say who called?'

'No, don't bother. Forget it.'

Walking a little faster, he made his escape. Thwarted, the neighbour slammed the window down.

That evening, soon after six, Ruth was serving in the saloon when the stranger came in and ordered a pint of mild. He was a fine figure of a man—in his early thirties, smartly dressed, with a bronzed complexion and a trim beard.

'Thanks a lot,' he said, as she handed him the beer.

She couldn't help being struck by his accent. 'You're not from round these parts,' she said.

He smiled back at her, showing a row of

464

white even teeth. 'Is it that obvious?'

'Are you over here on holiday, or business?'

'A bit of both, maybe. With any luck.'

'And is this your first visit to London?'

'Not quite—I've been here before.'

'Here, in this pub? I felt sure I knew your face. Didn't you come in once with Mr Cassidy?'

He cut in quickly. 'No, ma'am—I never set foot in here till tonight. And I'm not acquainted with any Mr Cassidy. You must be confusing me with someone else.' Then he took his drink and walked away from her, to the piano at the far end of the room.

'Oh, I beg your pardon.' Feeling she had been rebuffed, Ruth occupied herself with some glasses that needed washing.

It was strange. She still had a feeling she'd seen him before, and yet he'd never been in the Watermen and she'd never met any Americans, apart from Cassidy... The door opened again and a group of dockers came in, loud and hearty, clamouring to be served. By the time she had dealt with them and turned back for another look at the American visitor, there was an empty glass on top of the piano, and the stranger had gone.

While London sleeps, and all is light and gleaming
Millions of its people there lie sweetly dreaming.

Lil thought of her parents, who would be busy in the pub at this time of night, and of Danny and Huw, and felt a stab of longing for them all. London seemed very far away.

She was sitting round the bonfire with a mixed group of youngsters, middle-aged women and a couple of older men, watching the firelight play over their faces as they swayed and sang together.

Some have no home, while others softly weep. Others laugh and play the game, while London's fast asleep.

It was a melancholy tune, but with a gentle sweetness that went straight to Lil's heart, and she sighed happily. This was the best time of the day, when the work was over and they could sit round the fire, enjoying the freedom of this extraordinary gypsy life.

At first she wasn't at all sure she was going to like it. It seemed very rough after the comforts of home. She had been horrified to find that she would be sharing a little wooden hut with four others—Auntie Florrie, two elderly female neighbours and Sharon. She had thought for an awful moment that Matt would be sleeping there as well, for in many of the huts, men and women, boys and girls were thrown together indiscriminately—and she was relieved when, since Matt had joined the party at the last moment, he was sent off to share a tent with some other chaps.

There were no proper beds, either. As soon as they arrived, they were given big sacks made of striped ticking, like eiderdown covers, which they had to stuff with straw. These, along with a couple of thin blankets, were their only bedding.

Aunt Florrie and the other women slept 'on the shelf'—a square wooden platform raised off the ground. Sharon and Lil slept together with nothing but a waterproof sheet between their straw palliasse and the trodden dirt floor. Lil hoped that no mice would venture into the hut while they were asleep.

Each day followed the same pattern: they were awoken at half-past six and 'blown on' to the hop-fields by the farm-manager, who had an ancient brass bugle. The older women packed a basket of food for the day and filled a kettle with water, then they set off for the fields, where they worked for two hours. At nine they stopped for a breakfast of bread and cheese, with tin mugs of tea brewed in the billy-can over the fire. It had milk and tea and sugar boiled up in it and tasted disgusting, but by that time they were so thirsty, as long as it was wet and warm they were glad to drink it.

The work was simple enough, but it was monotonous and very hard.

Down the long alleys between the hop-vines, huge sacking bags had been set up, supported on trestles; these were the bins, which had to be filled by the pickers. In their different family groups, they stripped the hops from the bines and filled the bins; picking was mainly done by the women, while the younger men, like Matt, were employed as 'pole-pullers'. Their job was to cut the bines from the supporting poles and pull them down so the women could reach them.

Lil envied the men, and wished she could

be a pole-puller, going from one group to the next; it seemed a lot easier than picking, for the bines were harsh and covered in prickles which cut her hands. Some women preferred to wear gloves, but that meant picking more slowly, and they got paid according to how many bins they filled.

At intervals during the day, the farm-manager sent round 'measurers', to check on their progress; it was the measurer's job to record the weight of the hops that had been picked, filling bushel-baskets from the bins and entering the tally in their account-books. At the end of each week, the pickers would be paid their wages, according to the amounts that were entered.

The working day finished about five o'clock, and every afternoon Lil waited for the measurer's welcome cry: 'Pull no more bines!' as if it were a reprieve.

There were other things she hated. They had no proper lavatories, only a shed with a bucket in it, which was emptied infrequently. On some farms, Florrie said, they had to use a hole dug in the ground. There was no warm water to wash in; sluicing her hands and face in the icy-cold stream running along the bottom of the field was the best Lil could manage, yet washing was essential, for the bines left a dark brown stain that was hard to scrub off.

But though the days were long and strenuous, and the life was spartan, there was another side to it.

Lil had never been out of London before, and the countryside seemed like paradise; the flowers in the hedgerows, and the brilliant green leaves and grass, the smell of fresh air—the pungent, intoxicating scent of hops, which surrounded them all day and all night—and the amazing freedom that came from spending so much time outdoors. It was a different way of life altogether.

Best of all were the evenings. They always had a good supper of stewed meat and vegetables which had been simmering all day in an iron pot over the fire, then the men, and some of the women, would go off to the nearest village for a drink, while the rest sat round the fire, swapping stories, telling jokes, joining in the choruses...

Our lovely hops—our lovely hops.
When the measurer he comes round,
Picking 'em up—off of the ground,
When he starts to measure, he never knows when
*   to stop.*
So jump right in, and fill up yer bin
With our lovely hops.

Lil looked round the circle of faces. She couldn't see Sharon—perhaps she'd gone off with some of the kids from another family party. That was the nicest thing about hopping. Everybody was so friendly, you could wander round and talk to anybody, whether you knew them or not.

She couldn't see Matt either, but she guessed he would be at the pub. She had hardly spoken to him since they arrived. During the day the pole-pullers were kept busy, touring the fields, and at night they all went out drinking together.

By the time Matt returned, it was getting late and one of the older men was stamping on the red ashes of the fire. Once the flames were out, the night seemed very black; suddenly Lil was startled to see what looked like a cluster of tiny stars, winking and dancing, coming towards her.

Matt emerged from the darkness; in the light of the dying embers she saw that he was carrying Sharon on his back. Aunt Florrie pounced on her crossly.

'You naughty girl, wherever have you been? Going off like that without telling anyone...'

'It's all right. She was with me—we was catching fireflies,' Matt explained, as Sharon scrambled down.

She had a jam-jar in her hands, and inside the jar half a dozen fireflies circled one another in an eerie glow of cool, greenish light.

'I'm going to take them home to show Papa,' she said.

Matt guffawed. 'They won't live that long! But we'll get some more tomorrow, eh?'

Half an hour later, Lil and Sharon settled down for the night under their two blankets. The other women were already asleep; Lil could hear them snoring. Not wanting to disturb them, she asked in a whisper, 'How did you happen to meet Matt? I thought he'd gone drinking with his pals.'

'I didn't meet him. He came up after supper and asked me if I'd like to go for a walk. He said he'd got something to show me.'

'The fireflies?'

'Don't be daft!' Sharon giggled. 'That was later on, when we were coming back afterwards. Matt found that old jam-jar, so he put the fireflies in it.'

'What do you mean—afterwards? After what?'

'After we'd been playing about.' Sharon spoke very softly, but her voice was full of mischief. 'He's wicked, he is. Do you know what it was he wanted to show me? He took me behind a hedge, then he undid his trousers and he said: "Here, cop hold of this".' The straw mattress rustled, as Sharon convulsed with laughter.

'But that's dreadful! Whatever did you do?'

'Oh, nothing much. We just played about for a bit, that's all. It was rather silly, really.' Sharon yawned. 'Goodness, I'm so sleepy—all that fresh air. I can't keep awake a minute longer. Good night!'

Lil lay awake for a long time. She was very shocked—how could Matt do anything so horrible? And with Sharon, too, who wouldn't be thirteen till next month. She knew that men could be sent to prison for doing things like that with little girls. She decided that she didn't like Matt at all. She would never speak to him again, as long as she lived.

Thinking it over, she decided she didn't like Sharon much, either.

Next morning, another taxi drew up in West Ferry Road and the man in the gaberdine coat and snap-brim hat climbed out, paying off the driver.

471

He could walk to Millwall Road from here; it would be less conspicuous. As the cab drove off, he made his way towards the old shop on the corner, but as he got nearer, his footsteps faltered. Had he made a mistake? Could he have taken the wrong turning?

No, of course not. He knew his way round the Island like the back of his hand. But the shop had changed—it was now a ladies' hairdressers. He walked a little nearer and peered in through the windows.

Inside, Gloria was putting rollers in a customer's hair, about to give her a perm. She turned to pick up the setting lotion and noticed the silhouette of a man outside on the pavement, but as she glanced at him, he moved away quickly.

Twenty yards along the street, a rag-and-bone man was pushing a barrow piled with rubbish, and the stranger stopped him.

'Excuse me,' he began awkwardly. 'The shop on the corner—it used to be a dry-goods store, I mean a grocery.'

'S'right.' The totter hawked and spat into the gutter. 'Old Emily Judge used to run it. Give it up, she did, years ago. It's her daughter what runs the place now.'

'Ah yes, I see.' He stroked his beard thoughtfully. 'Can you tell me—Mrs Judge had a daughter-in-law who lived with her, a young lady—slim, fair-haired, very pretty—is she still there?'

'Would that be Maudie Judge?' The old man eyed him doubtfully. 'Nah—moved away, she did. You'll find her at number seventeen, Denmark Place. Second on the left, then first right.'

'I know where it is. Thanks a lot—I'm obliged to you.' He walked on quickly, leaving the old man staring. Now he was so near his journey's end, he could not bear to waste another moment.

He reached the house and knocked, waiting in a fever of impatience.

The door opened, and Maudie stood there. She was no longer the slim girl he remembered, but at the sight of her his heart leaped, and he forgot everything he had been planning to say.

'Maudie,' he began, and his voice was thick with emotion. 'Thank God I found you.'

They had both changed so much, yet she knew him instantly.

'Oh, Tommy,' she said, and held the door wide. 'Come in.'

As soon as the door shut, they were in each other's arms as if they had never been parted. When they could speak, he said breathlessly: 'I've got so much to tell you. So much has happened.'

'I've got things to tell you too,' she broke in, but his words overlapped hers.

'What are you doing here? Why are you living in Uncle Josh's house?'

Then the tears came, and Maudie fell into his arms again, seeking the comfort of his embrace and weeping. 'I didn't know...I thought you'd never come back...Josh is my husband.'

17

They lay naked in each other's arms after making love again and again—Maudie had no idea what the time was, or how long they had been together—until at last there was nothing they could do except hold one another and look at one another, sharing the wonder of it and the joy.

It had been inevitable. They had not stopped to think or to question it, but had gone straight up to the bedroom, kissing and embracing, caressing and undressing each other, and falling into bed.

Joshua's bed...

Slowly, as passion faded like an ebbing tide, Maudie began to realise what she had done. She had been unfaithful to her husband; she had broken her marriage vows.

'We shouldn't have,' she said in a small voice.

Tom drew back his head so that he could look her full in the face, as if she had said something meaningless.

'We had to,' he said.

'Yes, I know, but—'

'But what? Don't tell me you're sorry—you can't be sorry.'

'No, of course not. It was wonderful, the most wonderful thing...but it was wrong, wasn't it?'

'How could it be wrong? Did it feel wrong to you?'

'No.'

'Of course it didn't. Because it was right. Because you and me, maybe we weren't married in church, but we were married in heaven, in the eyes of God. I always knew that. You must have known it, too—you knew I'd come back some day.'

'I was afraid you'd found somebody else. I thought you'd forgotten me.'

'How can you say that? I wrote to you—I told you I'd come back. The first time was when I'd been in the States about a year, but you never answered my letter. So then I waited a while, and a couple of years later I wrote again. That letter came back through the mail marked *Not known at this address—gone away*. After that I didn't know where the hell you were.'

Maudie stared at him. 'That must have been after I moved, after I married Josh. But everybody knew where I'd gone—why didn't they send the letter on to me?' Then she broke off. 'Why are you looking like that? What is it?'

He turned his head away. 'The idea of you marrying Joshua. I still can't believe it.'

'Tom, I'm sorry, please forgive me. I'd never have married him if I'd known. I never loved him...not like you...not like this.' She clung to him in despair. 'And now it's too late.'

'It's not too late! We can put things right; we'll start over again.' He stroked her arm, lazily and lovingly. 'This puts me in mind of

475

those nights when we lay together like this, with little Trev in the next room. How's the boy doing? He must be a big lad by now.'

She buried her face in his shoulder and gave a sob, between laughter and tears. 'You don't seem to realise how long ago it was. Trevor's a grown man now and—he's left home.'

She told him what had happened as well as she could, and he tried to comfort her, his lips nuzzling the nape of her neck. 'Things will be better from now on, I promise. Like I said, we'll start all over—you must divorce Joshua, then we can be married.'

Lifting her head, she saw the certainty shining in his eyes. She longed to share it, but could not.

'I can't,' she said at last, and her voice was just a thread of sound. 'I've given my word, I promised I'd stay with him always. He loves me, Tom, and I think he needs me.'

'Don't I love you? Don't I need you? I've spent the last fifteen years waiting for this moment—the day I'd come back and find you again. I worked hard, I saved every penny I could, I got promoted each year, and now I'm a company manager in charge of the whole office.'

He looked round the ordinary little bedroom at the fading flowered wallpaper, the drab curtains, the old-fashioned furniture.

'I'm not exactly a rich man, Maudie, but I can give you a better life than this.'

'But this is the life I chose. I don't deserve anything else.'

'Will you hush up and listen? Let me tell you the way it was. When I first got to the States, I didn't aim to stay there long. I planned that when I had some cash saved up, I was going to come back here and tell the truth about what happened at Cyclops Wharf, fifteen years ago. I wanted to clear my name.'

'Oh yes, you must do that—tell everyone the truth!'

Tom interrupted her. 'But as time went on, I realised it was hopeless. Saul Judge was dead, and there were no other witnesses to what happened. Maybe my dad might have tried to back me up, but I had a feeling he wouldn't be around too long. I guess he's dead by now, isn't he?'

'Oh, Tom—I should have told you.' Contrite, Maudie embraced him again. 'There's so much you don't know.'

'That's OK. I reckon I kind of knew it; he was a very sick man when I went away. But that's how it was—I didn't have any evidence on my side, so why should anyone believe my story? I was afraid the police might send someone to find me. I kept remembering how they caught Crippen and brought him back.'

Maudie was horrified. 'Don't say that! He was a murderer! You didn't mean to kill Saul, did you? I've always believed that. Your mum, Aunt Emily, Ruth—we all knew it must have been an accident.'

'But don't you see? I could never prove it. That's why I decided to change my name. Everyone in Yonkers knew me as Tim Jackson—I even think of myself as Tim Jackson now. I had to tell a whole string of lies to the authorities out there. I said I'd run away to sea from an orphanage—that's why I had no papers. It was a lot easier to get into the USA in those days.' He kissed her gently. 'I want you to come back there, to come and live with me. We'll tell everyone you're Mrs Tim Jackson—nobody need ever know any different.'

'I can't. I told you, it's impossible.' Maudie wriggled out of his arms and sat up. 'We must get dressed and go downstairs. Suppose somebody should call in and find you here?'

'That's OK—you can tell 'em I'm a distant relative come over on a visit from New York. Hey, listen—you mentioned Ruth a little while back. I called in at the pub last night, and she didn't recognise me. Let's face it, I was still a kid when I left home.'

'Oh, you shouldn't have—you were taking a dreadful risk.' Standing by the bed, she began to pull on her clothes. 'How long are you going to stay in London?'

'Till you agree to come back with me. I'm going to ask you every day till you say yes.'

In spite of her anxiety, she smiled. 'I don't think you've really grown up at all. You're still just a kid really—wanting things you can't have.'

He threw out an arm, catching her round the waist. 'I seem to remember I generally got what I wanted, didn't I?'

'Now, Tom, stop that!'

'Tim! Tim Jackson—your second cousin from

478

the States.' Naked, he sprang to his feet. 'OK, let's get some clothes on, then I'll help you make the bed. After that we're going out for a walk. You've got to give me a guided tour—take me around the neighbourhood! I'm a stranger in these parts, remember?'

They wandered through the Island in a kind of dream. He tried to show some interest in the changes that had taken place, but they only had eyes for each other—nothing else seemed real. The hours passed like minutes, and it was after six when they returned to Joshua's house...and found Josh already there, in the kitchen.

'What time do you call this? We had to make our own tea,' he began, then stopped in surprise as a bearded young man followed Maudie into the room.

With a sinking heart she began timidly, 'We went out for a walk.'

Tom cut in: 'I should explain—I'm a distant relative of Mrs Judge, second cousin, twice removed. Just got in from the States, so it seemed only right to look up some of our British connections.'

'Oh, yes? I never knew you had any relatives in America, Maudie.' Josh attempted to be sociable, and held out a hand. 'Aren't you going to introduce us?'

'Yes, of course. This is Mister...' She stared at Tommy in dismay, her mind a complete blank.

'Tim Jackson.' Swiftly, he supplied the details. 'From New York. Glad to make your acquaintance, sir.'

As the two men shook hands, there was a thunder of feet on the stairs, and Jimmy and Bertie tumbled into the room. They too stopped short, staring at the stranger. Once again Maudie performed the introductions and they shook hands ungraciously.

'I'm sorry I was late getting tea ready,' Maudie apologised. 'If you'd like to sit down, I'll be as quick as I can.'

'We've eaten,' said Jimmy. 'We helped Dad finish up the veal and ham pie. We're not stopping.'

'Not stopping,' echoed Bertie. 'We've got a meeting tonight.'

'Going to the Brotherhood?' asked Tom, trying to show polite interest.

As the words left his mouth, he realised his mistake; the three men gazed at him in undisguised amazement.

'How d'you know about the Brotherhood?' Jimmy asked.

Tom thought fast. 'Maudie happened to mention it. We have Guilds back home where I come from. I'm a strong Union man myself.'

'Oh, yes? Anyway, this isn't a Brotherhood night,' Jimmy told him.

'Not tonight—we're going to a political meeting,' added Bertie. 'Over Hackney way, so we'll have to get a move on. Ta-ta.'

When they left the house, Joshua cleared his throat. 'Well now, Mr Jackson, sit down—make yourself at home. I should say this calls for a celebration, wouldn't you, Maudie?'

He went to the sideboard, taking out a bottle

and some glasses. Behind his back, Maudie caught Tom's eye, shaking her head vigorously and saying, 'Mr Jackson can't stop. He's got to get back to—where is it you're staying, Tim?'

'I'm putting up at a hotel off Theobalds Road, but you're quite right, I said I'd be back in time for supper, so you'll have to excuse me.'

Cradling the whisky in his arms, Josh expressed his disappointment. 'Sorry to hear that, Mr Jackson. But I hope you'll be calling in again, while you're in London?'

'Oh yes, I will, Mr Judge. I will indeed. Good night.'

As Maudie followed him to the front door to see him out, he added under his breath: 'Tomorrow, and every day. I told you!' Then, loudly, 'Be seeing you, Maudie. Good night!'

When she returned to the kitchen, torn by conflicting emotions, she found Josh had already filled his tumbler with whisky. He looked up, saying, 'Pity he had to rush off like that. I don't much care for Yankees as a rule, but he seemed pleasant enough. Perhaps he'll stay longer next time.'

Tom was as good as his word, and called at Denmark Place the following morning.

Lying awake half the night, wrestling with her conscience, Maudie had made up her mind that this was to be the very last time. She would explain to Tom that this must be goodbye for ever.

Within half an hour of his arrival, they were

in bed again, and again he asked her to go back to America with him.

'You know I can't.' She did not understand how it was possible to be so ecstatically happy and in the depths of despair at the same time. Lying in his arms, she protested helplessly, 'Why can't I make you see? You must never come here again. I bet the neighbours are gossiping already, peeping through their lace curtains.'

'All right—tomorrow you can come up to Theobalds Road and meet me at the hotel instead.'

'I couldn't do that!' She was very shocked. 'Whatever would people say? Besides, tomorrow's Saturday—Josh will be at home.'

'OK, so you can take me sightseeing— Westminster Abbey, the British Museum—all that stuff. Or do you think Joshua would like to come along as well?'

'I'm sure he wouldn't.'

'Fine, then you'll have to show me around on your own, won't you? And Sunday we'll go on a river-steamer, how about that? Or take a stroll through Greenwich Park, maybe. We used to go there, in the old days, remember? When am I going to get it into your head that I mean what I say? One way or another, you're going to see me every day from now on and that's that.'

On Saturday afternoon, the hop-pickers returned from Kent. Florrie delivered the two girls to the Watermen, but refused Ruth's invitation to go in for a cup of tea; she was afraid of Marcus's wrath, if he ever found out she had entered the public-house.

Sharon, clutching a bunch of tired dahlias that she had wheedled out of the farmer's wife, said: 'I won't stop either, Auntie Ruth, thanks all the same. Mumsie will be expecting me.'

'Of course she will; she'll be wanting to hear all about your holiday. Did you have a lovely time?'

'Oh, yes we did, didn't we, Lil?' Sharon smiled.

'Yes,' said Lil briefly. ''Scuse me, I must take my case upstairs.'

Later, she told her mother, 'Parts of it were nice. Parts of it were awful...I don't think you'd have liked it much.'

'I expect it was hard work. How did Matt like hopping? I thought you'd have brought him in for tea. Didn't he come back on the same train as the rest of you?'

'Oh, yes—but he wasn't in the same carriage. He was playing cards with some of his pals.'

'I see. But he enjoyed himself, did he?'

Lil shrugged and said, a little too casually, 'I don't really know. Matt wasn't working with us. I hardly saw him all the time we were there.'

Ruth looked at her more closely, and Lil turned away, unwilling to meet her gaze. So that's it, Ruth thought. She and Matt must have had a tiff—well, I'm not sorry.

She was aware of the friendship that had sprung up at one time between her daughter and Glory's son, and she had always felt uneasy about it. Matt was a difficult, unpredictable boy, and she did not consider him to be nearly good enough for Lil. If something had happened during the past fortnight to drive them apart, so much the better.

At the weekend, Matt went off on another expedition, to Petticoat Lane. On Saturday night, some of his drinking companions at the Ferry House tipped him off that there was going to be 'a bit of fun' at the Sunday morning market, and after a fortnight of country life, he was ready for the kind of excitement that the city had to offer.

Petticoat Lane was a lively place at any time, but Matt's friends had heard a rumour that something out of the ordinary was going to happen.

They roamed through the maze of stalls for a while, keeping their eyes open. At first it seemed to be just like any other Sunday—the same old hustle and bustle, the same old stall-holders keeping up their quick-fire patter:

'I'm not *selling* these canteens of cutlery, lady—I'm *giving* 'em away! Made from the very best Sheffield steel, the same eating-irons what the King and Queen use at Buckingham Palace. Nothing but first-class merchandise here—no rubbish! And I'm not asking the usual purchase price, neither. I'm not even offering them at half-price. I'm begging you on my bended knees to make me an offer... What am I bid for this thirty-six-piece set of solid steel cutlery? What'll you give me?'

Suddenly a harsh voice rang out from the back of the crowd. 'How about a punch in the throat?'

This was followed by a volley of tomatoes,

taken from a greengrocery stall on the other side of the Lane. The salesman flung up his arms to protect himself from this onslaught, dropping the canteen of cutlery which exploded with a crash, spilling knives and forks over the paving-stones.

Immediately there was an uproar. Women screamed and ran for shelter as half a dozen young men in black shirts and trousers pushed through the crowd, snatching more boxes of cutlery from the stall and flinging them aside in a glittering shower of metal.

'Hey, you—stop that! What the hell d'you think you're playing at?' exclaimed the salesman. 'Somebody call a copper!'

'Shut your face, Jew-boy!' retorted the leader of the gang. He signalled to his cronies and they put their shoulders to the ramshackle wooden stall, overturning it.

Matt and his friends joined in, whooping and laughing; this was what they'd been waiting for.

'Let 'em have it!' they shouted, and set up a singsong chant: *'Go—go—Ikey-Mo... Get the yids out—go, go, go!'*

Following the Blackshirts, they ran down the street, weaving in and out of the crowd and picking on the Jewish stall-holders, leaving a trail of havoc. Imitation fur coats, lengths of furnishing fabric, books and gramophone records were tossed left and right; further along they reached the food stalls, and sacks of rice, flour and sugar were toppled and spilled, pastries and bagels trampled underfoot.

It all happened so fast, the invaders had passed on before anyone could stop them, but a few moments later the sound of police-whistles cut through the hubbub and blue-black helmets appeared, bobbing above the crowd—but by that time the damage was done.

'Look out!' One of Matt's pals grabbed him, panting: 'There's coppers working down the Lane from both ends—don't let 'em get you!'

Matt ducked and swerved, taking a short cut through a side alley, then he stopped dead, afraid that he had run straight into a trap. A black saloon car barred his way; the doors were open, the engine already ticking over. As he hesitated, not knowing which way to go, a young man hailed him from the car.

'Hey, Matt! Climb in. We'd better get you out of here.'

With a shock, Matt recognised his cousins, Jimmy and Bertie; they too were wearing black shirts and trousers, and black leather Sam Browne belts.

The police-whistles sounded nearer. Matt needed no second bidding, but scrambled into the big saloon. It was packed with young men, breathless and grinning. The excitement of the chase intoxicated them—their eyes glowed with triumph.

Jimmy put his foot on the accelerator, and the car roared off. Matt realised that it had been waiting there to pick up the leaders of the raiding-party and help them make a swift getaway.

'You're all in this together?' he asked.

'Course we are, we're going back to Head-quarters now.' Jimmy smiled. 'I saw you doing your bit out there—why not come and join us? The party's always on the look-out for keen young chaps like you.'

On Monday afternoon, Florrie went to have her hair washed and set. She visited the salon once a month; Gloria charged her a special cut-price rate, as she was one of the family.

They talked for a while about the hopping expedition, and Florrie complained that it wasn't like the good old days when she was a girl. There were a lot of common people about nowadays. Some of the men had gone off and got drunk in the evenings, and behaved in a very vulgar way afterwards.

'Far as I remember, blokes often used to get a bit of how's-yer-father when they'd had a skinful,' Gloria pointed out. 'Still, it's true what you say, there's some real hooligans about. Did you hear about what happened down the Lane yesterday morning? Attacking the Jews, they were—knocking things over—they ought to be locked up.'

The two women agreed; times were certainly changing, and not for the better. Florrie wanted to know what else had been happening on the Island during her absence, and Gloria said, 'Nothing out of the ordinary. Oh, except for Maudie's American cousin turning up.'

'American cousin?' repeated Florrie in astonishment. 'I never knew she had any cousins in America.'

'Yes, it was a big surprise all round. Breezed in out of the blue, he did, one day last week. I haven't met him myself, but they say he's a proper gent—pots of money, by all accounts, stopping in a hotel up West somewhere. But he took the trouble to come and call on his relations—that shows a good heart, doesn't it? I believe he took Maudie out on a river-steamer yesterday. It's his first time in London, so she's showing him around.'

Glancing in the mirror, she saw a very strange expression on Florrie's face.

'A cousin—from America—taking her out?' Florrie asked. She spoke more slowly than usual, as if her words could not keep pace with her thoughts.

'That's right—what about it?'

'Oh, nothing,' said Florrie, with an effort. 'Like you said, it must have been a big surprise for Maudie.'

As soon as she left the salon, she made straight for Denmark Place. She hammered on the door-knocker and when this produced no result, she knocked again, even more loudly. After a few moments Maudie opened the front door. When she saw Florrie on the step, her face froze.

'Oh, it's you,' she began uncomfortably. Her hair was untidy, and she began to pat it into place.

Florrie eyed her suspiciously, and then her gaze fell upon the heart-shaped pendant on the silver chain hanging round Maudie's neck—and she knew for certain.

'Where is he?' she said.

'Where's who?'

'Don't you play games with me, young woman!'

Florrie pushed past Maudie and went into the kitchen. A bearded man sprawled untidily in the armchair, his tie undone and his shirt unbuttoned. When Florrie entered the room, he scrambled to his feet.

They stared at each other in silence, and then Florrie said, 'So here you are. I guessed as much.' She walked up to him, peering into his face. 'Perhaps the others don't recognise you, but you didn't think you could fool me, did you?'

'Hello, Mum,' he said quietly. 'It's been a long time.'

'Is that all you've got to say for yourself Coming back here with your smart clothes, and a Yankee way of talking—and never a word to me in all these years?'

He tried to explain. 'I went to your house, but they said you were away, so—'

She swept this aside, looking him over critically. 'I'll tell you one thing—them whiskers don't suit you. But I suppose you had to disguise yourself, to be on the safe side—seeing as how you're a wanted man.'

Maudie tried to bring the situation down to something approaching normality, saying with desperate politeness: 'Won't you sit down? Can I make you a cup of tea?'

'I don't want tea. I don't want anything from you, my girl,' snapped Florrie, but she pulled out a chair and sat at the table all the same, folding her hands tightly and never taking her eyes from her son's face. 'In all these years, you couldn't even send me a postcard to tell me how you were getting along, but you managed to write to your fancy woman, didn't you?'

Tom grabbed the chair at the opposite side of the table and flung himself into it, spurred by sudden anger.

'So it was you! You took those letters I wrote to Maudie and you destroyed them! You'd no right to do such a thing.'

'Don't you start telling me what's right and what's wrong. Just look at you, carrying on with a married woman behind her husband's back, making yourself free of this house... Or have you moved in already? Are you sleeping here as well?'

'If you want to know, I'm staying at the Kenilworth Hotel, off Theobalds Road. Ring up and ask if you don't believe me!'

'Don't you give me any back-answers. You're glorying in your sinful wickedness, that's what you're doing. But you won't get away with it. Everybody knows you killed a man, and the police are still looking for you. When I told your dad you'd written a letter, it upset him that much—well, I wished afterwards I'd never told him. I still believe it was the shock of it that did for him, 'cos by next morning he was gone. How does it feel to have two men's deaths on your conscience, eh?'

'Don't say that. It's wicked of you,' Maudie broke in fiercely.

490

'You keep out of this!' Florrie turned on her. 'It was you led my son astray in the first place. Emily told me how you'd been carrying on with him, when you was both living there, over the shop. He was no more than a boy—and you a married woman with a child of your own!'

'I was a widow! When Arnie was killed, I had nobody to care for me...only Tommy.'

'We loved one another then—and we still do,' said Tommy. 'That's why I've come back for her.'

'Are you off your head? Don't you realise she's married again, with a husband and a home of her own? You should never have come here. You must go back where you came from, and never show your face here again.'

'When I go, I'll take Maudie with me,' he said.

'Oh, no, you won't. I won't let you!' She gripped the edge of the table, and her knuckles were white. 'Haven't you brought enough shame upon your family already? I'm telling you—you'll go back to America, here and now, or it'll be worse for you!'

'What do you mean?'

'You'll not commit any more crimes, not if I can help it. Just clear out and leave us in peace, because if you don't I shall go straight to the police and tell them everything.'

Her face was set in deep lines of hatred and bitterness; all colour had drained from her skin, leaving it a muddy grey, except for two spots of vivid red upon her cheekbones. Hanging on to the table, she pulled herself upright, adding,

'They'll take you off and lock you up, and they'll charge you with murder. Get out of here now—today—this minute—or you'll swing for it, my son!'

She spat out the final words, then walked from the house, with a curious stiff-legged gait, and the slam of the door echoed behind her. Terrified, Maudie flung herself into Tom's arms.

'She means it. She really means it...I knew you should never have come back. You must do what she says! You must go away!'

'Not till you come with me,' he repeated firmly. 'She can do what she likes; I'm not leaving without you.'

That afternoon, when the pub shut, Connor and Huw went downstairs to the cellar. Connor led the way with Huw following more slowly, since he still found the steps difficult to negotiate with his bad leg.

'You're sure you feel up to tackling this?' Con asked, switching on the single overhead light. 'It's going to be a massive job.'

When he reached the bottom step, Huw paused and looked around. The cellar ran the entire length of the building, with short tunnels leading off the central area, some of them stacked with barrels of beer, others used as fuel-bunkers beneath the pavement coal-holes. The light could not reach the furthest corners, and the combination of dust and cobwebs, grit and coal-dust made the whole place a cavern of darkness.

492

'It's like the black hole of Calcutta, only not so warm!' Connor went on. 'Danny promised he'd give me a hand at weekends, so if you think it might be too much for you...'

'Not a bit of it.' Huw put aside his stick and began to roll up his sleeves. 'I'm looking forward to some real work for a change. Between us, we'll soon lick this lot into shape.'

'You're a born optimist. Ah well, I suppose we can make a start.'

The cellar was in need of a thorough clear-out; after the night of the Thames flood, it had been drained and cleaned and disinfected, but since then it had been left to accumulate a collection of junk and a thick coating of grime. All the rubbish would have to be thrown out, the floor scrubbed and the walls whitewashed; this job would not be finished in a hurry.

At the end of an hour, they seemed to have made very little impression on it, and when Ruth called down the cellar steps to ask how they were getting along, Connor shouted to her: 'We're doing fine, but you're not to come and look at it yet. We want it to be a surprise!'

Ignoring this, Ruth continued down the steps, carrying a tray, then exclaimed: 'But you haven't even started!'

'That's the surprise,' Huw told her.

'I thought I was supposed to provide refreshments for workers, but since you don't seem to have done anything, I might as well take this tray away again,' she retorted.

'Don't you dare. My gullet's thick with coal-dust already—I'm dry as a bone.' Connor helped himself to a mug of tea. 'As a matter of fact, we've done quite a lot. It just doesn't show, that's all.'

Ruth ran her fingertips over the wall, and inspected the result. 'Filthy,' she said. 'But then London's a filthy place.'

'You never spoke a truer word,' agreed Connor. 'Have you noticed the change in our Lil since she went away? Two weeks in the hop-fields, and she's come back a different girl. Brown-skinned, clear-eyed—that's what living in the country does for you. I tell you this, the day I retire and give up the pub, we're going back to Ireland; that's the greenest place on God's earth.'

Ruth sighed. 'It's also a long way off! If we could just get out of London for a day, it would be something.'

'And why not?' Huw asked suddenly. 'Why don't we all take a day off, once in a while? Catch a bus and travel down to Kent—or Surrey, or Essex—anywhere, so long as we can walk on grass and smell the flowers. We could put up a notice in the window: *Closed for the day*—and give ourselves a holiday, the three of us!'

Ruth turned eagerly to Connor. 'Could we really? It would be so wonderful.'

But Connor was shaking his head. 'The Brewery wouldn't be best pleased. It's our job to stay open seven days a week; we can't turn business away. Besides, the summer's over now. It's the first day of October tomorrow.'

'October can be beautiful,' said Huw. 'When

494

I was a boy, in the valleys, we used to call it the golden month... Wouldn't your mother and father mind the pub for you, just the one day?'

'Da's not strong enough to handle the work now, and it wouldn't be fair to Mam, leaving her carrying all the responsibility.'

'Right, then. I'll stay, and you and Ruth go off on your own.'

'Thanks, Huw. It's a nice thought, but as long as I'm landlord of the Watermen, my place is here—but why don't the two of you go without me? Like you said, a day in the sunshine would do you both a power of good.'

Ruth and Huw looked at one another, and there was a moment of absolute stillness in the cellar, then Huw said softly, 'That'd be fine by me. How about it, Ruth?'

Her mouth felt dry. She licked her lips, unable to reply—and was saved by a voice calling to her.

'Ruth, are you down there?' Mary O'Dell stood at the top of the stairs. 'There's a visitor here to see you—Mrs Judge.'

Ruth moved swiftly. 'My mother wants me. Something must have happened—excuse me,' and she made her escape up the wooden steps.

But it wasn't Louisa Judge; it was Maudie Judge, pale and anxious, who met her in the kitchen.

'I'm sorry to trouble you when you're busy, Ruth, but I must see you.'

'Yes, of course. What's the matter?'

Maudie threw a sideways glance at Mary

O'Dell. 'It's sort of private. I wondered if we could go and talk somewhere?'

Mystified, Ruth took her sister-in-law up to the front bedroom, and sat on the end of the bed, leaving Maudie the stool by the dressing-table—but Maudie could not sit still, preferring to pace up and down.

'It's so hard to know where to begin,' she said. 'I've been worrying myself sick. I don't know what to do, and there's no one else I can turn to...I want to ask your advice.'

'Why, what's wrong?'

Maudie could not meet her eye but moved restlessly about, looking out of the window, picking things up from the dressing-table and putting them down again as she told her story.

'A long while ago, after Arnie was killed, I met somebody. His name's Tim Jackson—you don't know him, but he used to live round here. And we—we fell in love... We had to keep it a secret, 'cos he was too young to get married—he's five years younger than me. Anyway, not long afterwards he went off to America. He thought there'd be more chance for him out there, and he was right. He's done very well for himself—he's got a good job now, with plenty of money. Last week, he came back to London on a visit.'

Ruth interrupted: 'Just a minute, I think Glory said something the other day. Isn't he a relative of yours?'

Maudie stammered, 'Oh yes, that's right—a distant relation. Second cousin, something like that. Only we hadn't seen each other for fifteen years. It's funny, he talks American now, and—and he still loves me. Of course he didn't know I'd married again, but now he wants me to leave Josh and go away with him.'

'But you love Josh, don't you? You must love him.'

Maudie's face was flushed as she struggled to tell the truth, or as much of it as she dared. 'I never really loved Josh. He's been good to me, I don't deny that, but it wasn't love. Not the way I loved Tim—they way I still love him. I told him Josh will never agree to a divorce, but he says he doesn't care about that. He wants me to go with him anyway, back to America. He comes to see me every day; he says he'll never leave me till I say yes.' She turned to face Ruth at last, and the words burst from her in a torrent. 'And I want to. I want to so much, it's driving me mad!' Then she fell on her knees, clasping Ruth's hands. 'Tell me what I should do!'

Ruth tried to collect her thoughts; on the mantelpiece, the bedroom clock seemed to be ticking much more loudly than usual, nearly as loud as the words that kept repeating in her brain, over and over: *He's five years younger than me...*

Could Maudie know somehow that there was a difference of five years between her and Huw Pritchard? Could she possibly be hinting? No, of course not; she mustn't let her imagination run away with her. In any case, she had done nothing to be ashamed of.

Still clasping her hands, Maudie said, 'You're

497

so cold. Your fingers are like ice—aren't you feeling well?'

'I'm perfectly all right.' Ruth took a deep breath, then went on. 'I think you know in your heart what you have to do. You married Josh for richer or poorer, for better or for worse. You made a promise to him, and to God. Whatever this other man says—whatever you feel for him—that doesn't give you the right to leave your husband. You must be strong; you have to do your duty.'

Maudie's face crumpled, as she tried not to cry. 'Yes, I know. I've known that all the time. P'raps I needed somebody else to say it to me.' She fumbled in her sleeve. 'Oh dear, now I can't find my hankie.'

Ruth produced a clean handkerchief, and Maudie wiped her eyes. Ruth put her arms round her, holding her and kissing her; on her cheeks, Maudie's tears were mingled with her own.

Some time later, when Maudie had gone home and it was time to open the pub for the evening, Huw drew back both the bolts on the front door, top and bottom, then limped across to the bar, where Ruth was putting the cash float into the till.

'Did you think over what Con was saying?' he asked her. 'About the day out? How about next Sunday, if it's fine? We could go down to Dorking—Box Hill's very nice, and I know a hotel where we could have a bite to eat.'

Ruth slammed the cash-drawer shut and turned away, saying over her shoulder, 'I'm sorry, Huw. I couldn't possibly go with you—not without Connor. You know that.'

And she went out of the saloon without looking at him.

On Tuesday afternoon, Tom called at Denmark Place for the last time. He took off his hat and coat and threw them on to the kitchen table. 'This is the day,' he said.

She looked at him sadly, knowing what she had to do. 'What do you mean by that?'

'Our last day in London. We can't go on like this. We're wasting time—wasting our life together. This is the day when you're coming with me.'

'No, Tom. I've told you over and over—I can't.' She screwed up the last ounce of her strength. 'This is the day we have to say goodbye.'

He took a step towards her. 'Are you saying you've stopped loving me?'

'No.'

'And you know I love you more than ever. Are you saying you don't want me?'

'Yes. Well, no—not exactly—but it's got to finish, Tom. You're going back to America and I'm staying here, with Josh.'

'Are you trying to tell me you'd let me go? That we're never to see each other again?'

She lifted her chin bravely. 'Yes,' she said.

He came nearer still, so close, she could not look at him, but shut her eyes. She could feel the warmth of his body, so close to her own, and she could smell the thrilling, masculine smell of him, and feel his breath upon her cheek.

'Kiss me goodbye then,' he said, and took her in his arms.

At six o'clock, Josh came home from work. He was not altogether surprised to find the kitchen empty and the table not laid; no doubt Maudie's damned cousin had taken her out again. She'd come home soon, pink and flustered, apologising for being late.

He frowned uneasily when he saw the letter on the sideboard, propped up against the biscuit-barrel. Tearing the envelope open, he started to read; then he sat down slowly and began to read it all over again, from the beginning.

He did not hear Florrie when she knocked at the front door; she knocked three times, growing more and more impatient. Suddenly she remembered that she still had a spare key to Josh's house, though she had not used it since he married Maudie. She found the key at the bottom of her purse, and let herself into the house.

Joshua was still sitting at the table, a bottle of scotch beside him and the letter in his hands. He did not look up when Florrie came in, asking urgently, 'What's happened? Where's Maudie? Is she with—that man?'

In answer to her questions, Josh passed over the letter without a word. When she had read it, she exclaimed shrilly, 'Well, don't just sit there! You must go after them—fetch her back!'

Josh spoke with difficulty, in a voice distorted with pain. 'What's the use? She doesn't want me... She's made that clear enough.'

'Don't be a fool, she's your wife! I know where they've gone. I know the name of the hotel. You must go to the police and have them took up!'

'She doesn't want me,' he repeated. 'Maudie's gone—let her go.'

'But the police can arrest him. They'll put him in prison, and it's no more than he deserves. If you won't do it, then I will!'

She was already at the front door when another thought occurred to her, and she paused with her hand on the latch. If she told the police all she knew, the whole story would have to come out. That would mean still more scandal for the Judge family—and what good would it do, in the long run? Once it was common knowledge, Josh could never take Maudie back, it would be too humiliating... Better for him to build a new life, without her.

Slowly, she retraced her steps and said carefully: 'I've been thinking—you're probably right. She was always a cheap, flighty girl; she was never a good wife to you, Josh—you're well rid of her. But don't you worry, you're not alone. I'm still here to look after you, and I won't ever let you down.'

After Maudie's unexpected visit to the pub on Monday afternoon, Connor had asked Ruth: 'What was all that about? Mam said she seemed

501

a bit upset. It's not that boy of hers again, come home to make trouble?'

So Ruth had to tell him that it was nothing to do with Trevor. An old flame from Maudie's past had turned up from nowhere—a young man she knew before she married Josh, begging her to run away with him to America... And Maudie had been tempted to go.

'So what did you say to her?' Con had asked.

'I told her she shouldn't even consider it, of course. I said she should stay with her husband.' Ruth looked at him in surprise. 'What else could I say?'

'I don't know.' A fleeting smile crossed Connor's face, but it was gone before she could interpret it. 'I just hope she was grateful for your advice.'

They heard no more from Denmark Place until Wednesday evening, just before closing-time. Ruth was helping Con in the saloon, and Huw came through from the public bar to get some silver, because his till was running out of change.

As Connor counted out five pounds in shillings and sixpences, the street door flew open and Josh appeared. When he lurched across to the bar, they all saw that he was drunk.

'Give me a pint, and a double scotch as a chaser. Here, take it out of this,' he said, fumbling in his pocket and slapping a handful of notes on the counter. 'Oh, and whatever you're having yourselves. Join me in a little—little celebration, will you?'

Ruth began gently, 'Josh, you've already had a few by the looks of it, and it's getting late. Don't you think you ought to be heading for home?'

'No, not yet.' Josh winked, putting his finger alongside his nose. 'I know better'n that—I can't go home like this. She doesn't approve of me drinking, you see. But if I leave it till later, with any luck Florrie will have gone to bed already.'

'Did you say Florrie?' Ruth asked sharply. 'You mean Maudie, don't you?'

'Oh, no. Florrie moved in this afternoon; she's taken the spare room in the attic. She's going to be our new housekeeper—that's what I'm celebrating,' he explained thickly. 'Come on, Mr O'Dell. Better get those drinks in before you call time.'

'But where's Maudie?' Ruth wanted to know.

'Haven't you heard? She's gone away—gone to America with her Yankee cousin. I thought everyone knew that. Gone off with the man she loves.' As he uttered the last word, his body twisted and his shoulders hunched forward. He hung his head, so they should not see the grief in his face.

They averted their eyes. Ruth, Connor and Huw all turned away from the spectacle of this sad, lonely man—and found themselves staring at each other in the engraved glass mirrors round the walls of the saloon. Wherever they looked, they could see nothing but endless reflections of one another.

18

Sunday, 4 October, 1936 was a milestone in the history of London, for it was the date of the so-called Battle of Cable Street.

In the popular mythology of the East End, Cable Street remains a heroic landmark; a bloody conflict between Oswald Mosley and his British Union of Fascists on one side, and the mass of working-class Londoners on the other.

The reality was rather different.

By late September, the BUF periodical *The Blackshirt* was putting out announcements of a march through East London, starting at the Royal Mint and proceeding via Shoreditch, Limehouse and Bow to end in a mass meeting at Victoria Park.

Anti-Jewish feeling had been whipped up by the Mosleyite agitators; messages like *Get rid of the yids* and *PJ* (for 'Perish Judah') appeared on hoardings everywhere.

Among the anti-fascists, feelings were equally intense; everyone knew about the Spanish Civil War between the left-wing Popular Front and Franco's Nationalist Party. The defiant Communist slogan, *They shall not pass,* had become famous, and that autumn it began to appear all over East London, whitewashed on walls and pavements. As the day of the march drew near, loudspeaker vans patrolled the streets, calling on all sympathisers to rally to the defence lines; they were determined to block the roads at Cable Street and Gardiner's Corner.

The BUF march had been given official permission by the Commissioner of Police, and six thousand officers were posted at strategic points between Tower Hill and Whitechapel; every policeman in the metropolitan area was called in for duty on 4 October.

By noon on Sunday, the Blackshirts were mustered at Royal Mint Street. Their leader arrived later and the march, due to set off at two o'clock, was not ready to start until three-thirty.

The police struggled to clear the crowds in Cable Street, where willing hands had put up barricades. Worn-out furniture, piles of builders' material, corrugated iron sheets and an overturned lorry were blocking the road. Behind these defences stood an army of determined men; Irish Catholics like Danny, Communists like Huw and Jewish protesters like Ernest and Abram stood shoulder to shoulder.

When they defied the order to withdraw and let the planned march go through, the police used force, charging them again and again with fixed batons, and a pitched battle broke out.

Sympathetic bystanders joined in, hurling stones and brickbats at the police. Ordinary housewives, looking down on the scene from upstairs windows, added to the tumult, flinging empty milk-bottles and old tin cans on to the policemen down below. Soon the roads and

505

pavements were running with blood, and helpers did their best to rescue the wounded and carry them to hospital.

At Tower Hill, where the Blackshirts waited impatiently, the Commissioner finally made up his mind; in the interests of public safety, the proposed march must be cancelled—and Mosley had no choice but to agree to this decision.

The anti-fascists, bloody but unbowed, withdrew their forces and the Battle of Cable Street was over—for the time being.

But that was not the end of it.

A week later, the triumphant East-Enders held a victory parade, impudently electing to follow an identical route from Tower Hill to a mass meeting in Victoria Park. This was sanctioned by the authorities, and the march went ahead as planned, with police escorts smiling jovially, side by side with the same protesters they had been fighting seven days earlier.

From Tower Hill to Victoria Park is a distance of three or four miles, and Danny persuaded Huw that he shouldn't attempt it.

'Being part of a human barricade is one thing,' he told him, 'but you're not going to set yourself up as a marathon walker, are you?'

Instead, he took fifteen-year-old Abram to keep him company and, against his better judgment, though nothing short of brute force would have kept her away, his sister Lil.

They were half-expecting trouble, but on the outward march there were no problems. At some street corners, they noticed groups of youths who shouted rhythmically: *The yids—the yids—we gotta get rid of the yids!'* and raised their arms in the fascist salute, but the marchers ignored them, and a young police constable who was keeping pace with them remarked, 'There won't be any trouble today. They know better than to start any rough stuff while we're around.'

'Oh, thanks very much, officer,' said Danny, with an exaggerated display of gratitude. 'If it wasn't for you, we'd be shaking in our shoes!'

The policeman smiled, then added, 'I believe I've seen you round the Island, haven't I? Aren't you Connor O'Dell's son?'

'That's right,' agreed Danny, rather surprised. 'And this is my sister Lil—and Abram Kleiber, who's a cousin of ours.'

'Glad to know you,' said the constable. 'I've had the pleasure of meeting your dad a couple of times. The name's Burns, Mike Burns. Remember me to him, will you?'

But Mike Burns's prediction of a trouble-free march proved to be wrong. As soon as the marchers were out of sight, the corner-boys went into action. For more than half a mile, they tore along the road, wrecking every Jewish shop-front they passed. Armed with sticks, iron bars and hatchets, they smashed windows and scattered merchandise; a hairdresser who stood watching them from his doorway was picked up and hurled bodily through the window of a nearby tailoring shop, then the gang seized a little girl and threw her in on top of him. Amazingly, in the middle of so much broken glass, neither of them were seriously injured.

The tailor's car was parked at the kerb, and this too became a target; they surrounded and overturned it, and as petrol streamed out of the tank, one of them tossed down a lighted match, and the car went up in a sheet of flame.

Less than a mile away, at the entrance gates of the park, the police were unaware of this frenzy of destruction. As the protesters marched in through the gates, a loudspeaker-van gave out instructions: 'This is to be an orderly meeting... There must be no disturbance... If there is any fighting to be done, the police are here to do it... Nothing must discredit today's march.'

It was when the meeting was over that the real confrontation began.

When Danny and Lil marched out of the park, they were faced by an angry crowd of young men and women who shouted: 'Up the fascists! Down with the dirty yids!'

Abram began to run towards them, shaking his fist, but Danny grabbed him and dragged him back, saying, 'Don't be a fool! You wouldn't stand a chance against that lot.'

As he spoke, the mob began to pelt them with sticks and stones, rotten apples and rashers of stale bacon, singing loudly and discordantly: 'We are the boys of the Bulldog Breed,' and following this up with a version of the National Anthem. Between each verse they pressed forward to spit in the faces of the marchers, while the police tried desperately to keep order.

Half a dozen young men broke through the police cordon, charging into the procession, and Lil called urgently: 'Danny—take care!'

508

Just in time, he ducked to avoid a slashing blow from an open cut-throat razor. He threw his arms protectively round his sister, then he recognised his attacker. It was Matt Judge.

Matt recognised Danny and Lil at the same instant. His mouth sagged open in dismay, and the razor fell from his hand, to be kicked away under the feet of the crowd.

'What are you doing here?' he asked.

'We're making a protest!' retorted Danny furiously. 'What d'you think you're doing, for God's sake?'

The crowd surged suddenly, and they clutched one another, knowing that if they lost their footing, they could all be trampled to death.

'Come on, let's go,' growled Matt. Lowering his head, he charged into the writhing mass of bodies like a knife through butter, leaving a passage behind him so that the others could follow.

An hour later, Danny and Lil got back to the Watermen. The pub didn't open till seven on Sunday evenings, and Huw was alone in the saloon when they went in.

'Where's Mum and Dad?' asked Danny.

'Upstairs—they'll be down in a minute.' Taking in their dishevelled appearance, Huw whistled. 'What the devil have you two been up to?'

Quickly, they told him about the violent climax to the 'victory parade'.

'We were lucky—we got through without a scratch, but a lot of people were beaten up,' Danny told him. 'Abram was OK too, except the sleeve of his jacket was ripped by a broken bottle. I don't know how he's going to explain that to his mum.'

'You'd best slip upstairs and get changed yourselves, before anyone sees you like that,' began Huw.

'Yes, in a minute. We've got something to tell you,' Lil interrupted. 'Something else we found out... Matt Judge has joined the fascists. He came at us with a razor, but when he saw it was us, he changed his mind. It's funny—I used to think he was a friend of mine, isn't that weird?'

'He's always been like that—all muscle and no brain,' said Danny. 'Still, he helped us get through the crowd and I suppose we should be grateful for that... But who d'you think got him into the BUF in the first place? Jimmy and Bertie Judge! He told us they're both full members of the Blackshirts.'

Huw spoke quietly, but his voice was bitter. 'So that's what the Brotherhood's turned into. They're not just against the Left Wing now, they've become Mosley's biff-boys. My God, if I'd been able to get some real evidence against them that time, I'd have put a stop to their tricks once and for all...'

For a moment, the men had forgotten Lil until she broke in: 'What do you mean? What sort of evidence?'

They exchanged glances. 'I'll tell you later,' said Danny. Then, as they heard the sound of a door opening upstairs, he concluded quickly, 'That'll be Dad now. Better nip into the scullery and get tidied up before he comes down.'

As it happened, it was a false alarm. Connor and Ruth did not come downstairs till the stroke of seven, and when they did, they looked unusually serious and preoccupied.

'Something wrong?' enquired Huw.

'It's Con's da,' said Ruth. 'That chesty cold's giving him a lot of trouble. He can't seem to shake it off.'

'He'll be fine,' Connor assured her, with more confidence than he felt. 'Mam's going to give him some Friar's Balsam—that should clear his tubes.'

'Yes. I'll boil up some water for her.' Ruth went through into the kitchen. 'Why do these things always happen on a Sunday, when the chemists are shut and you can't get a doctor?'

Next morning, Patrick O'Dell was still no better, so Ruth offered to go round to Dr Mackay's surgery and ask for a prescription.

There were several people already in the waiting-room, but she found a vacant chair next to a big, burly man with greying hair and a florid face. As she sat down beside him, he shifted ungraciously to make room for her, and with a shock she realised that it was her brother.

'Josh!' she exclaimed. 'Fancy seeing you!'

For a moment he stared at her through bloodshot eyes, as if he had difficulty in focusing, then he forced a smile.

'Ruth,' he said. 'Well, well. What are you doing here?'

She explained about her father-in-law's illness;

he muttered some conventional good wishes, then fell silent again. Ruth felt impelled to ask, 'And how about you? How are you keeping?'

'Me? Oh, I'm not so bad—mustn't grumble.'

Guiltily, she realised she hadn't seen him for a very long time. They had met in the street occasionally, and snatched a few words in passing, but she hadn't really talked to Josh since Maudie left him.

'Just dropped in to ask the Doc to give me a tonic,' he continued. 'You know how it is. We're none of us getting any younger, are we?'

Looking at him, Ruth could think of nothing to say in reply. He seemed to have aged a great deal in the past year. His face was flabby and his nose red and swollen, marked with broken veins. She had seen enough heavy drinkers in the pub to recognise the tell-tale signs.

'How are you getting along at home?' she ventured. 'How are the boys? And Florrie?'

'Oh, we're rubbing along pretty well, considering. Florrie's a bit too fond of talking for my taste, but she's a good worker, I'll say that for her. Anyhow, I'm out most evenings.'

'I see...' Ruth tried to think of a more cheerful topic, and remembered suddenly. 'You've got a birthday coming up soon, haven't you? The middle of October?'

'Fancy you remembering! Yes, next weekend I'll be celebrating my fiftieth—it's going to be a great occasion.'

'Fifty. I can hardly believe it—where have the years gone?'

'It's a solemn thought, eh? Half a century...'

He tried to make light of it. 'We're going to have a bit of a do; as it happens, we'll be making some changes at the Wharf as well. I dare say young Daniel will have told you?'

'I believe he did say something about rebuilding.'

'Our old offices are practically falling down and there's plenty of space that could be put to better use, so at the end of the week we'll be moving out into temporary quarters in one of the warehouses, while they start rebuilding. The boys suggested throwing a party, Saturday night, to mark my half-century and a farewell to the old premises, too. They're dead set on doing it in style—a few drinks, music and dancing—that sort of thing.'

'Wine, women and song? What will Father have to say about that?'

Josh winked at her. 'Father's not invited! Between you and me, the old man doesn't know what's going on half the time. Spends most of the day studying the Scriptures. Now and then he hobbles out for an hour or so, to set up his soapbox at some street corner and preach another hellfire sermon—and generally make a nuisance of himself.. No, I shan't be asking Father.'

Then he turned to Ruth. 'But how about you? You're still family, no matter what Father says. Why don't you bring Connor along, and the youngsters? You'd be more than welcome.'

'Oh, I don't know. It's good of you to ask us, but Saturday's our busiest night—and what with Con's father being poorly, and everything... But

I'll certainly pass on the message; it's kind of you to think of us.'

When she got home, with medicated wadding for Patrick's chest, a tin of ointment and a bottle of medicine—it took a lot of coaxing before he would consent to taste it—all thought of Joshua's birthday party went out of her head.

It wasn't until supper-time, when she dished up yesterday's cold beef and bubble-and-squeak to the family, that she remembered the invitation.

Connor dismissed the idea out of hand. 'Saturday? Not a chance,' he said. 'But you could go without me—why don't you?'

'I shouldn't enjoy it. It wouldn't be much fun on my own.'

'You won't be on your own. Didn't you say he'd asked Danny and Lil? Come to that, why don't you take Huw along in my place?'

Huw looked up, then said flatly, 'Sorry, I'm afraid I shouldn't be much use to Ruth as a dancing-partner.'

She concentrated on the plate in front of her, carefully cutting up a slice of meat... Did Connor know what he was saying? Or had he been reading her thoughts? Did he guess how she sometimes dreamed about dancing with Huw? There were times when she ached to touch him, to hold him in her arms—even now, the idea sent a shiver of excitement through her.

'No,' she said, without looking up. 'I can't possibly go. You'll need all the help you can get on Saturday night.'

At the other side of the table, Huw added, 'Anyway, I doubt if they'd welcome me with open arms at a Brotherhood party. Danny, could I trouble you to pass the sauce-bottle?'

Danny did not respond immediately, and they all looked at him.

'Danny?' Lil nudged her brother. 'Huw wants the brown sauce.'

'Eh? Sorry, I was thinking about something else.' Danny passed the bottle, then gave Huw a meaning look. 'If Lil and me are invited, I don't see why we shouldn't accept their kind invitation, do you? Matter of fact, I'd quite like to have a last look round the old Office, before they move out.'

Red sails in the sunset, way out on the sea.
Oh, carry my loved one safe homeward to me.

The Jubilee Wharf had never known an evening like it. Within the gates, a marquee had been erected, and inside the marquee a temporary wooden floor had been varnished and polished until it was smooth enough for dancing. At one end of the tent, a cold buffet was laid out, and a bar dispensed drinks; at the other end, a four-piece band sat on a built-up rostrum, pumping out recent popular songs.

When Lil and Danny arrived, the nightwatchman on duty directed them into the Guild Office, now converted into a cloakroom, where they left their hats and coats. They were both looking very smart; Danny had on his best blue suit and Lil wore a new dress in lime-green shantung, bought with money she had saved up from her wages. They passed into the marquee, where Uncle Joshua greeted them cheerfully, if a trifle vaguely.

'Ah, Daniel! Come in, lad, come in. And your sister—beg pardon, my dear, I'm a terrible one for names. Lilian, of course... Come in, both of you—eat, drink and be merry! Sorry your mum and dad couldn't be with us, but it can't be helped.'

Danny and Lil had visited the People's Palace in the Mile End Road with their friends, and sometimes partnered one another, so they joined the crowd on the dance-floor.

Night and day—you are the one.
Only you beneath the moon, or under the sun.

Although the day had been sunny, an autumn breeze was blowing from the river and it grew chilly once the sun had gone down, but oil-stoves were set up at various points around the tent, and the dancers soon warmed up.

Josh leaned against the bar, chatting to his sons. When Danny and Lil left the dance-floor, he beckoned them over.

'Come along, you two—what'll you have to drink? Jimmy—Bertie—don't let your cousins stand there without a glass in their hands. Look alive, boys!'

'Do you want a lemonade, or would you prefer something stronger?' Bertie asked.

'I'll have a beer, please,' said Danny. 'Lil doesn't drink.'

'Course, I was forgetting—she's only a baby!' Bertie's face creased into an oily smile. 'Lemonade or soda-pop for the little lady?'

'Don't you be so cheeky!' retorted Lil. 'I'm sixteen—I can have a real drink, if I feel like it.'

'Ah, but do you feel like it?' Jimmy teased her.

'Yes, I do—so there!' She saw an older girl sipping a red drink with bubbles fizzing in it. 'I'd like that, whatever it is.'

'Sparkling burgundy for Lilian, why not?' Jimmy gave the order to the barman. 'One sparkling, and one beer.'

Leaning back with her elbows on the bar, Lil felt very grown-up and said, 'I'm enjoying this! Uncle Josh ought to have a party every year!' She took the glass Jimmy gave her, and raised it in a toast: 'Many happy returns, Uncle. Chin-chin!'

Somehow she had expected it to be sweet, like Cherryade; the strong, dry tang of burgundy surprised her, but it was not unpleasant and she took another gulp. Above the rim of the glass, she caught Danny's eye and read the message he was sending her. She nodded imperceptibly—she knew what she had to do now.

Emboldened by the drink, she set herself out to be very sociable, saying to Joshua, 'I haven't seen Auntie Florrie yet. Isn't she here tonight?'

Bertie sniggered. 'Can't you just picture her, dancing cheek-to-cheek with Dad?' and Jimmy guffawed.

517

Josh's smile was wiped off, and he reprimanded his sons. 'That'll be enough of that. No, Florrie's not with us this evening—it's not really her sort of party.'

'Tea and biscuits at the Mothers' Meeting—that's more her style, eh?' Bertie chipped in.

'I said give it a rest!' Awkwardly, Joshua moved away to greet some newcomers. 'Hello, there. Glad to see you—come and have a drink...'

Jimmy glanced round. 'Where's that brother of yours? He was here a minute ago.'

'Must have slipped away somewhere,' said Bertie.

'I expect he found himself another dancing-partner,' said Lil. 'There's such a crush on the floor now, you can't see everybody.' She moved closer to Jimmy. 'It's funny—though we're cousins, we've never really got to know each other very well, have we?'

'Well, now's the time to put that right.' Jimmy smiled at her. 'How are you getting on with Gloria at that hairdressing parlour?'

'All right. You ought to drop in some time. If you ever feel like a shampoo and set, we'll give you a special rate!' She was trying to be as entertaining as she could, to distract his attention from the fact that Danny was no longer in the marquee.

If anyone asked him what he was doing, Danny was going to say he'd gone to the cloakroom to get a handkerchief from his coat-pocket, but there didn't seem to be anyone about. Going through the outer office, he tried the inner door—and found it locked. Well, that would have been too much to hope for... Retracing his steps, he slipped round the outside of the building, looking up at the row of windows. He couldn't see in, for the blinds were drawn, but luck was on his side, as one of the sashes had been left a few inches open at the top. If he pulled himself up on to the sill, he should be able to slide it down and—

'Hello! What's all this, then? Trying to break in, are we?'

He whirled round; he was faced by four members of the Brotherhood, led by Bertie Judge. Danny backed against the wall, thinking fast.

'No, of course not. I saw someone had left the window open and I was going to shut it.'

Bertie snorted with laughter. 'That's a good one, that is. You don't suppose we're going to fall for that, do you?'

'What d'you mean?' protested Danny, and made to walk past them. 'I just went to the cloakroom. I'm going back to the dance now.'

A heavy hand stopped him. 'You're not going anywhere, Sunny Jim,' said Bertie. 'We know all about you—don't we, Cheesey?'

Danny was well aware that Cheesey Cheshire disliked him, ever since the night when he'd had to confess he was afraid of ghosts; so he couldn't expect any sympathy from Cheesey, nor from Bertie's other henchmen.

'We know who your friends are, an' all,' sneered Cheesey, moving closer. 'We saw you last Sunday marchin' with them—lefties and yids, all of 'em.'

'And we don't like your cheek, coming here tonight where you're not wanted,' continued Bertie.

'I was invited. Your dad asked us to his birthday party!'

'Don't give me any lip! You came here because you wanted to snoop round the place. Peeping and prying, trying to stir up trouble,' said Bertie. 'OK, lads—let's teach him a lesson.'

He could not make a run for it. He tried to fight them off, but they picked him up bodily and carried him round the back of the building, over the cobblestones and out along the jetty. If he yelled for help, no one would hear him. In the distance, the sound of the band slowly faded:

Horsey, honey, don't you stop.
Just let your feet go clippety—clop...

'What are you going to do?' Danny asked breathlessly; the words were jerked from him as they humped him along like a sack of potatoes.

'You'll find out,' said Bertie, and he giggled again.

Danny's guts twisted with fear. He remembered the Punishment Squad, and the death of Izzy Kleiber... Was he too about to be tied up, dropped in the Thames and left to drown?

No. Danny was small fry—he did not merit such a drastic sentence. Instead, four pairs of

520

hands lifted him up, and Bertie's voice rang out: 'One—two—three—*go!*'

They swung him high and let him go. He fell down—down—into the river below. As it happened, the tide was going out, and close to the dock-wall it was no more than six feet deep. Icy water closed over his head and soft, oozing mud embraced him; with one strong kick he propelled himself upwards and broke the surface again, their laughter still ringing in his ears.

This was to be his punishment—jeering humiliation, and a cold bath. They left him to extricate himself as best he could, and he began to swim past the slimy river-wall until he reached a landing-stage where a dinghy bobbed at its moorings. Sodden and shivering, he scrambled out and made his way up a flight of wooden steps, while the dance band went on playing faintly in the distance:

Your tail goes swish, and the wheels go round.
Giddy-up, you're homeward bound!

Inside the marquee, Jimmy and Lil were laughing. He had been telling her a joke, but the music was so loud and the guests were making such a din, she couldn't hear all the words—but she laughed anyway.

'I mustn't have any more to drink—I'll get squiffy!' she said.

'Why not?' He pressed another glass into her hands. 'That's what we're here for, to enjoy ourselves!'

At the far end of the bar, the nightwatchman had come into the tent, looking for Joshua. Josh had to cup his ear and tell the man to speak up before he could make out what he was saying.

'Your father—Mr Marcus—he's outside, carrying on again.'

'How the hell did he find out?' grumbled Joshua, but he went to investigate.

It was a bizarre spectacle. Marcus Judge stood between the open iron gates, holding up his painted banner—*The End of the World is Nigh*—and leaning upon the pole. There was nobody about; no one was listening to him as he declaimed in a cracked voice that was no more than an echo of its former glory: 'Behold the heathen in their wickedness, bringing shame upon the land. Behold the undutiful son who has brought down his father's grey hairs in sorrow to the grave. Behold the evil-doers in their sinful lechery and drunkenness.'

Joshua walked up and stood face to face with the old man. 'Nobody's paying any attention to you, Father. Why don't you give it a rest?'

Marcus continued as if Joshua had not spoken: 'Woe to that man who hath his father's curse upon him, for he shall meet his doom. He shall be cast into the everlasting furnace and perish in the flames of hellfire.'

Calmly and deliberately, Joshua took the banner from him; without its support, Marcus swayed and would have fallen, but Joshua steadied him, saying wearily: 'Come on, Father —I'll see you home.' But when he tried to help him, Marcus shook him off.

'Take your hands from me! You've been drinking again—you reek of alcohol. I want nothing to do with you. You're no son of mine.'

Using the banner as a staff, he began to propel himself slowly along the street. Joshua hesitated, uncertain whether to go after him, then abandoned the idea and went back to his birthday party.

Got a date with an angel,
Gonna meet her at seven.
Got a date with an angel,
And I'm on my way to heaven.

Jimmy and Lil were dancing now. She was happy and excited, and more than a little confused. The drink had gone to her head and she kept tripping over Jimmy's feet. Each time she did so, he chuckled and held her more tightly.

She felt dizzy; conflicting emotions were sweeping through her, leaving her more confused than ever. She told herself that she hated Jimmy Judge and everything he stood for. She hated his bully-boy politics and his strong-arm tactics—and yet she couldn't help enjoying the sensation of those strong arms around her, and the warmth of his body moving against hers... She had come to this party for one reason only. Danny had told her about the Punishment Squad, and the evidence he needed to prove that Izzy Kleiber's death had not been an accident. It was up to her to keep Jimmy and Bertie entertained while Danny went to search the Guild offices... The trouble was, she couldn't keep track of both brothers at once, and Bertie seemed to have disappeared. Besides, it was difficult to think clearly while the blood was racing through her veins, and the beat of the music was carrying her away, and her legs felt so very unsteady and peculiar...

Thank goodness—there was Bertie at last.

He threaded his way through the dancers and came up to them, tapping Jimmy on the shoulder.

Jimmy began to object. 'This isn't an excuse-me,' but Bertie whispered something in his ear. Jimmy nodded thoughtfully, then said, 'OK, leave it to me.'

Bertie disappeared into the crowd once more, and Jimmy steered Lil away from the dance-floor, saying: 'I just heard—your brother's not too well. He's feeling sick—let's hope it wasn't anything he ate in the buffet. Anyhow, he didn't fancy coming back inside, so he's taken himself off home.'

'Oh, poor Danny. I must go and find him!'

'No, don't do that. He's been gone ten minutes or more; you'd never catch up with him. And he left a message to tell you he didn't want to spoil your fun; he'd like you to stay here. He knew we'd take good care of you.' Taking Lil to a table near the bar, he helped her into a chair. 'I'll get us both a drink, then we can sit and talk for a while, how about that?'

Sitting alone, Lil tried to sort out her muddled thoughts.

Poor old Danny—feeling sick—gone home. That means it's up to you now, my girl, she told herself. Somehow you've got to find that discipline thingummy. Get the evidence.

When Jimmy rejoined her, he had a tot of whisky for himself and another sparkling burgundy for Lil.

She said weakly, 'I shouldn't really,' but she sipped it, playing for time. Putting on a bright smile, she said suddenly: 'I'm sure your work here must be very interesting. You must tell me about it.'

He began to talk about life on the docks, but she urged him to tell her more details about the Brotherhood.

'It's not like the other Unions, is it? I know that much. I mean, it's more like a secret society, with its own Rules and Regulations. I wish you'd explain them to me.'

'If I did, they wouldn't be secret any more, would they?' he countered.

'Stop teasing! You can tell me—I'm your cousin, and I know the Brotherhood was started by your grandfather. He's my grandpa as well, so I've got as much right to know about things as you have. In fact, I could be a sort of sister in the Brotherhood, couldn't I?' she suggested.

Jimmy smiled. 'Yeah, that's an idea. All right then, what do you want to know?'

'There's something called the Punishment Squad, isn't there?' She knew it was very important to get this part right, and she made an effort to pronounce each word clearly and correctly. 'For dealing with offences against

Guild Rules... Danny told me that.'

'Your brother should learn to keep his mouth shut,' said Jimmy.

'He knows he can trust me. Besides, if you let me join the Brotherhood I'll have to know all the Rules, won't I? Is it true you write down all the punishments in a Dissy—Dishy,' at the third attempt she got as far as, 'the Discipline something?'

'The Discipline Register?' He threw her a quick glance. 'Why do you want to know about that?'

'Oh, I just think it's interesting. I'd really like to see the Register—do you think I could?'

'If that's what you want, I don't see why not. Mind, you'll have to become a member of the Brotherhood first! The very first sister to join the Brotherhood.' And he smiled again, reaching across the table to squeeze her hand.

'Finish your drink, and come with me,' he said.

Joshua was taking a stroll outside the marquee when he met Bertie and one of the other lads—what was his name?—Cheshire, that was it... Cheesey Cheshire, the boys called him.

'Hello, Dad,' said Bertie, looking very pleased with himself. 'Where are you off to?'

'Nowhere special, just getting a breath of air. That jazz band's a bit too noisy for my taste and it's getting very warm in the tent.'

'We're just going in for a drink—d'you want me to bring one out for you?' Bertie enquired. 'Or have you had enough?'

526

Joshua straightened up. 'Are you saying I can't hold my liquor?' he demanded. 'I'll be with you in a minute—set one up for me, will you? And make it a double. Dammit, this is my party!'

Bertie turned to go and found himself face to face with Danny, who had just walked in through the gates. He was soaked to the skin and shivering, but he would not run away.

'Where the hell did you spring from?' Bertie asked. Then, as Danny stepped forward into the lamplight, and they saw the water streaming off him, collecting in a puddle at his feet, he began to laugh. 'Blimey, just look at you! Has it been raining?'

Cheesey was laughing too, but Danny ignored them and spoke to Joshua. 'Silly of me—I was walking along the jetty when I tripped on the cobblestones and fell in the river... No harm done—I got out all right, but I had to come back and find Lil. I think it's time we were leaving.'

'You'd better get into some dry clothes before you catch cold.' Josh squinted at his nephew in bewilderment. 'Bertie, don't stand there grinning. Go and find the girl—what's-her-name—tell her her brother's waiting.'

'I can't do that.' Bertie stopped laughing, but his face was still gleeful with malice. 'She's not here.'

'What? Where is she?' said Danny.

'I thought you'd gone home—that's what I told her. So she went off on her own to find you. If you hurry, you might catch her.'

'Thanks very much.' Danny turned his back

on Bertie. 'Good night, Uncle Josh—and thanks for the party.'

Lil followed Jimmy into the outer office, where hats and coats hung on makeshift rails; a hanging oil-lamp threw heavy shadows, and she shivered.

'What's wrong? Not scared, are you?' said Jimmy.

'No, of course not. It's a bit cold in here, that's all.' She gripped the back of a chair; her head was swimming. 'Is this where they keep the Register?'

'All the secret documents are locked up in the other room; it's a good job I've still got the key.' He walked over to another door and unlocked it. Looking past him, Lil saw that the inner room was in darkness. 'After you,' he said.

She took a few steps towards the doorway, then stopped on the threshold. 'Aren't you going to turn the lights on?' she asked.

'They're not working; the gas has been turned off. Those wall-brackets were daft, old-fashioned things. When they start rebuilding, they'll rip them out and put in electricity—and about time too. In you go.'

Lil took one more step, then stopped again. 'It's so dark,' she told him. 'How can we look at the Register in the dark?'

'We'll manage,' he said, taking her arm and easing her gently into the room. 'Go on—ladies first.'

She walked forward, and saw in the faint

glow from the outer office that the room had already been cleared; the carpet was rolled up, and chairs were stacked on top of a long, semi-circular table. Only then did she realise that he had tricked her.

'There's nothing here,' she began, turning to face him.

As she did so, he closed the door behind him, and then there was no light at all. His voice came to her through the darkness.

'There's you and me,' he said. 'That's all we need. If you're going to join the Brotherhood, you have to go through the initiation first.'

'No,' she said, and her heart was pounding. 'I don't want to. I want to go home.'

'Not yet,' he said, and she heard him walking towards her. 'Stay where you are. I'll show you what to do.'

She tried to move away from him without making any noise; she held her breath, praying he would not find her. When he spoke again, his words took her by surprise, coming from another direction.

'So that's the game, is it?' he asked, with rising excitement in his voice. 'Hide and seek—or cat and mouse. But I'll soon find you, never you fear.'

Her lungs were bursting; she had to take a breath, but she was afraid that he would hear her. Still moving away from him in silence, she thought that if she could get close to the wall, she might be able to slip past him and reach the door.

She had forgotten the rolled-up carpet.

Tripping over it, she fell back, with a smothered cry.

She heard him laugh—a single bark of triumph—and before she could pick herself up from the floor, he was on top of her.

'Now for the initiation,' he said, and his mouth was very close, his breath hot upon her cheek. 'You will repeat after me: *I, Lilian O'Dell...*'

'Let me go! Please, Jimmy.'

He slapped her across the face—without much force, but the blow was so unexpected she gasped with pain, and he exclaimed, 'Do as I say, and you won't get hurt! Repeat after me: *I, Lilian O'Dell...*'

'*I—Lilian O'Dell...* Jimmy, let go!'

'*Do hereby solemnly swear...*'

His body was hard, thrusting against her, and though she struggled to get free, he was too strong and too heavy; his hands moved rapidly over her, clawing at her dress. She heard the fabric tear, and felt clumsy fingers exploring her breasts.

'*Do hereby solemnly swear*—let me go home, and I promise I'll never tell anybody.'

'*To obey all commands given to me by those in authority...*'

Then the hands went down to her thighs, pulling up her skirt, fumbling with her knickers, and she began to sob with fear as his voice went on, thick and ugly: '*If I should ever break this solemn promise, I shall be duly punished.* Say the words after me, you little bitch! *If I should ever break this solemn promise...*'

530

'*If I should ever—ever break this*... No, Jimmy! Stop, please, you must stop!'

His saliva dribbled on to her mouth, tasting of whisky, and she gagged, jerking her head away.

'Don't pretend with me. You're loving it—you know you are...' Urgently, he thrust her legs apart, and the ritual phrases became meaningless as he gabbled them faster and faster. '*I shall be duly punished—for all my misdeeds*—oh, yes, you're a right little tease. Go on, admit it—you've been asking for this all night, and now you're going to get it.'

And as the pain began, she could still hear the strains of the dance band, very far away, playing a jolly tune.

Who's afraid of the Big Bad Wolf
The Big Bad Wolf, the Big Bad Wolf?
Who's afraid of the Big Bad Wolf,
Tra-la-la-la-la...

When Danny arrived at the pub, he knew at once that something was wrong.

Unusually, there was a saloon car parked at the kerb—an old, sturdy Lanchester. Danny felt sure he had seen it before, though he could not place it. He couldn't go into the saloon in his sodden clothes, but looked in through the windows and saw his father serving alone behind the bar, grim-faced and not like himself at all.

He went in through the side door, then hung back, keeping out of sight as his mother passed from the kitchen and up the stairs, carrying a pile of clean towels. She too looked very

531

grave, and he was glad she had not noticed him standing in the shadows.

As soon as she had gone, he started cautiously along the passage; he had to get up to his room and strip off his wet clothes before anyone saw him.

He moved quickly past the open archway that led into the bars then, as he reached the foot of the staircase, Huw came up the cellar steps carrying a crate of bottles. Huw still had difficulty climbing stairs, and with both hands full, he had to rest his shoulder against the wall to steady himself.

'Here, let me have that,' said Danny, taking the crate from him.

Huw looked at him, and blinked. 'What in God's name have you been up to? You're wet through.'

'Bertie and his pals were playing games,' said Danny. 'I'm OK.'

'Bloody hell.' Huw clenched his fists. 'Those bastards!'

'Never mind them,' Danny interrupted. 'Have you seen Lil?'

'I thought she was with you, at the party.'

'We sort of separated. She left before I did...isn't she here?'

'She may be upstairs. The whole place is at sixes and sevens tonight—we're short-handed anyhow, and with your ma helping with the old man—'

'Why, what's happened?'

Huw shook his head. 'I don't know the details, but they think it might be pneumonia.

The doctor's up there now with him.'

Of course. At last Danny identified that old Lanchester—it belonged to Dr Mackay. 'But he is going to be all right?' he asked anxiously.

'I can't tell you. Your gran's up there as well—I dare say Lil's with them. I can't stop, they're waiting for these in the public.' With that, Huw grabbed the crate of bottles once more and limped off through the archway.

Danny ran upstairs. When he had towelled himself dry and put on some other clothes, he went and knocked at the door of his grandparents' room. Looking in, he saw Ruth and Mary O'Dell and the doctor gathered round the bed where Patrick lay back against the pillows, his face grey and shining with sweat and his eyes closed—asleep or unconscious, Danny could not tell. Totally concentrated on the invalid, the others did not even look round, and Danny closed the door again quietly.

Lil was not with them, and when he went to her room, there was no sign of her there either. He decided to go out and look for her, but though he roamed the streets until long after midnight, he could not find her.

When Lil got away from the Jubilee Wharf at last, she thought she was going to die—and for a while wished she could.

Her whole body was aching and pain cut through her groin like a knife turning in a wound. She was still shaking all over and she wanted to be sick. She longed to vomit out the taste and smell and filth of the man who had

533

raped her, but she was too weak to do more than retch and bring up a little bile.

Worst of all was the feeling of being soiled—soiled so deeply, she felt she could never be clean again.

Exhausted, she leaned against the dockyard wall, and when her legs would no longer hold her up she slid slowly down until she was sprawled on cold paving-stones; rough bricks grazed her shoulders through her thin, tattered dress, but she scarcely noticed.

She did not know what to do.

Her entire life seemed to have reached a dead end; the sixteen years that had led up to this moment seemed to count for nothing. Nothing remained but shame and disgust, and the sense of degradation.

But there was a more immediate problem. What could she do in the next few hours? Where could she go?

She couldn't go home, that was certain. She could not face Mum and Dad and the rest of the family. At the thought of them, she uttered a small, hopeless cry; she could never let them see her in this state. She felt a wet, warm trickle between her thighs and, fearfully investigating, found that she was bleeding. No, she could not go home.

She tried to sit up, and for a second everything went black. The wall, the pavement, the street—everything was spinning slowly like a nightmare merry-go-round. With an extra pang of self-disgust, she realised that she was still half-drunk.

Then a man's voice broke in on her misery. 'Hello, what's all this? Are you all right, miss?'

Looking up in terror, she found a uniformed policeman standing over her.

'Go away,' she muttered. 'Leave me alone.'

'Can't do that, miss—looks like you need some help. Do you think you can stand up, if I give you a hand?'

'I said *leave me alone!*' She tried to push him away, but she had no strength left. He lifted her gently to her feet, and a ray of light from a street-lamp lit up her face.

'I know you,' he said. 'You're Lily O'Dell.'

'Not Lily,' she corrected him resentfully. 'Lilian. And who are you?'

'The name's Burns. I met you on the march last Sunday. I landed night-duty this weekend.'

She closed her eyes. 'Let go of me. Please, just go away.'

'Your mum and dad wouldn't like that. Come on, let's get you home.'

She struggled in his arms. 'No! I'm not going home! I don't want them to see me drunk.'

He frowned. 'You shouldn't be hitting the bottle at your age. Not used to hard liquor, I dare say?'

'Shut up! And don't you dare tell Mum and Dad about this, d'you hear?'

'I hear you.' Another idea struck him. 'You work for Gloria Judge, don't you? At the salon.'

'What if I do? It's no business of yours.'

'No, listen, hang on a minute. How about if I took you there instead?'

For the first time she looked him full in the

535

face. 'Auntie Gloria? Yes, all right.'

He kept one arm round her shoulders and she stumbled along beside him. Each time she lost her footing, he had to hold her up. Eventually they reached the shop in Millwall Road, and he rang the doorbell.

It was nearly half-past eleven, and Gloria had gone to bed. They had to wait until she came downstairs in a dressing-gown, with her hair in a slumber-cap and no make-up. She looked old and tired, and far from pleased to be dragged out of bed.

'Who is it? What's going on? Do you know what time it—' Then her face changed. 'Oh, my God. You'd better come in.'

She helped the constable bring Lil through to the kitchen, and lit the gas. In the hard yellow light, the girl's face was deathly pale, tear-stained and blotched with dirt.

'You poor kid—whatever happened to you?'

Lil would not reply; she averted her face and Gloria turned to the policeman. 'Where did you find her?'

He told her as much as he could, then he said that Lil appeared to be the worse for drink. Glory exclaimed angrily, 'That's a lie! She wouldn't—she's not that sort...' but when she leaned over Lil, she sniffed then sighed. 'I'd never have believed it. You've been a silly girl, haven't you? Trying to be grown-up, like all the rest? What are we going to do with you?'

Lil still refused to answer, and the constable explained: 'She wouldn't let me take her home, so I brought her here instead.'

536

'I'm glad you did. All right, leave her with me. I'll get her cleaned up and give her a bed for the night. Her mum must be off her head with worry. Never mind, duck—I'll ring her and explain you're staying with Auntie Glory, and tomorrow I'll get Matt to see you safely home.'

The effect was electrifying. At the mention of Matt's name, Lil recoiled violently.

'No—not Matt! I don't want him to touch me!' She seemed to grow physically smaller, shrinking away from them and shielding her body with her hands. For the first time Glory saw the bloodstains on the tattered lime-green dress.

'God in heaven—who's done that to you?' she whispered.

Too tired to resist any longer, Lil broke down in tears and told them what had happened. When she had finished, Gloria cradled the girl in her arms, saying, 'There, there, my duck. It's all over now. You'll be all right.'

Then she looked up at PC Burns and said quietly. 'You heard what she said—this is police business. It's up to you now.

19

'What time is it?' asked Patrick drowsily.

'Half-past eight,' Connor told his father.

'In the morning?'

'In the evening.'

Patrick nodded; he did not have much idea of time any more. After a moment he frowned. 'What are you doing upstairs at all? You should be down in the bar, not sitting around here doing nothing.'

'Don't you trouble yourself, Da. Huw's in the public, Ruth's in the saloon and Danny's giving her a hand too, so I can sit with you and Mam for a while.'

Satisfied, Patrick shut his eyes, drifting off to sleep again. Connor and his mother exchanged glances. During the long winter of 1936 to 1937, time had seemed to stretch out interminably at the Watermen. Ever since Patrick's first bout of pneumonia last October, he had been a very sick man; although Dr Mackay pulled him through, the illness had taken its toll, leaving him very weak. Sometimes he would rally a little, and the family told themselves the old man was on the mend at last, but then he would relapse, prey to another infection—and the hard weather of January and February did nothing to help him.

In March he had suffered a second battle with pneumonia, and the doctor warned Connor that it had put a severe strain on the old man's heart; the end might come at any time.

Lately he had been sleeping a great deal, but when he awoke he always wanted the reassurance of someone close by, so they took it in turns to sit with him. Now, as they watched, he stirred restlessly and opened his eyes again.

'Half-past eight at night, d'you say?' he enquired. 'What's business like this evening?

Have we plenty of customers below?'

'The usual Saturday night crowds,' Connor assured him. 'And in a few weeks we'll be busier than ever. This time next month we'll be run off our feet with the celebration.'

'What's that?' Patrick's eyes, once so sharp, were misty and unsure. 'What celebration would that be?'

'The Coronation,' Mary reminded him. 'We talked about it the other day, don't you remember? The Duke of York's the new King, and he's to be crowned next month. They're throwing a street party outside that day. Perhaps if the weather's fine, you might feel well enough to sit out in your easy chair.'

The old man pulled down the corners of his mouth. 'A street party? I'm not in favour of that—taking our customers outside, eating and drinking. It'll be bad for business.'

'Trust you to think of that!' Connor gave a half-smile. 'But how about if we supply the drinks to them, at a special price?'

'Well, it'll need some working out.' Patrick's eyelids were drooping again. 'I'm too tired to calculate it this evening. I'll think about that tomorrow.'

But for Patrick O'Dell, tomorrow never came. As his wife and son kept their vigil, they saw a change come over him; the lines of weariness and anxiety that seamed his face were gradually smoothed out, and his shallow breathing became more and more imperceptible—until at last they realised he was making no sound at all.

Mary leaned over him, listening intently, then

539

she kissed him on the brow. When she turned to Connor, her eyes were bright with tears.

'You must send for the doctor—and the priest too,' she said. 'But he's gone already.' Gently, she pulled up the sheet to cover his face. 'He had a great heart in him,' she said, 'but by the end it was worn out... Leave me to be with him now, will you?'

Connor embraced her without a word, and went downstairs to tell Ruth.

As a mark of respect, they closed the pub and the customers went home. Connor telephoned Rosie, and she said she'd come right away; Ruth took Danny and Lil upstairs to see their grandfather for the last time. Afterwards, Danny chose to stay and keep his grandmother company by the bedside, holding her hand.

While Huw was locking up for the night, Lil boiled a kettle and filled the teapot, and Ruth and Connor sat at the kitchen table.

'Are you all right?' Lil broke a long silence, bringing them their cups of tea. 'You're not saying anything.'

'There's not much to be said,' Connor told her. 'We'd been expecting it, but even so—when it happened...' He fell silent again and began to stir his tea, and went on stirring it for a long time.

The sound of the teaspoon in the cup grated upon Ruth, but she realised that Con didn't even know he was doing it. He did not look at her, and she wondered what he was thinking.

His face was unreadable; at moments of crisis, he seemed to retreat into himself. She wished he would talk to her, and felt he was hardly aware of her presence. Was this what all marriages became, in the end? Two strangers, living under the same roof—sharing a bed, but never sharing their thoughts? Yet Mary and Patrick had been close to one another in spite of everything, right to the end.

Even during that dreadful time, long ago, when the truth about Patrick's brief affair with Mary's sister had exploded like a time-bomb, threatening to shatter their peace of mind for ever, Mary was still able to find it in herself to forgive her husband, and they had remade their lives together...

There was a gentle tapping at the door, which opened a few inches. Huw looked in, saying tentatively, 'I've locked up and I've cashed up. Is there anything else I can do for you? Either of you?'

'Nothing else.' Connor pulled himself together. 'Thanks, lad—you might as well get off home now.'

Huw looked directly at Ruth—a long look, full of sadness and sympathy. She knew he wanted to help her in some way, but there was nothing he could do or say. He had to be content with, 'I'll see you in the morning, then. Good night.'

When Huw had gone Ruth said quietly, 'There's nothing anyone can do, but there's still so much to be done. The doctor, the undertaker, the registrar... And the funeral, too—we'll have to talk to your mother about the arrangements.'

541

'I was wondering about that.' Connor sipped his tea. 'It crossed my mind that maybe we should let Aunt Moira know?'

Ruth turned to him quickly. 'How strange,' she said. 'I was thinking of her too. I'm afraid Mam won't want her at the funeral, but all the same...'

'Yes, she ought to be told.'

On Sunday mornings, Ruth and Mary usually went to early Mass together, so they had plenty of time to prepare the dinner afterwards. This week, Ruth had persuaded her mother-in-law to have a lie-in for once, and go to a later Mass with Connor; Danny and Lil accompanied Ruth to church instead.

As they walked back from St Anthony's, they met Mike Burns—off-duty and in plain clothes.

'Good morning,' he said. 'I hope you won't think this is an intrusion, but I heard the news last night and I wanted to tell you how sorry I am. Please give my condolences to Mrs O'Dell.'

They murmured conventional acknowledgments, and the young policeman added, 'If there's anything I can do—anything at all—you only have to say.'

'That's kind of you,' said Ruth, 'but everything's pretty well organised. Thanks all the same.'

Mike glanced at Lil and addressed her awkwardly. 'I was just thinking, if you've nothing special to do, it's a nice morning, so... Do you feel like a walk through the Gardens?

542

The daffs are all coming out. I mean, it might take your mind off things...'

Lil looked at her mother uncertainly. 'I don't know, what d'you think? Would you sooner I came home and helped with the dinner?'

'No, you go. The walk will do you good.'

So Mike and Lil made their way down Manchester Road towards the Island Gardens. Ruth turned back to watch them, saying to Danny, 'I'm glad Lil's taken a liking to Mr Burns. He's a pleasant chap, and she doesn't have many other friends.'

'You mean boyfriends, don't you?' Danny asked.

'I don't mean anything of the sort!' Ruth reproved her son, as they set off together. 'Lil's too young to be thinking about boyfriends. I just meant friends generally. It's strange—she used to be so bright and sociable but these last few months she's been a different girl altogether.'

'It was that damn party that did it,' Danny commented, with the worldly wisdom of his eighteen years. 'She was so ashamed of herself for getting squiffy that night, she's never got over it.'

'Well, at least she learned her lesson, that's some comfort,' Ruth agreed. 'And don't let me hear you swearing again, if you don't mind!'

In all the upheaval over Patrick's first bout of pneumonia, Gloria's phone-call to the pub explaining that Lil was safe and well and spending the night with her was accepted almost with relief, as one thing less to worry about. Only later did Ruth stop to wonder why her

543

daughter should suddenly decide to turn up uninvited on Glory's doorstep. Glory helped Lil to concoct a half-truth: she had been silly and indulged in a few glasses of wine, and not wishing to go home tipsy she had sensibly turned to Gloria instead, to sleep off her thick head.

This also helped to explain her pallor next day, the dark rings under her eyes and her general state of misery.

Lil could not bear to tell her parents what had really happened. After all, the story was only partly a lie. If she had not been drinking, things might have been different...

Gloria had been kind and understanding, backing up Lil's story, but she had also urged Mike Burns to take some official action against Jimmy Judge. It was his duty to put a stop to such things, she told him—and surely a slip of a girl like Lil could be protected from public scandal? They could keep her name out of it, couldn't they?

Mike said he would make some enquiries. A few evenings later, he had called in at the salon as Glory and Lil were shutting up shop, and talked to them both in confidence.

'It would be difficult to make a case against Mr Judge without bringing Lilian into court,' he began. 'In fact, pretty well impossible. Not only that, but we'd probably never get him in the dock in the first place.'

'What do you mean?' Gloria stared at him. 'We know he's guilty.'

'What we know, and what we can prove, are two different things,' said Mike. 'I've

544

been making some enquiries. I went round to Denmark Place yesterday evening, and I managed to see Mr Judge on his own. I asked him to give me an account of what happened last Saturday.'

'And I suppose he denied everything?' The memory of that night was reflected in Lil's panic-stricken face, and Gloria gripped her hand. 'Well, that's not surprising, he'd say anything.'

'Yes, no doubt, but... I know this is painful for you, Lilian, but I have to ask... Didn't you tell me that the assault took place in darkness?'

'That's right.' Her mouth was dry; it was hard to bring out the words. 'He—he said the lights weren't working.'

'So when he attacked you, you couldn't actually see his face?'

'No, but I knew it was him. Of course I did, he took me there!'

'Did anyone hear him offer to take you to the Guild Office? Did anyone see you going in?'

'No, I don't think so.'

'Did anyone see you leaving the marquee together?'

'I don't know. I don't remember it very well.'

'Yes, I see.' Mike shifted uncomfortably; he had taken a seat in one of the customers' chairs, and looked out of place in his uniform against a background of shampoo bottles and hair-driers. 'In fact, it's true to say you'd had a bit too much to drink?'

'What are you saying?' Gloria broke in. 'Whose side are you on?'

'I'm just putting the case any defence lawyer would make for his client. Lilian had too much to drink, she couldn't identify the man who assaulted her with any certainty and, to make matters worse, Mr Judge told me his brother and half a dozen other friends are ready to swear he never left the marquee all the evening.'

'He's lying!' exclaimed Gloria.

'It seems to be impossible to prove, one way or the other,' said Mike sadly. 'I'm sorry, Lilian, but I can only advise you. We haven't got a hope of convicting him.'

'Thank God!' Suddenly Lil burst into tears, hiding her face in Gloria's shoulder. 'Oh, thank God. I never asked you to do anything like that. I just want to forget it ever happened...'

Above her bowed head, Gloria's eyes met Mike's. They both knew Lil would never forget it, as long as she lived.

Today, six months later, Mike and Lil walked side by side through the Island Gardens, enjoying the shimmer of green on the trees and the splashes of yellow daffodils in the flowerbeds. They were content, but they hardly said a word to each other; though they had become friends, there was very little spoken communication between them.

Lil threw Mike a sidelong look, with something that was halfway to a smile. 'Thank you,' she said.

'What are you thanking me for? I've done nothing.'

'Then I'm thanking you for what you don't do. You don't talk much; I like that.'

He smiled back at her. 'Just as well, probably. I don't have much to say for myself.'

After another pause, Lil pursued the subject a little further. 'I was noticing Mum and Dad last night. They don't say much either, when they're together.'

'I expect they understand each other by now, without needing to talk.' Leaving the Gardens, they approached the main road. 'Perhaps it's the same with us?'

He was nearly twice Lil's age, and he felt protective towards her. As they reached the kerb, he put his hand casually upon her shoulder. At once she flinched, moving away from him.

'I'm sorry. I didn't mean—' he began.

'No, I know, and *I'm* sorry. It's just—I can't bear people touching me,' she blurted out.

He didn't need any explanation. He knew she liked him well enough, but he also knew how she felt about men. He would have to go on waiting, and try to be patient.

'I think I'd better be getting home,' she said. 'If you don't mind.'

They began the return journey to the pub. A bank of cloud had drifted across the sun; it was beginning to get quite chilly.

The funeral took place the following Thursday.

'Lord, hear our prayers...' The parish priest had difficulty in reading the words from his missal as the wind whipped the flimsy pages over, between his fingers. 'By raising Your

Son from the dead, You have given us faith. Strengthen our hope that Patrick, our brother, will share in His resurrection...'

The graveyard behind St Anthony's Church was small, and shaded by a line of stunted trees. On the other side of the fence was the flat expanse of Mudchute; not long converted from an urban wasteland of mud dredged from the river, and clinkers from industrial boilers, it had become a grassy plateau where allotment-holders toiled to produce a patch of potatoes or a row of cabbages.

Open to the winds from all directions, it was a favourite haunt of the gulls that flew up from the estuary, swooping and wheeling with harsh, screeching cries.

Ruth pulled her summer coat a little more tightly round her, standing with the rest of the family at the graveside.

The slow, solemn ritual continued. The coffin was lowered by the pall-bearers; a spadeful of earth fell on to the lid with a hollow, rattling sound that made Ruth shudder. She stole a look at Mary O'Dell, who was leaning on Connor's arm, her head held high and her eyes fixed upon the scudding clouds. How could she remain so confident, so undiminished by her husband's death?

The priest's voice rolled on, lifted against the gusts of wind that tore at his words: 'I am the resurrection and the life, says the Lord. If anyone believes in Me, even though he dies, he will live. Anyone who lives and believes in Me, will not die.'

Of course that was the answer. Mary's faith gave her unshakeable trust in the life to come; Patrick was not trapped in that plot of earth—he had gone before, to his everlasting reward, and in God's good time Mary knew she would be reunited with him.

On the other side of Mary O'Dell, Rosie stood with Ernest and her children. Abram was tall and slender, and Ruth noticed that as he grew older, he was beginning to look very like Ernest's brother Izzy. His dark curly hair contrasted strongly with his sister's: Sharon had recently had a peroxide treatment at Glory's salon and was now almost unrecognisable in yellow ringlets... Rosie herself stepped forward, carrying a sheaf of white narcissi; her cheeks shining with tears, she scattered the flowers into the open grave.

'Lord God... May the death and resurrection of Christ, which we celebrate, bring our brother Patrick to the peace of Your eternal home.'

When the ceremony was over, they remained in silence for a few moments longer, each one remembering the old Irishman, then they turned away, moving off in ones and twos.

There had been a large turn-out of mourners—neighbours from all over the Island and regulars from the Watermen. Apart from all the others, one figure hung back under the trees, trying not to be seen; a woman in black, with a black veil pulled down over her face.

But Mary knew her at once. Two dozen yards away, as Connor helped her along the gravel path, she stopped and stiffened. The stranger looked about for escape, but there were too many people clustered between her and the churchyard gate, and she could not slip away quickly.

As she hesitated, not knowing where to go, Mary moved towards her and said in a low voice, 'Is it yourself, Moira? I wondered if you might be here.'

Her sister lifted the black lace veil; she was very pale, and her hands trembled. 'I hope you won't think it was wrong of me...but I had to come.'

The two women looked at one another for a long moment, then Mary said simply, 'I'm glad you did. He would have been pleased. Thank you, my dear.' She put her arms round Moira, and they kissed for the first time in nearly twenty-four years.

'You came on your own, then?' Mary continued. 'You haven't brought your husband with you?'

Moira bit her lip before replying. 'Henry died three years ago. So I know a little of what you must be feeling now.'

They embraced again, then Moira greeted Ruth and Connor, and was introduced to their grown-up children.

'It's a fine family you have,' she said. 'That's something I envy you, Mary—' but at that moment the words died on her lips, for Rosie's family were following them up the path. At first Rosie did not recognise her natural mother. She wore a polite, conventional smile—and then the truth dawned upon her and the

550

smile disappeared instantly, leaving her face cold and hard.

Moira flinched, as if she were in physical pain. They all stood frozen in a grotesque, artificial tableau.

Mary O'Dell was the first to speak. Taking Rosie's hand, she said, 'Won't you say hello?'

Rosie seemed unable to move or to reply, yet she could not take her eyes from Moira's face. Almost in a whisper, Mary urged her softly, 'Please, darling. Remember your da—this is for him.'

She drew Rosie forward, joining her hand with Moira's, and they greeted one another at last—tentatively, awkwardly—but perhaps taking a first step towards love and understanding. Rosie managed to say, 'Thank you for what you did for us, when we opened the shop.'

After that she introduced Moira to Ernest and the children—Abram shy and watchful, hanging back slightly—Sharon shaking hands with great aplomb and a dazzling smile—and the ice was broken. By the time they got back to the Watermen, they had begun to talk like friends.

Mary and Ruth were determined that Patrick should have a first-class send-off, and there was a wonderful spread in the saloon of cold meats and salad, bottles of port and sherry, home-made soda bread and a splendidly light madeira cake.

As the guests ate and drank, the melancholy mood lifted and became something nearer a celebration. Someone at the piano began to play the old Irish songs, and Sharon said to Rosie, 'I wonder if he knows *On the Good Ship Lollipop?* I could do my Shirley Temple impression.'

'Not today, dear,' said Rosie. 'Another time.'

Sharon shrugged, tossing her bright blonde curls, and turned to Danny and Lil. 'Oh well, there isn't really enough room here. I need plenty of space for the whole tap-routine. Will you be coming to the Coronation Gala at the Town Hall? Miss Grosvenor's in charge, and she's given me two of the best spots on the programme. You will come and see me, won't you?'

The Gala was held on the Friday evening before Coronation Day; Danny and Lil went along to the concert together.

The hall was packed with the performers' relatives, who kept telling each other that this was every bit as good as a professional show. There was no orchestra, but below the front of the stage Miss Hilda Grosvenor—younger than her sister Ethel and lacking some of that lady's determined energy—provided a painstaking piano accompaniment to every item, from the gentleman who played *Roses of Picardy* on the musical saw, to the entire team of Grosvenor Babes who lined up to form a tap-dancing train, their elbows revolving to the rhythm of the wheels, for *Shuffle Off to Buffalo*. Sharon's talent and vivacity were immediately noticeable—not only because she was the leader of the troupe but also because, rising fifteen, she was

552

a head taller than any of the other tiny tappers.

'That's funny,' said Lil, studying the programme. 'All the other Babes have got their names printed, but Sharon isn't in the list.'

'You don't think it might be because she's too modest?' suggested Danny, solemnly.

They looked at one another, and Lil smiled. 'I don't really think so. There's a girl called Sally King who's down to do *The Good Ship Lollipop* instead of Sharon—I don't understand it.'

The first half of the show reached a glamorous climax with *A Tribute to Hollywood*, in which various members of the company gave impressions of such stars as Fred Astaire and Ginger Rogers, Nelson Eddy and Jeanette Macdonald. But when the Shirley Temple number began, there was Sharon—blonde ringlets bouncing and diamanté tap-shoes twinkling—making a song and dance about the delights of bonbons, candy-shops and Peppermint Bay.

'She's a bit old for Shirley Temple, isn't she?' asked Danny, under his breath.

'Well, yes, but you've got to admit she does it well,' Lil said defensively. 'I remember now, she once told me she wanted to go blonde and change her name for the stage and now she's done both.'

The concert ended on a patriotic note with a selection of songs from *Merrie England*; Sharon/Sally performed a pas-de-trois on points with two other girls, while a buxom contralto dressed as Good Queen Bess sang *O Peaceful England*.

Then the entire company lined up along the footlights, suddenly bursting into a spirited version of the National Anthem. Taken by surprise, the audience shuffled to its feet and joined in raggedly.

When the curtains closed and the lights went up, Lil asked her brother, 'What did you think?'

'Quite good, I suppose—but I'm glad it's over. Can we go now?'

'In a minute. We ought to stay behind and see Sharon first, to tell her we enjoyed it.'

They made their way out of the hall and along the street to a side entrance marked *Artistes Only—No Admittance,* where they stood with a little crowd of mums and dads, waiting proudly for their offspring.

There were some cars drawn up at the pavement's edge, but Lil did not give them a second glance. Then, in the doorway, she saw Sharon emerging, carrying a big box of chocolates with a red ribbon bow, talking to an elderly lady in gold pince-nez, a mulberry velvet dress and a fringed shawl.

When she saw Lil and Danny, Sharon waved and beckoned to them. 'Oh good, you did come after all!' she exclaimed, when they squeezed through the crowd. 'Well? Did you enjoy it?'

'It was a very good show,' said Lil, and nudged her brother. 'Wasn't it, Danny?'

'Yes, I know,' Sharon pressed on impatiently, 'but what did you think of me? Was I the best?'

'You were all very good,' said Danny.

Sharon's smile froze slightly, and she turned to the lady beside her. 'Miss Grosvenor thought I was marvellous, didn't you? She gave me these chocs as a special thank-you. Oh, by the way, these are my cousins.' She introduced them briskly. 'Lil and Danny—Miss Ethel Grosvenor.'

'You must be so proud of Sally, I'm sure.' 'Miss Ethel's eyes bulged with enthusiasm behind her pince-nez. 'We're absolutely certain she has a wonderful future ahead of her. Having been in the profession myself, I shall be able to give her some useful introductions.' Then she broke off to wave to someone through the crowd. 'Aha! There's our friend Mr James in his car, Sally dear. You mustn't keep him waiting.'

Sharon heaved a happy sigh. 'He's offered to give me a lift home, 'cos Mumsie and Papa couldn't come tonight—wasn't that kind of him? Sorry I can't stop. See you soon. Nighty-night, Miss Grosvenor—cheery-bye!'

She hurried away, clutching her chocolates, and they watched her climb into a large black saloon at the kerb. Lil only caught a brief glimpse of the driver as he leaned across to open the door for her, but a sick fear gripped her stomach and she turned to Miss Grosvenor.

'Did you say "Mr James"?' she asked.

'That's right. Mr James Judge—such a charming man. I believe he's involved in local politics, and very influential. I know he's terribly busy, but he's been a very good friend to the Grosvenor Academy. He's always so interested in our young dancers. He often drops in to watch the rehearsals, and sometimes he takes one or two of the girls out to tea, if he thinks they deserve special encouragement. Naturally, he's particularly interested in dear Sally. He told me himself: "That young lady could go far"—those were his very words.'

Lil said nothing, but moved away, averting her face. Danny muttered 'Good night,' to Miss Grosvenor, and chased after her.

'Hey, that was a bit sudden, wasn't it?' he asked. 'What's wrong?'

'Didn't you hear what she said? That man with Sharon—it was Jimmy Judge.'

'I know. I've seen him before, driving that black car. I think he borrows it when he's travelling to his damn party meetings... But I didn't know he took an interest in dancing, or do you think it's the dancers he's interested in?'

He grinned, and Lil burst out vehemently, 'It's not funny, Dan—it's terrible! It could be dangerous.'

'What are you on about?' He stared at her. 'You look sick as a dog—are you OK?'

'No, I'm not.' She tried to conceal her revulsion, saying quickly, 'I feel a bit dizzy, but I'll be all right in a minute. Let's go home.'

On Sunday afternoon, Lil went to Silmour Street hoping to see Sharon.

Ernest's business was prospering. He had put in a new shop-front and the old name-board had been replaced by a smart modem fascia with the words *Happy Snaps!* emblazoned above the door. The windows were filled with cameras of all kinds and different prices, together with some enlargements of Ernest's own work—mainly portraits and wedding-groups.

In the middle of the pictures there was a study of Sharon in her ballet tutu, poised in a classic arabesque. Lil looked at it for a long moment, and her heart sank.

She rang the bell, and presently she saw Abram coming through the shop to unlock the door.

'Hello,' she said. 'Is Sharon at home?'

'No, she's gone out with Papa. But Mama's upstairs—would you like to come in?'

They went up to the flat, where Lil found Rosie putting on a black hat and coat in front of a mirror; she was still in mourning for her father.

Rosie turned and greeted her niece. 'Lil dear, what a nice surprise! But I wish you'd let me know you were coming; I'm just going out. Aunt Moira's invited me to her house for tea. You know we met at the funeral? Well, she's been asking and asking me over to Greenwich ever since, but we've been so busy in the shop I haven't had a minute. But today, with Ernest out, it seemed like a good opportunity.'

'Abram tells me Sharon's out as well,' said Lil.

'Yes. It's a shame—she'd have loved to see you, but she makes herself useful when Ernest's taking pictures; she helps carry spare rolls of film and lenses and all that.'

'And he often includes her in the pictures,' added Abram. 'She likes posing for photographs.'

'Well, Papa says a pretty girl adds human interest. He's going all round Poplar and Limehouse today, taking shots of the Coronation decorations. With any luck, he'll probably sell a few to the local papers.'

'I saw the one in the shop window, of Sharon in her ballet-dress,' Lil said. 'What a pity you and Uncle Ernest couldn't get to the Gala concert. It was very good.'

'Miss Grosvenor always puts on a good show but we couldn't go, it being a Friday—the Sabbath, you know. Ernest's quite strict about that.'

Again Abram chimed in: 'And anyhow he doesn't approve of Sharon changing her name and dyeing her hair. He says she shouldn't be ashamed to be Jewish.'

'What nonsense! She isn't ashamed, and her hair's not dyed, it's been bleached, that's all... I tried to explain that if you want to take up the stage as a career, you have to make a few sacrifices, but I'm afraid he's a bit old-fashioned.' Rosie glanced at her wristwatch. 'Help, I must go, it's later than I thought. Don't feel you've got to run away, Lil. Stay and have some tea. Abram will put the kettle on, won't you, Abe?'

Rosie kissed Lil, then ran downstairs and they heard the shop door closing. The two cousins looked at one another and Abram asked, 'Would you like some tea?'

'Not really. We always have dinner late on Sundays and I don't want anything.' Lil took her courage in both hands and continued, 'I hope Sharon got home safely the other night, after the concert?'

He looked puzzled. 'I think so. A friend of Miss Grosvenor's gave her a lift in his car.'

'Yes, I know. I saw him. As a matter of fact, I know him.' This was more difficult than she had expected. 'That's why I came round today. I wanted to tell Sharon about that man. I wanted to warn her.'

'Warn her?'

'Would you give her a message from me? Tell her she mustn't go out with him again. He—he's not to be trusted. I do know about him, because he's one of my cousins too, on the other side of the family.' She forced herself to go on, hating even to say the words. 'His name's Judge... Jimmy Judge.'

At once Abram's face changed. 'Joshua Judge's son?'

'Yes, why? Do you know something about him?'

'No. But I know something about his father ...something about the Brotherhood. Danny knows it, too.'

'This is nothing to do with the Brotherhood. I'm really worried about Sharon—you will tell her what I said, won't you?'

'I'll tell her, but I don't know if she'll take any notice. Generally she does whatever she wants.'

'But this is important!' Lil felt the same sickening fear rising within her, but she could not stop now. 'If I tell you what happened to me, will you promise me you'll tell Sharon?'

Her face was red and her palms were sweating, but she made herself tell Abram her story. When she had finished, he sat gazing at the pattern in the rug, unable to look at her. Then he said huskily, 'I'm so sorry... So very sorry.'

'Thank you. I'm all right now—and my family don't know about it, but ever since I saw Sharon with him the other night I've been so afraid for her.'

It was a beautiful afternoon. Moira Marriner's garden was looking at its best, brimming with forget-me-nots and vivid tulips, and scented by clumps of wallflowers. An early bee bumbled through the flowers as Moira and Rosie sat out on two canvas chairs, taking tea at a white-painted iron table.

Afterwards, when the maid removed the tea-things, Moira looked at her daughter and smiled—a smile that was edged with sadness.

'We can talk out here; they won't hear us in the kitchen... You and I can talk at last.' She looked down at her thin, bony fingers, twisting her wedding-ring round and round as she continued. 'I know how much you hated me, for such a long time, too, and I realise it's no more than I deserved.'

'Don't say that,' said Rosie. 'I was stupid—and very selfish. At first all I could think was that you'd lied to me, you and Patrick. You were my mother and father, and you didn't want me; you gave me away. That hurt—it hurt badly—and the hurting made me hate you.'

'I thought I'd never see you or speak to you

again, and it nearly broke my heart—and I had
no one but myself to blame. I'd cheated Mary,
I'd cheated Henry Marriner, and worst of all
I'd cheated you—the only child I'd ever have.'

'Didn't Mr Marriner want a family?'

'I don't think so—we never really talked
about it. We loved one another in our way.
He admired me and respected me, and set me
up in this house and garden. I never wanted
for anything...but he wasn't able to give me a
child. You were my child, and I had to watch
you from a distance, growing up in the O'Dell
family—never able to love you as a mother
should love her daughter.'

'And my father—did you love him?'

Moira sighed. 'Not the way you mean. Our
affair wasn't really love—it was something that
flared up in one night, then burnt itself out. Oh,
I was fond of him—you couldn't help being fond
of Patrick, but as for love, no, it was never that.
He loved Mary, no one else. And then, when
you were growing up and the truth came out
at last, I lost all of you at one stroke. Mary,
Patrick, my nephews—and my own daughter.
From that day to this, I've never ceased to
regret it. That's why it's so wonderful for me
to be able to sit and talk to you now, hoping
you can find it in your heart to forgive me,
after twenty-four years.'

Rosie moistened her lips with her tongue. This
was the moment she had been dreading.

'I didn't hate you for twenty-four years,' she
murmured. 'Like I said, I was angry and
selfish—my pride took a knock. Yes, I hated you

561

for a while, but nothing like twenty-four years. Three years at the most, no more than that.'

Moira stared at her. 'But all this time you refused to have anything to do with me! When you found out I'd helped to set up Ernest's shop, you refused to take my money. You still hated me then!'

'No, that wasn't hate. It was guilt, and shame. For twenty-one of those twenty-four years I hadn't the courage to face you.'

The bee buzzed and flew off, spiralling away into a neighbouring garden, and then there was no sound but the leaves whispering in the soft springtime air, as Moira struggled to understand.

'What are you telling me?' she asked.

'Did you know I'd lived with Ernest after the war began, before he was sent away to that internment camp? I loved him very much—I still do—and when the war separated us, I thought it was the end of the world. I was sure I'd never see him again, and that was when I found out I was pregnant...'

'During the war?' Moira could not make the dates fit. 'But Abram wasn't born till 1921, long after the war finished.'

'I'm not talking about Abram. This was 1916; I'd left the Island and taken a job in Gamages' fashion department. That's when I realised I was going to have a baby. I made up some story, and told them I was ill. I left London and went into the country, to a quiet cottage hospital where nobody knew me. I gave a false name and pretended I was a war-widow. I don't know if they believed me, and I didn't really care. And afterwards, when the baby was born, I—I...'

A sob rose in her throat, nearly choking her. She forced herself to continue: 'I did what you did. Now you know why I couldn't face you, all these years. I called you a bad mother because you abandoned me, and yet when it came to the point, I was no better. I gave my baby away to be adopted.'

If Mrs Marriner's domestic staff were spying from the kitchen window, they must have been very puzzled to see two grown women sitting side by side, holding hands and weeping.

'You never told Ernest?' Moira asked.

'That I'd given his child away? How could I?' Rosie shook her head. 'I've never been able to tell anyone—till now. It's a secret I've had on my conscience for half a lifetime.'

Moira put her arm round Rosie's shoulders.

'At least it's a secret we can share,' she said.

Late that evening, a few yards from the Island Gardens, Abram stood concealed in the shadows beside the little pavilion which housed the lift to the pedestrian tunnel under the river. Across the water, he could see the bobbing lights of boats at their moorings on the opposite bank. A freighter was heading slowly up-river in the deep central channel, its portholes gleaming; a threatening blast from the siren made Abram's heart beat faster—his nerves were already on edge. Ever since Lil left the shop, he had been trying to

563

decide what he should do. Now he had made up his mind—he had to go through with it.

He heard footsteps approaching. A figure materialised from the darkness into the lamplight, and he saw with relief that it was Danny.

'Abram?' Danny looked round uncertainly.

'I'm here.' Abram stepped forward. 'You got my message, then.'

'Yes—what's it all about?'

Abram hesitated. The winding-gear whirred and clanked as the lift rose to street level, the iron gates rattled open and a few passengers emerged, dispersing in different directions. The lift stood waiting, and the attendant raised an enquiring eyebrow.

'Going down?' he said.

'No.' Abram took Danny's arm, leading him out of earshot. 'We can't talk here—come on.'

They walked a little further, to the point where the road opened out on to the river and a slipway ran down to the water's edge. At their feet, ripples broke over the stones with a sound like ghostly hands clapping.

'What's up?' Danny asked again.

Abram took a deep breath, and began to explain. He told him of Lil's visit to Silmour Street, and her fears for Sharon's safety—and he told him of Lil's ordeal with Jimmy Judge.

Another ship hooted mournfully a long way upstream, and the little waves slapped and gurgled on the shining stones. Danny said in a fierce whisper, 'That bastard! That stinking, lousy bastard. I'll kill him!'

Abram shook his head. 'There's another way.

We can put paid to him and his father, too—the whole rotten Brotherhood—once and for all. And I know how to do it.'

Wednesday was the great day.

The Coronation celebrations began early in the morning, as willing helpers set up trestles and table-tops outside the Watermen; people brought out chairs from their houses and bed-sheets to use as tablecloths, lending their cutlery, cups and plates. Ruth and Connor were kept busy, in the pub and outside it, serving drinks and sandwiches, cutting up slices of pie and setting out iced buns and chocolate wafers for the children. Lil and Danny did all they could to help, while in the kitchen Mary O'Dell made endless pots of tea and buttered innumerable slices of bread—and Huw seemed to be everywhere at once, doing the work of a dozen men in spite of his lame leg.

When the midday meal was over at last, everything had to be cleared away again, because there was to be a sports contest for the neighbourhood children, with all kinds of races up and down the street—and in the evening they would shove the piano out of doors and hold a dance under the fairy-lights and coloured bunting, while a grand firework display was to take place along the river.

But before that, there was an awful lot of washing-up to be done.

They all took it in turns, and at some point in the afternoon, Lil found herself at the sink, with Huw beside her, drying dishes.

Passing him a pile of wet plates, she said cheerfully, 'I notice our Daniel seems to have made himself scarce. Trust him to slope off when there's scullery-work to be done! Go and round him up, Huw, and tell him he's got to come and do his share.'

Huw gave her a mysterious look, then glanced over his shoulder to make sure the kitchen door was shut and no one was listening.

'I can't tell him anything,' he said. 'He's not here.'

'Well, that's a fine thing, I must say!' Lil pulled a face. 'Where's he gone?'

'Nobody's supposed to know, but there's no harm in me telling you,' said Huw. 'I mean, you were in on the plan last time, at the birthday party, and if things hadn't gone wrong, Danny would have got hold of the evidence that time.'

Lil recoiled from the memory of that night, but she hid her feelings. 'Go on,' she said levelly, and carried on with the washing-up.

'Dan's determined to have another go at getting that damn Register. He says there'll never be a better time. Tonight everyone will be out on the razzle, getting drunk and enjoying the fireworks, and there'll be nobody on duty at the Wharf. He's going to break in, while the coast's clear.'

Horrified, Lil stared at him. 'He mustn't do that, it's too risky!' she gasped. 'He can't go in there all by himself.'

'He's not by himself—he'll have young Abram Kleiber with him. The two of them have it all worked out. That's where Danny is now—he went round to Silmour Street about an hour ago.'

Swiftly, Lil dried her hands on the scullery towel. 'Tell Mum I'm sorry I couldn't finish the washing-up—say I had to go out. Don't tell her anything else. I'll be back as quick as I can.'

'But—just a minute! Lil...'

'Sorry, can't stop!' She disappeared through the back door into the yard, and was gone.

It was about a quarter of an hour's walk to Silmour Street, but she got there in nine minutes—running, then walking, then running again.

As it was a national holiday the shop was shut but she rang the bell and waited. For a long time nothing happened, which gave her a chance to get her breath back, but she was just beginning to think that the Kleibers must all be out, joining in the celebrations elsewhere, when at last Sharon came downstairs and opened the door.

She was half-dressed, with a pretty kimono thrown over her petticoat, and her blonde hair untidy, needing a comb.

'Oh, it's you,' she said blankly.

'Yes. Is Danny here?' asked Lil. 'I'm sorry to bother you, but it's very urgent. I believe he was coming to see Abram.'

Sharon glanced up and down the street, then drew her inside and shut the door.

'I must look a perfect sight!' she said. 'I was just changing my dress. I'm getting ready to

567

go out—I'm off to a party with some friends of mine. We're going to see the fireworks later on.'

'Can I speak to Danny?' Lil cut in.

'Oh, no, I'm sorry, he's not here. There's nobody at home, I'm all on my own. Mumsie and Papa have gone over to Greenwich to spend the day with Auntie Moira. Danny was here about an hour ago, but then he went out with Abram.'

'Already? Where have they gone?'

'I couldn't tell you, I'm sure. They said something about meeting some friend of Abram's—I don't know his name, but I believe he's a wherryman. Abram was talking about borrowing a boat from him. I expect they're going on the river.'

'Oh, no.' Standing at the foot of the stairs, Lil felt as if her legs would give way, and she sank on to the bottom step. 'That means I'm too late to stop them.'

'Whatever's the matter? Is there something wrong?'

'They could be in danger—both of them. They're planning to break in to the Jubilee Wharf.'

'Break in? You mean—like burglars? Abram wouldn't do a thing like that!'

'It's not exactly burglary. There's something they're trying to find, some important papers. Dear God, if anyone catches them, they'll be in terrible trouble.'

'Oh, dear. I'm ever so sorry, but I'm afraid there's nothing I can do about it.' Sharon caught sight of herself in a mirror, and automatically patted her ringlets into place. 'Goodness, my hair's a mess. I wish I could help, but I must get dressed. You do understand, don't you?'

'Yes, of course.' Lil had not seen Sharon since the concert, and she asked suddenly: 'Did Abram tell you what I said? About Jimmy Judge?'

Embarrassed, Sharon lowered her eyes. 'Yes, he did, but you needn't have worried. It was all right. I mean, you know, nothing happened.' She escorted Lil firmly to the door. 'Anyway, I hope you find Danny and Abram. Good luck!'

As soon as Lil had gone, Sharon locked the door after her then went quickly upstairs. When she reached the landing, she exclaimed: 'Ooh, you made me jump, lurking about like that! How long have you been standing there?'

'Long enough,' said Jimmy Judge.

He was in his drawers and undervest, and Sharon protested, 'You don't have to get dressed. She's gone now!'

'I know, I heard what she said.' Sitting on the edge of Sharon's bed, he began to put on his socks. 'I recognised her voice right away. That was Lilian O'Dell, wasn't it? What's she been saying to you about me?'

'Oh, nothing much.' Sharon tried to pass it off with a little laugh. 'She said you were a bit naughty sometimes, that's all. I didn't really take much notice.'

As he fastened his sock-suspenders, Jimmy

asked curiously, 'How do you come to know her, anyway?'

'She's my cousin. You know Connor O'Dell at the Watermen? Well, he's Mumsie's brother.'

Jimmy raised his head and looked at her—an incredulous look, as if he had never seen her before.

'You mean Rosie O'Dell?' he said. 'The girl that married Ernest Kleiber?'

'That's right. He's my father.'

'But your name's Sally King!'

'That's just my stage-name. I'm Sharon Kleiber really, only Sally King looks better in the billing.' Sharon came across to the bed and put her arms round him. 'What are you so cross about? I thought we were going to have a nice time. Come on, let me help you get undressed.'

'No!' He pushed her aside and stood up, pulling on his shirt. 'I've got to go now.'

'You don't have to. I told you, we'll have the place to ourselves for hours.'

'Don't be a fool, didn't you hear what she said? Her brother—your brother—they're out to make trouble for me... Well, they're in for a big surprise.'

'What do you mean?'

'When they get to the warehouse, they'll find a welcoming committee waiting for them.'

'No, you mustn't go, I won't let you. Stay here with me!'

She clung to him, but he threw her off. Turning his back on her, he began to pull on his trousers.

570

'Sharon Kleiber...' He repeated her name slowly and contemptuously, as he buttoned his fly. 'I should have realised—that's why you were so easy. You dirty yids are all the same.'

20

When Jimmy got back to Denmark Place, he expected to find Bertie there, but there was no one in the kitchen except his father and Florrie, sitting in armchairs at either side of the fireplace.

'Where's Bertie?' he asked Florrie, for his father appeared to be dozing. 'Up in his room, is he?'

'He's gone out. Him and his friends went to see the fireworks.'

'Already?' Jimmy scowled. 'Damn...'

'Language!' said Florrie reproachfully. 'Yes, they said they were going early to get good places. If you want to join them later, they'll look out for you.'

Regardless of his aunt's feelings, Jimmy cursed. 'Bloody hell!'

Florrie gave a little shriek of horror and Joshua blinked, roused from his nap.

'What's that? What's going on?' he asked.

'I'm trying to find Bertie and the rest of the lads. There's some mischief planned for this evening at the warehouse,' began Jimmy.

Joshua frowned, making an effort to concentrate, then shook his head. 'No, not

571

mischief—fireworks. Thass wass planned for tonight... On account of the corry—coronation... Firework display.'

He closed his eyes again and Jimmy growled, 'Drunk as a lord... Fine thing.'

'You didn't ought to talk like that about your father,' Florrie scolded him. 'We was listening to the wireless—the Royal Family all come out on the balcony at Buckingham Palace—you should have heard the crowds cheering! And your dad said he had to drink a loyal toast to Their Majesties—that's when he opened the bottle. Very patriotic, your dad is.'

The bottle of whisky on the table was now half-empty, and Jimmy exclaimed impatiently, 'I haven't got time to argue—I've got to get to the Wharf. Where's the old man's keys?'

Joshua's jacket was hanging on the back of the kitchen door, and Jimmy began to rummage through the pockets while Florrie protested: 'You can't do that! You mustn't take his keys without asking!'

'Fat lot of good asking, when he's dead to the world!' Finding the heavy bunch of keys, Jimmy concluded, 'That's all right—I'm off. I don't know what time I'll be back.'

The slam of the front door woke Josh again; he looked round blearily, expecting to see his son. 'Where's he gone? He was here a minute ago...'

'He's gone to the warehouse—he took your keys out of your pocket. I tried to stop him, but he wouldn't listen.'

Slowly, heavily, Joshua pulled himself up on

to his feet, muttering, 'Took my keys, did he? We'll see about that.'

It was nearly dark when Danny and Abram arrived, mooring the wherry at the landing-stage below the outer wall of the dock.

'Lucky for us it's high tide,' said Danny. 'A few hours earlier and we'd have had to wade in over the mud-flats. Here—take the painter and make her fast to one of those iron rings on the wall.'

The wherryman had agreed to lend his boat for a small consideration, as he would not be plying for fares on the river this evening. Like almost everyone else in the Island, he was intending to go out and enjoy himself.

'We won't see a soul here tonight,' said Abram, tying the knots. 'The Wharf will be deserted.'

'There might be one or two crewmen left aboard the ships, on watch,' Danny pointed out. 'But I don't expect they'll bother us. Come on.'

They mounted the wooden steps, and slipped over the wall. It was getting murky now, and they fell silent as they walked along the narrow jetty. Suddenly Danny felt uneasy. At first he could not think why, and then he remembered another night, some years earlier, when he had walked along this jetty alone—but not quite alone. He remembered the old man's words—'*Between sundown and first light—just at the turn of the tide...*'

He would not look at the river-wall, but fixed

his eyes on the outline of the berthed ships ahead of them. However, his blood ran cold and his footsteps faltered.

'What's up? What's the matter?' hissed Abram.

'Nothing. Keep going... Don't look round!' Danny rapped out these commands as they walked on. 'Keep looking straight ahead, whatever you do.'

Out of the corner of his eye, he could just see a shape—the shape of a man, rising above the river-wall. He dared not look at it directly, but he was aware of a grey face and shiny black hair, clinging wetly to the scalp; a face that seemed to be watching their progress, urging them on...

'What d'you mean?' Abram glanced towards the river. 'I can't see anything.'

Danny turned his head—and let out a deep breath. 'No. There's nothing there. I must be imagining things.'

They passed the ships and reached the line of warehouses; high roofs black against the night sky.

'Where did you say the Guild Office is?' asked Abram.

'Till they finish the new buildings, they're using the top floor of Number Three Warehouse. Here we are.'

They stopped, looking up. Five storeys high, Number Three towered over them like a red-brick cliff, the long façade broken with lines of arched windows.

'How will we get in?' Abram wanted to know.

'I'm going up the fire escape and over the roof. You'll stay here on guard, in case anyone comes along. If you see somebody, give me a whistle, then nip back to the boat and wait for me there.'

Abram tried to argue. Wouldn't it be better if they went in together? But Danny was in charge now. He knew his way around; it would be quicker and easier for him to go in alone.

He began to climb the outside staircase, trying to make as little noise as possible, but his steel-tipped boots rang out on the metal steps. When he got to the top, he reached up to the parapet and heaved himself over the edge, on to the slates. A sloping skylight shone dimly, reflecting the last glimmer of light over the western horizon.

Danny wrapped his scarf around his fist, and punched in one pane of glass, which tinkled down inside. He put his hand through and opened the catch, then eased up the window-frame. When he had propped it open, he swung his legs over the edge, let himself down as far as he could, then dropped to the floor below.

It was very dark in the office, but he pulled a torch from his pocket and switched it on. Playing the thin beam of light round the room, he found the desk he was looking for, and went straight to it.

As he was about to open the top right-hand drawer, a loud explosion made his heart miss a beat. He held his breath, and a few seconds later, a bright crimson glare lit up the broken skylight. Of course—the firework display...

Reassured, he pulled open the desk drawer and found a set of cloth-bound books. Flicking over the pages by the light of his torch, he went through them rapidly—*The Brotherhood... Rules and Regulations... Membership List... Discipline Register...*

As he opened the book, a voice spoke from the darkness behind him.

'You didn't have to break the window, O'Dell,' said Jimmy Judge. 'I left the door open downstairs... I've been expecting you.'

At the Watermen, the bar staff were run off their feet; customers kept milling in and out through the street doors with drinks in their hands, in spite of Ruth's warning cry: 'No glasses outside, if you please, gents!'

They came in to replenish their mugs, then went out again to watch the play of coloured lights flaring up and drifting down over the rooftops. In the saloon, the pub pianist tinkled out various patriotic ballads, while Connor and Ruth tried to deal with the orders. In the public, Mary had volunteered to help Huw keep the beer-pumps flowing.

So Lil was by herself in the kitchen—alone, and worried half to death about her brother and about Abram. What could she do, except tell Huw, when she could speak to him privately? But what could Huw do on his own? The only possible solution would be to tell the police, but that would land the boys in still more trouble...

The sound of music and laughter from the bars was so loud she didn't hear the knocking at the side door at first. When at last she went down the passage and opened it, Sharon tumbled in, breathless and indignant.

'I've been knocking for ages—what took you so long?' Without waiting for an answer, she hurried on, 'Where can we go? I must talk to you!'

'Come into the kitchen—everybody else is on duty,' Lil told her. 'Has something happened?'

Sharon sank into a chair at the kitchen table. 'Wait till I tell you—it's the most terrible thing! We've got to help them before it's too late!' she exclaimed.

There was no doubt that she was upset, yet a part of her was enjoying the excitement of the situation, extracting the last ounce of drama from it.

'I've been awfully frightened!' she continued, putting her hand to her heart. 'I'm so afraid he might kill them!'

'What are you talking about? Who might?'

'Jimmy Judge...' Sharon would not look at Lil, but traced the woven pattern in the tablecloth with her forefinger. 'He was there, you see, upstairs—when you told me about the boys.'

'Upstairs, with you?' Lil stared at her, aghast. 'Sharon? Oh, no!'

'Yes, he was. He heard everything you said...and you were quite right about him, I know that now. He's a horrible man—beastly and wicked, and he said some terrible things to me. I don't care how important he is, I'm never going to have any more to do with him as long as I live!'

'Never mind about that!' Lil grabbed her by the shoulders, forcing her to stick to the point. 'Do you mean to tell me Jimmy Judge knows Danny and Abram have gone to the Wharf'

'That's the terrible part. He said he'll be there, waiting for them. They've walked straight into the trap!'

'What's all this?'

The girls' heads turned simultaneously. Behind them, Lil's father stood in the doorway.

'Suppose you tell me what's been going on,' said Connor. 'Right from the beginning.'

Abram tried to read the time from his wristwatch, but the occasional rocket-bursts and showers of gold and silver high overhead were fleeting and inadequate. He felt sure it must be getting late; he seemed to have been waiting outside the warehouse for a long time.

The night wind nipped his ankles. Abram shivered, and wondered yet again what Danny was doing inside the building. He was tempted to follow him up the fire escape to find out, but if Danny left by another exit, they could easily miss one another in the darkness.

A series of roman candles shot stars of red, white and blue into the heavens, each in turn dissolving into a storm of glittering diamonds.

And then Abram noticed something else.

There was a light, moving inside the warehouse: he could see the yellow glow swinging to and fro, through the arched windows on the ground floor. The windows were nearly four feet above him, so he could not see in—just an irregular patch of light swaying across the ceiling.

He knew that Danny had a pocket torch with him, but a torch wouldn't produce that kind of light. So if it wasn't Danny in there, who else could it be?

Abram decided to investigate. He had never set foot in Jubilee Wharf until tonight, so this was all unknown territory to him—but there had to be a way in somewhere. Walking round the building, he found a doorway; he turned the handle and discovered that the door was unlocked. Cautiously, he went inside.

The ground floor of Number Three Warehouse was being used as a grain store, and the air was heavy with the strong, nutty smells of wheat, rye and barley; full sacks were piled high on all sides, with narrow walkways in between. There was no illumination, except for one moving patch of light cast by a hurricane lamp.

Holding the lamp aloft, Joshua Judge lurched unsteadily between the grain sacks, searching for his son.

He did not like visiting the Wharf so late; he had never liked it, since that night nearly twenty-four years ago, when the Punishment Squad had disciplined Izzy Kleiber with the worst penalty in the Rule Book... It was Josh's hands that had lashed Izzy's wrists to the iron rings in the river-wall, and Josh's hands that had untied him next morning—no longer a man, but a water-sodden corpse. Israel Kleiber had met his death at the hands of Joshua Judge.

The crime had haunted him ever since. He avoided the Wharf after dark, as far as possible. Tonight he understood in a fuddled way that there was trouble afoot, so he had to try and deal with it, whatever it was—but he couldn't stop thinking of Izzy Kleiber. He would not go near that jetty by night, not for a king's ransom. The story had got about, of course. Someone had talked, and many tongues had built it up—now there were even tales that the Wharf was haunted, that at certain times of the night, Izzy's ghost had been seen along that jetty, rising from his watery grave...

A sharp fusillade of explosions startled him, and he stared up at the windows, seeing the sky outside turning red—then blue—then green.

Slowly, in these changing lights, he saw a figure coming towards him along the alleys of grain sacks—a figure with dark curly hair—a face that glowed with a deathly green pallor. *The face of Israel Kleiber.*

Joshua screamed with terror. 'Keep off! Keep away from me!' And he flung the hurricane lamp at the apparition.

Equally terrified, Abram ducked and fled; the lamp burst as it struck the floorboards, and burning oil spread in a pool of liquid flame among the dry, bulging sacks.

The first time Jimmy Judge hit him, Danny was taken off guard. The two young men had been fencing verbally for several minutes, after Jimmy had grabbed the Discipline Register from Danny's hands.

'You know you're wasting your time, don't you, you and Pritchard and Kleiber, and the rest of the lefties...' he sneered. 'Do you think we'd be fool enough to put things in writing which could make trouble for the Brotherhood? Anything that goes into the Register goes down in code, my friend—we're not idiots.'

Danny pretended not to understand what he was talking about, and they circled the desk warily while Jimmy threatened to send for the police and have him taken up for breaking and entering.

'Go ahead, why don't you?' Danny asked, but did not get any answer. Jimmy was not anxious to set off a police investigation. Keeping the beam of his torch fixed on Jimmy's hard, set face, Danny went on: 'All right then, if you won't do it, how about if I go and give myself up? They'd be interested to hear what you just told me...'

Jimmy's expression changed to anger, and he lunged at Danny across the desk. The first punch landed full in Danny's face, rocking him back, and he dropped the torch. It skidded to the floor, throwing a ray of light uselessly into a corner of the room, and the fight continued in darkness.

Danny fell back against the wall, losing his balance and falling sideways; Jimmy was on top of him before he even hit the ground.

There was a difference of eight years between them. Jimmy was older and heavier and more confident, while Danny was tall and muscular, but he had inherited his mother's slim build, not his father Sean O'Dell's broad shoulders and physical weight. It was an uneven contest.

For the first few moments, Danny was also handicapped by an instinctive assumption that this would be a fair fight. He was not prepared for Jimmy's ruthless tactics—kicking, punching low, gouging at his eyes, kneeing him in the groin—and when they rolled over together, knocking down a small side table, Jimmy did not hesitate to snatch it up and use it as a weapon, bringing it down again and again, trying to batter Danny's skull.

Luckily, in the darkness his blows were wide of the mark, and Danny heard the wood splinter on the floorboards, inches from his ear. He knew then that he was fighting for his life.

'You're bloody mad, you are,' he gasped. 'If you kill me, you'll swing for it!'

Another punch silenced him; guided by the sound of Danny's voice, Jimmy hit him in the mouth with the full force of his clenched fist. As pain flared up in Danny's face, he tasted blood and spat out a broken tooth. Instantly, Jimmy followed up his advantage. Before Danny could defend himself, he punched him again, in the pit of the stomach.

As Danny heaved and retched, groaning for breath, Jimmy grabbed him by the throat, and for a second Danny thought he was about to be choked to death; instead, he was dragged to his feet. Still winded and scarcely able to stand, he slumped against Jimmy, who hauled him across the room.

One of the arched windows beneath the eaves stood open; suddenly Danny realised what Jimmy planned to do. He struggled as hard as he could, but in his weakened state he was no match for Jimmy.

The older man laughed, panting. 'By the time the police get here, you won't be able to tell them anything. Attempted burglary—entering over the roof—trying to make a getaway through this window... Pity you fell and broke your bloody neck.'

He began to heave Danny backwards over the low sill. That was when they both heard a voice shouting, five floors below.

'Fire! Help—Danny—the warehouse is on fire!'

Jimmy hesitated. Leaning across Danny, he looked out of the window, suspecting some trickery—but then he saw the glare reflected on the paving-stones and heard the roar of the flames.

'Jesus Christ!' He spat out the words, releasing his hold on Danny. In half a dozen strides he was out of the room, through the emergency door and on to the fire escape. Dazed, Danny realised that he was free.

Still struggling for breath, he ignored the pain in his jaw and the blood trickling down his chin, and followed Jimmy on to the iron staircase. He expected to be met by cool night air, but it was uncomfortably warm outside; already the reek of smoke was rising from the lower floors, as Danny picked his way down five flights, clutching the hand-rail.

At ground-level, Abram was trying to tell

Jimmy what had happened. 'Your father saw me, and that seemed to drive him crazy. He yelled at me to go away, then he threw the lamp... That's how the fire began. I ran out, but when I had turned back, I could see him standing there—on the other side of the fire and the smoke. He didn't even try to get out. He looked kind of dazed, as if he didn't know what was happening.'

As Danny joined him, Jimmy said curtly, 'My father's in there.'

Fearfully, they approached the open door and looked inside. The fire had taken hold by now, and there was no sign of life—nothing could be seen but a sheet of flame. Danny took a few steps into the building, but the heat and the thick, choking smoke drove him back. Then a hand fell on his shoulder, and a familiar voice said, 'Don't try it, son.'

Danny whirled round in astonishment. His father looked him over, with a mixture of fondness and pride.

'Holy Mary, you've taken enough punishment for one night by the looks of you,' said Connor. 'Who's in there? Joshua? I'll see to this.'

More men came running; one of them carried a fire-bucket full of water, but as he was about to chuck it through the doorway on to the flames, Connor took it from his hands.

'That's not going to do much good,' he said. 'Let me have it.'

He was wearing a thick woollen jersey; stripping it off quickly, he soaked it in the bucket, wrung it out, then pulled it on again, partly covering his face and masking his nose and mouth.

Then he walked into the blazing warehouse.

At the Watermen, fifteen minutes later, the street door burst open and Danny ran into the saloon.

Ruth was serving behind the bar with Lil helping her—illegally, for Lil was too young to be working as a barmaid, but at a time like this nobody gave that a second thought.

The noisy crowd fell silent when Danny arrived, not only because of his headlong speed but because of his injuries—his face was bruised and his mouth was caked with blood. Smoke grimed his cheeks, but tear-stains traced pale channels through the dirt. He had stopped crying now, but his words were thick with grief as he spoke to his mother.

'Can I talk to you, on your own?'

Ruth knew something terrible had happened, but she tried to speak calmly. 'Yes, of course you can. Lil—stay here and look after the bar, there's a good girl.'

She followed Danny into the kitchen and shut the door. 'It's your father, isn't it?' she said. 'What's happened?'

He pulled out a chair and made her sit down. He, too, was trying to be calm and sensible, but the tears began again as he told his story.

'...and then he went back inside the warehouse ...into the fire.'

Ruth's voice was expressionless. 'Didn't anyone try to stop him?'

'It all happened so fast, we couldn't think straight. Abram ran to get help. I think somebody called the fire brigade—'

'But your dad,' she interrupted him, but still in the same level tone. 'What about Dad?'

'I don't know how long he'd been in there. It may only have been a few minutes—it seemed like hours. I never thought the warehouse would burn so fast. I mean, it's made of brick, with steel joists holding up the floors—but the floors are wooden planks, so...they caught fire as well. We stood there watching and we saw the first floor go up in flames. It just seemed to cave in and collapse. Then there was nothing but fire—everywhere.'

'And that's all?' She sounded very faint, as if she were far away.

'Somebody said "That's the end. There can't be anyone alive in there." So then I came home and—' His voice broke. Bowed over the table, he buried his face in his arms.

She put her hand on him, stroking his hair and saying gently, 'Yes, I see. Thank you for telling me. Will you do something else for me? Huw's in the public; ask him to come here, would you? I shall need him—to help me break the news to the others.'

For some time she sat alone in the kitchen, staring at the dresser with its rows of plates and cups—Connor's own cup, especially large, never used by anyone else—but she did not see any of it. She could see nothing but Connor's face.

There had been no time to say goodbye before he went out to the Wharf—before he set off to rescue Danny and Abram. She remembered that as he went out, he had looked back over his shoulder, throwing a half-smile that said: 'Don't worry, I'll be back soon. It'll be all right...'

Now she knew that it would never be all right again.

It had not always been a perfect marriage, with some dark unhappy days when they seemed to be far apart from one another, but tonight she could not remember the bad times—only the hours when they were happy together, a happiness she had never known with any other person.

She thought of the night she first saw Connor, battered and beaten up after his expulsion from the Brotherhood—how she had helped him back to his room, here at the pub; how she had helped him to undress—his strong, firm body shining in the lamplight, the muscles sliding under smooth, glistening skin.

That called up other memories, of their wedding night—their bodies meeting nakedly for the first time, the revelation of a whole world she had never even dreamed of... A love she had never known before, and would never know again.

The door opened, and Huw came into the room.

'Danny just told me,' he said. Moved by love and pity, he came close to her, taking her in his arms, holding her tightly. 'My dearest, what can I say? What can I do to help? I know how you must feel.'

How strange, she thought. How many times

in the past few years I've lain awake at night, longing for this—aching for Huw's arms around me, to have him close to me—and now he's here, and it means nothing at all.

'No,' she said quietly. 'You don't know. I didn't know myself, till tonight. And now, God forgive me, it's too late.'

Gently, she withdrew from his embrace and rose to her feet. 'I'm sorry, Huw. You know I'm very fond of you—I always will be—but I love Connor, nobody else.'

Slowly, she left the room and went along the passage to the side door, taking down her coat from the hat-pegs.

Huw followed, completely at a loss. 'Where are you going?'

'To Connor.' Seeing his expression, she added, 'Oh, don't worry, I know he's dead. But I have to go to him.'

'Do you want me to come with you?'

'No. This is something I must do by myself.' She walked out into the alley, and he had to let her go.

When she reached the dock entrance, a police constable was holding back a small crowd of curious onlookers, though from the gates there was nothing to be seen but the bright orange glow and the pall of black smoke overhead.

The constable stopped Ruth. 'Mrs O'Dell, you shouldn't be here.'

She recognised him then; it was PC Burns. She said simply, 'My husband's somewhere in there. I must find him.'

Mike tried to say something, but could

not—and he let her go through.

As she reached the Wharf, a last dazzle of rockets exploded in the distance; the twin bascules of Tower Bridge stood out in silhouette against the gaudy sky. Ruth turned away from the spectacle. It was hard to believe that the festivities were still going on. In another place, in another world, it was still Coronation Day.

Here were no fireworks, nothing but fire itself, and everything that went with it—uniformed men running to and fro, playing out hoses, playing fierce jets of water on to the blaze, surrounded by steam and smoke. Two ambulances were drawn up beside the river-wall, and two men carried a body on a stretcher, shrouded in a blanket.

She walked up to the ambulance-men and said: 'Let me see him, please.'

One man shook his head. 'We can't do that, lady. He's a goner.'

But his colleague recognised Ruth from the Watermen and broke in. 'She has a right. He was her brother.'

Her hand outstretched to pull back the blanket, Ruth stopped. 'What do you mean? He's my husband—Connor O'Dell.'

'No, ma'am. It's your brother Joshua. Mr O'Dell's in the other van.'

She began to run towards the second ambulance; the back door was open, and as she was about to climb inside, a figure came out to meet her.

'What the hell are you doing here?' asked Connor.

He was almost unrecognisable. His head was bandaged, his skin was black and some of his clothes had been burned away; his torso was scorched and blistered. Behind him, another ambulance-man protested: 'Mr O'Dell—come and lie down! We have to take you to the hospital.'

'No thanks, lad, I've changed my mind.' Connor stood there, swaying a little. 'My wife's come for me, you see, and if she doesn't take me home, there'll be the devil to pay. But if you were to be good enough to offer us a lift back to the Watermen, I wouldn't say no.'

He remained deaf to all argument and medical advice. Tonight, he was determined to sleep in his own bed.

Finally one of the men drove them back to the pub and helped Ruth to undress Connor, wash him and apply ointment to his burns, and put on fresh bandages. It took a long time, but at last everyone else had gone, and Ruth was able to undress and slip into the double bed beside her husband.

Then he told her the rest of the story, as far as he could recall it.

'When I got into the warehouse, I thought I'd made the biggest mistake of my life—and the last! The heat was so powerful, the air seemed to scald me, and though I was breathing through the wet jersey, my lungs felt like they were red-hot. For a moment, the flames were so fierce, I was blinded—but then I made out one small space close to the wall, and I managed to squeeze through. That was when I saw your brother, just a couple of yards from me—standing there like a man in a nightmare, unable to speak, unable to move—and the clothes already alight on his back.'

He paused to catch his breath, recollecting that moment. The memory was so vivid, he could still feel the unbearable heat burning his skin as the raging inferno surrounded him. He had always thought fire was yellow, or orange, or red; he had never imagined anything like the incandescent, white-hot glare that confronted him. He couldn't tell Ruth about that—he could never put it into words. Instead, he continued:

'I threw my arms round Joshua, trying to smother the flames on him. I don't think he knew who I was—and I couldn't have spoken to him, for the roar of the fire was like one long thunderstorm raging about us. Your brother was a big man, sure enough, but by then he'd no more strength in him than a baby, so I picked him up and I carried him with me, through the flames... I couldn't turn back; the ceiling above was giving way. I felt a blast of burning air rush by me like an express train as it fell in behind me. All I could do was keep going, hoping for another way out. By the mercy of God, I found a back door and kicked it open—and we got out of that hell...'

Then he corrected himself. 'No, that's not true. I got out—Joshua didn't. By the time I laid him down on the ground, he was already dead.'

There was a long silence, and then Ruth said slowly: 'I want to tell you something. Tonight,

I thought you were dead—and that's when I realised something I should have known all along. I loved you from the first minute I saw you, only for a long while I was too stupid to understand it. And long afterwards, when we were married, I sometimes took that love for granted. I forgot what our love meant—I forgot how much you meant to me. But tonight God gave me another chance, so now I can tell you—I love you with all my heart, and all my body, and all my soul...'

He uttered a strange sound; something between a chuckle and a sob. 'How'd you like that?' he murmured. 'I've never loved you so much as I do this minute—and the state I'm in now, I can't even touch you.'

She moved a little closer, and raised her head. In the darkness, her mouth found his, and she kissed him softly on the lips.

'We have the rest of our lives,' she said.

Danny never went back to work at the Jubilee Wharf, but found himself a job elsewhere, and was taken on at the Royal Victoria Docks as an apprentice engineer. Before he signed on, he made one last visit to the Jubilee.

There were new buildings now at the front entrance, replacing the old rooms where he had originally joined the Brotherhood. Further along the Wharf, he saw scaffolding pricking the sky—another warehouse would soon be going up on the burnt-out site.

When he entered the Office, he found Jimmy seated at a streamlined modern desk. Bertie, assisting his brother, was putting some papers away in the drawer of the steel filing cabinet. They looked at Danny, then at one another; they had not seen or spoken to him since the night of the fire.

'Well?' said Jimmy.

'I'm returning these,' said Danny. 'I shan't be needing them now.'

He turned out his pockets, placing two objects on the desk-top—the brass tally with his number on it, and the wicked, curving spikes of the claw.

'You're resigning from the Guild?' asked Jimmy. His voice was clipped, giving nothing away.

'Yes, we heard you'd been taken on elsewhere,' added Bertie, curling his lip into the semblance of a smile.

'That's right. I had a feeling you wouldn't be sorry to see me go,' said Danny. 'I think the time's come for the parting of the ways, don't you?'

'I dare say.' Jimmy was still noncommittal.

'I suppose you heard Jimmy's been elected as Chairman, in Dad's place?' Bertie indicated their surroundings with a wave of his hand. 'What do you think of our new premises?'

'Very smart,' said Danny politely. 'I wish you well.'

Bertie held out his hand uncertainly. 'Do we shake on it?'

'No!' Jimmy cut in harshly. 'I don't think so.'

Danny studied him thoughtfully, then said,

'Perhaps you're right. I don't suppose our paths are likely to cross in the future, anyhow. Goodbye.'

When the door shut behind him, Bertie asked, 'Why wouldn't you shake hands? It don't mean anything—and he won't cause us any more trouble. That's all over and done with.'

'Think so?' Jimmy looked up at his brother with such intensity in his eyes, Bertie was taken aback. 'Are you turning soft, or what?'

'No, of course not,' Bertie stammered, 'but O'Dell's father did go in to rescue Dad. He tried to save his life!'

'He didn't manage it, did he?' Jimmy's face darkened. 'If it hadn't been for Daniel O'Dell breaking in that night, that fire would never have started. O'Dell cost us Dad's life—and one day he's going to pay that debt.'

On an October evening, Lil and Mike were walking in the Island Gardens.

This had become a regular arrangement; they met once a week, generally on Sunday afternoons when Lil had some free time. They never met in the evenings because she did not enjoy going out after dark—even with someone she liked and trusted.

But in one respect things had changed. For a long while Mike had never put his hand on her, and she had never touched him—until one day, when she slipped her arm casually through his as they strolled along. He said nothing, but waited to see if it might happen again. The next Sunday, she took his arm as a matter of course, and now they always walked with their arms linked companionably. It gave him some hope for the future.

They never discussed the understanding between them; several times Mike had been tempted to question Lil, in order to discover her feelings about him, about their relationship—but each time he held back, aware that by asking such questions he risked putting an end to any relationship at all.

But today he would have to say something...

They had been admiring the beds of Michaelmas daisies in the Gardens; bright pink and mauve and purple, massed together. Summer was long gone, and now autumn was ebbing away, but it was going out in splendour.

They turned a corner, facing the vista across the river—the view of the Royal Naval College; in the setting sun, the fairy-tale palace looked like burnished gold.

'Isn't that beautiful?' Lil's hand tightened on Mike's arm. She turned to him, her eyes dancing. 'I'm happy—and I know I'm happy.'

He smiled back at her, but there was a sadness in his smile. 'I must tell you something,' he said. 'We won't be able to go on taking these walks together—not for a while, anyway.'

She looked frightened. 'What do you mean?'

'I've applied for a transfer to the River Police. It's been approved.'

The Thames Division of the Metropolitan Police patrolled the fifty-four miles of river from Staines Bridge to Dartford Creek.

'But that's good news.' Lil was confused. 'It's a sort of promotion, isn't it?'

'It'll be a change from pounding the beat, I'll say that!' he agreed. 'Yes, it's something I've been wanting for a long time. The only thing is, they're sending me away to do my basic training. I'll be attached to the station at Shepperton for six months.'

'Where's that?' Anywhere up-river, past Tower Bridge, was a foreign country to Lil.

'Hampton Court way. Not too far, really, but I'll be living in digs. I shan't get back here often. I don't know when I'll see you again.'

'I'm sorry.' The light went out of her eyes. 'I mean, I'm pleased for you—but I'm sorry for me.' Her hand slid down his arm, resting lightly on the back of his hand as she added, 'I shall miss you.'

He felt a sudden surge of hope, as he said, 'Will you write to me?'

'Of course I will. Let me know your address and we'll write to each other. We'll keep in touch.'

In late November, Connor and Ruth were taking the same afternoon stroll. She had been cooking the Sunday joint all the morning, and when that was eaten, the washing-up had taken longer than usual. She said she was tired of looking at four walls and felt like a breath of fresh air before it got dark.

For her sake, Connor had forgone his usual Sunday siesta, and they were taking a turn in the Gardens.

It was a grey afternoon; a shower of leaves fluttered from the trees, piling up in drifts on the grass. Though they didn't know it, Con and Ruth had reached the same vantage-point as Lil and Mike, a few weeks earlier; standing by the river-wall looking across to Greenwich.

'Soon be winter,' said Connor.

'Don't say that. I hate winter—fogs and frost, everything dark and miserable.'

'There's still some brightness about.' Connor picked up a handful of dry leaves; they had turned colour and the green had become a brilliant crimson. 'Are these cheerful enough for you?'

He handed them to her as if they were a bouquet; she selected a couple, tucking them into the lapel of her coat.

'Thank you.' She smiled. 'And thanks for coming out with me. I know what a sacrifice it is for you to give up the *News of the World!*

Connor shrugged. 'I took a peep at it while you were washing up. There wasn't much cheer in that, either.'

'Why? What's happened?'

'It's more like what's going to happen. The Government's announced this week that they're going to build air-raid shelters all over the country, and they're giving two million sandbags for the Civil Defence—that's what they call it. There's plans drawn up for London to be evacuated in an emergency.'

'An emergency? Is that a way of saying another war?'

Connor nodded. 'You heard what Ernest

Kleiber said. The way things are now in Germany, anything could happen.'

'What will we do?' Ruth looked at him. 'If there is a war, what's going to happen to us all?'

'God only knows...but I do know one thing—we'll get through it somehow, just like we've always done. Whatever happens, we'll face it together—you and me.'

Ruth looked down at the bright leaves; taking them from her coat, she dropped them over the wall. A sudden gust took them, circling and spinning down until the waves snatched them. They floated away, eddying among the ripples, disappearing for a moment, then bobbing up again—two flashes of red in the grey-green current that carried them downstream. Ruth strained her eyes, watching them until they were out of sight.

Then she took Connor's hand in hers and lifted her chin, facing the river breeze.

'Time to go home,' she said.

This Large Print Book for the Partially sighted, who cannot read normal print, is published under the auspices of

THE ULVERSCROFT FOUNDATION

Other MAGNA Romance Titles In Large Print

ROSE BOUCHERON
The Massinghams

VIRGINIA COFFMAN
The Royles

RUTH HAMILTON
Nest Of Sorrows

SHEILA JANSEN
Mary Maddison

NANCY LIVINGSTON
Never Were Such Times

GENEVIEVE LYONS
The Palucci Vendetta

MARY MINTON
Every Street

Other MAGNA Romance Titles In Large Print

CATRIN MORGAN
Comfort Me With Apples

JEAN SAUNDERS
All In The April Morning

JUDITH SAXTON
Nobody's Children

HELEN UPSHALL
A House Full of Women

ANNE VIVIS
Daughters Of Strathannan

DEE WILLIAMS
Carrie Of Culver Road

MARY WILLIAMS
Castle Carnack

Other MAGNA Romance Titles
In Large Print

MARGARET BARKER
Surgeon Royal

MARY BOWRING
Vet In Charge

FRANCES CROWNE
Dangerous Symptoms

ANGELA DEVINE
Crock Of Gold

HOLLY NORTH
Nurse At Large

ANNA RAMSAY
The Legend Of Dr Markland

JUDITH WORTHY
Locum Lover